THE STREET

Kay Brellend, the third of six children, was born in North London but now lives in a Victorian farmhouse in Suffolk. Under a pseudonym she has written sixteen historical novels published in England and North America. This is her first novel set in the twentieth century and was inspired by her grandmother's reminiscences about her early life in Campbell Road, Islington.

KAY BRELLEND

The Street

HARPER

This novel is entirely a work of fiction.
The names, characters and incidents portrayed in it are
the work of the author's imagination. Any resemblance to
actual persons, living or dead, events or localities is
entirely coincidental.

Harper
An imprint of HarperCollins*Publishers*
77–85 Fulham Palace Road,
Hammersmith, London W6 8JB

www.harpercollins.co.uk

A Paperback Original 2011
5

A catalogue record for this book
is available from the British Library

ISBN 978 0 00 735863 2

Set in Meridien by Palimpsest Book Production Limited,
Falkirk, Stirlingshire

Printed and bound in Great Britain by
Clays Ltd, St Ives plc

FSC is a non-profit international organisation established
to promote the responsible management of the world's forests.
Products carrying the FSC label are independently certified
to assure consumers that they come from forests that are managed
to meet the social, economic and ecological needs
of present and future generations.

Find out more about HarperCollins and the environment at
www.harpercollins.co.uk/green

For Mum, to finish what you started

For Dad, to keep a promise

For Nan, Granddad, Great Nan, Great Granddad, remembering you with love and pride

For everybody who ever spent time in Campbell Road, later Whadcoat Street, a.k.a. 'The Bunk'

ACKNOWLEDGEMENTS

I owe my gratitude to the following:

Jerry White for his wonderful study on
Campbell Road, Islington

Gary and Louise for kindly sharing their research and
knowledge of family history

Basil Clarke, war correspondent during WW1

Getting Older

1913

ONE

'Shut that brat up or I will . . . fer good.'

'You don't mean that, Mum. Little 'un's hungry. I've been waiting up for you to come home so's you can feed her. Why do you say horrible things?' The small girl's expression was a mixture of contempt and sorrow as she challenged the woman swaying on her feet. In fact she knew very well why her mother turned mean and brutal: it was due to the amount of Irish whiskey she had tipped down her throat in the hours since she'd left this squalid hovel that was their home.

Tilly Keiver narrowed her glassy gaze on her daughter. 'You got too much o' what the cat licks its arse with, my gel.' The words were slurred but menacing. Unsteadily she shoved herself away from the doorjamb. 'If I weren't dog tired you'd feel the back o' me hand and no mistake about it.' She raised a fist raised to emphasise it was no idle threat. Slowly she let the hand fall so it might aid the other in grappling with the buttons on her coat. Irritably she shrugged the garment off and left it where it fell on rag-covered floorboards. Small, careful steps took Tilly on a meandering path towards the iron bedstead. It was the dominant piece of furniture in a room cluttered with odd, dilapidated pieces.

Alice Keiver watched her mother, listening to her swearing beneath her breath as she bumped into a stick-back chair and sent it over. Then her ample hip met the wardrobe. If Tilly felt the hefty contact there was no sign: the volume of cursing remained the same. She was soon within striking distance and Alice shrank back into the armchair. She'd been huddled within its scratchy old embrace for two long hours whilst awaiting her mother's return. Her thin arms tightened about the fretful infant wriggling against her lap. To soothe the hungry baby and quieten her mewling she again stuck the tip of her little finger between tiny lips. Little Lucy pounced on the fruitless comfort and sucked insistently.

Alice knew that once her mother had reached the bed and sunk onto the edge she was unlikely to rouse herself to retaliate, whatever she heard in the way of complaints. Soon that moment arrived.

'You're not tired, you're drunk as usual.' Despite Alice's frail figure her accusation was strong and she lithely sprang to her feet, clutching the precious bundle of her baby sister protectively against her ribs as she paced this way and that.

'Get yerself in the back, 'fore I use this on yer,' her mother slurred, showing her a wobbling fist. But Tilly's chin was already drooping towards her bosom.

Alice made a tentative move forward, and then tottered quickly back as her mother snapped up her head but, as she had correctly assumed, Tilly made no move to rise from the bed once she'd settled into the comfort of its sagging edge.

'You're a bleeding nuisance, you are. Worse'n all the rest put together. Now git! Let me get meself to bed. Cor, I'm all in.'

Tilly Keiver was a big-boned woman with a florid face topped by reddish-blonde hair. Usually she kept her beautifully thick mane under control: plaited and coiled in a neat bun either side of her head. But a night of roistering with her cronies in the Duke pub, and a painful stumble on the way home, had resulted in her crowning glory resembling a fiery bird's nest. She yanked out two pins from one side of her head and a thick plait uncoiled sinuously onto a shoulder. She left it at that. The other side was forgotten.

After a few quiet minutes Alice thought her mother had dozed off where she slouched. But before she could act, Tilly managed again to rouse herself and, having folded forward, her callused fingers began pulling at her footwear.

Tilly's new boots had been got, against fierce competition, just that afternoon from Billy the Totter. Carefully she tried to unlace them but the fancy double bow she'd fashioned when sober got the better of her. In a frenzy of impatience she used toe against heel to squash down the leather and prise them off. The last one freed was tossed from her foot against the wall in a fit of temper. Even in her inebriated state Tilly regretted rough-handling her prized possession. Her frustration resulted in coarse cursing that continued as she fumbled with her heavy skirt. She managed to work it to her ankles and shake it away. Done with undressing, she swung her feet up onto the mattress and momentarily lay quiet and still; the only sound from that side of the room was the settling bedsprings.

Alice moved quietly closer to help her mother cover herself. But Tilly's flopping hand had finally located what it sought. After a few attempts she managed to swing the solitary blanket high enough to drift about her body.

'Don't go to sleep yet, Mum. Lucy needs feeding,' Alice pleaded in a whisper. 'And there's no milk left. There was only a drop that'd gone sour and Dad put it in his tea before he went off to work.' She gently shook her mother by the arm to rouse her.

Alice knew her mother was conscious but choosing to ignore her pleas, so now she must wait. In a very short while Tilly would sink so deeply into sleep that she'd hear and feel nothing. Alice gently placed little Lucy on the bed a safe distance from her mother's twitching, and started to tidy the room. She must loiter until she heard her mother snore.

She picked up Tilly's best coat from the floor, shook it, and draped it across the end of the bed. The small-back stick chair had been made even more rickety by rough treatment; nevertheless Alice moved it to neatly join the three still pushed under the table. The precious boots were collected and placed together out of sight beneath the bed. A rumbling sound drew her back, on tiptoe, to her mother.

'Mum?' she tested quietly. There was no response. Even when baby Lucy let out a wail Tilly stirred only to suck in another ragged breath. Alice tested her mother's consciousness again, this time with more volume to her voice. Tilly snored on.

Quickly Alice's nimble fingers unbuttoned her mother's blouse. Deftly she positioned the baby close to a plump breast to nurse. Alice froze stock still, her fingers covering the baby's mouth to stifle her whimpers. One of her mother's hands had fluttered up as though she might swipe them both away, but after a moment, hovering, it fell back to the mattress.

Little Lucy's face had become crumpled and crimson as though she sensed imminent comfort slipping away. But Alice was sure now that her mother was sufficiently stupefied. With furtive care she guided the baby close then snatched away her fingers, allowing the baby to latch on and feed.

Slowly Alice sank to her knees by the bed, feeling quite weak and exhausted. She guessed it must be past midnight. She began to gently move straggly hair away from her mother's bloated face and when done with that she ran loving fingers over the fleece covering her little sister's bony head. The gentle hum created by her mother's rumbling breathing and her sister's enthusiastic suckling made her drowsy and her lids fell a few times. She forced herself back to wakefulness before her forehead touched the mattress. Feeling chilled, she crept to the end of the bed and put on her mother's coat. It pooled on the floor about her and she used the material to cushion her bony behind as she sat on the rough boards and looked about for something to do whilst she waited for her sister to finish her feed.

Drawing one of the boots from under the bed, she slowly turned it to inspect its fine quality. The laces had been tightened into small, hard knots by her mother's clumsiness. Patiently she picked at them until they loosened. Smiling at the bows she had tied, she began to pull the leather at the heels until the ridges started to disappear. Satisfied with her handiwork, she slipped it onto her skinny foot and extended her leg to admire the boot, waggling it this way and that to inspect it from different angles. One day she'd buy herself such things . . . better things, she promised herself.

They were good boots. Quality. Billy the Totter had said he'd got them from a woman over Tufnell Park way. Alice knew a lot of women hereabouts charred for posh ladies over there in the better district of North London. But he'd said that they weren't even that lady's property. She'd got them off her sister who lived in Mayfair in one of the houses with pillars out front and servants out back. Alice reverently smoothed the soft leather with her fingertips.

Barely were the boots neatly back in position beneath the bed when she suddenly shot up to a crouching position. A loud thud from the floor below had curtailed her yawning and startled her into wakefulness. Her eyes darted to the bed but nobody was stirring.

The tenement house in which they had rooms was never peaceful. Day or night people came and went and constant noise was only a minor inconvenience to an existence in what was known as Campbell Bunk. In the rooms below lived her aunt Fran and her husband Jimmy. Alice had been partially aware of the ebb and flow of an argument issuing from those rooms the whole time she had waited for her mother to come home. But now it seemed the ruckus was about to turn nasty.

Aunt Fran and Uncle Jimmy were always at it and, judging by the increased din, their disagreement was about to take its usual turn and become violent. Even knowing it, Alice again jumped in her skin at the unmistakeable clatter of a missile striking a wall. Screamed abuse from her aunt immediately followed. Alice shot across the splintery floorboards on her bony knees to stare unblinking at her mother's sagging face. But Tilly remained oblivious to her warring relatives, and her soft snores continued unabated.

The noise below had worsened and Alice was relieved to see that little Lucy had finished feeding and was also sleeping quite soundly, undisturbed by her aunt and uncle fighting close by. Alice remembered that she'd witnessed her aunt Fran pull a knife from a drawer in the table and rush at her uncle Jimmy. She remembered too that her dad had had his hand cut when he took it off her.

Nervously Alice shifted the baby aside, keen now to get herself and little Lucy to bed. She pulled her mother's gaping bodice together and painstakingly refastened the buttons. Then the stiff, worn blanket was properly pulled over her so it might be of some small benefit against the cold March night. Alice opened out her mother's coat to act as an extra blanket and spread that on top. Finally she did as her mother had told her over an hour ago and went into the back room.

'Is Mum home? Heard something like a row goin' on.'

'Yeah, she's back.'

'Been boozin', I s'pose, has she?' the sleepy voice enquired from the murky shadows.

Alice looked towards the double mattress she shared with her sisters. It was the elder who had spoken. Sophy was almost a year and a half older than her. Bethany was just over three years younger. The sleeping infant in her arms was almost seven months old.

''Ere . . . make room,' Alice grumbled and gave Sophy a nudge so she would shift over.

The elder girl squeaked indignantly. 'Oi, get yer elbow out me face, will you.' She, in turn, gave Bethany a little shove and the girl rolled over, still asleep, with a thumb trapped in her mouth.

'What's all the row about, anyhow?'

'It's Aunt Fran and Uncle Jimmy. They're at it again.'

'S'pose he's been up the corner gambling and she's found out . . .'

'S'pose,' Alice agreed and, having undressed to her undergarments, got beneath the covers. She immediately huddled close to Sophy for warmth and pulled one of the old ragged coats that served as makeshift blankets up to her chin. Carefully she drew baby Lucy into the protective nest of her arms.

'Is Dad back?'

'No,' Alice replied. 'He won't be back for a long time yet.'

Their father had found himself a few days' work at the market and would help overnight setting up the stalls for the following day. If he was lucky, he might stay on and take half-profits for helping old Mr Cooke sell his fruit and vegetables. Of course, if trade looked to be slow and pickings were hard, their dad would be sent home before ten o'clock with very little in his pocket for his night's work.

'Dad'll go mad at her if she's spent his bacca money on booze.'

'I know,' Alice whispered into the dark.

'How old do you think we'll be before we get out of this dump? Really old, I suppose. Might even be sixteen. Four-eyes Foster was sixteen before she got enough saved up to get a room in Playford.'

Alice laughed soundlessly. She knew bespectacled Annie Foster, of course. For as long as Alice could remember Annie had lived just a few doors away in Campbell Road. On Annie's sixteenth birthday she'd finally dodged her step-father's fists by running away from home. 'That's just round the corner!' she derisively pointed out whilst frowning at the shadows on the ceiling. In her estimation, scarpering to Playford Road was hardly escaping. 'When I go I'm going a real long way . . . a *real* long way. I'm makin' a move when I'm thirteen. You can come too if you like.'

Sophy raised herself on an elbow and peered through the gloom at Alice. 'Run away?' she scoffed. 'When you're thirteen? You only just turned twelve last week and you've got no money.'

'I've saved a few bob from me doorsteps, and I know old Miss Murphy wants me to do her brasses reg'lar. Done 'em once before and she said they'd never rubbed up so good.'

'How much she give you?' Sophy was most interested to know. Any chance of earning regular money from a good paying customer was news best kept to oneself. Sophy shifted closer, peering down into Alice's face.

Alice pulled the coat up higher to her sharp little chin. She turned over, settling her head into her hand, regretting that she'd been unwisely boastful. 'Go to sleep,' she hissed over a raised shoulder. 'We'll never get up for school if we don't get some shut-eye.'

'Go on! How much did old Murphy give you to do her brasses?'

'Ain't saying, so don't ask.' Alice curved her small, thin

body about her sleeping baby sister and determinedly closed her eyes.

'I'll come with you, if you like, when you go,' Sophy promised quietly. 'I'm older'n you and I know a lot more than you do.'

'About what?' Alice asked dubiously.

'About everything,' Sophy boasted. 'I know about workin' in good houses, which you don't 'cos you're not old enough to go. Mum's took me loads of times to Highgate when she were working for Mrs Forbes and her daughter.' Sophy paused, unsure whether to let on a secret of her own. 'I got meself a nice few handkerchiefs out of Tufnell. Sold 'em for a good price, too.'

Alice immediately turned her head to stare through the gloom at her sister. 'You don't want to let Mum hear you say that. She won't half have yer hide if she knows you've been pinching off her clients.'

'What she don't know don't hurt. 'Sides, it were ages ago now.' Sophy was quiet for a moment. 'Don't you let on, right, 'cos I still got a little put by and she'll want it. And she won't stop till she finds it, neither.'

''Course I won't say,' Alice snorted. Should their mother find out any of them had a few bob saved she'd turn the place upside down looking for it. Alice had known her dad, who was a painter and decorator by trade, hide a half a crown in a tin of paint in the hope it would be safe from his wife till he got home. Alice squirrelled further into the bed but there was no warm spot lower down on the freezing mattress. Quickly she drew her knees back to her chest. 'Well, what else d'you know?' she asked after a few minutes of trying to get off to sleep.

'Lots of things,' Sophy insisted. 'Know about boys too.'

'Well, you can keep that to yourself,' Alice said with genuine lack of interest.

'You'll change yer mind soon enough,' Sophy chuckled. 'Once you start using the jam rags you'll know what I mean.'

'Oh, shut up, will you,' Alice groaned, disgusted. She knew what her sister meant and she had no wish to ever get involved with all that messy stuff every month. It made her feel quite queasy to think about it.

'I reckon Tommy Greenfield is soft on me. He keeps watching me all the time. His sister said she reckons he likes me too.'

'He got Maisie Brookes into trouble,' Alice hissed. She turned slowly to widen her eyes expressively. 'You want to watch yourself. Mum'll kill you if she finds out you've been knockin' around with him.'

'Ain't been knockin' about with him,' Sophy muttered defensively. 'Just said he'd been looking at me, that's all.' Sophy lay her head back down for a second. Then she leaned close to Alice to add, 'Anyhow, everyone knows that Maisie's a slag. Weren't the first time she'd dropped her drawers.'

Alice grunted noncommittally in response and closed her eyes. A moment later they flicked open and she groaned.

'What now?' Sophy asked.

'She's wet,' Alice said. She felt for the rag that served as Lucy's nappy and her fingers encountered the warm, soggy cloth.

'Hope that's all it is,' Sophy garbled in real alarm.

Alice climbed out of bed and, shivering in her underwear, quickly unwrapped the wet cloth whilst trying to keep little Lucy's damp bottom protected from the frosty air with a coat. She searched by touch in the gloom and finally located a fresh rag at the foot of the bed. Carefully she wiped the baby dry with it then she turned it, shaped it, and skilfully secured it about Lucy's fragile pelvis.

Speedily she jumped back into bed and moved Lucy between herself and Sophy. 'Quick, keep her warm or she'll wake up and start yelling. Then we'll know it. We'll not have a wink of shut-eye.'

Sophy grunted and made room. ''Spose we'll all stink of piss again tomorrer.' It was her final comment before she fell asleep.

TWO

'Where's the money?'

An apprehensive look slipped between Alice and Sophy. They each picked up a slab of bread from the plate on the table and started to chew. Bethany slipped down from her chair, murmuring about needing the privy.

'I said, where's me bacca money?' their father suddenly roared. He shook the empty tin in his hand and glared at his wife. With an almighty crash he slammed the tin onto the mantelshelf.

Tilly Keiver settled baby Lucy more firmly on her jutting hip. 'What bleedin' money? Weren't no money in the tin. You had it out Monday. I saw you.' She swivelled her hips from side to side, rocking the baby, even though little Lucy seemed unconcerned by her father's fury.

Jack Keiver approached his wife. He was a well-built man in his early thirties. His features were regular and the only blemish on his handsome face was a small, odd-shaped area of freckled skin that ran along his jaw. Presently the birthmark was stretched by the grim thrust of his chin. 'You lyin' cow. I wouldn't take money out when you was around to see where it was hid. You think I don't know you by now?'

He stared angrily at the empty tin as though he might get his three shillings back if he wished hard enough for it. 'You've had it, ain't yer?' Suddenly enlightenment erased the weariness from his rugged features. 'You was out boozing again last night, wasn't you?'

'Ain't been nowhere,' Tilly snapped back. She turned to squarely face her husband, her figure stiff with belligerence. She'd fought with him before and would do so again if necessary. 'I've been stuck in this dump, ain't I,' she lied without a flicker of guilt altering her wide blue gaze. Her eyes darted to her two eldest daughters, settled fiercely on Alice. Both girls kept their heads bowed and sipped at their lukewarm tea.

'I'm warning yer, gel, don't drag them into it.' Jack's lips were rimmed white with wrath. 'Soon as me back's turned you're thievin' and off out.' He thrust his hands deep into his pockets and paced to and fro. 'Well, if you think I'm working nights again for old man Cooke for a pittance so's you can tip me takings down yer neck . . .'

'If you get yourself some proper work you won't need to be Cookie's sidekick for a measly few bob.' Tilly blocked his path and shoved her face up to his. 'I told you that Mr Keane wants one of his houses in Playford painted out.'

'And I told you that I'll not knuckle under for him . . . or you.

'You selfish git. You sit around moaning you ain't got no work then don't want a good job when I find it for you.'

'I can get me own.'

'Yeah, I noticed. You're fuckin' useless, you are.'

'You keep a civil tongue in front of the kids.' Jack Keiver's dark brown eyes narrowed coldly on his wife.

The warning had been issued in a voice that Alice strained to hear yet it made a shiver slip down her spine. She looked at her father from beneath her lashes, watching him swing away and pick up his coat and hat. He'd been in barely fifteen minutes and he was not intending to stay. A sorrowful sob was stifled in her chest. She wanted to run to him and throw her arms about him, tell him she had a little bit put by and he was welcome to it to spend on whatever he liked. But she sat still and simply watched as he opened the door.

'I'm off out.' He looked back at his sullen-faced wife. 'I know you've been boozing, Tilly,' he said dully. 'You reek of it.'

'Yeah, well maybe I wouldn't need it if I had a man bringin' in proper wages and helping out now 'n' again.' That was muttered at the door Jack had banged shut behind him. Tilly shook back her tangled fiery hair and spat out a curse to hurry him on his way. Then she turned about with her chin up to face her daughters.

'Come on . . . what you two waiting for? Christmas? You should've been out from under me feet by now. Get off to school and quick about it.' Tilly deposited Lucy on the bed, and started gathering up the crockery on the table. It needed rinsing under the tap on the landing so they could use it at dinnertime. She shoved the little pile of plates and cups towards Alice. 'Here, get this done 'fore you disappear. I've got to nip downstairs and see your aunt Fran about some work I've found her.'

As Tilly sped down the stairs she thought about Jack. Regret was writhing in the pit of her stomach, making her irritable. She could have owned up and said she'd taken his money for her boots. He might not have minded that so much; it was his belief that she'd stolen it for whiskey that made him mad. Yesterday, when she'd got the boots off Billy the Totter, she'd meant to show Jack what a bargain she'd found. But he'd come in and gone out to work down the market without seeing her. She hadn't intended to go to the Duke at all. She'd had no money for a start. Then a friend had called by and offered to stand her a drink. It'd been Kitty Drew's treat for she'd been promoted to supervisor at the Star Brush factory. It was a celebration . . . a time for a bit of fun. Gawd knows there was little enough of that to be had round here!

Tilly loved Jack and she knew he loved her. She knew she did things she shouldn't. She said things she shouldn't. And as for that temper of hers . . . it was a bitter consolation reminding herself that he was far from perfect. If he'd taken on that job for Mr Keane it would have seen them straight for several weeks. He'd let his blooming pride get in the way of a bit of decent grub on the table.

With a savagery born of frustration Tilly hammered loudly on a door. She got no response to that so, after a moment or two, made to walk in unannounced. The door was locked. 'You in, Fran?' She rattled the handle. Still no one came to open it so she gave the panels another thump. 'Fran? Jimmy? Anyone home?'

'Saw him go out,' a voice behind Tilly informed her.

Tilly turned to see Mr Prewett locking his door. He had the room in front of her sister Fran's. Tucking his walking stick beneath his arm he began to limp down the stairs. He hopped down a step at a time with the aid of a rickety banister that seemed to hang in space. Over time the spindles had been prised free and used as firewood by tenants desperate to keep warm. 'Surprised I was, I can tell you, to see either of 'em walkin' after the bleeding commotion coming out of there last night.' Having made his complaint, Mr Prewett hopped down another tread.

'They was at it last night?' Tilly demanded, frowning down at the top of his shiny head.

'Thought the whole road must've known what went on, the row they was making.' Bill Prewett settled himself firmly on one foot and looked up at her. 'Banged on their door meself, I did. You gorn deaf or summat?'

'I was out for a while . . .' Tilly explained.

'Oh . . . out, was yer?'

The knowing tone made Tilly itch to run down and slap his smug face for him. She knew that it was common knowledge around here that she liked a drink. So what? So did most people struggling to survive in this shit hole.

'Anyoldhow,' Bill went on quickly, having recognised the dangerous glint in Tilly's eyes, 'I saw Jimmy slope off around seven this morning. He looked alright, as far as I could tell, but that don't mean nuthin'.' With that he eased himself forward and carried on his slow descent of the stairs.

Tilly turned back to the locked door and renewed her efforts with both hands. Her concern for her younger sister's welfare had put a fire in her belly. 'Fran? Open the door if you're in there.' Her fists were raised to recommence the assault when her sister finally opened the door a crack. 'Let me in, you silly cow.'

'Only if you promise not to go mad and start shouting. Me head's fit to explode as it is.'

Tilly gave an impatient sigh and shoved past Fran into a room as dingy and depressing as the one she'd just left on the floor above. She turned about and gave her sister's appearance a thorough inspection. Her back teeth began to grind but she fought down her anger and simply continued to stare at the sorry sight before her. The light was poor but even so Tilly could see blood spatters on Fran's blouse and her bruised and battered face. Calmly she asked, 'What the fuck started him off this time?'

'He's a bastard.'

'Yeah, I know that.' Tilly waited, hoping to hear a better explanation for Jimmy's savagery. None was forthcoming.

'Look at the state of you, fer Gawd's sake,' she burst out. 'Didn't you try and belt him back?'

'Just makes him worse.' Fran grimaced in pain. 'Besides, me arms hurt too much. Felt as though he'd twisted them out of their sockets. He had them right up behind me back.' She tried to ease her shoulders but even small movements made her gasp. 'I'll get him one o' these days,' she vowed shakily. 'I'll creep up on him with a knife when he ain't expecting it. You see if I don't.' Her bravado flagged and she slumped against the wall. 'We're finished this time, in any case.'

'You said that last time.'

'Now I mean it 'cos he's give me no wages in over a week. I know where the money's gone, too. I know for sure he's got a fancy piece.'

'You said you was finished last time when you found out he had a fancy piece,' Tilly reminded her a mite too sarcastically.

'It's alright for you,' Fran shrieked, stretching her cut lips. 'We ain't all lucky enough to have a decent man like Jack.' Gingerly she raised her fingers to her face as she felt the warm wetness on her chin. 'Me mouth's started to bleed again,' she wailed and bent her head to a cuff to staunch the flow.

'Where's the boys?' Tilly asked after her two young nephews.

'Got them off to school somehow. Bobbie's gone off bawling fit to burst. Stevie's wet the bed. I gotta get that cleaned up before Jimmy turns up. If he finds out he'll give him such a hiding.'

'I'll change the sheet,' Tilly promised. 'And if Jimmy turns up, I'll see to him too,' she vowed grimly. 'First, let's see to you.'

'I'm alright,' Fran muttered and again brought her cuff up to her face. 'Nothing I ain't dealt with before.'

'Come upstairs.' Tilly got hold of her sister's arm but, hearing Fran cry out in pain, she instead slipped a hand about her waist. 'Come on,' she urged and tugged her gently towards the door. 'Let's get some tea on the go and we'll sort it out.'

'I reckon he's got a woman round here this time. That's where he's spending his money.' Fran dipped her head to hide her weeping eyes.

'We'll sort it out,' Tilly repeated firmly. She opened the door and propelled her sister out onto the landing.

Alice and Bethany were sharing the job of wiping the crockery dry and stacking it on the battered old dining table. Sophy had said she'd done her stint washing up yesterday and had got going to school. When their mother reappeared with Fran in tow both girls stopped what they were doing to gawp at the state of their aunt's face. One of her eyes was puffed to a slit, her lips looked gigantic and her jaw was red and grazed from chin to ear. She greeted her nieces quite jovially even though her eyes were suspiciously wet.

'You two still here? Bobbie 'n' Stevie been gone to school a quarter of an hour or more. You'll be late, y'know.'

Having heard their cousins had already left, the girls looked at one another. It was not unheard of to get a blackboard rubber aimed at your head by Rotten Rogers if you were last in for registration.

'We're just going,' Alice said and dropped the towel she'd been using to dry up. Bethany followed suit.

Both girls knew that big trouble was afoot, and the two women would want to discuss in private a plan of how to put right whatever had now gone wrong between Aunt Fran and Uncle Jimmy.

'Where's Sophy?'

'Gone to school,' the sisters chorused in reply.

Moments later Tilly surprised them by saying, 'You'll have to stop home.' She caught one of Alice's elbows in a strong grip. 'You get going.' Tilly tipped her head at the door indicating that Bethany should immediately use it.

With a quick, sympathetic look at her sister Bethany did as she was bid. School was a pain, but at least you could have a laugh with friends on the way there and back. Staying home and caring for Lucy was, to Bethany's mind, utterly boring. And she knew that was why Alice was being kept off school.

'Do I have to, Mum?' Alice asked plaintively. Usually when they had women's talk they liked to be alone. But there had been one other time Alice had been kept home to act as nursemaid to Bethany when Aunt Fran had problems; it had been years ago before Lucy had been born. On that particular day the whole house had seemed to shake with the commotion that'd gone on.

Uncle Jimmy and her dad had come to blows because Jimmy had accused Tilly of poking her nose in his business. Naturally, her dad had backed her mum although Alice had sensed he thought Jimmy had a point.

Alice was glad her dad had gone out now. At least he would be spared any nastiness that might occur if Jimmy turned up hollering for his missus as he had last time. Not that her mum was unable to stick up for herself. She'd witnessed her fighting in the street with men and women. She'd seen her put a poker over the head of Bart Walsh when he'd refused to pay his rent and had spat at her. Her mum had looked big as a house on that occasion. It'd been only a day or so after that Lucy had been born.

'Yeah, you do have to stay home today,' Tilly told Alice. 'Me 'n' your aunt Fran have got to go out a bit later and you've got to take care of Lucy 'cos we can't drag her round with us.' Tilly sweetened the dictate with a promise.

'Tell yer what, Al; if you're a good gel I'll get you some chips dinnertime. There, how's that?'

Alice gave a faint smile. In fact it was a nice bribe. They'd had very little to eat yesterday. Dinner had been bread and a scrape of jam. There'd been no jam left for this morning and a slab each of bread with the mould cut off the crust had been their breakfast.

'I've got a couple o' coppers for you too,' Aunt Fran said and attempted a smile. The small movement made her wince and moan and hold her jaw.

Alice knew things must be serious if she was getting treats. She didn't know where her mum and Aunt Fran were heading but guessed it would be to locate Uncle Jimmy. A dingdong was sure to ensue. Alice went to the bed and looked down at Lucy. The baby was gurgling quite contentedly, her thin legs kicking energetically. Alice gave her little sister a tickle then put a finger onto one of her curled palms. Immediately Lucy gripped it, still giving her a gummy smile. Soon the baby would want a feed and become fractious and her mum was bound to be busy elsewhere. 'Did Dad bring in any milk?'

'Don't think he did, love.' Tilly grimaced in exasperation. She ferreted in the pocket of her apron and pulled out coins in a fist. 'Here, nip to the shop and get some and we'll all have a cuppa tea.'

Despite her mother frequently going to bed under the influence she mostly got up in the morning good as new. To Alice it seemed that two different people lived in her mother's body. One could be quite nice; the other could be a monster. Today she seemed to have recovered better than usual. The thought of sorting out Jimmy had obviously put her in a good mood.

Alice took the money and, having pulled on her coat, went out. They lived on the top floor of the house in a front and back room of about equal size and state. Now she skipped down the dank staircase and rushed towards the light streaming in through the doorless aperture at the bottom of the flight. Once the building had had a front door but it had been damaged in a ruckus many years ago and never repaired. The remnants had then been hacked off the hinges and used as firewood.

The bitter cold atmosphere outside was preferable to the gloom and stench that shrouded their home. Alice sniffed in crisp, clean air, thrust her hands in her pockets and set off on a brisk walk towards the shop.

Either side of the street loomed terraced houses set behind railings, similar to the one from which Alice had just dashed. Campbell Road marched from Seven Sisters Road at one end to Lennox Road at the other and was cut in half by Paddington Street. The tenements were overcrowded, without adequate washing facilities for either people or equipment. Added to a permeating smell of grime was an atmosphere of rising damp and overflowing privies, for the buildings were badly maintained. The majority of the landlords felt under no obligation to do repairs until threatened by a visit from the sanitary inspector.

The Keivers lived in what was known as the rougher end of The Bunk close to the junction with Seven Sisters Road. That territory had always been intended to house the impoverished. The top half of the road had been built with a better class of occupant in mind. But those people had long since decamped in search of respectable neighbours, leaving their properties to be divided and colonised, often by as many as thirty poor people.

As Alice walked, hunched into her coat, she caught sight of her friend, Sarah Whitton. She called out, waved and darted over to the other side of the road to talk to her. 'You not at school either?'

Sarah aimlessly juggled the few groceries she'd just bought from the corner shop. 'Mum's took bad again this morning.'

Alice grimaced in sympathy. It was well-known by her neighbours that Mrs Whitton hadn't been right since her son passed away. He'd caught the whooping cough and died, making the whole road fearful of going the same way. Lenny Whitton had been a strapping lad of fourteen and the consensus of opinion had been that if it took him out, anyone was fair game. In fact only one other person had succumbed and she had been sixty-nine and already in poor health.

Now Sarah's mum suffered with *nerves* and spent most of her time shut indoors. She survived by living off her three daughters. Sarah, who'd not yet had her twelfth birthday, spent the weekends doing whatever odd jobs she could find. Ginny Whitton's husband had departed shortly after Lenny. But he'd gone just around the corner to Lennox Road and a woman who was less trouble to live with.

'Why aren't you at school? You bunkin' off?' Sarah asked.

'Nah! I've got to look after Lucy 'cos there's trouble brewin'.'

'Yeah? What?' Sarah had immediately perked up at the prospect of a bit of gossip.

'You should've heard the racket going on in ours last night. There won't half be big trouble when me mum 'n' Aunt Fran catch up with Uncle Jimmy.' Alice's blue eyes grew round in her pale face. She leaned forward to confide, 'Should see the state of me aunt Fran! She looks like she's been street fighting with a pro.' Alice whipped a chilly hand from her pocket to demonstrate her poor aunt's disfigurement. 'Lip out here and eye like that 'n' already going black.'

Sarah's jaw dropped open. 'Yer dad going after him?'

'Dad don't know yet what's gone on. Me mum'll get Jimmy first, anyhow, if she can find him.'

'I know where he is,' Sarah gasped triumphantly.

'Where?' Alice demanded with a grin.

'Seen him go in number fifty-five as I was coming out of the shop. It was only a few minutes ago.'

Alice blinked at a house a few doors away. 'Cor! Dunno why he's hiding in there. You'd have thought he'd scarper further'n that. Nellie Tucker lives there, don't she?' Alice didn't know much about Nellie Tucker other than she worked nights and lived with her old mum. Although she did recall that a lot of the women round here seemed to have taken against her since she moved in about six months ago. But then feuds between people were commonplace in The Bunk. She shrugged. 'Suppose I'd better get going. Gotta get some milk. See yer, then.'

When Alice returned home she found her mum in the process of bathing Aunt Fran's face with a cloth.

'Hold still,' Tilly ordered as Fran tried to duck from the pressure on her cuts and bruises.

Alice put the milk on the table and watched.

'Get the tea goin', Al, there's a good gel.'

Alice obediently set the half-full kettle on the hob grate. 'I just saw Sarah Whitton. She's off school 'n' all.'

'Her mum bad?' Tilly asked whilst still patting gently at Fran's closed eye.

'Yeah. She just saw Uncle Jimmy going in number fifty-five.'

Tilly halted with the cloth poised above her sister's face. Both women swivelled to look at Alice. 'You sure about that, Al?' her mum asked whilst from a corner of her eye she gave Fran a significant look.

'That's what she said. Why's he gone in there?'

Tilly dropped the cloth back into the basin.

'I reckon I can guess why he's gone in there,' Fran choked out through her fat lips. 'The bastard! With that scabby bitch!'

'Come on. Let's get this done,' Tilly announced briskly and started rolling up her sleeves.

When they'd gone Alice went to check on baby Lucy. She was still in exactly the same position as when last she'd seen her. But now her tiny face was crumpling and she was making little whimpering sounds. Alice knew she would soon start to wail. Picking up the rag her mum had used on Aunt Fran, she looked for a clean edge. She tore it away then dipped the end into some of the milk she'd just bought. Gently she inserted the milky cloth between Lucy's lips and watched her suck.

Having satisfied the baby for a moment, she went to the window and angled her head to try to see her mum and aunt. But number fifty-five was too far away for her to catch sight of what might be going on. She pulled a chair close to the window and stood on it but her view was no better from the top sash. Her curiosity was getting the better of her and she quickly found a shawl and wrapped Lucy in it. Then she whipped off her school pinafore and tucked Lucy into that too. Impatient to be outside, Alice scrambled into her coat and, bundling Lucy onto her shoulder, she darted out of the room and down the stairs.

THREE

A little jeering crowd had already gathered about the railings outside number fifty-five. Soon Alice was close enough to see what entertained them. Her mum had hold of a fistful of Nellie Tucker's fair hair and was dragging her head down close to the pavement. Her other hand was busy delivering swift punches to Nellie's face. Uncle Jimmy looked embarrassed and keen to get away from Aunt Fran, who was waving her arms and ranting at him.

Alice knew that Uncle Jimmy had beaten his wife, and that it wasn't the first time. It seemed hard to believe he could ever do such a thing. He always had a laugh and a joke for her and Sophy when they met him. She could see now that he had that soppy smile on his face. It looked like he was puzzled as to what the fuss was all about. Alice edged nearer, hoping to find out what had started this latest upset.

'Yer fuckin' whore. Get yerself back down Finsbury Park. Keep to reg'lar clients, or yer'll have more o' the same.' Alice recognised her mum's raucous voice.

As if to make her point Tilly landed one final blow on the side of Nellie's head before letting go of her hair. Nellie tipped forward onto all fours. To add insult to injury, Tilly sent the woman crashing down onto her chin by kicking her up the behind. A hoot of laughter erupted from the assembled throng. A few of the women started to clap. 'New position for you, love, eh? Or perhaps you like it up the jacksie,' someone shouted.

Another time Tilly might have joined in the banter but she was in no mood for it today. She stuck her hands on her hips and swiftly got her breath back before swinging about. She immediately stalked after her brother-in-law. 'You fuckin' animal.' One of her thick fingers was up close to Jimmy's unshaven chin. 'Find yourself another place and another punch bag. Come back here again and touch me sister 'n' you'll be leavin' in a pine box.'

Bright colour started to creep up under Jimmy's collar. Having a brawl in the street with a man was one thing; being threatened by a woman in front of an audience was another. Tilly bloody Keiver was making him into a laughing stock and he didn't even have the consolation of knowing that later he could, behind closed doors and at his leisure, kick the words back down her throat. She wasn't his to tame, more was the pity. Only once had she been at his mercy and if he'd known what a thorn in his side she'd become over the years he'd have done a far better job of making sure she gave him respect and a wide berth in the future. That soft sod she'd married let her get away with too much and she'd got cocksure.

He took a furtive glance to right and left to see who was witnessing his humiliation. One of his drinking pals from Lennox Road was laughing openly at him and it made his gut start to writhe. He'd have to give Tilly Keiver a smack in public just to save face.

With his fists tightening at his sides he marched after Tilly to confront her. 'You interfering bitch,' he enunciated in a furious whisper whilst swaying on the balls of his feet, ready to strike. 'Why don't yer piss off home and sort out your own business?'

'This is my business, you bastard,' Tilly snarled and lunged forward, her fingers curled. Before she could tear into him she was grabbed from behind and hauled clear of Jimmy's swinging fist.

Jack Keiver held onto his struggling wife, his arms hooked under hers so she could do nothing but kick out in frustration and punch her hands in the air. Ignoring her threats and curses he simply said one word, 'Twitch.' It was enough to immediately calm her down and quieten the crowd.

The little group of spectators started to shuffle, then disperse. In less than a minute only Nellie, still on her hands and knees and whimpering, remained with the Keiver clan when the two constables reached them.

'What's going on here?'

The officer who had spoken was Constable Bickerstaff, nicknamed Twitch by inhabitants of The Bunk on account of a recurrent tic that regularly brought one of his shoulders and ears together. He spasmed and cast a stern look at the dishevelled woman crouching on the floor. 'What's going on?' he again demanded to know. He fiddled with the truncheon on his hip as though to reinforce his authority and hurry an explanation.

'Nuthin'.'

The single word was chorused by all, even Nellie. Twitch turned to his colleague. Constable Franks was more interested in eyeing a comely woman across the road than bothering with this rabble. Connie Whitton had been watching the spectacle at a distance. The little tease knew he liked her and tauntingly flicked up her skirt to give him a glimpse of her knees before having a raucous laugh with her friends at his expense.

'What d'you reckon about all this?' Bickerstaff asked Franks. 'It looks like more than nothing to me.'

'I reckon it's nothing if that's what they all say it is,' the younger man replied flatly, then looked around, his expression displaying disgust at his environment. The depressing, rotten houses marched off either side of the road as far as the eye could see, interspersed here and there by shops that seemed to make little effort to draw in customers, judging by their gloomy window displays. Franks had been transferred from Hampstead so was quite new to this beat. He knew they were required to walk this route but he saw no reason why they should linger unnecessarily in the worst street in North London.

Campbell Road, so he had been told by long-serving colleagues, and some of The Bunk's inhabitants, was home to the most notorious criminals: thieves, prostitutes, fraudsters – every sort of rogue and vagabond drifted through this slum. Unbelievable as it seemed to Franks, some had settled and been resident a very long while. If a couple of women – one who looked like she'd had seven bells beaten out of her – wanted to set about a well-known brass, it didn't take a genius to work out that one of their old men was playing away. Bickerstaff might be a stickler for doing things by the book but, in the great scheme of things, this was a petty domestic incident. The Bunk community had its own system of justice. Franks agreed with it: leave them be to shovel up their own shit.

'Well . . . right . . . come on, then. Get on home, the lot of you, before I change my mind and get out my book.' Twitch earned his nickname again. He didn't want to start an argument with Franks in front of this crowd. But back at base he'd have something to say about his colleague's lack of support. To his mind, the new recruit was too keen on warming his arse on a chair and his hands on a mug of tea.

Jimmy Wild needed no further telling. With a sly, poisonous look encompassing his wife and his in-laws he sauntered off towards Paddington Street. Tilly and Jack took up position either side of Fran and, linking arms, they started off home.

Twitch made to follow Franks who'd also moved away, impatient to get back to the comfort of the station. He hesitated and stooped to take a look at Nellie, who was still huddled on the pavement. Not a soul had come to her aid, even to get her to her feet. The worthless scumbag who'd caused the trouble had been the first to skedaddle.

Sidney Bickerstaff had been pounding this beat for very many years. He knew the people round here. He knew Wild. He was a womanising thug who had once put his wife in hospital because he couldn't control his temper or his fists. Yet the policeman had seen the weasel turn and flee rather than stand his ground when an irate fellow accused him of touching up his wife. Sidney came across many Jimmy Wilds in his line of work. Every one was a charming fellow on the surface. But underneath was a despicable coward who enjoyed beating up women because a fair fight with another man terrified him.

Sidney had guessed at once what had gone on. He took another look at the grizzling tart. Presently she was trying to keep her tangled blonde hair from sticking to the blood on her face. A clump of it was on the road beside her.

'Need a hand, love?' Sidney Bickerstaff stooped to proffer an arm.

'Fuck off, copper,' she replied and, clearing her throat of congealed blood and mucus, spat it onto the ground by his feet.

Twitch looked at the mess an inch from his polished shoes. 'Lucky you missed, or you'd be licking them clean,' he threatened softly.

'If it ain't yer shoes you mean it'd cost you a lot more'n you could afford, mate.' Nellie managed a coarse laugh but it hurt, so she stopped. 'Fuck off, copper,' she repeated more quietly.

'Mum! Mum, come and see, quick!'

It was a Saturday in spring and some balmy sunshine had drawn Tilly's three oldest daughters out into the air to sit on the pavement with their cousins. Now Alice bolted upright from her squatting position on the kerb and hared into the house. She met her mother flying down the stairs when she was halfway up.

Tilly had immediately responded to her daughter's urgent summons. 'What the bleedin' hell you bawlin' out fer? What's up?'

'There's a little crowd comin' up the road! Come 'n' see. The man shouted at us asking if we know where he can get rooms.' The information had streamed out of Alice, leaving her gasping for breath. It was not only the thought of a bit of entertainment to liven the humdrum routine of the day that had propelled her inside. Her mum rented out rooms for Mr Keane, so the prospect of work and money was in the offing too. Alice was very conscious of how precious was that opportunity to her family.

Mother and daughter emerged from the hallway of the tenement house into the sunshine. The sight that met Tilly's squinting gaze caused her to blow out her lips in astonishment and mutter to herself, 'Well, what in Gawd's name have we got here now?'

A small, wiry man was pushing a pram, hobbling with the effort as he clearly had an injured foot. His wife, for Tilly guessed that was who the poor ragbag was, trailed behind him, holding the hands of two children. They dragged either side of her like lead weights. Behind that sorry trio slouched two bigger kids, both boys, who looked to be teenagers, carrying between them a sack. It doubtless held the family's possessions.

As they came to a stop by her, Tilly peered into the pram. Two more children were in it, one each end, with a bag squashed between them.

'We've been tramping fer days. D'you know where we can get a room or two? Cheap it'll need to be,' the man announced without preamble.

Tilly had been busy doing Fran's washing. Her sister was in no fit state to lift wet sheets. Weeks had passed since Jimmy's attack but Fran's arms were still weak from the sprains her husband had given her. Now Tilly plonked her soap-chapped hands on her hips. Her expression betrayed her amazement. The Bunk was known to take in stragglers with nowhere else to go yet even for this depressed area of Islington this family was a very sorry sight. 'Where've you lot travelled from?'

'Essex,' the man answered and leaned on the pram handle to ease his bad foot off the ground.

'You walked from *Essex?*' Tilly squeaked in astonishment.

The man nodded and took a glance at his listless wife. She seemed exhausted beyond speech or expression. 'When we got to Highgate some people knew about this place and directed us here.'

For a moment longer Tilly roved a sympathetic eye over them. Then she got to business. 'Well, you can have a couple of rooms next door. Front and back middle.' She tipped her head to indicate the tenement house.

'You own houses?' the man said, fixing an interested look on her.

'Nah!' Tilly barked a laugh. 'I manage 'em for me guvnor. I've got these two here and a few others for Mr Keane. He owns a lot of property roundabouts.'

'How much?' He automatically rocked the pram up and down as one of the babies let out a piercing wail.

'Can let you have it fer a shillin' a night. Or five shillin' a week paid up front, however you want to do it.'

'Ain't got five shillin' but that's the way I want to do it.'

Tilly fixed her canny gaze on him. 'Well now, might be able to help you on that score 'n' all. I can let you have somethin' to pawn at a cheap rate so that's all right.'

The man stared at his brood of silent children huddled about his wife. 'Any work hereabouts?' A pessimistic look met his question and made his mouth droop.

'Some . . . but nothing much good,' Tilly told him straight. 'Looks like you'll need a tidy bit more'n what half-profits down the market pays to keep this lot.' Tilly cocked her head to look at the woman. An idea came to mind. 'Your wife after work?'

''Course,' the man roundly answered for his silent spouse.

His wife sent him a sullen stare from beneath low lids.

'What's your names, then?' Tilly asked whilst giving Bethany a cuff, as she'd started to whine for a penny for the shop. 'Get off up the road a while,' Tilly snapped at her daughters. 'I'm doing business here.'

The two older girls, who had been interestedly watching and listening to the exchange, each took one of Bethany's hands and began swinging her between them as they strolled off up the street.

'What's yer name again?' Tilly raised her voice to make herself heard over the screaming child in the pram.

In exasperation the fellow snatched up the fractious infant then introduced himself. 'Bert Lovat is me name and this here's me wife, Margaret. Be obliged if you'd show me these rooms. Won't go through all the kids' names. If we stay here long enough you'll come to know 'em, I expect.'

'I'm Tilly Keiver. I live here with me husband Jack 'n'

our girls.' She flicked her head to indicate the house next door. 'Wait here and I'll just nip indoors to fetch the key.'

Within a few minutes they were climbing up a dilapidated staircase in silence. By the time they reached the first-floor landing Bert could no longer conceal his dejection.

Despite the bright and sunny day the interior was so dismal it was hard to discern where doors were set in the drab-coloured walls. A stained sink was set against a wall on the landing and for a few moments the only sounds were a dripping tap and Tilly's efforts to turn a key in an awkward lock.

'What a shit hole,' Bert bluntly commented as he and his wife drearily looked around.

'Yeah,' Tilly agreed over a shoulder. 'But beggars can't be choosers, right?'

'Yeah . . . I ain't choosy,' Bert sourly agreed.

Tilly led the way into the room's grimy interior. A few sticks of ancient, battered furniture were pushed against the walls. A fiddle-backed chair that once might have belonged to a nice set now had stuffing leaking from a corner. A wardrobe that had only one door of its pair remaining had been shoved aside to allow an iron bedstead to dominate the centre space. Beneath its springs, resting on bare boards, was an additional flock mattress. A square table with a dirty, fissured top took up the rest of the wall space.

'Let's see the other,' Bert muttered in a resigned tone.

They trooped in single file into the back room. Again the man's eyes pounced at once on the sleeping quarters: a double bed with a smaller mattress pushed underneath. 'Big enough for the four old'uns, I suppose.' He came back into the front room and looked at the hob grate powdered with grey ash. 'Where's the water?' He swung his eyes to and fro.

'Didn't you see the sink on the landing? You've got to

share with other people.' Tilly could tell he was bitterly disappointed at the accommodation. 'That's why it's cheap,' she said with a sympathetic grimace. 'Got another of Mr Keane's houses up the better end o' the road. But that'd cost more. Got a ground floor front and back. It's a bit bigger and better furniture and a few sheets 'n' blankets to go with it. I could do that at seven bob fer the week . . .'

'Nah!' Bert harshly interrupted, shaking his head and slipping a sideways glance to his wife, for she had sunk to sit on the bed edge. 'This'll do. It'll have to do.' He shifted the baby in his arms, still rocking it to and fro although it had quietened.

'One thing I won't do is get meself in trouble with me guvnor,' Tilly said firmly. 'I collect his rent and I ain't losing me job. So you've gotta pay me what's due when it's due or it's trouble for everyone. That clear?'

Bert nodded and cast a wary eye at the war-like woman confronting him. He reckoned she looked like that Boadicea in a chariot who'd fought the Romans. He remembered his oldest, Danny, had brought home a book when he'd been learning about history at school. Tilly had leaned forward slightly, fists on hips, whilst awaiting his agreement. 'Bring the stuff up,' Bert ordered one of his sons who'd been hovering by the open door. The youth stared sulkily at his father before turning about and doing as he was told.

Bert put the baby down on the bed next to Margaret. 'I'm off to try 'n' find some work,' he said bluntly. 'I'll take a job clearin' pots in a pub if it comes to it.'

'That's what it always comes to,' his wife muttered acidly at his back as he limped out of the room.

'You want any work, duck?' Tilly settled herself on the bed next to Margaret Lovat. 'Might be able to help, y'know.'

'What's goin'?' The woman raised her eyes and pushed a stand of lank brown hair behind her ears.

'Might be able to find you something this afternoon if you like. It's graft but better'n nothing if you need a few bob urgent.'

'Washing?' the woman guessed with a dead-eyed look.

Tilly nodded. 'Me sister Fran's work but she ain't fit and her client wants this back by seven tonight. Well-to-do lady she is, out Tufnell Park. Might lead somewhere.'

Margaret Lovat turned a jaundiced eye on Tilly. 'You reckon I'm daft enough to believe I've got a chance of taking yer sister's best touch?'

Tilly crossed her arms and gave Margaret a keener appraisal. So she wasn't the mouse she'd seemed. She'd come back with that quick enough. 'Take it or leave it.' Tilly stood up. 'No skin off my nose either way. Ain't my client.'

'I'll do it.'

'Come next door when yer ready. I'll show you what's gotta be done.'

Margaret Lovat followed her to the door. 'Where's the privy?'

'Out back. Go down the stairs and do a left till you come to a door; that'll take you out to the courtyard.' She made to go then hesitated and said with a hint of apology, 'I'll prepare you fer the state of it. It's full of Mr Brown. I've been on at Mr Keane fer weeks to get a plumber to fix it.' She nodded to the landing. 'There's the sink. Shared with a couple called Johnson. You won't have no trouble off them. He's got reg'lar work on the dust and she hardly comes out the room. Got bad arthritis,' she added by way of explanation. 'Back slip room's just been took by a single lady. Don't see nuthin' of her. Think she's a waitress up west and that's why she comes in all hours of the night.' Tilly raised her eyebrows at Margaret in a way that fully exhibited her suspicions.

'How nice,' Margaret sighed with weary sarcasm. 'Stuck between a totter and a prossy.'

'She's a looker too, is Miss Kerr, so keep an eye on yer old man.' Tilly issued the warning with a grin.

'Ain't worried about him!' Margaret snorted derisively. 'She's welcome to him. Give me a break at least.'

'Yeah . . . I noticed he don't hang about,' Tilly said, amused. 'Not much of a gap between your two youngest, I'd say.'

'Thirteen months,' Margaret sighed. 'Little Lizzie's just three months. I'm bleedin' knackered, I can tell yer.'

The two women exchanged a look of cautious camaraderie.

'It's me eldest, Danny, I'm thinkin' of. He's fifteen next birthday 'n' comin' of age, alright. The boy's always got his hand stuck down the front of his trousers.'

Tilly cackled a laugh. 'I noticed he's a strapping lad.'

'He is,' Margaret said, her face softening with pride. 'Nothing like his old man. Takes after my side. Me dad was six foot and built like a brick shit house. Danny's bright too and was doing well in school till . . .' She shrugged and turned away.

'All gone sour for yers in Essex?'

'Yeah . . . won't be going back there no more.'

Tilly looked at Margaret's averted face and felt sorry for the woman. Obviously there was a tale of woe to be told. But then everyone in Campbell Road had one of those. Tilly felt sorry for every poor sod that turned up in The Bunk looking for somewhere cheap to stay and a job of sorts to keep the kids fed. Sympathy was of no bloody use when what was needed was hard cash and a bit of luck for a change.

'Yeah . . . well . . . anythin' else you need to know, I'm just next door.' She wiped her hands on her pinafore. 'See yer downstairs in a bit, alright?'

FOUR

'Gonna let me in, then?' Tilly asked impatiently as her sister simply gazed at her. She'd come to tell Fran she'd found someone to take on her washing.

Slowly Fran stood aside and Tilly swept in. Fran's bruises had almost disappeared, but a sallow colouring around her eyes and jaw was a reminder of the beating she'd taken. Her arms were healing more slowly and the muscles were still stiff and sore from being brutally treated.

'What you looking so shifty about?' Tilly asked bluntly.

Fran simply shrugged.

'A new family's moving in next door. They've not got a pot ter piss in. The woman wants work urgent so she's doing your washing. We'll get it finished and back to Tufnell in plenty of time.'

Fran gave a weak smile and muttered her thanks.

Tilly sensed something was not right and then her nose told her what it was. 'He's been in 'ere, ain't he?' she accused, taking another sniff. 'I can smell bacca.'

'Don't go mad, Til,' Fran started to wheedle but was soon interrupted.

'Yeah, don't go mad, Til,' Jimmy Wild echoed, emerging

from the back slip room where he'd been hiding himself. He walked closer and slung an arm about his wife's frail shoulders. 'We've made up, ain't we, gel? I'm back home where I should be with me family.'

'He's said he's sorry and he won't do it no more. The kids need their dad.' Fran was unable to meet Tilly's eyes and stared at the floor.

'You fuckin' idiot,' Tilly exploded. 'How many times have you heard him say sorry 'n' it won't happen again?'

Fran narrowed her eyes on her sister. 'I can't manage on me own. I got kids and debts.'

'Yeah, 'n' he's gonna add to them for you,' Tilly said on a harsh laugh. 'Just like before.'

She gave her brother-in-law a hate-filled look. He winked back, making her fight down her need to pounce on him and punch the smirk from his face.

Jack Keiver was just at that moment on his way up the stairs. Seeing the door open to his sister-in-law's room he poked his head in to say hello. The greeting died on his lips. The scene in front of him made him hasten further into the room. He drew Tilly's arm through his in an act of restraint and solidarity. He'd immediately guessed what had gone on. His brother-in-law had managed to squirm his way back home with lies and promises.

'Come on, Til, leave it. We've been through all this before. Let 'em stew. It's their business.'

For a moment Tilly stood undecided before allowing her husband to lead her to the door. Jack was right, but still she felt betrayed and angered by her sister's weakness. She felt now more inclined to shake her than punch him.

Jack turned and looked at Jimmy. He raised a threatening finger. 'We ain't finished. I ain't forgot you tried to take a swing at my missus. And all on account of some poxy brass.'

'I was wrong.' Jimmy gestured an apology with his flat palms. 'I swear on the Holy Bible it won't happen no more. All in the past, mate. I'm back and it's gonna be alright this time.'

'Yeah, 'course it is,' Jack muttered sarcastically as he led Tilly out.

'What d'you think of that Danny?' Sophy asked Alice as they made their meandering way back home from the shop. They'd bought a penn'orth of liquorice and sucked on it while talking. Bethany put up a hand and Sophy obligingly wound a black string onto her palm. Their young sister then skipped happily in front of them, head back and the liquorice dangling between her lips.

'Who?' Alice asked with a frown.

Sophy tutted and her eyes soared skyward. 'The new family what turned up yesterday. The biggest boy's name's Danny. He kept lookin' at me. I think he fancies me.'

'You think all the boys fancy you,' Alice chortled.

'Look!' Sophy hissed and nudged Alice in the ribs. 'Here he comes now with his brother! I bet they've been following us.'

Alice gave her elder sister a look. Sophy's cheeks were turning pink and she was scraping her fingers through her brown hair to tidy it. In Alice's estimation the new boys were probably just off to the shop. She decided not to dampen Sophy's excitement with that opinion.

The Lovat boys made to walk past without a word and with barely a sullen look slanting from beneath their dark brows at the Keiver girls. Alice sensed her sister's disappointment at their indifference and bit her lip to suppress a smile.

Alice's mild amusement stoked Sophy's indignation. She swung herself into the boys' path and adopted a belligerent stance she'd seen her mum use, with hands plonked on her thin hips and chin jutting forward. 'Why've you come all this way from Essex? You lot in trouble?'

'What's it ter you?' the boy called Danny snarled and aggressively looked her up and down.

'We don't want no scumbags living next door,' Sophy told him, her lip curling ferociously.

'Nah . . . by all accounts you've got "em livin' in the same house,' Danny let fly back, making his brother Geoff guffaw.

Sophy turned crimson. She'd not meant to start a proper argument with him. All she'd wanted was for him to stop and say a few words, but now she'd started this ruckus she couldn't back down. 'You wanna watch what you're saying. Me dad'll have you.'

'Yeah . . . and I'll have him back,' Danny said. 'We ain't scared of nobody, you remember it.'

Alice, who had up till now been watching and listening, decided to give her sister some support. 'You ain't scared 'cos you ain't been here long enough,' she piped up. 'Wait till you meet the other boys; they'll beat you both up, you give 'em lip.'

'Yeah.' Sophy nodded. 'Wait till you meet a few of 'em. Robertson brothers wot live across the road'll thrash you good 'n' proper. Let's see how big yer mouth is then.'

Danny hooted and began to act palsied. 'Look! I'm shakin' in me boots.'

'You will be!' Sophy answered but she was already edging away, aware that no gains were to be made.

The Lovat boys began to shift too. One last challenging stare over their shoulders and they were carrying on towards the shop.

Sophy stared boldly after them. 'Knew I wouldn't like 'em soon as I saw 'em,' she announced loud enough for them to hear.

'Don't think they're bothered whether we like 'em or not,' Alice muttered. 'Don't think they like us either.'

'Good!' Sophy flounced about. Grabbing Bethany's hand she yanked on it and they headed off home.

They were close to the junction with Paddington Street when Alice spotted Sarah Whitton outside her house with one of her older sisters. Louisa Whitton looked to be in a fine temper and Sarah was scooting backwards away from her, obviously to escape a whack. Louisa was a hefty, sweaty girl of about eighteen, not too bright and known to use brawn rather than brain. All of a sudden she lunged at Sarah and swiped her across the face, making her young sister howl and rub frantically at a scarlet cheek.

'Wonder what's goin' on?' Sophy murmured to Alice. Her features had transformed from moodiness, brought on by the confrontation with the Lovats, to anticipation. Family fights in the street were a common occurrence in Campbell Road and provided a bit of light relief for people living with the monotony of poverty.

'Come on, let's go 'n' see,' Sophy urged. They started to walk faster, Bethany lagging behind. As they got closer they could hear Louisa's raucous accusations as she stalked her sister with her fists at the ready.

'Thievin' li'l bitch! Give it me back or I'll lay you out, right here ''n' now.'

'Ain't got it . . . ain't got it, I tell yer. Let me go in . . . Mum'll tell you, I ain't got no money.'

'What's up?' Alice called and ran closer to her friend. She liked Sarah and felt concerned on her behalf. She also wanted to help if she could. A worm of guilt was already squirming unpleasantly in her belly as an idea of what might be wrong entered her mind.

'Keep yer nose out,' Louisa bawled at her and wagged a threatening finger. She came close enough for it to land and shove against Alice's nose. 'You Keivers need ter mind yer own.'

'You don't want to let me mum hear you say that,' Sophy piped up then piped down as Louisa shot her a pugnacious look.

'Give me the money you got fer it, you li'l cow.' Louisa advanced again on her snivelling sister.

'What's she on about?' Alice demanded of her friend as Sarah cuffed snot from her top lip.

'She reckons I took her new blouse down the secondhand shop in the Land. I never did, I swear.'

'You lyin' mare. If you didn't who did, then? 'Cos I just been down Queensland Road 'n' saw it in the winder and that's where I just got it from. Solly said he remembers a girl about your age took it in. Cost me two 'n' six to buy back me own soddin' blouse. And he wanted more for it!'

Alice suddenly went very pale and very quiet. She looked at Sophy to see that her sister seemed to be engrossed in this spectacle. So were various other people who had lazily propped themselves against doorjambs or railings to watch what was going on.

'Go on . . . give her another dig,' one of the boys from Sophy's class at school called out mischievously.

'I'll give *you* a dig you don't shut up, Herbert Banks,' Alice yelled angrily at him.

'One more chance then I'm gonna really set about yer,' Louisa warned.

'Mum!' Sarah wailed in anguish. But everyone, even Sarah, knew that help from that quarter was very unlikely. Ginny Whitton's *nerves* kept her prostrate on her bed for hours on end with just a bottle of gin for company. At this time of the afternoon it was unlikely she could hear much at all through her booze-induced meditation.

'I'll get your two 'n' six,' Alice blurted and rushed forward to step between the two sisters.

'What's it to you?' Louisa dropped her hand and stared at Alice.

'Nuthin' . . . she's me friend. I'll get your money. Just leave her alone.' Alice felt one of her sister's hands gripping her elbow and Sophy tried to yank her away.

'You ain't got half a crown,' Sophy hissed. 'Now she's gonna lamp you instead, stupid.'

'Shut up,' Alice muttered and, shaking off her sister's fingers, she turned and sprinted for home.

'None of our business.' Tilly cut Alice short as her daughter neared the end of her breathless tale of woe.

'But it is, Mum. Sarah's gonna get a hiding and it was me took that blouse in to Solly's place for you and we only got one and six for it.'

'Yeah, and it was Ginny Whitton give it to me in the first place to sell for her. If Louisa's got a beef it's with her mother, not with us.'

'Will you come and tell her that? She's waiting for half a crown.'

Tilly transferred baby Lucy from one hip to the other and sipped from a cup of lukewarm tea. She was drinking it in the hope it might take the whiff of whiskey from her breath before Jack got home. 'I got things to do,' she answered irritably. 'Besides, I got enough o' me own wars to sort out without gettin' involved in the Whittons' dingdongs.' Inwardly Tilly was still brooding on her sister's monstrous stupidity in letting Jimmy come back.

Since marrying Jimmy Wild it seemed that the pretty, confident young woman Fran had once been had all but disappeared. It infuriated Tilly to know the pig had such power over her sister that he'd started to alter her character.

Yet she blamed Fran too for allowing him to return again and again to crush her more firmly beneath his boot.

'Can I have half a crown then to get Louisa off Sarah's back?' Alice pleaded. 'It ain't fair. She ain't done nuthin'.'

Tilly choked on her tea. 'Get out of here before I land you one, you little tyke!' she shrieked. 'Give yer half a crown, indeed. If I had half a bleedin' crown I'd be down the shop with it and get something fer yer teas tonight.'

Alice knew she was wasting her time. She'd thought straight off that her mum had been drinking from the way she was a bit unsteady on her feet. Now she knew for sure. She was obviously in a bad mood; if she'd had half a crown she'd be down the Duke with it, not down the shop buying bread and jam.

'Louisa said us Keivers ought to mind our own,' was Alice's final tactic in trying to rouse her mum's temper into action.

But Tilly was sunk in her own thoughts. One day she'd have that bastard Jimmy, she promised herself. She'd have him locked up so he'd never hurt Fran or her kids again.

Alice slipped out of the door and met her mother's nemesis on the lower landing.

'Alright, Al?' Jimmy greeted her with his soppy, wonky smile.

Alice nodded but her eyes were bright with unshed tears.

Jimmy blocked her way. 'Woss up, little 'un?' he crooned.

'Need half a crown urgent,' Alice blurted. 'Mum won't give it me.'

'Half a crown, eh?' Jimmy fished in a pocket and produced a silver coin. 'There yer go,' he said, handing it over with a flourish.

Alice raised a wondrous, grateful smile to her uncle's face. Half a crown was not easily come by. It had taken her two months to save that from her doorsteps and now she regretted spending it on going to the flicks and chips on the way home just last week. She'd treated Sarah too as she never had more than a few coppers to call her own despite doing odd jobs most evenings. She'd heard her dad say it was bloody astonishing that Ginny Whitton could recover well enough to wrestle away her daughters' wages before she suffered a relapse.

'I'll give it you back, promise,' Alice gasped at her uncle then fled with the coin clutched tightly in her hand.

Jimmy watched her go with a crafty smile on his face. He then raised his eyes to the landing above. He was just biding his time with that mouthy bitch . . . just biding his time . . .

Having hared back along the road as fast as she could, Alice soon saw that she might be too late. A fight was still going on but now it was between Louisa Whitton and her sister Sophy. Louisa had hold of Sophy's hair and was dragging her along by it. Sophy was screeching and trotting to keep up as Louisa sadistically speeded up her pace. Their sister Bethany was standing on her own, grizzling, her chin on her chest. From the sidelines came various raucous suggestions as to how Sophy ought to retaliate.

'I told you to keep your nose out of me business. If yer sister don't get back here with me money you get the hidin' instead.'

Alice launched herself at Louisa, punching ineffectually at the rolls of fat in her back. Suddenly she was whipped away by an arm girdling her waist. She landed on her feet and turned about to swipe out but the younger Lovat boy dodged aside so her fist smacked air rather than him.

'You'd better let her go, fatso.'

Alice gasped in a breath and simply gaped at the two Lovat boys. Danny had spoken; he was standing looking quite nonchalant, his eyes fixed on Louisa. But there was something menacing about him that quietened the crowd. Danny Lovat's face might betray him as about fourteen but he was a strapping lad, easily five feet eight inches tall. And that was quite lofty for a man, let alone a youth, around these parts where stunted runts abounded.

'What're you going to do about it, little boy?' Louisa jeered but she didn't sound so confident now and her grip on Sophy's hair loosened a bit.

'Well, I don't usually hit girls, but you're so big 'n' ugly I'm gonna make an exception.' Danny didn't respond by as much as a blink to the laughter his comment produced. 'Let her go, fatso, 'n' piss off home. Or I'll have to make you.'

Louisa considered herself to be a bit of a rough handful. She wasn't going to let a kid who might still be at school make a monkey out of her. Shoving a flat palm against Sophy's skull, she sent her tottering backwards to crash to the ground. She then turned to swing a left at Danny that barely connected with his shoulder as he swayed like a pro. Quite gracefully he then stepped back in and floored her with a single punch on the chin. It was obvious he'd put little weight behind it and, after a stunned moment, the crowd showed its appreciation with a smattering of applause before dispersing.

Alice rushed to Sophy to try and get her up off the ground. She noticed that a clump of her sister's hair was straggling on her shoulder where Louisa had yanked it out. Before Sophy could see it Alice brushed it off and stamped her foot on top of it. 'Where's Sarah gone?' Alice asked.

'She scarpered after you went and left me with that maniac,' Sophy sobbed. 'She's nutty, that Louisa. She needs lockin' up.'

'You alright?' Danny asked gruffly and stuck out a hand to help Sophy.

'Yeah . . . thanks,' Sophy mumbled. She ignored his hand and sprang up in an ungainly jumble of limbs.

He shrugged and he and his brother were soon heading down the road.

'Oi . . . you two . . . you can't just go off like that,' Alice shouted spontaneously after them.

The boys sauntered back and looked questioningly at them. 'What d'you want, then?'

Alice flushed. Now they'd come back she didn't know what answer to give. 'What's his name?' She pointed at Danny's brother, who was unconcernedly chewing as though he'd never hoisted her to safety from Louisa's fat back.

'Geoff,' Danny said while Geoff gave Alice a long look.

'And how d'you come to fight like that?'

'I'll have yer next time, yer bastards.'

Danny stuck two fingers up at Louisa without bothering to even glance her way. 'Done boxin' in Essex,' he told Alice whilst looking at Sophy.

Sophy continued fiddling with her hair to try and tidy it, blushing furiously. She grabbed at Bethany's hand and shushed her to stop her crying

'You get going home now, Beth. Sophy's alright, see.' Alice wiped her younger sister's face clear of tearstains with her thumbs. Then she turned her about and gave her shoulder a little push to start her off home.

'You got blood on your lip,' Danny neutrally told Sophy.

'Did you do boxing 'n' get paid?' Alice asked interestedly, cuffing away her sister's blood on her sleeve when she saw Sophy searching in vain for a handkerchief.

'Yeah . . . sometimes,' Danny replied. 'Never saw no money though. The old man soon had any purses.'

'Ain't worth workin',' Sophy chipped in. 'Never get to keep nuthin'. They always have it off you.'

'Why d'you come here then?' Alice asked. 'Ain't nothing worth having round here.'

'Got in a fight with the landlord where we lived. Broke his jaw. He threw us all out then the coppers got involved when it all turned nasty.' Danny saw Geoff frown at him as though warning him to hold his tongue. Danny shrugged in response. He didn't see the point in trying to hide it. The Keivers knew they'd only have tramped miles because something serious had happened.

Alice's eyes grew round. 'Did your dad go mad at you for getting you all thrown out?'

'Nah . . . was his fault. If he hadn't borrowed money off the landlord none of it would've happened. Had the money for almost a year and never paid none back, y'see. Never could 'cos he lost his job when he done his foot in.'

'How'd he do it?'

'Cart fell on him down the market.'

'You turned fourteen yet?' Sophy asked shyly.

Danny nodded. 'While back.'

'You're lucky. No more school,' Sophy said wistfully.

'You going to get work round here?' Alice asked.

'Soon as I can find something decent. Don't want no dead-end errand-boy capers. Want me own business.' Danny looked about with disgust in his eyes. 'Then when I've got a few bob I'm moving on, going home to Essex. Can't wait to get out of this dump.'

'Me neither . . .' Sophy and Alice chorused passionately.

Feeling quite relaxed in their camaraderie, Alice opened her palm and showed her half a crown.

Three pairs of hungry eyes darted to it.

'Where d'you get that?' Sophy gasped. 'Mum never give you it.'

'Uncle Jimmy did,' Alice said. ''Spose I should give it back, 'cos I ain't giving it to Louisa after what she's done.'

Nobody said anything, they all kept their eyes pinned on the shiny silver coin.

'Let's go and get some chips.' It was an impetuous decision. 'You two can come 'n' all,' Alice magnanimously said to Danny and Geoff.

'When you was boxing did you get knocked out much?' Sophy asked Danny before chewing on a chip.

The four of them were lined up, sitting on a low wall in Blackstock Road with scrunched newspapers filled with chips and meat pies nestled on their laps.

'Reckon that's insulting,' Danny said, all solemn.

'No . . . didn't mean you weren't no good, or nuthin',' Sophy blurted, and quickly turned to give him an earnest look. 'Just wondered if you ever got injured, that's all.' The last thing Sophy wanted to do was start another row with Danny.

Danny and Geoff exchanged a look and laughed.

'He's winding you up,' Geoff said easily and tipped his head back to swig from a bottle of pop.

'Undefeated champion, weren't I?' Danny said, deliberately puffing out his chest to make the girls giggle. 'Mind you, weren't no reg'lar fights I got into. More like bare-knuckle street scraps where bets were took off the audience. Well-arranged, though, they were. Had to be, of course, 'cos the law would've put a stop to it if they'd found out. Could make fifty quid a night . . . sometimes more.' He looked off into the distance. 'Should've stuck with it. Might've got a backer who'd have took me pro. A couple of fellers showed an interest in managing me. But me mum wouldn't have it. Said I was too young. Could've ended up like Kid Lewis 'n' made some *real* money if I still had them contacts.'

'Could've ended up all bashed about 'n' all,' Sophy lectured. 'You're lucky yer nose ain't all squashed and yer ears shaped like cauliflowers.'

'You sound just like our mum,' Geoff said wryly and slid his brother a significant look before he turned his attention to Alice, sitting rather quietly beside him.

'When you leaving school?' he abruptly asked.

'Not for ages.' Alice grimaced sadly. 'Not even thirteen yet.' She frowned again at the crumpled newspaper on her lap containing her delicious food. It had seemed like a good idea to come and have something to eat with the Lovat boys. But now doubts about what she'd done were worming into her mind. In her pocket she had change from the half crown her uncle had lent her but she knew she must offer him back the whole amount and she'd no idea where she'd find that money. She was regretting having shown off and offered to be generous with money that wasn't hers to spend. If her mother ever found out what she'd done she'd be for it.

FIVE

'There . . . take yer poxy half a crown!' Tilly roared. She drove a fist into her pinafore pocket, pulled out a coin and lobbed it.

'No need to be like that, Til,' Fran said, swiping the money off the dirty floorboards. 'I'm just saying that your Alice has took what's rightfully mine. Jimmy's give me no money and the boys need something for tea.'

'Well, ain't that a surprise . . . Jimmy's give yer no money!' Tilly sarcastically echoed her sister's words back at her.

'Well, perhaps he would've done if your Alice hadn't been out beggin' and got to him first.'

Tilly turned her savage, narrowed gaze on her sister, making Fran flinch. 'My kids don't beg, and don't you ever say they do. He should've told her no when she asked.'

'He's got a kind heart.' Fran coloured at the sound of her sister's scoffing hoot of laughter.

'He's a fuckin' animal and you know it,' Tilly spat. 'He's deliberately making trouble between us, you know that too.'

'Don't talk about him like that. He's me husband,' Fran shouted, narked.

'Yeah, he's your'n alright, more fool you,' Tilly replied and turned her back on her sister. 'Shut the door on your way out.'

'Oi . . . you . . . here!' was the greeting that Alice got when she returned home with Sophy.

Immediately Alice felt her stomach lurch. She knew straight away from her mother's voice and fearsome look that she was in for a hiding and she could guess why.

'You two in back,' Tilly commanded her other daughters.

'You been asking Uncle Jimmy for money?'

'No!' Alice protested. 'I didn't ask him for nuthin'. He give it me.'

'But you was telling him our business, and that I'd not give you money you'd asked for. You took his half crown.'

Alice nodded then howled as a rough hand swiped her cheek.

'You tell him nothing, you hear? Never tell him what goes on in this place. Have you given that half a crown to fat Louisa on account of her blouse going missing?'

Alice miserably shook her head. She knew she was in trouble whatever she said. All she had left to return to her uncle Jimmy was a shilling and threepence in change. 'I didn't give Louisa it. When I got back she was beating Sophy up and Sarah'd scarpered.'

Tilly's features tightened on hearing that Sophy had been set about. 'Right. Give it here, then,' she ordered and stuck out a hand to take the coin.

'Spent it,' Alice muttered and hung her head.

'You . . . done . . . *what?*' Tilly demanded in genuine astonishment. She grasped her daughter's chin and forced it up.

'Bought chips; we was hungry.' Alice knew that wasn't

explanation enough to satisfy her mother. A few penn'orth of chips didn't make half a crown. She'd bought pies and pop too. 'Bought some for the new boys too 'cos Danny was on our side and knocked down Louisa for what he did to Sophy.'

'Feeling generous, was you?' Tilly's hand cracked against the other side of Alice's face this time. 'You little pest. Give 'ere what's left of it. Every penny.'

Alice dropped the coins into her mother's waiting palm. 'I'll pay back the rest from me doorsteps,' Alice mumbled while the tears rolled down her scarlet, stinging cheeks.

'Too bleedin' right you'll pay it back,' her mother agreed harshly. 'Now get out o' me sight else I'll really give you something to cry about.'

Alice sank onto the bed in the back room and shrugged off Sophy's comforting hand. She turned her face into the musty old mattress and closed her hot, dribbling eyes.

'Wish I was old enough to leave school,' she muttered. 'I'd be out of here and miles away by tomorrow.'

'Me 'n' all,' Sophy agreed. 'Hope Danny gets a decent job soon.'

Alice turned on the bed to look at her sister. 'Won't help you what job he gets,' she said shortly and cuffed the wetness from her face.

'Might do . . .' Sophy looked away. 'Only just met him but I know he likes me and I like him,' she said a bit defensively. 'Can't wait to get away from this dump and nor can he. When he goes home to Essex I'm going with him.'

Alice levered herself up on an elbow, momentarily shocked into speechlessness. Her sister looked oddly calm and confident and there wasn't a sign of the self-conscious smile that usually accompanied her daft hopes. 'I never heard him say you can,' Alice reasoned. 'Anyhow, you don't hardly know him.' She'd spluttered that with a grin, already recovering from her mother's chastisement. It wasn't an unusual occurrence for any of them, even Bethany, to get a good belt off her when she was het up over something. And she had given her mother something to get very het up about. Inwardly her stomach squirmed in regret because she knew the money must be found from somewhere to pay back Uncle Jimmy. He wouldn't wait for payment while she did her doorsteps for the next few months. Alice focused on her sister's expression, considered the meaning behind it. She looked secretive but in a nice way. Danny *did* like Sophy. He'd made that pretty obvious this afternoon by the way he was looking at her and touching her. At one point Alice had feared he might try and kiss her behind a wall in Seven Sisters Road. And Sophy had just let her know . . . as if she hadn't already guessed . . . that she liked him right back. 'You reckon he'll marry you or something?' Alice asked. 'You're not even old enough to leave school.'

'Soon I will be.' Sophy nodded in emphasis. She glowered fiercely at Alice. 'Don't you go telling Mum I like him. She'll put a spoke in. She can't wait for us to get out to work neither but only so's she can have our wages off us.'

Alice knew that was true. Even the little bit they managed to make on their odd jobs was under scrutiny from their mother. They'd learned to hide very well their few coppers for their mother had been known to prise up floorboards searching for them.

'You could marry Danny's brother Geoff, if you like,' Sophy said, revelling in her romantic daydream.

Alice snorted. 'I'm not getting married for a long while. When I get a job and get some money I'm getting meself some decent clothes from Chapel Street. I'm never going in the rag shop again once I'm working.' She paused and thought about being married and found the idea of it didn't seem as ridiculous as once it would have done. She wondered if it was because in her mind she'd pictured Geoff sitting opposite her at the table, drinking tea in his vest. 'And I'm saving too,' Alice rushed on, feeling confused. 'I'm saving as much as I can to get away from here.'

'Shall I go out now?' Bethany suddenly piped up. She'd been fidgeting on the bed for a while. 'I want to go and see me friend Sally over the road. Is Mum still on the warpath?'

Alice encouraged Bethany to go away. She was quite enjoying this talk with Sophy. They'd never before chatted for so long about their plans for the future. Before, getting work and being a grown-up had all seemed to be a long way in the distance. Now, for some reason, it didn't.

'Danny probably won't take you with him anyhow.' Alice hoped in her heart that she was wrong. She hoped Sophy got to live her little dream, if that's what she wanted.

'We'll see . . .' Sophy said and with that she lay down on the bed too. She rolled over and stared at Alice, her eyes wide and concerned. 'I bet he don't know.'

'Don't know what?'

'He don't know to keep his mouth shut about where he lives. If he tells people he's living in Campbell Road he'll never get a decent job.'

'It's too late to go after a job today,' Alice wisely pointed out. 'You can tell Danny all of that tomorrow.'

'What in Gawd's name is that?'

'What's it look like?' Jack asked, still smiling widely.

Tilly had a look on her face halfway between disbelief and despair. 'It looks like a bleedin' piana,' she roared at him. 'Don't dare tell me that you've paid good money fer it.'

Jack knew that before Tilly got worked up enough over wasted cash to launch herself at him he must stop teasing her and reveal his good news. In fact he'd no need to say anything at all. He simply shoved a hand in a pocket. When it reappeared it held several pound notes.

For once in her life Tilly Keiver was momentarily dumbfounded. They were stationed on the pavement just outside their home. At the kerb was a cart that Jack had just pulled up the road. Tilly had seen him from the window when he came round the corner from Paddington Street. After a stunned few minutes gawping at her husband ferrying a gleaming piano on an old cart she'd flown down the stairs to confront him over it. Her eyes darted about the street as though she reckoned someone might be close by and spot her husband had a wad in his pocket. As far as she knew Jack had been working as a runner for a bookie because nothing better had presented itself. That paid shillings not pounds. 'Put that away for Gawd's sake,' she squealed.

Jack obligingly shoved the cash back where it came from but said, 'Let 'em see. I come by it fair 'n' square.'

'Did you now?' Tilly sounded sceptical. 'What you done? You pulled a stunt?'

'No . . . I ain't pulled a stunt. I ain't been gambling neither. I got work, Til. I got good work from Basher Payne.'

Basher Payne had started out with just one horse and cart. He now owned half a dozen and hired them out. He also owned doss houses in Campbell Road and the surrounding streets. He protected his little empire fiercely despite the fact he stood little more than five feet four inches tall, and had earned the name and reputation of a formidable fighter.

'What work's he given you?' Tilly eyed her husband suspiciously.

'I've been painting out his places in George's Road 'cos the sanitary inspector's been in and condemned 'em. I started Monday. I kept it as a surprise for you. He's pleased as punch with what I've done so far.' Spontaneously Jack pulled Tilly in to a hug. 'He paid me this on account.'

Energetically Tilly elbowed free of her husband's embrace, not yet convinced that such good luck could be theirs. She needed more information. 'So you got a job off Basher and a sub off him so thought you'd buy a joeyanna with it to celebrate.'

'Why not?' Jack asked simply. 'You want a bit of a drink and a laugh, don't you?' He grinned at her. 'Well, I don't mind if I join in. No need to go down the Duke all the time. We can have a few bottles and a singsong right here. The kids can stay home instead of dawdling in the corridor of the Duke or out on the pavement.' He plunged a hand into his pocket and scrunched the notes till they crackled. 'Ain't as if I spent it all. Supper from the chippy tonight. Kids'll like that.'

'Yer daft git,' Tilly said quite affectionately. 'We ain't got room enough upstairs to swing a cat and you bring us home this monstrosity. Where we gonna put it? Out on the landing?'

Jack bent to snatch a kiss from his wife. 'You're pleased really, ain't you?' he teased. 'If Basher keeps me in work for a good while perhaps we'll finally get out of here 'n' get up the other end of the road in something bigger 'n' better.' He ruffled her thick, fiery hair. 'This Saturday we'll have a bit of a knees-up. Ask a few of the neighbours over.'

'You daft git,' she repeated with a grin. She slipped her fingers over the glossy lid of the piano. 'How we gonna get the bugger upstairs?'

'I'll see if Jimmy's in,' Jack said. 'He can give us a hand with it.' He disappeared into the dank interior of the house, whistling cheerfully.

The smile on Tilly's face faded at the mention of her brother-in-law. She wouldn't ever forgive Jimmy for beating

Fran, or for causing trouble over the half crown he'd given to Alice. Several months might have passed, and things might have calmed down between them all, but Tilly knew it wouldn't be long before Jimmy was up to his old tricks again. Jimmy was work shy. He also thought he was a bit of a hound round these parts and the fact that he had a wife and kids relying on him wouldn't stop him poncing about doing nothing or showing off to his mates . . . most of them younger than he was by some years. When he thought he could he'd take up with fancy women again and generally act flash with the bit of cash that should be given to Fran as housekeeping. And if Fran didn't like it, he'd show her who was boss . . . in the way he always had . . . with his fists.

A few minutes later Jack reappeared with Jimmy loping at his side. It was early summer and Jimmy had on just a vest belted into his trousers. From his lips dangled a stumpy crumpled roll-up.

'Alright, gel?' he greeted Tilly.

She mumbled a response, her eyes flashing dislike at him.

Jimmy smirked and unconsciously flexed the muscles in his naked arms. He knew Tilly despised him yet it didn't stop him preening. Such was his conceit that he thought every woman must find him irresistible. He'd plenty of time on his hands to keep himself in shape by sparring with the lads at the YMCA in Pooles Park. His eyes lingered on Tilly, running over her top to bottom. He was just waiting for the right opportunity to impress on her once again he was a bloke you didn't mess with. He'd done so once before,. She'd deserved another lesson on numerous occasions since. It might have been a while ago but he hadn't forgotten the way she'd showed him up in the street when he'd been caught out with Nellie. His pals still ribbed him over it and made him feel a bloody fool. He was more careful with

Nellie now. They'd had to make use of alleys and dark corners instead of her room along the road.

But Nellie was pulling in a good few quid a week from working the streets up west and sometimes Jimmy thought he might be better off moving in with her. He didn't see why he should knock himself out acting as Jack's labourer doing painting and decorating, or helping Billy the Totter for a few measly bob a day, if he could act as Nellie's manager and take a bit of commission off her.

'Oi, daydreamer . . .' Jack called and started Jimmy from his brooding. He undid the rope that had lashed the piano to the cart.

'Where d'you get this fucker then, Jack?' Jimmy enquired past the drooping dog-end in his mouth.

'Off old man Bailey. He said he'd give me first refusal on it. He kept to his word. Been put by since Christmas.'

'You give him a deposit?' Tilly demanded shrewdly. She knew that Victor Bailey had a secondhand furniture store in Holloway Road. She knew too that he wasn't generally soft-hearted. He was a wily businessman.

Last Christmas things had been tight for money and the kids had had just one stocking, filled mainly with bruised fruit and a few liquorice sticks, to share between them. If she thought for one moment that money that could have been well spent had been put down on a piano and left there for six months she'd put a hammer through the poxy thing right now.

'I didn't give him nuthin',' Jack soothed, knowing the way his wife's mind worked. 'He kept to his word 'cos I did him a favour and mended the lock on his door when he was burgled.'

Tilly's acceptance of that explanation was limited to a jerk of her chin. She watched as the two men proceeded into the house lugging the piano between them. She glanced around to see that they had drawn a few spectators. She threw back her fiery head and gave a loud chuckle. 'What's up? None of yers seen a bleedin' piana before?' she bawled out, spinning on the spot in glee. Then gripping her skirts she followed Jack and Jimmy in to the house.

'Mum . . .'

Tilly gathered up the old sheet in her arms then spun about to look at Alice. She narrowed her eyes on her daughter. 'What's that look fer? What you after?'

Alice chewed her lip. 'Don't go mad . . . but . . .'

'Spit it out, girl,' Tilly said and folded her arms with the sheet bundled against her chest. 'I ain't got all day to stand about.'

They were in the bedroom that Alice shared with her sisters. Tilly had got hold of a decent sheet off Billy the Totter to replace the threadbare scrap that had covered the dirty mattress the girls slept on. Alice had just helped her mother put the new one on the bed whilst trying to pluck up courage to ask the favour that had been playing over in her mind. Oddly she thought she had a good chance of her mum agreeing to what she wanted. She could be awful in some ways but nice in others.

'It's about Sarah . . . she's got in right trouble again.'

'Oh, yeah?'

'Well, you know I said she'd moved round the corner to stay with her dad 'cos Louisa won't leave her alone and keeps hitting her over that blouse?'

'Yeah . . .' Tilly said in a drawn-out way.

'Well, she can't stay with her dad no more 'cos he's moving to Bethnal Green to get a job and if Sarah goes she'll have to go to a different school and she don't want to 'n' nor do I want it 'cos she's me friend.' Alice drew breath to renew her appeal. 'She can't go home 'cos of Louisa and also 'cos her mum's took in Louisa's friend who pays rent. There's no room there now.'

'And?'

'Can she stay here for a while? Just till . . .'

'Just till what?' Tilly asked, but she gave a rare smile. 'You're too soft, my gel. It's gonna do you no favours when yer older.'

'So can she stop here for a while? Till the lodger moves out?'

'Just for a while till she gets it all sorted out. I'll take Beth in our bed fer a bit. Sarah can kip in with you 'n' Sophy. But you tell her that if she's gonna expect a bit of grub Ginny'd better stump up the necessary. You tell her or I will.'

Alice rushed to her mother and hugged her about the waist. 'Thanks, Mum.'

'Get off with you.' Tilly elbowed herself free. 'Now let's get on. Yer dad'll be back soon and wantin' something to eat.'

SIX

'I'm arresting you lot if that fire's not out by the time I come back.'

'You 'n' 'oose army, rozzer?'

Constable Bickerstaff took a threatening step towards the bonfire, fingers stroking the truncheon on his hip. Through a mirage materialised two men's faces, their grins highlighted by fierce flames.

'Aw, c'mon, mate . . . just roastin' me chestnuts . . .' one of the men lewdly implored for lenience.

'You know rules are no street fires; now put the bugger out,' Twitch bellowed. 'It's hot enough tonight as it is without you making it worse than it needs to be.'

As though to reinforce his argument Sidney Bickerstaff peeled his serge collar away from his sticky skin and wiped it with a handkerchief. He took a glance about. It was ten o'clock on a Saturday evening in late summer and dusk had settled long ago. It might have been three o'clock in the afternoon. Campbell Road never slept. At any time of day or night you might find it bustling with people young and old, and reeking of unwashed humanity and indeterminate rotting debris. At the height of summer the stench and noise was just so much worse. The domestic cacophony escaped through windows and doors flung wide in the forlorn hope of letting in fresh air. It wasn't unusual at this time of year to see people sleeping on carts in the street to escape the stifling conditions in the overcrowded houses.

Sidney Bickerstaff and Ralph Franks had just passed a grizzled old fellow playing a barrel organ and stopped a group of louts from tormenting him and his monkey. The boys had scattered, shouting abuse, but Twitch knew if he turned around he'd see them peeping round the corner of Paddington Street at him. They'd simply wait till he disappeared into Seven Sisters before looking for mischief again. He knew too the street gamesters who'd hared off, after grabbing up dice and cards and coins that'd been strewn on the pavement, would reconvene on the corner outside the doss house as soon as the coast was clear.

'I'm sweltering here,' Constable Ralph Franks complained as he sought his older, stouter colleague as lee from the illegal bonfire. 'We're not coming back this evening, so might as well turn a blind eye.' He turned to squint at the blaze. 'Leave 'em be. With any luck they'll burn the whole bleeding street down and do everyone a favour.' He broke off grumbling as he glimpsed the girl he found attractive. She'd seen him too and was casting sideways looks his way while chatting to another girl. The one he fancied was a definite looker whereas that lump of lard standing next to her was ugly enough to put a bloke off his beer.

As the young constable turned away from her Connie Whitton smiled and wondered what coppers got paid and if that particular copper had a wife or sweetheart. If he did, it wouldn't stop her. It wouldn't stop him either; the randy git couldn't keep his eyes off her when they met. If she took up with him, or any copper, she'd get the cold shoulder round here. That wouldn't worry her. She was itching to get away from the lot of them. Her mother was driving her mad, taking all her wages, then collapsing on the couch she used as a bed. She never stopped drinking and moaning. Her sister Louisa stank the place out because she sweated so much and never bothered to wash. She looked across the road and saw her sister Sarah sitting with the Keiver kids on the steps outside their house. Sarah had been living away from home for months and it didn't seem to bother her younger sister one bit to be away from her family. Connie knew how she felt.

On noticing the two policemen were heading off in Sarah's direction, Connie sauntered over to say hello to her sister and put herself in the young constable's way again.

'What d'you want?' was Sarah's blunt reply to her sister's cheery greeting.

'Party goin' on in there, is it?' Connie cocked her head to listen to the unmistakeable sound of a piano being thumped and some raucous singing accompanying it.

'What if it is? You ain't invited, anyhow,' Sarah flatly told Connie.

'No need to be like that, Sar,' Connie complained. 'Ain't my fault Louisa set about you and started it all off. Ain't my fault either that Dad moved off to Bethnal and left you behind.'

'He didn't leave me,' Sarah muttered. 'I wanted to stay behind.'

'What's all that racket?' Twitch asked, earning his nick-name twice in rapid succession. He'd crossed the street to stand and glare up at the open window out of which, at that precise moment, sailed an empty brown bottle. It narrowly missed Alice's head and smashed on the pave-ment. Alice jumped up and scraped shards together with her foot.

'Just me mum 'n' dad 'n' a few friends having a singsong,'

Alice cautiously told Twitch, still shifting broken glass. She knew, as did everyone in these parts, that you had as little as possible to do with the law. She sat down again and one of her hands dived into the newspaper containing the chips she was sharing with Sarah. They'd been sitting on the pavement for some while talking about this and that and every so often going indoors to jig about on the fringes of the adults or snatch a drink of lemonade. But this weekend the temperature had soared and it was too crowded and hot in there for the youngsters to want to stay too long. They got crushed and elbowed by adults boozing and swaying and roaring out songs.

Since Jack had brought home the piano it had been a regular occurrence on Saturday evening to have a get together – and it went on for as long as limited space and sobriety would allow. Usually by the early hours of Sunday the guests who were still standing had stumbled off home and an uneasy peace was to be had till morning.

Twitch continued to gaze at the window with his hands clasped behind his back. It was a racket, no doubt about it, but if Bunk residents stayed on their own patch it meant he and Franks encountered fewer disorderly drunks while on the beat. And Tilly Keiver was one of the most difficult drunks to deal with. About to share that observation with his colleague, Twitch realised Ralph had wandered off and was talking to the pretty Whitton girl.

'You're fairly new around here, 'n't yer?' Connie struck up conversation and lowered her eyelashes. Close to he wasn't bad looking at all for a flatfoot.

'Yeah . . .' Ralph said. 'And I wish I wasn't.'

Connie glanced up from beneath her lashes. 'Stay long enough you might just find something about The Bunk you like.'

'Like what?' Ralph eyed her calculatingly. 'You know of

some sort of compensation for me being stuck in the worst street in North London on a Saturday night?'

'Yeah . . . might do . . . might know of something . . .' Connie pouted. 'What's your name?'

'Ralph Franks.'

'I'm Connie . . . Connie Whitton. I live up the other end a bit; better end, you might call it.'

'I might,' Ralph said sarcastically. 'But I doubt it.' He moved away from her, conscious of his colleague's ears flapping.

'Well, might see you again . . . when you come back for your compensation,' Connie added slyly.

'Ready to go then, are we?' Twitch asked with a very old-fashioned look lifting his brows beneath his helmet. 'Able to march back to the station, are you, with your balls on fire?' he added with acid amusement as they plodded on towards the corner that turned into Seven Sisters Road.

Franks scowled and said nothing but his restless hands plunged a little deeper into his pockets.

'So . . . found something desirable about the place, have you?'

'She's probably on the game . . . hard to know with any of that lot what they get up to.' Ralph frowned into space.

'If she was on the game, son, she wouldn't be hanging around here on a Saturday night. She'd be up west somewhere earning a fortune with those looks.'

'Are they trouble?'

'Who, the Keivers? I wouldn't mess with them for no reason.'

'Nah. The Whittons.'

'The Whittons.' Twitch grunted a laugh. 'Now let me see. What you've got there is one mad old mother, a father who's had sense enough to have it away on his toes before he goes crackers too, a son dead of disease and three daughters.

Lenny died of something or other when he was just about old enough to go to work. I think that's what sent the mother into a decline . . . the thought of his lost wages. As for the girls . . . you've got a fat ugly one, a skinny schoolgirl and the novice tart you just spoke to. So, all in all, I suppose you'd have to say they're a pretty average mob for around here.'

'Come 'n' play us a tune, Al,' Jack called to Alice as she tried to slip past him in the crowded room. Jack pulled her onto the stool beside him and affectionately ruffled her dark hair.

'Don't know any tunes, Dad,' Alice said with a grin but she plinked and plonked up and down on the ivories, making some inharmonious noise while her dad took a break from performing. He flexed his fingers then supped from the pint glass on top of the piano. The other men might drink straight from the bottle but her dad liked to take his ale with a bit more style.

'Come on, Jack, get goin' again while I'm in the mood,' Jimmy Wild yelled before swigging from the bottle in his fist.

Alice swivelled on the seat to look about. Her eyes met Jimmy's and he gave her a wink. Not so long ago she would have shared the private moment and winked right back. But now, since he'd got her in to trouble with her mum over that half a crown, she felt differently about him. She was beginning to understand that Uncle Jimmy wasn't as nice and friendly as he liked people to think. She was coming to believe that perhaps it wasn't half a dozen of one, six of the other when he and Aunt Fran were going at it hammer and tongs. And perhaps Bobbie and Stevie hadn't misbehaved enough to deserve the bruises she'd seen on them at school. She suspected that her uncle just needed to be in a bad mood over something to act mean.

He'd been mean to her. He must have known that she'd get a wallop off her mum for taking his half a crown. She'd thought that a little secret existed between them yet he'd told on her straight away. His wink and that secret stare now made an odd feeling squirm in her stomach. She half-smiled at him but looked away quickly, her eyes flitting about the cramped room.

She'd left Sarah on the pavement and only come in to get them a drink of pop . . . if any was left in the bottle. If not she was going to ask her dad for a bit of money so they could get some from the shop. Since her dad had got a good job with Basher Payne money hadn't been so tight and being cheeky and asking for a few coppers didn't naturally get you a clip round the ear. Her dad had waylaid her and she'd stopped where she was rather than slipping back outside because she enjoyed having his attention.

'Come on, give us a little tune, Monkey,' her dad fondly invited her, using the pet nickname he had for her.

'Alright, Freckles,' she teased him back and rubbed a tickling finger over the speckled skin on his jaw. 'Glad I'm not a Freckles,' she said provocatively.

Jack touched the mark. 'It's me beauty spot,' he said, as he always did when ribbed over the blemish. 'I know you'd like one just like it really.'

Alice chuckled and picked out a simple chord that he'd taught her when they'd first got the piano. Her dad accompanied her lightly, encouraging her to try again when she hit a wrong note. Finally Alice gestured she'd had enough and looked around for her mum. She was squashed up against the mantelpiece with Aunt Fran. Both of them drinking whiskey by the look of it. Aunt Fran's best skirt barely outlined the little mound of her pregnant belly. Most of the people who had lodgings in the house were either crammed into the room or were out on the landing. Even old Mr Prewett from the landing below – who was known to be a bit of a misery guts – was sitting on the bed edge, tapping his good foot in anticipation of her dad soon starting to play a new tune.

Margaret Lovat bent her head close to Alice's and shouted over the rollicking din, 'You seen my Danny, Alice?'

'He's just outside on the pavement with all of us,' Alice answered.

'Tell him to nip next door 'n' see to the little 'uns, will you, in case Geoff's gone out.'

Alice got up from beside her dad and slipped out and into the back room. Mrs Lovat had just reminded her that her baby sister might need her attention. It was usually her job to make sure that Bethany and Lucy were taken care of while the adults enjoyed themselves and got drunk. Not that her mum asked her to do it. She was probably too under the influence to even remember she had kids some of the time. She just assumed Alice would look out for the younger ones.

By the light of a tiny flame in an oil lamp balanced precariously on the seat of a chair Alice could see Bethany was dozing on the bed next to Lucy. The room stank and the unmistakeable sound of flies could be heard buzzing. Alice turned up the flame. She looked down at Lucy. She was awake and smiled at her despite the fact that a fly crawled in the milky sick on her chin.

Alice flicked it away and found what she needed to clean her up. She wiped her face with a rag then attended to her bottom end. Alice felt herself gag as the stench intensified. Quickly she bundled the filthy nappy onto the floor and cleaned Lucy's bottom. She then put a clean scrap of cotton on her and picked her up.

'When I go . . . I'll take you with me,' she promised her. 'I'll always be around if you need me,' she whispered against her soft, musky cheek. She put her back down on the bed close to Bethany then, picking up the stinking nappy, she took it out, hoping that most of the flies would follow.

'Lucy's nappy,' Alice said by way of explanation as Sophy wrinkled her nose at her. Alice had tried to rinse her hands under the tap on the landing but the place was so packed it was hard to get to the water and wash properly. She felt a little embarrassed and annoyed at Sophy for miming she stank in front of Danny. 'Anyhow, your mum said you've got to go 'n' check on the little 'uns,' she told Danny.

Danny muttered beneath his breath but got to his feet.

'I'll come with you,' Sophy immediately volunteered.

A significant look seemed to pass between the two of them. 'Nah . . . 's'alright,' Danny mumbled. 'Geoff might be in there. Not seen him go out. Not that he's any bleedin' use with the kids. He's probably akip.'

'You two been making plans then?' Alice asked when they were alone. Sarah had gone off to the shop with her sister Connie to get some sherbert.

Alice knew that Danny had just started a new job down the market helping on a costermonger's stall. Despite having boasted months ago he wouldn't be taking dead-end errand-boy jobs, that was what he'd started off with. To save face he said he'd taken it because he got a bike to use for deliveries. He'd bring the bike home at dinnertime and give the Keiver kids and his brothers and sisters lifts on the cross bars up and down the road. But misuse of the bike wasn't why he'd got the sack. The grocer had got suspicious about the amount of stale loaves and broken biscuits that went missing rather than being sold on at a discount. Of course, he couldn't prove that Danny had had them . . . but he reckoned it'd seemed odd that Mrs Lovat never seemed to need to buy bread to go with her margarine and jam.

SEVEN

'I'm going to ask you a straight question and you'd better give me a straight answer.' Tilly was talking to Sophy but she suddenly shot a frown at Alice. 'Wait outside.'

Alice did as she was told and descended the stairs. She loitered first in the musty hallway then, when the sensation of debris, blown in by the wind, fluttering against her feet began to irritate, she went to breathe in the sweeter atmosphere of a dull and misty mid-November morning. She stuffed her hands in her pockets and shivered against the chill whilst her mind began turning over possible reasons why her mum would want a private talk with Sophy. From several painful experiences Alice had learned that usually no good reason prompted their mother to get you on your own.

She heard a clattering of footsteps on the stairs and saw her cousins Bobbie and Stevie emerge from the murky hallway. Alice noticed that one of Stevie's cheeks looked red.

'Your dad clouted yer?' Alice asked him sympathetically.

Stevie sniffed and cuffed at his nose. 'Nah . . . got it off me mum,' he said.

'He wet the bed again,' Bobbie said and dodged as his

brother swung out at him. 'He'll get a belt off dad 'n' all tonight if he smells piss on the sheet.' Bobbie started trotting down the road.

'Why don't you shut yer gob,' Stevie snarled after him before he slunk past Alice.

Various people were coming out of the tenement houses: adults going off to work, children on their way to school. Alice returned a simple greeting to people who hailed her whilst her mind still brooded on what was going on upstairs. She gazed up at the battered sash window as though wishing to peer in it and ease her curiosity. It seemed she'd been waiting ages for Sophy. Slowly her faraway vision dropped, focused on Sarah Whitton who was on her way down the road towards her.

Sarah had lodged with the Keivers until last month. Then Tilly had said enough was enough. She'd wanted Beth out of her bed and again in the back room with the other girls. So Sarah had had to return home. Sarah had wanted to stay but Alice had been oddly relieved and had only half-heartedly backed her friend's pleas to stay. Since the piano had arrived and taken pride of place in the front room their home was even more cramped than usual. But it certainly had been well used and even her mum had grudgingly said it had been worth shelling out for.

'What you hangin' about for?' Sarah asked as she drew level with Alice. 'Be late if you don't get going.'

'Waiting for Sophy. Mum's got her upstairs . . . talking to her,' Alice added darkly.

'She in trouble?' Sarah asked with a grimace.

'Dunno . . . hope not,' Alice replied and sent another look up at the top-floor window. She suddenly realised that she needed to get rid of Sarah so that when Sophy eventually appeared she could find out what'd gone on. Sophy would clam up in front of Sarah. Their mum had drummed into them enough times that you never let anyone, including your friends, know too much about your family's business. 'You'd best be getting off or you'll be late. Don't hang about waiting for us.'

Sarah gave a shrug as though indicating she wasn't too bothered about being late for registration but, after a few silent minutes, she sensed Alice's withdrawal and mumbled a farewell. Alicc watched her friend go and then took a few paces towards the desolate hallway. She wondered whether to creep back in and listen on the stairs to try and find out what was going on. She decided not to bother. If her mum were in any sort of paddy she'd be able to hear all about it just where she was.

'I know you 'n' Danny Lovat have been friendly for a while and I ain't put a stop to you seeing him because I ain't seen you misbehaving.' Tilly paused and considered. 'Ain't seen him misbehavin' either. Fact is he's been alright giving you bits 'n' pieces he's got hold of.' Tilly remembered that Danny had given Sophy bread and biscuits when he'd worked at the grocery store. Now he was helping out old Mr Greene on his market stall, Sophy often brought in a bit of buckshee fruit or salad stuff. In fact, Tilly had been happy to foster the little romance between her eldest daughter and the lad next door. But something was niggling at her and Tilly's way was to have it out rather than brood on it.

'Have you let him touch yer?' Tilly demanded to know. She fixed on Sophy a stare that made her daughter blush crimson and fidget on the spot.

''Course not,' Sophy spluttered, guessing at once what was worrying her mother. She'd thought she might not have noticed. Recently their mother had been boozing most nights now they were more flush with money. Their dad was working late distempering and so on and getting more of Basher Payne's houses ready for the sanitary inspector. But, drunk or sober, it seemed Tilly managed to keep an eagle eye on all that occurred, or didn't occur, in the Keiver household.

'I've not seen you take any rags out the drawer this month.' Tilly continued cutting bread for Bethany's breakfast but she slid Sophy another piercing look. 'You'd better not be lying to me, my gel,' she said in a quiet, sinister voice, so unlike her usual harsh tone. 'I've told you what happens when boys take liberties with gels. The gels get in the family way 'n' then it's right big trouble. So even with boys you really like you don't ever let them take liberties like that. Right? Remember what happened to Maisie Brookes?'

Sophy nodded, quickly edging towards the door. She remembered that alright. It'd gone round their school like wildfire that poor Maisie had almost died to get herself out of the trouble that Tommy Greenfield had got her into. But Sophy knew she wasn't that daft. She and Danny had already worked that one out and knew what to do. 'I'd better get going to school,' she said. 'I'll be late.' She shoved an arm into a sleeve of her coat.

'Yeah . . . well, end of this month you won't have no more school. The day you turn fourteen you're out 'n' earnin' full-time,' Tilly called after her. 'Christmas ain't far off 'n' we need all the wages we can get to make it a good 'un fer once.'

Sophy gave a nod. She was glad to change the subject. 'I'm already keeping me ears 'n' eyes open for something.'

'I've been looking too. Don't yer worry about that, my gel.' Tilly gave a rare smile. 'I think I've found something for you to start off with. Rag shop in Fonthill Road needs a sorter. One of 'em's leaving to have her baby come the end of the month. I already put your name forward fer it.'

'I ain't doing that!' Sophy stopped her sidling towards

the door. She showed her mother an expression of total disgust. 'I ain't coming home stinking 'n' dusty 'n' covered in fleabites for a measly seven bob a week. I'll stick with me doorsteps if nothing else turns up.'

'You'll take whatever full-time you can get hold of. If you want to keep your doorsteps then do them Saturday morning or give 'em to Alice to take on. Doorsteps are kids' work for weekends. You're out of here working every day, pulling in full-time, or you're outta here fer good. I mean it.'

'I'll sort out me own work,' Sophy mumbled and slipped out onto the landing before adding, 'Pam Greenfield got a job packing in the laundry in Fonthill Road. I can try there.' She turned and was soon hurrying down the stairs.

'I already tried the laundry. They don't want no one else right now,' her mother yelled after her.

'What's she on about?' Alice asked Sophy as they started trudging down the road towards school.

'Reckons she's got me a job ready 'n' waiting in the rag shop in Fonthill Road for when I turn fourteen. Fine birthday present that'll be! Ain't havin' it 'n' that's that. I'll try one of the factories for a job as a tea gel. But I ain't workin' in no poxy rag shop sorting stinky old clothes for a pittance.'

Alice looked sympathetic. In just over a year's time, it would be her turn to try and winkle out a reasonable job for herself. Searching for decent work around here – especially when employers guessed you came from the Campbell Bunk – was like finding a gold ring in the gutter.

'You could go try in the factory that makes toys,' she suggested to Sophy, but not very enthusiastically.

'Connie reckons that's what sent her sister Louisa so nutty. It were three years ago but she's never been the same since, Connie says.'

'Louisa's always been a mad cow.' Alice chuckled. 'Anyhow

you don't want to go talking to Connie now she's seeing that copper. Mum'll go mad if she thinks you've been telling her anything. She calls her the copper's nark.'

'Haven't told Connie nuthin'. Hardly ever talk to her. She thinks she's something, she does, now she's moved in with his family.'

'They sound horrible anyhow,' Alice said, wrinkling her nose. 'Connie told Sarah his mum's stuck up and calls her common as muck. His dad keeps touching Connie up.' Alice looked thoughtful. 'I don't suppose she'll decide to come back here though.'

After they'd walked a distance in silence Alice shot a shrewd look at Sophy. 'Is that all Mum wanted with you? To talk about getting work?'

Sophy pursed her lips before starting to chew at the lower. 'Wanted to know about me 'n' Danny being sweet on each other . . . you know . . . about us kissing 'n' so on. She's guessed me monthlies are late.'

Alice felt a hard lump jump to her throat. Sophy had already confided that to her but had said there was nothing to worry about because she'd been late before and in the end it came alright. But if Sophy had done something really silly, like dropping her drawers for Danny and going all the way, Alice didn't even want to consider what the outcome of that might be.

When Tommy Greenfield had got Maisie Brookes in the family way all hell had broken loose. The Brookeses and Greenfields had been fighting in the streets every other day for ages. Then Maisie's mum got what she wanted out of the Greenfields. She got some money and took Maisie to see someone in King's Cross and when they got back Maisie wasn't expecting any more.

'D'you ever find out what happened to Maisie when she got pregnant?' Alice slid a fearful look at Sophy.

'Her mum took her to some sort of doctor down in King's Cross.' Sophy pulled a face. 'He stuck something like a skewer inside her ter get rid of the baby and it all came out in sort of big bits of liver. That's what I heard anyhow.'

'Must've hurt terrible,' Alice whispered with a shudder. She'd guessed it had been something awful because Maisie had looked like death warmed up for ages afterwards.

Sophy sensed Alice's frightened eyes on her. ''S'alright,' she reassured her but with a smile that wobbled on her lips. 'We always do it standin' up. Danny said you can't ever get pregnant like that.'

'You sure about it?'

Sophy nodded miserably, her eyes darting about as though she feared they were being watched. But at the moment the Fonthill Mews, where she and Danny had stationed themselves to talk in private, seemed to be quiet enough. 'Sure as I can be. I know me aunt Fran was being sick when she was first expecting though she's alright now she's big as a house. Her baby's due in a couple of months, me mum says.'

'Can't see nuthin'.' Danny eyed Sophy's belly. 'Just 'cos you've been sick a few times don't mean yer in the family way.' He sounded desperate to believe his own reassurance and he scraped the fingers of one hand agitatedly through his hair.

''S'not just that. Me monthlies haven't come for ages . . . must be almost three months now.'

'Can't be,' Danny said then followed it up with, 'Shit!' He looked bleakly at Sophy. 'Ain't getting trapped in to stayin' round here,' he warned her through gritted teeth. 'Ain't ending up in some poxy room in a dump like this with no money and whining kids. Already got that back there and it's driving me nuts.' He jerked his head towards Campbell Road.

He raised a hand to touch Sophy's face as he watched her lower lip wobble. 'Love you, Sophy, honest I do, but we can't get tied down yet or we'll have nuthin', just like the rest o' the sad gits here. Be trapped in The Bunk forever, we will, if we can't get decent jobs and get a few bob behind us before we get wed.'

Sophy nodded and bit her lip. She knew Danny was right, but she knew too she was pregnant. She felt different, she was getting fat, so a baby must be growing inside her.

It was mid December and many weeks had passed since her mother had interrogated her that morning and made her late for school. Tilly had managed to wangle her a good job at the Star Brush factory because she'd called in a favour from Kitty Drew, one of the supervisors. Sophy was only making tea and doing a few odd jobs but she liked it and the wages at eleven shillings were better than she'd expected to start off with. Not that she got to keep much of it. Her mother soon had her pay packet off her on a Friday and woe betide if she tried to slip a bit out before handing it over. Sophy knew that to lose such a good job would be a disaster. She knew she *would* lose it if she were pregnant. She glanced at Danny; he was still staring at her, white-faced and frowning, as though he was desperately trying to think of a reason why she might be wrong.

'Can't you *do* something?' Danny burst out and then relief lifted his countenance. 'You're supposed to drink gin, or something like that,' he rattled off. 'I remember now when one of me friend's brothers got a girl knocked up he got her a bottle o' gin.'

'Did it work?' Sophy asked, brightening a little.

'Dunno . . . we're here now, ain't we, not in Essex. It don't notice,' Danny added quickly as Sophy looked as though she might burst in to tears. 'You can get rid of it before anyone knows . . . only us'll ever know.'

'Me mum's gonna kill me if she finds out.' Sophy snuffled on her sleeve.

'I'll get you a bottle of gin soon as I can,' Danny promised. He leaned forward and pecked at her lips.

'Gedoff!' Sophy shoved him away. ''S'how I got in trouble.' She pushed him more purposefully as he persevered in trying to kiss her. 'Got to get back to work anyhow. Me dinnertime's over.' They walked to the end of the Fonthill Mews. 'You'd best get me that gin then,' Sophy ordered grumpily before they turned in opposite directions.

'Fuckin' fine New Year this is goin' to be.' Tilly's shrieked exclamation reverberated about the room. It had been loud enough for every person in the tenement house to know something bad had happened to the Keivers.

Sophy cuffed her wet face and tried to escape her mother's swinging fist by dodging behind her father.

'Get off her and calm yourself down,' Jack bawled at his wife as Tilly lunged at Sophy again. He grabbed at Tilly and, planting his palms on her shoulders, shoved her down on the edge of the bed.

Sophy was sobbing quietly, one of her palms fastened to a cheek reddened from her mother's hefty blow.

'You stupid little cow,' Tilly spat between her thin lips. 'I warned you . . . I warned you what'd happen if you let him . . .'

'Shut up,' Jack snarled at her. He might have seemed more in control of his temper than his wife but he was equally shocked and angry. 'If I'm going to cause a war . . . and it will be a hell of a war,' he stressed to his oldest daughter, 'I need to know I'm doing it for a real reason.' A paternal eye examined Sophy's body. He noticed the thickening about her usually skinny hips and the buttons stretched across her bosom. 'You sure, Sophy?' he asked unnecessarily; his eyes had told him the awful truth.

'She's just been sick again,' Tilly pointed out, kicking at the bowl on the floor that held the vomit and sending it over. 'That's the third time this week. She's missed three monthlies. What more proof d'yer need that she's knocked up?'

Jack swiped up the half-empty bottle of gin that Tilly had found hidden under the mattress in the back room. ''Course she's been sick if she's been downing this stuff.'

'Why do you think she's been downing that stuff?' Tilly bawled scathingly. 'To try and get rid of it, that's why.' She shot to her feet. 'If you ain't goin' after Danny Lovat, I'll do it meself. If those bastards think they've got a roof over their heads after today they can think again. They're out on the streets and I'll make sure nobody else round here takes them in. They'll bleeding well suffer fer doin' this to us.'

Jack again slammed a hand on Tilly's shoulder and pushed her down. He swiped fidgeting fingers over his bristly jaw. 'No need to be spiteful, Til. Seems it's as much Sophy's fault as his. Sophy ain't accused Danny of forcing himself on her.'

'He didn't . . . I swear . . .' Sophy squeaked from behind her father.

'Keep quiet,' Jack barked at her and continued reasoning with his wife. 'I'd say Bert 'n' Margaret are going to be as done in as we are when they find out. They're not going to want this trouble any more'n we do. They don't need another mouth to feed any more'n we do.'

'There ain't gonna be another mouth to feed,' Tilly spat out. 'She's only fourteen 'n' she's getting decent wages down at Star Brush. Whatever needs to be done'll be done.'

'If you mean what I think you mean,' Jack said through gritted teeth, 'you'll do it over my dead body.' He glared ferociously at Tilly. 'Abortionist ain't getting nowhere near her, and that's the end of it.'

'We'll see about that,' Tilly muttered.

Tilly got up and this time when Jack made to push her back down she thumped him in the chest double-handed. 'I'm going round to see the Lovats. If you think you can stop me, just try. I'll have you first if yer like.'

'Can't always sort out everything by lashin' out, Til,' Jack said quietly. 'This is our daughter and our first grandchild we're talking about here. Danny might do his duty by her. They're both old enough to be wed, if not wise enough.'

'Stupid, sentimental git!' Tilly exploded. 'What they supposed to do fer money? Neither of 'em's got a pot to piss in. We got no room to have them here and the Lovats are worse off'n we are.'

Tilly transferred her glare to Alice, who had been standing still and silent in a corner of the room, watching and listening in fascinated dread to this latest upset in the Keiver household. Alice had been awaiting this showdown. For weeks past she'd feared it to be looming menacingly just a few days away.

'You know anything about all this?' Tilly demanded.

Alice shook her head and her anxious gaze darted back to Sophy. It wasn't wholly a lie. She'd guessed, of course, at the awful truth as soon as she'd noticed Sophy's belly getting bigger. But Sophy had said nothing and acted quite normal. She hadn't confided in her even when she'd hidden the bottle of gin under the bed. Alice had just thought she'd started to drink because she was showing off now she'd got a good job.

So all the time Alice had hoped and prayed that she was wrong and Sophy was right: her sister might be getting a fat boozer but she couldn't possibly be pregnant because she'd always done it standing up with Danny, so that was alright.

It was a Sunday afternoon in late January and despite

the freezing cold weather a lot of people would be about in Campbell Road. That wouldn't stop Tilly causing a rumpus out there in front of them. You kept to yourself and dealt in private with what you could, but when you couldn't you might as well let the whole world know what you were up to, and why. That way they'd know you weren't a mug and easily messed with. Tilly started for the door, rolling up her sleeves to her elbows as she went.

'I'll go next door. You stay here,' Jack directed her grimly and stepped in front of her. It wasn't that he feared for his wife's safety. He knew she could look after herself, as did most people who'd been about The Bunk long enough to get on the wrong side of her. But he was still head of the household and as such it was his place to confront Danny.

'I'll be right behind you then,' Tilly said forcefully. She let Jack go out then grabbing Sophy by the wrist she jerked her forward. 'You can come 'n' all,' she barked. 'You've had your fun, now see what it cost. After that I'm gonna pay you fer this.'

EIGHT

'Looks like trouble's on its way.'

Geoff Lovat had made that muttered observation before turning from the window and staring meaningfully at his older brother. Unfortunately Danny missed his warning. He seemed to be lost in a world of his own and continued gazing at the cold tea cupped between his palms.

Their parents, ever alert to the word trouble, had both shot up from the table and elbowed Geoff out of the way. His mother had got there first. She was faster on her feet than his crippled father. Soon Bert had caught up and was squirming for a space at the window so he could peer out.

Moments before Geoff had been watching the street scene, yawning. Then he'd spotted the Keivers and his jaw had clacked shut. Jack Keiver was marching ahead with his wife right on his heels, dragging Sophy by an arm.

Instinctively Geoff had guessed what the problem was. He knew that when their parents had been getting a skinful on a Saturday night in the Keivers' place Danny had been getting to grips with Sophy in their place. It hadn't happened for a while now, probably because Sophy had panicked when she'd guessed she was up the duff and put a block on it.

Often on a Saturday evening Geoff had been obliging enough to take himself off to give the lovebirds more time alone. Geoff had been glad to get out of the fleapit and hand over responsibility to Danny for their young brothers and sisters while he met a few mates for a crafty drink and smoke.

Finally Danny looked up. Geoff realised from his bleak expression that his brother had already guessed he was in for it and it was too late to try and scarper.

Margaret Lovat swung back to glower at her oldest son, her face taut with disbelief. She'd just caught a glimpse of Tilly Keiver's savage features and Sophy's beetroot-red face before they disappeared from view into the hallway below. No explanation for such a scene was needed. Not when Danny was looking cornered and had an odd, apologetic expression hooding his eyes. There was only one reason she could think of why a mother would drag a howling teenage daughter towards the house where the girl's sweetheart lived.

'The Keivers are on their way looking like they're on the warpath. Sophy's with 'em. You want to tell me why that might be?' Margaret whipped at Danny.

'What's goin' on?' Bert Lovat asked, looking puzzled as he limped back to the table to get his cup of tea.

Margaret shot her husband a despising look. Already she could hear the tramp of boots on the stairs. The next moment the door was taking a hammering fit to have it out of its frame. 'Got anything ter say?' Margaret asked Danny, her eyes bulging furiously at him, her lips a thin white line.

Danny did have one word to say. 'Shit!' It exploded through his teeth and his eyes closed.

'I reckon that's what you're in alright,' his mother told him. 'But remember this . . . you're stopping here with us. Your family here needs you more'n them next door. You ain't goin' nowhere.'

'Danny Lovat, come out here now,' Jack shouted through the door.

Without allowing her husband's demand time to work Tilly followed up with, 'Open the fuckin' door, or it comes off its hinges.' She rattled furiously at the doorknob.

'Get the kids in the back room,' Margaret said to Geoff as she went to the door and unlocked it. She was sent stumbling back as the Keivers burst in.

Jack held his arms out to either side in a futile attempt to keep Tilly in check behind him. 'I'll see to it,' he snapped at her from a corner of his mouth as she banged forcefully against his restraint.

'You know why I'm here, don't yer?' he said to Danny.

Danny pushed himself up from the table and nodded. His eyes darted to Sophy's blotchy, puffy countenance. It was obvious she'd taken a lot of stick already. He knew he ought to act the man, say something to protect her, but all he managed to mutter was, 'I thought we was always careful.' He frowned apology at Sophy.

'You weren't careful enough, were you, yer bastard,' Tilly thundered. 'She's three months gone 'n' been bringin' up her guts every morning this past week.' After a small pause to suck in breath she roared, 'And what d'you mean by getting her gin? Daughter of mine knows better'n to start drinkin' at her age . . .'

'Pity she didn't know better'n to keep her legs closed at her age, ain't it,' Margaret retorted sourly.

Jack caught Tilly under the arms and dragged her back as she lunged towards Margaret. 'Everyone calm down,' he said through his teeth then followed that with a heavy sigh.

Margaret slammed the door shut in the faces of the gawping neighbours who'd been steadily gathering on the threshold to listen. Entertainment such as this was enough to give the pubs a run for their money on a Sunday dinnertime.

'Danny says he was careful,' Margaret said, pushing forward and planting herself in front of her son as though to shield him. 'Perhaps he ain't the culprit. You thought to ask her who else might be responsible?'

With a roar Tilly had dodged past Jack and caught a fistful of Margaret's lank hair. She yanked her face close to her own. 'You saying my Sophy's been knockin' about with other boys?' Tilly dragged Margaret's head about so she was looking at her eldest son. 'There's yer culprit. The dirty little bleeder.'

It seemed Bert had nothing to say. He simply gaped at Margaret, waiting to hear what she'd come out with next in the Lovat family's defence.

'They're young but if they're old enough to bring a kid in to the world I reckon they're old enough ter get wed.' Jack swung a bleak look between the downcast couple.

'He ain't getting wed,' Bert said with dull finality when he realised his wife was momentarily lost for words. 'He's stopping right here where he's needed. And you lot can do what yer like about that.'

Margaret vigorously nodded her agreement to her husband's announcement whilst glowering at Tilly.

'He's needed by Sophy 'cos he's got her in the family way,' Jack argued back. 'It ain't good and it ain't right for either of them. But that's how it is as far as I can see. They get wed and we'll have to club together 'n' do what we can for them to start 'em off in a room of their own. Won't be no fancy celebration . . .'

'Won't be no celebration fancy or otherwise,' Margaret declared bluntly. 'He's going nowhere. You take him . . . what've I got left to keep us lot fed 'n' a roof over our heads? Ain't fair.'

Tilly threw back her head and barked a harsh laugh. 'Life ain't fair,' she blasted. 'But there it is. He's taken advantage of our Sophy and now she's having his kid. That ain't fair if it comes to it.'

'Little whore . . . I knew you was trouble from the start, the way you was always throwing yourself at him.'

As Tilly surged forward Margaret tried to rake her nails down her opponent's cheek.

Despite the attempts of their husbands to drag them apart, and disentangle their thrashing limbs from the toppling furniture and washing that'd fallen from chair backs, the fighting women continued to roll back and forth on the dirty boards. It was Sophy's shrieking that finally got them apart. Tilly rose, panting, onto her knees and stared at her daughter, as did every other person in the room.

'I ain't getting married to no one.' The look of relief that passed over Danny's face made a sob swell in her chest. 'I ain't getting married,' she repeated less vociferously as she realised she had everybody's attention. 'Ain't being stuck with a skewer neither to get rid of it. Gonna have it then let the welfare take it away. That's what I'll do. If any of you try 'n' stop me I'll go to the cruelty man and put meself in the workhouse till it's over.' With that she rushed to the door and yanked it open. Bursting a path through the knot of eavesdroppers congregated on the landing, she was soon down the stairs and out into Campbell Road.

As Sophy rushed towards home Alice rushed into the street and they met by the railings. 'Mum still in there?' Alice gasped as Sophy made to whisk past her. Obliquely Alice realised that her sister looked to be in a right old state. Her eyes and nose were dripping wet and her face was crimson from crying. But she couldn't stop now to talk to her about any of it. While most of her family had stormed off to deal with one emergency another had started back home.

About ten minutes ago her Aunt Fran had let out a shriek fit to wake the dead. At first Alice had decided to mind her own business in case her aunt and uncle were having one of their usuals. When no other noise was heard, until a shrill scream a minute or two later, Alice had decided to leave her two younger sisters on their own. She'd flown down to Fran's room in case Uncle Jimmy had killed her. He was nowhere to be seen. The baby was coming, her aunt had whimpered as Alice tentatively poked her head about the door. Fran had begged her to fetch her mum to her straight away because Jimmy had gone out and the boys were out in the street somewhere, playing.

Alice now flew into the dingy corridor next door and met her parents clattering noisily down the bare stairs. 'Aunt Fran's having the baby,' she gasped. 'She sent me to find you. Uncle Jimmy's out . . .' she finished in a pant. Her wide eyes took in her mother's dishevelled state. Her blouse was gaping where buttons had been ripped away and her coarse, fiery hair was messed up and falling all over her face. It was obvious to Alice that she'd been scrapping.

Tilly gawped at Alice then pushed past, muttering, 'Fuck's sake! I hope she's got it wrong. Baby ain't due for at least a month, I'm sure of it.' As an afterthought she turned back to Jack. 'Better get that good fer nuthin' home just in case the baby *is* coming. See if you can find him, Jack, will you?'

Once Tilly had headed home Jack drew Alice to him with an arm about her shoulders. 'Have a look for your uncle Jimmy on the corner, Al, will you? He might be gaming. I'll try the Duke. Best get him home in case it ain't a false alarm.'

Alice nodded and trotted off towards Paddington Street whilst Jack went in the opposite direction to look for his brother-in-law.

Soon Alice's questing gaze found the doggers out – kids who were stationed about here and there keeping an eye peeled for the law while a gaming session was on. Then she heard the croupier calling out numbers before she caught sight of about a score or so men who were hunched over the pavement watching rolling dice. Further into Paddington Street she saw her uncle lounging against the wall of the doss house with a fan of cards in one of his hands. Several other men were crouched down, encircling an upturned box with a mound of money on it.

'Aunt Fran wants you to come home,' Alice gasped out.

'Alright, love.' Jimmy gave Alice a crooked smile then ignored her and continued to play cards.

''S'important,' Alice cried. 'Baby's coming.'

That got Jimmy's attention, and that of the other fellows. Just for a moment they stared at her, then at him before their eyes returned to their hands. 'Alright, Al . . .' Jimmy said with another lazy smile that didn't quite light his eyes. 'Tell her I'll be along in a minute. Off yer go, there's a good gel.' His tone had changed too. He was telling her to piss off.

Alice shrugged hopelessly and dashed back the way she'd come. Outside their house she found Bobbie and Stevie. Both the boys were shuffling about on the pavement, darting in and out of the hallway. As she came closer Alice noticed how scared they both looked. In a moment Alice knew why. A horrible moan issued forth from the interior of the building.

'Aunt Til told us to come out.' Bobbie explained their presence on the pavement.

'She gonna die?' Stevie asked Alice, his eyes huge in his thin, pale face.

'Nah . . . 'course not . . .' Alice reassured them. But she too had grown anxious on hearing that awful sound.

She remembered when her mum had had Lucy that there'd been a lot of noise and mess. But her dad had been with her mum all the time and a great deal of help Alice thought. He'd only left her to boil up some water when old Lou Perkins had turned up and taken charge. She lived up the top of the road and apparently knew all about bringing babies in to the world. Alice wondered if perhaps she ought to go and see if Lou Perkins was in. If she wasn't she'd probably be found in the Duke Tavern. On a Sunday dinner-time a good deal of the residents of The Bunk who had the cash to buy a drink or two could be found there, or one of the other pubs close by.

Leaving Bobbie and Stevie on the pavement Alice scampered up the stairs, forgetting in her haste to avoid the spot in the landing floorboards that was broken. She stumbled, rubbed her shin, and tiptoed towards Aunt Fran's door. She peeped around it, searching for her mum.

Tilly was sitting on the edge of the bed, bending over Fran who was restlessly twitching on the mattress. At that moment a groan issued from between Fran's bluish lips.

'Shall I go and see if Mrs Perkins is home?' Alice volunteered in a quiet hiss.

'Is your dad back with Jimmy?' Tilly frowned over her shoulder at her daughter.

Alice shook her head. 'Uncle Jimmy's up the corner. I found him. He said he's coming in a minute.'

That information made Tilly's eyes and mouth narrow but she was soon swinging her attention back to her sister. Fran had dug her heels into the bed as a contraction took her huge belly arching towards the ceiling.

'S'alright . . . 's'alright,' Tilly soothed Fran while pressing her palm to her hot forehead. She looked back at Alice. 'Yeah . . . would you go 'n' see if Lou's in, Al? Then get your dad back here quick as can be. When you pass the corner if

Jimmy's still there tell him he's needed home *now* or I'll come 'n' fetch him back meself.'

Alice had turned to go but her mother called her back.

'Al . . . Al . . . wait a minute. Before you go, get that kettle set to boil and get some more water from the sink in that there bowl.' She nodded her head at a tin bowl on the table that held dirty crockery.

Alice unloaded the plates and cups and quickly did as she was told. As she was about to leave for the second time her mother stopped her again with the instruction, 'Shout up the stairs fer yer sister. Sophy'll have to get down here with me and keep the hot water coming in case I need it soon. Beth'll have to see to Lucy for a while.'

Alice nodded and hared up the stairs, garbled out to Sophy what her mother had told her then ran down again and out into the wintry air.

She gasped out to her cousins where she was going and made no objection when the two boys started running behind her as she went on her errand to fetch Lou Perkins.

As they passed the gamblers' corner Alice called to the boys behind. 'Go 'n' tell yer dad it's urgent and he's got to go home straight away or me mum's after him.' Stevie and Bobbie seemed for a moment as though they would do so. They hesitated; then having stopped and considered, they speeded up and caught up with Alice again. They both knew that telling their dad something like that was likely to get them a good cuff in front of everyone, then more later in private.

Alice banged on the door of number ninety-two. 'Is Mrs Perkins at home?' she panted out at the old man who'd opened the door. He removed the pipe clenched in his yellow teeth to croak, 'No, she ain't.' He made as though to shut the door.

'Baby's being born down the other end. D'you know where she is?'

The old man opened the door a little wider. 'Poor little mite,' he grunted in his tobacco-roughened voice. 'Might find her at the Duke or the Pooles Park.' Having aired his sympathy, and his opinion on Lou's whereabouts, he closed the door without any further ado.

Eventually Alice ran Lou to ground at the Pooles Park Tavern. She was merry but not drunk. Not the sort of drunk state that Alice had seen her mum in, anyhow. She came with them and puffed behind the trotting youngsters, gasping at intervals, 'Bleedin' 'ell, slow up; me legs ain't as young as your'n, y'know.'

As they turned the corner Alice saw her dad pacing back and forth outside on the pavement. As soon as he glimpsed them he strode to meet them. Something in his demeanour seemed to give Lou her second wind and she speeded up. A grim head flick and a muttered, 'First floor, second door,' from her dad and the woman disappeared in to the sombre interior.

'That's what happens sometimes,' Tilly said quietly to Sophy. She had taken her daughter into a corner of the room because Sophy had started to sob uncontrollably. The atmosphere in the confined space was heavy with the reek of sweat and blood. By the bed Lou Perkins was cleaning up Fran, who was lying quite still now, her greyish countenance turned away to the wall. Lou dipped the rag into tepid water that had long ago turned crimson and again wiped Fran's encrusted thighs.

Tilly knew her sister was lucky to be alive. The baby girl had been breech and stillborn after struggling for almost two hours to get its tiny body free of its mother's hips.

Sophy's wide-eyed stare was fixed on her dead cousin. The baby girl had been wrapped in a pillowcase and placed at the foot of the bed. 'Why'd she have to die?' Sophy gurgled. 'Ain't fair.' She swiped a hand over her runny nose.

'Sometimes it's more'n fair,' Tilly contradicted her harshly. 'Sometimes it's a blessing. When it's your time you should wish yourself so lucky.'

NINE

'Don't want to interrupt, but ain't it about time you took yourself off home to see yer wife?'

It was softly spoken sarcasm but had the required effect of making the couple immediately scramble apart. A moment before they'd been locked together, the woman with her back to the wall and her arms and legs encircling her partner. Jimmy Wild glanced over his shoulder, cursing under his breath. He'd recognised his brother-in-law's voice straight away. Nellie Tucker jerked together the edges of her coat and tightly belted it over her rucked-up dress. It was late afternoon and dusk had already descended, bringing with it a clinging icy mist that had shrouded the furtive pair from prying eyes, or so they'd hoped. But Jack had spotted them . . . eventually.

It was over five hours since Fran had given birth to her dead daughter. Since that time Jack had been out searching for Jimmy to tell him the awful news. Having looked for him in all his usual haunts he'd been about to give up when, quite by accident, he'd finally run him to ground. Cold and hungry, and hunched into his coat, Jack had idly glanced into an alleyway he'd been passing on his way back to

Campbell Road and caught a glimpse of what looked to be a courting couple bumping against the wall. After a moment or two of observation he'd realised his search for his bastard of a brother-in-law was at an end. So carried away had Jimmy been that he'd not even heard Jack call out to him the first time.

'No need to be sarky, mate,' Jimmy said easily. 'Ain't as if Fran's never had a kid before. She knows what to do. I'd just get in the way.' He gave a conspiratorial chuckle. 'Last time, with Stevie, I got told ter stay outside and didn't do nuthin' but go up and down the stairs.'

'So this time you thought you'd go up 'n' down with that old bag instead, did yer?'

''Ere . . . you . . .' Nellie started to protest at the insult. She surged forward but was shoved stumbling back against brickwork by Jimmy.

'If I was you,' Jack told her with silky menace, 'I'd get meself off home sharpish, just in case I copped a stray one.'

'That don't sound like you, Jack.' Jimmy sneered a laugh. 'I know you ain't got the balls to clump a woman even when the bitch deserves it.'

'Whereas you have, eh?' Jack said quietly. 'Nellie know that?' He jerked his head at the sullen-faced tart. 'She know how much you like using yer fists on a woman 'n' telling her she deserves it so you can be the big man?'

'What you so riled up about?' Jimmy snarled. He came closer, belligerently thrusting out his chin. 'I don't see what my missus droppin' her nipper is to do with you anyhow.'

'You don't see nuthin' at all, do yer, Jim?' Jack said. 'You're too busy poncin' about ter notice anything what goes on.' He controlled his temper with difficulty as a vision of Fran's deathly pale face crept into his mind. Then came the memory of Lou Perkins carrying a bowlful of rocking red water down the stairs to empty it in the privy in the yard.

He focused his gaze back on Jimmy. 'While you been pokin' this old brass,' he said bitterly, 'your wife's been having a real bad time . . . I mean *real* bad. She's torn ter bits and lost a lot of blood. Your daughter's stillborn.'

'Stillborn?' Jimmy looked confused then he stalked closer to Jack with a grim frown. 'She's killed our kid?' He sounded peeved and disbelieving.

'You nearly lost your wife, you fuckin' bastard!' Jack raged. 'The baby was round the wrong way and if it hadn't been for Lou Perkins knowing what to do, you'd be putting two in the ground, not one.' Jack saw that finally he'd shocked his brother-in-law. 'You'd best see Lou alright for what she did for you today. Woman's been a diamond and stayed and helped Tilly clean up yer place.'

Jimmy tickled at his chin with nervous fingers and darted a look at Nellie. She seemed dazed by what she'd just heard.

'First you'd best get home and see Fran,' Jack prompted Jimmy. 'She's still in a dreadful bad state. She's been askin' after you. She needs some comfort and you'd bleedin' well better give it to her.'

Jimmy pushed roughly past Jack and had managed a couple of steps before Jack, following silently, spun him around by the shoulder, and landed one on his chin. It was a short jab; just enough to make Jimmy stagger and understand that there'd be more to come.

'Just fer starters,' Jack promised. 'We'll finish it another time.'

Jimmy put a hand to his cut lip and gave Jack a vicious smile. 'Yeah . . . we *will* finish it another time 'n' all, mate.' He strode away without sending a look or word Nellie's way.

'I didn't know it was her time, honest; he never said nothing to me,' Nellie started to whine.

''Cos it would've made a difference, eh?' Jack sneered. 'Bet the fucker ain't paid you neither, has he?' He smiled with sour amusement then turned on his heel and headed for home.

'See you this Saturday night?' Bill Prewett called up to Tilly but continued his hop down the stairs.

'Nah . . . we're giving it a bit of rest for a while yet.' Tilly had leaned over the banister to tell her neighbour that there would be no weekend parties going on at the Keivers' for the foreseeable future.

'Oh . . . yeah . . . right. See what you mean. How is Fran?' Bill Prewett stopped and rested his weight against the rickety stairs. 'Not seen nothing of her. Take it she's still laid up?'

'She's doin' alright, considering,' Tilly replied whilst absently swinging the kettle she held in one hand. She'd been about to fill it from the tap on the landing. 'Doctor's been in a couple of times and given her some jollop for the infection. Wanted to take her into the 'ospital for a rest and so on, but she won't have it.'

Bill Prewett nodded his head sagely then shook it. 'You wouldn't get me in there willing neither. No workhouse, no 'ospital. At my age you gotta avoid both of 'em like the plague 'cos you don't never come out again 'cept in a pine box.' He frowned up at Tilly. 'Lucky she was, your sister . . . very lucky.' With that he continued to hobble on out into the cold, damp street.

Tilly rested the kettle in the stained sink and turned on the tap. She looked about at the dilapidation, her eyes darting from one sombre locked door to another. Usually she didn't study the depressing environment, it was just there. Now it sent a soft sigh blowing through her lips. Hurriedly she turned off the tap as the kettle overflowed. She went back into the room and put it onto the hob to boil for tea. Bobbie and Stevie were sitting at the table with Bethany. They were all looking at her expectantly. Her nephews had practically moved in with her since Fran had lost the baby several weeks ago now. Fran was still fighting infection and too weak to get up for more than a few hours a day.

When Tilly's nephews weren't at school they pottered about between the two households. Bobbie slept in his own room downstairs as the Keivers' sleeping areas were already cramped. Stevie had refused to leave at night. Tilly had gruffly said he could stay if he could find himself a space. She knew the poor little blighter would sooner kip on old coats on the floor than go home and get bashed by his father for having wet the mattress again. And he'd wet himself almost every night since his mum got ill. In fact once he'd done more than that. Annoyed as Tilly had been, she'd bitten her tongue when he started to grizzle, and cleaned him up for school.

She pushed cups of weak tea in front of the boys and Beth and cut hunks of bread to go with it. A scraping of jam on top made it a bit more of a palatable breakfast for them. 'Hurry up and get it down yers,' Tilly ordered briskly. 'Time's marchin' on.' She scooped Lucy up off the floor where she'd been toddling and dragging a shoe along by its laces. She plonked her in the middle of the bed and gave her a finger of bread and jam to chew on, hoping to keep her occupied while she got the kids off to school.

Soon Tilly's thoughts were again turning to her sister. She wished Fran *would* go into the hospital for a while; at least she'd get a bit of decent grub and a rest. She was looking pale and scrawny and Jimmy never made life easy for her. It set Tilly's teeth to scraping when she thought how popular and outgoing Fran once had been. As teenagers they'd gone together to dances and Fran, being blonde and pretty, had always attracted the lads. But she'd fallen for Jimmy Wild, despite a couple of his past fancies warning her he was a bully who'd steal her last farthing. Then she'd got herself in the family way and was trapped with him. He'd be different with her, Fran had boasted. He was going to get them a nice place down Highgate way and get himself a good job to pay for it. Within a very short while Fran had learned the hard way how false was his smile and how empty his promises. Then over years she'd discovered, painfully, what she'd get . . . or the boys would get . . . if ever she complained about Jimmy's lies and womanising. Tilly knew that the sadistic git wasn't above controlling Fran by punishing Bobbie and Stevie.

Now that Fran was laid up and bringing nothing in Jimmy had been forced to take regular work. Tilly knew he resented having to do that. One day last week he'd knocked off work early and had come stomping up the stairs looking for Fran in Tilly's place. He'd been moaning for his dinner then, uninvited, he'd slouched into a chair at Tilly's table, sucking on a dog end and brooding on the racing pages in the newspaper. Every so often he'd flung at Fran – who was gulping down her tea as quick as she could – a surly look and told her that the sooner she bucked up and got herself back out earning the sooner he'd be able to find decent work and be his own guvnor instead of some tosser's sidekick. Tilly hadn't known whether to shout him down or burst out laughing at that one. If a decent job kicked him up the arse he'd swear he hadn't felt it.

Tilly jerked her thoughts to the present. 'Come on, you lot. Should've been gawn to school by now.'

'Shall we wait for Alice?' Beth asked as she got to her feet and pulled on her coat. Bobbie and Stevie got down from the table too.

Tilly frowned. She'd been so occupied thinking about Fran that she'd not realised that the two older girls hadn't come out of the back room yet. Alice should have been about ready to go off to school and Sophy ought to have already left for work.

'You lot get going,' Tilly told them. In the next breath she yelled out, 'Al . . . Sophy . . . D'you know what time it is? Get yourselves up and out!'

Having bellowed her wake-up call she whipped Lucy into her arms and followed the younger kids down the stairs. She stopped by Fran's door. She guessed Jimmy would've gone to work by now. If he hadn't she'd be turning around and going back up the stairs again.

Jack had told her how he'd found Jimmy with Nellie Tucker on the day Fran nearly died in childbirth. Tilly had so far managed to hold her tongue because the last thing she wanted to do at the moment, while Fran was so low, was further upset her sister. When Fran was in good health she found it hard to stand up to the bullying bastard she'd married. Now she was weak and no match for him at all.

Tilly had been making an effort to avoid coming face to face with Jimmy because she knew that a confrontation over it all was brewing and she'd end up telling him his fortune. Tilly found Fran's door unlocked and her sister seated at the kitchen table, her elbows on wood and her head dropped in her hands.

'Feeling rough again this morning?' Tilly asked with gruff concern. 'Need anything from the shop?'

'Jimmy's left.' Fran's voice sounded toneless.

'Left?' Tilly echoed. 'What . . . for work?'

Fran shook her head, her loose fair hair swinging in strings about her pinched white features.

Tilly grabbed at one of Fran's hands and moved it away from her face so she could properly see her expression.

'He's gone . . . said I'm useless 'n' a parasite 'n' he ain't coming back.'

Tilly put Lucy on the bed then pulled out a chair and sat

down. After a silent moment she said bluntly, 'I ain't gonna tell you it's a shame, Fran.' She drummed a few restless fingers on the table. 'Ain't gonna tell you it's a surprise neither. Could see where this was heading straight off . . . soon as that work-shy layabout knew you wasn't up to grafting and supporting him no more.'

'He's me husband,' Fran cried and cuffed at her weeping nose.

'He's no good . . . never has been,' Tilly retorted. She got up from the table and came round and put two squat, work-roughened hands on her sister's shoulders. She squeezed fiercely to emphasise what she was about to say. 'You was always too good for him. I thought you might bring him up, you know; thought he might change, hoped he might for your sake. I know you believed in him, 'cos you loved him and you thought he loved you and he'd do right by all those lies 'n' promises he'd given you. But he ain't got it in him to change, Fran. He is what he is; it's in his blood. And he's got the bleedin' cheek to tell you you're a useless parasite!'

'He wouldn't even say where he's gone. Don't want me pestering him, he said. Just got his things together this morning and went.' Fran raised her swimming eyes to Tilly. 'I reckon he's got a place ter go. He's got a woman, alright.'

Tilly kept her thoughts to herself. Fran was already overwrought.

'What am I going to tell the boys about their dad?'

'Tell 'em he's gone and it's safe to come home,' was Tilly's acerbic answer.

'I know why he's gone . . . I know alright,' Fran said, pushing up from the table. 'I know I'm his wife and I should let him, but I can't though, Til. It hurts so bad when he comes near me. I just can't let him 'cos the bleeding starts again and then he gets mad anyhow 'cos of the mess in the bed . . .'

'Good riddance to bad rubbish.' Tilly enclosed her sister in an embrace. 'Hope he catches the pox off that scummy bitch.'

'He's gone to Nellie Tucker, ain't he?'

Tilly shrugged and tried to avoid Fran's eyes. 'Who cares where he's gone? He's left you alone and that's a good thing. You're not well enough to be doin' it, Fran,' Tilly said. 'If you fell straight away, it'd kill you fer sure.'

'You know he's been knockin' about with her again, don't you?' Fran ignored Tilly's wise words. 'He told me he's been getting what he needs off a real woman . . . rubbed me nose in it, he did. Made me feel I was nuthin'.'

'Bastard!' Tilly hissed through stretched lips.

'Why didn't you tell me if you knew?' Fran wailed.

'You've been ill; too poorly to bother about that slimy . . .'

'Shut up!' Fran wailed. 'He's a man . . . got needs; ain't his fault I got ill and can't do me duty.'

'Is that what he told you? You've let him grind you down, you silly cow,' Tilly said fiercely. 'Can't you see what he's doing? He's *glad* when you feel useless, he's hoping you'll do everything he tells you to. He's hoping you'll end up as his fuckin' slave. You can't let him do that to you, Fran,' Tilly emphasised with a thump of a fist on the tabletop.

Fran turned away and, lifting her pinafore, scrubbed her face with it. But she said nothing.

'When's he done *his* duty?' Tilly roared, incensed by her sister's apathy. 'Did he tell you that while you was struggling to bring his daughter in to the world he had Nellie Tucker up against the wall in an alley? Did he tell you that he knew for hours that you was in labour but he wouldn't come home?'

'He said no one could find him to tell him in time.' Fran turned a wide-eyed, disbelieving stare on Tilly. 'He said Jack caught up with him after it was dark.'

'Yeah . . . Jack did,' Tilly agreed caustically. 'But Alice told him when he was up the corner gambling, at about midday. After that he made sure he wouldn't get found. He made himself scarce alright.' Tilly picked up Lucy and wobbled her back and forth on her hip. She sighed and stared at the ceiling. She hadn't wanted to bring a fresh lot of tears to her sister's eyes. 'Let's get out of here for a while. You up to a walk to the shop?'

Fran shook her head miserably. She took her pinafore up to her face again, scrubbing at her wet cheeks.

'Yeah . . . you are . . . come on; let's get you out for a walk 'n' if I see him or Nellie fuckin' Tucker they'll get what's coming to 'em.'

'You reckon that's where he's gone?'

Tilly nodded and buttoned Lucy into her coat to avoid her sister's anguished stare.

'Come on, let's get out of this dump, just for a while,' she said forcefully.

Fran knuckled her teary eyes. 'Ain't got no money for the shop.'

'Me neither,' Tilly confessed with a wry grin. 'Old Smithie'll let us have a few odds 'n' ends on the strap. Then come dinnertime I'll use me few bob on a few drinks round the Duke. Might cheer you up a bit.' She helped Fran ease her arms into her coat. 'Jack's got no more work with Basher after this week. Thing's'll be tight again with us.' They went out onto the dark landing. 'But now Sophy's bringin' in a wage packet that's something.'

The two women started a slow descent of the stairs, Tilly encouraging her sister to lean heavily on her rather than use the rickety banister. As they neared the bottom, Alice appeared on the landing above.

'Not gone off to school yet?' Tilly yelled angrily at Alice.

'I'm going now,' Alice called down. 'I've been sitting with Sophy 'cos she's got belly ache and been sick.'

'Poor little cow still being sick?' Fran asked Tilly as they emerged into the dismal atmosphere of Campbell Road on a grey morning. There was no sign yet of spring arriving.

'Thought she'd got past all that throwing-up stage,' Tilly said with a frown. As Alice emerged behind on the pavement her mother turned to her.

'Is Sophy getting herself up and off to work?'

'Dunno, Mum,' Alice replied. 'She reckons her belly aches bad. But she wasn't sick that much. 'S'pect she'll be off soon.' With that Alice slipped past and trotted off to school.

The sisters linked arms and started towards the shop.

Halfway up the road they spied Margaret Lovat coming towards them. Tilly scowled at the woman.

Margaret turned her head and avoided her eye. Tilly Keiver was the landlord's rent collector. Margaret had lived in Campbell Road long enough to know that Tilly bore grudges. She'd expected the cow to have them put out on the street. But the Lovats still had a roof over their heads and she wanted to keep it that way.

After the confrontation between the Keivers and the Lovats that fateful Sunday morning in January an uneasy truce had settled between the families. An unspoken agreement had been reached with Sophy too. Not that any family discussion had ensued after the uproar on that day. The crisis with Fran losing the baby and being so ill had pushed all thoughts of Sophy's pregnancy to the back of everybody's mind for some days afterwards.

Then when things seemed to be getting back to normal Jack had got Tilly on her own for a quiet chat. What he'd had to say had been short and to the point, and he'd been in the sort of mood that Tilly knew well. She might get her way on some things with him, but on this she wouldn't. So she'd listened and just grunted at the end of his speech.

'Sophy's made her decision over it all,' he'd stated firmly, 'and it don't seem bad to me. No wedding, no abortion. Welfare'll get the kid as soon as it's born and that'll be the end of it. Fresh start for her and better for the baby 'n' all. So that's how it's going to be. Right?'

Getting Work

1914–1917

TEN

'Al!'

On hearing that brusque summons Alice emerged from the back room. She was pushing Bethany in front of her and continued plaiting her sister's long brown hair whilst looking enquiringly at her mother.

Tilly continued pouring tea for each of her nephews. Despite their dad having up and left them in relative safety some weeks ago Bobbie and Stevie still liked to keep to the routine of spending most of their time with their cousins upstairs despite the crush of bodies. When in their own home their mother seemed to be always bawling; either at them or into her pinny.

'Your birthday soon, Al,' Tilly stated.

Alice smiled. 'Oh . . . yeah . . . it is.'

'You're getting older, growing up.'

Alice nodded and looked wistfully into space for a moment. In just a few more days she would be a teenager. She focused again on her mum, a bit puzzled as to what had brought about this odd chat. At this time of the morning her mother was usually keen to get all the kids out from under her feet and off to school. Sophy had already left for work.

'I was talking to Annie Foster yesterday,' Tilly said. 'She's got a new job round in Thane Villas. The toy factory's takin' on.'

Alice raised her eyebrows. It was always interesting to know where work was available but she didn't see what it had to do with her. Annie Foster was a lot older than she was and not one of her friends. In fact since Annie'd bolted round into Playford Road to escape her brutal stepfather she'd only seen her about on odd occasions.

'Annie says they want people bad and aren't asking too many questions.'

Suddenly Alice had an inkling of what her mother was getting at. But she'd made a mistake in calculating her age. She gave her a grin. 'I'm thirteen soon, mum, not fourteen.'

'Yeah . . . I know that . . . but who's gonna know how old you are if they ain't taking birth certificates? You look a bit older than you are. You look a lot older than Sarah Whitton, fer instance.'

Alice stared at her mum; slowly she realised she was serious. 'What about school?'

'What about it?' Tilly turned from the table and stuck her hands on her hips. 'Staying on at school 'n' doing it all by the rules ain't done Sophy no good. Look at the mess she's got herself in.'

'I ain't getting meself in that sort of mess, ever,' Alice said emphatically.

'No, you ain't!' her mother replied with equal force. 'What you're getting, miss, is a full-time job.'

Tilly gesticulated with a thumb at the boys and Bethany to get off to school.

At the doorway Bethany turned back. 'Can I get a job too, Mum?' she asked plaintively.

'Wish you could, Beth,' Tilly sighed. 'But ain't sure we'd get away with that one. Now off you go.'

With a grimace of disappointment Bethany followed her cousins.

'You can stop home today,' Tilly told Alice once the door had closed. 'See if you can bump yourself into Annie at dinnertime outside the factory and find out all about it. She might know the name of the charge-hand doing the hiring.'

Having got over her astonishment Alice considered what her mother had said. It took little more than a minute for her to come to the wondrous conclusion that she didn't mind one bit starting full-time work before she was supposed to. She didn't even mind that the factory her mother was referring to was where Louisa Whitton – so it was rumoured – had gone mental. In fact excitement was tightening her stomach and curving her mouth into a surprised smile. Very shortly she might be properly grown up, earning good money, and wearing new clothes instead of cast-offs from Billy the Totter or from the rag shop.

Alice didn't always agree with what her mum did or said but on this she thought she was right: what was the point in staying at school for another year, till she was fourteen? More schooling wouldn't help get her a better job round here. She'd just be a year older . . . a year poorer. Her address would still be Campbell Road so she'd get shown the door by most employers unless she lied and said she lived elsewhere. It'd be a wasted year; a year spent just scrubbing doorsteps or rubbing brasses for measly half crowns at the end of a very long shift. And then you had to fight to get your clients, and keep them. Having mulled it all over in her mind for a few minutes Alice realised she was thankful her mum had made mention of it. The sooner she started earning, and saving, the sooner she could get herself out of The Bunk. And that was her dearest ambition. It'd gnawed away at her ever since she could remember.

When she'd been about five her mum and dad would

sometimes take her and Sophy on a trip out to a posh area in Highgate or Hampstead to do a bit of busking to earn cash. Alice could still remember the first few times she'd seen those wonderful big houses that had gardens with grass and flowers out front instead of muck stuck to iron railings. She remembered the scent of coloured petals and of the fine ladies who'd bend to press pennies into her small, outstretched hand while her mum rattled a tambourine and did a jig with Sophy, and her dad played a whistle.

They had not often trekked the miles there for Sophy and Alice quickly flagged during the tramp. But her mum would encourage her tired little legs to keep going by saying the rich pickings to be had off toffs would get them a fish 'n' chip supper. They didn't always get what they'd been promised if they passed a pub on the way home and their mother had a thirst and all the pickings in her pocket.

The memory had started in Alice a profound longing to have a place that was neat and tidy and had flowers growing. As she'd got older, and her dream expanded to include a husband and children, Alice had realised she must have a decent man too . . . not a man from around here. She didn't want a layabout or a gambler or a drinker or anyone who squandered precious money that was destined to give her children a different life to the one she'd known. She wanted a man like her dad . . . who really deserved to have done better for himself, or so Alice thought. And probably he would have done if he hadn't married her mum . . .

But, there was a fly in the ointment that Alice could see and she felt a surge of resentment on remembering it for it was spoiling her daydream, and her blossoming plans for her new life. She cast a look on her mother, wondering if she had overlooked it too.

'What about the school board man?' Alice ventured.

'There'll be trouble if I bunk off for so long. I ain't even thirteen for a few more days.'

'I'd say the school board man's got more on his plate than to worry about the likes of you,' Tilly briskly replied. 'By the time you get took on somewhere you'll be more'n thirteen anyhow. By the time the school reports you absent you'll be thirteen and quite a bit. Ain't worth their while to make a song 'n' dance over it. I know for a fact that Geoff Lovat next door ain't done more'n a couple of days' schoolin'. He's been working almost since the day they turned up last year. School board man ain't bothered him.'

Alice knew that was true. Geoff had done full-time work at thirteen – when he could get it. He'd done a bit of casual sweeping and so on down the coal yard; he'd been on a market stall with Danny when they'd had enough to invest in a barrow of their own for a few weeks. He'd also gone with Billy the Totter on his rag ''n' bone round till Billy reckoned too much stuff was going walkies. Geoff would go anywhere at all where he'd get a wage packet and no questions asked about his age, or whether he was bunking off school and likely to attract trouble. Like Danny, he was able to get work easily because he looked a lot older than he was and had the height and physique of a man.

'I'll get round to the factory gate and hang about dinnertime,' Alice promised her mum.

'Yeah, do that. If nothing comes of it we'll keep looking.'

'Ain't doing the rag shop though,' Alice said quickly.

Tilly raised her eyebrows at her daughter's obstinate tone. 'Best find yourself something quick then,' she replied. 'You're out to work now and that's that.'

Alice huddled into her coat and pulled the collar up to keep the breeze from buffeting her cold face. She looked again towards the iron gate as a few women hurried out, gossiping.

They were no doubt rushing home for a bite to eat at dinnertime before their afternoon shift started. But there was no sign of Annie Foster. Alice had already decided that if she didn't ambush her here, by the factory gate, she'd make the effort to find her in Playford Road. She was out to work now. Definite.

Another bunch of young women emerged from the old brick building and Alice felt a surge of relief. She recognised Annie; she stuck out because of her glasses. As the women stepped onto the pavement Alice called out. Annie changed direction and came over to her with a wave for her friends who'd headed off the opposite way.

'Thought you might turn up. Your mum said as you might be interested in gettin' a job,' Annie said without preamble.

Alice nodded. 'They still taking on?'

'I think they're pretty much done. You'll need to be quick.' Annie took a glance up at the wall where the board for vacancies had been pinned. It had gone. 'I know that Tina Baker's had enough. She's just put in her notice. She's leaving Friday 'cos she can't keep up and earn enough. It's piecework so it ain't easy money. Right boring too, it is.'

Alice nodded her understanding. 'Don't mind. It's a start.'

'Yeah,' Annie said wryly. 'It's a wage packet come Friday.'

'Who shall I ask for?'

'Mr Wright's the manager. He ain't bad actually. I'd get in there now if I was you, before they stick the vacancy notice back up on account of Tina quittin'. Also it ain't so mad busy over the dinnertime.'

Alice nodded, glancing apprehensively towards the ugly, squat building. She took an inspiriting breath.

'Don't say your proper age if he asks,' Annie instructed kindly. 'But he might not ask. He never did when I got took on. But then I'm older than you and I look it.'

Alice nodded again and muttered her thanks. Nervously she brushed down her coat to remove rain spots. She took another deep breath, about to move towards the gate but Annie stopped her.

''Ere, is it right what I heard that your Sophy's in the family way?'

'Who told yer that?' Alice demanded rather roughly. Immediate, instinctive loyalty to Sophy and her family had made her sound aggressive.

'Tommy Greenfield. He found out off his sister Pam. Me 'n' 'im are walking out together.'

'Oh yeah? Well, you want to watch him,' Alice said gruffly. 'Or he'll have *you* in the family way. Remember poor Maisie?' She threw that caution over her shoulder as she walked on without answering Annie's question.

Once inside the building Alice felt her confidence rapidly disappearing. The noise of machinery was thudding away somewhere out of sight. She sidled further in and passed a wall, the top half of which was a glass panel. She glanced in to see a couple of wooden desks jumbled with boxes of files and paperwork. A man looked up from where he was writing to frown enquiringly at her.

Alice froze. She'd hoped for a few private moments to get her bearings before someone spotted her. Determinedly she gripped the door handle and poked her head in. 'Excuse me. I'm looking for Mr Wright.'

'Well, you've found him. What are you after? A job?' he asked bluntly.

Alice nodded.

'Well, come in then and sit yourself down.'

Alice slipped through the door and after fidgeting on the spot, wondering which chair to choose, she sat on the closest.

'Not there. Here.' Mr Wright tapped a chair that was adjacent to his own.

Swiftly Alice did as she was told, aware that the fellow's eyes were on her. But he didn't look unfriendly; in fact he had quite a pleasant sort of face even though he was almost bald. He looked quite smart too in his dark suit of clothes. She guessed he was about as old as her dad.

'What's your name and how old are you?'

Alice's heart sank. Straight off, the first question he'd asked, when she'd been sure he might be more concerned if she came out of The Bunk. 'Alice Keiver and I'm fourteen,' she blurted but could feel her face heating because of the lie she'd told.

'Fourteen, are you?'

'Me friend Annie Foster recommended me to come and get a job,' Alice said quickly, for she'd heard the suspicion in his voice. 'She's been took on recently and said as you had vacancies. I work hard.'

'Know Annie, do you? Well, I can't complain about her. She does her quota and more.'

'I can do that too,' Alice promised eagerly.

Simon Wright gave a half smile. That sort of enthusiasm rarely lasted long in places like this. He guessed she was lying about her age but not by much. Alice Keiver could pass for fourteen, delicately built though she was. He often saw girls close to school-leaving age who couldn't be patient and wait those last few months. Usually he'd play it by the book. But the factory had a large order to meet and they'd be one short again with Tina leaving on Friday. At least with the younger girls they were glad of the work. At the beginning they expected less and did more than their older colleagues to keep their jobs.

'I'm not going to say it's the easiest work, or the most interesting, but you'll get your pay packet end of Friday's shift without delay. Ten shillings to start.'

Alice nodded eagerly.

Simon Wright picked up his pen. 'I need some details from you, Alice. Address?'

Alice gulped then quickly said, 'Campbell Road. But I'm moving soon . . . soon as I can.'

On turning into Campbell Road on her way home from the factory Alice stopped humming and waved frantically. She'd spied her mum marching purposefully down the road. Alice put on a spurt and went to meet her and tell her the good news.

As Alice got closer she slowed to a walk again and some of her high spirits evaporated. She could see her mother's expression now and read from it that something was definitely not right.

Tilly's lips were compressed tight and her blue eyes were narrowed dangerously. As her daughter reached her Tilly snapped out, 'You'll have to get inside and take Lucy off Fran. I've left her with your aunt while I've been doing me rent collecting. Now I've got to go and see Mr Keane and give him some real bad news.'

Alice guessed that the *real bad news* was to do with unpaid rents. It wasn't unusual for people around here to get in to arrears if they'd had no work. Usually her mum was quite lenient and would juggle figures this way and that for people she liked and who needed a bit of help for a few weeks. She'd been known to lend small items, like blankets, to women to pawn so they could scrape by till something turned up. But Tilly didn't take nonsense off anybody. Alice knew that often people were tempted to take liberties. They'd use money that had been put by for rent on frivolous things. Billy the Totter turned up each week in Campbell Road before rent-collection day. He'd made it his business to find out when each house manager did the rounds in the hope of getting in first and laying his sticky fingers on the cash before the landlord got it. Alice knew her mother wanted to keep on the right side of her boss, Mr Keane, because she wanted his work.

Tilly's thoughts were running along the same lines: she didn't want to lose her job. It was a good one with perks. She took liberties . . . but not too many. She knew Mr Keane had in the past cocked a deaf'n to tales about her. In a roundabout way he'd let her know so long as she delivered the rents due he didn't care too much how she got them, or how she robbed Peter to pay Paul. Of course he knew that she dipped in and fiddled here and there and had a little flutter with his money to try and make a bit of extra cash for herself; but as long as the figures tallied when the money was handed over he was satisfied.

'I got the job at the factory,' Alice ventured in the hope of lightening her mother's dark frown.

'Bleeding good job too,' Tilly retorted. ''Cos if I lose me job over this we'll need your money, every penny of it.'

'What . . .?' Alice started to enquire but Tilly soon cut her short and through gritted teeth told her what had gone wrong.

'Those Robertsons in number fifty-two have gone 'n' done a bunk. Bastards must've took off early hours of Sunday morning. Nobody seems to have seen them since Saturday.' Tilly stuffed her hands into her pockets to warm them. 'Old Beattie who lives a couple of doors away from them reckons the lads had a barrow pulled up outside ready 'n' waiting. When she asked what it was for they said they was setting up in rag 'n' boning. She didn't think no more of it, she said, or she'd have come and warned me.'

'Did they owe a lot?' Alice glanced across the road at the offending house. Usually she wouldn't have had the courage to question her mother about any of her business. It would have earned her a clip round the ear for cheek. But her mother had started the discussion, and it seemed that securing her first proper job was passage to being allowed to know such things.

'They owe a month; but it ain't just that. I lent Jeannie Robertson a blouse to pawn. Good 'un, it was. Won't see that no more. But that ain't the worst of it. They've done a runner with every stick o' furniture that was in the place. All of it Mr Keane's.'

Alice's jaw slackened and her eyes grew round. Naturally, it wasn't unheard of for people to do a moonlight flit around here. But usually they just scarpered with their own measly stuff, and owing back rent.

'That's why they hired a cart,' Alice ventured, and got a sour look from her mother for stating the bleeding obvious.

The Robertsons were known to be a family of ruffians. They were generally avoided as being the lowest of the low in a road where the dregs of society were said to congregate. Two teenage sons had lived with their mother at number fifty-two. Nobody knew where Jeannie Robertson's husband was, and nobody had cared enough to ask for she was a blunt, unfriendly type. They'd moved from Lorenco Road in Tottenham and had been tenants for about two years. Since that time the boys had been known as violent troublemakers. They'd both been up before the magistrate recently for smashing the windows of St Anne's church round in Pooles Park. The Lennox Road Mission had also been targeted when the boys were banned from the youth club because of their bad language and behaviour. Alice and Sophy had been warned repeatedly by Tilly to stay away from them, and they had.

'Get in and take Lucy off Fran's hands or she'll be moaning and kickin' up a stink,' Tilly directed Alice. 'Time she got off her arse and bucked herself up a bit,' she muttered, and set off down the road.

Alice knew then that her mother was well and truly riled. She was never usually out of patience with her sister Fran, or if she was she kept it to herself. Alice felt the criticism was justified. In her opinion it was time her aunt got herself some proper work instead of cadging all the time. It was about time too that Bobbie and Stevie spent more time in their own place. It was a constant crush in the Keivers' rooms.

Alice entered the dim hallway of her home silently praying that her mum would not lose her job over this. She knew too well what would happen if she did: she'd have to hand over every penny she earned from the factory job and manage to put nothing by for her new life.

As Alice knocked on Fran's door to collect her little sister she realised why the Robertsons had gone on a Saturday night. They'd known that the Keiver household would be in drunken uproar. Now that Fran was over the worst, the Saturday night singsongs had started up again. The Keivers, and a good deal of the neighbours, wouldn't have been in a fit state in the early hours of Sunday morning to notice a thing that went on.

ELEVEN

'Mr Keane ain't pleased but then I expected that. I told him straight: it's not my fault. We don't take references around here. I can't guess any more'n him what the bleeders'll get up to.'

The relief in Tilly's face matched Jack's feelings. If his wife lost her work with Mr Keane, when he was still raking around for a bit of proper pay, it would have been hard on all of them. 'Is old Keane sending the boys out looking for the Robertsons to get his stuff back? Don't suppose they've gone far.'

'Doubt he'll bother unless he wants to stop anyone else doing likewise.' Tilly shrugged. 'The stuff they took was only fit for burning. The old table was full o' worm and the chairs no better. The bed was scrap iron, and no door on the wardrobe. They had that off for firewood day after they turned up. You turned up anything today, Jack?' Jack shook his head and accepted the cup of tea that Tilly held out to him. 'I saw Jimmy today,' he said, hoping to avoid further discussion about his lack of success job hunting. 'Walkin' arm in arm he was, with Nellie down Finsbury Park way.' He shook his head and muttered, 'Out walking bold as you like with a prossy. What's he come to?'

'Nuthin',' Tilly stated sourly. 'That's what he's come to. And I ain't wasting me breath talking about him. Have you been back to Basher to see if he's got any work coming up in his houses?'

'I've been putting meself in his way every day. Once his Brand Street places have been fumigated he says there might be a sniff of something. Bet he's sick o' the sight of me.'

'Well, I ain't sick o' the sight of you, Jackie boy.' Tilly knew she'd got off lightly with Mr Keane and relief had put her in a good mood. In a rare show of affection she grabbed one of her husband's arms and rubbed her cheek on his rough shirtsleeve. 'I still got me job with Mr Keane, thank Gawd, and sooner or later I'll have them Robertsons for doing the dirty on me, you see if I don't.'

Jack planted a kiss on top of his wife's fiery head. 'You will 'n' all, gel, won't you.'

'I feel sorry that Fran didn't find herself someone like you,' Tilly muttered against his arm. She felt his muscle flex beneath her cheek as he happily registered her compliment. Then a few of his fingers sank into her hair, tilting up her head so their eyes collided.

'You don't want to go sweet talkin' me, Til,' he growled, his eyes alight with amusement. 'Not unless you're prepared for a bit of a lie down in the middle o' the afternoon.'

She went on tiptoe and kissed him full on the mouth. 'That's all yer getting,' she warned, sliding a teasing finger between their lips. 'We got one swollen belly in the family 'n' that's enough fer me . . .' She gave a squeal as Jack tried to wrestle away the hand fending him off. A moment later they'd broken apart and Tilly was rolling up her sleeves and stacking crockery in the bowl.

'Got a job, Dad,' Alice announced proudly as she came into the front room. She'd been up the road to the shop with Lucy toddling at her side. Now she put tea and bread on the table and lifted her little sister onto the bed to rest her little legs.

'More doorsteps?' her dad asked interestedly. 'Ain't you got enough chores to do on a Saturday morning, Al?'

'And that reminds me,' Tilly butted in, clattering cups. 'Beth can take on your doorsteps now you don't want them, Al. Don't let nobody else take 'em on. Beth's plenty old enough to be doing more'n running old Beattie's errands for a few coppers.'

Alice nodded then resumed her conversation with her dad. 'I've got a proper job. At the toy factory, working full-time.'

Jack laughed. 'You're not old enough to work full-time in a factory.'

'She's old enough. She got offered the job,' Tilly said firmly, her eyes clashing on her husband's. 'She starts Monday.'

Jack stared in disbelief. 'She only turns thirteen tomorrow,' he spluttered. 'What about school?'

'She's finished her schoolin',' Tilly stated. The deed was done and it was staying done, no matter what Jack said. 'She's learned enough . . . all she needs to know. Now she's working.'

Jack looked thoughtfully at Alice and for a moment said nothing. 'You alright with that, Alice?' he finally asked.

Alice grinned. 'Yeah, I'm alright with it, Dad. Can't wait to tell Sarah. She'll want a job as well. But I got the last one, I think. I turned up right on time, just as Tina Baker told Mr Wright she was leaving.'

'Well, what d'yer know . . . Keivers had a bit of good luck for a change,' Tilly muttered wryly.

On Monday morning Alice was up bright and early even though she didn't need to report to Mr Wright's office till eight-thirty. He'd said that straight off he'd introduce her to the forelady in charge of her section. She needed to be shown what to do on the first day and get used to the machinery. She'd probably do packing to start while she learned the ropes, he'd told her.

Alice dressed in her good skirt and clean white blouse and was tying back her dark hair neatly when Sophy opened the door.

'Forgotten something?' Tilly demanded to know why Sophy had returned home. She'd only set off for work about fifteen minutes ago.

'Feel bad, Mum,' Sophy explained faintly. 'I can't go to work. Ain't up to it. I came home 'cos I feel like I'm gonna pass out.' Sophy rubbed at her belly and grimaced in pain.

Having studied her eldest daughter's face Tilly decided she wasn't pulling a fast one. She did look a strange colour. 'Get yourself in bed for an hour or so then.' Tilly impatiently flapped a hand at the back room. 'But you'd better do a shift this afternoon. Y'know your dad's scraping around for decent work now Basher's put him off.' In a temper Tilly started grabbing plates and cups and banged them into the tin bowl. 'You got yourself into this mess, my gel, you'll just have to put up with the consequences. Hard lesson to learn, ain't it!' she shouted as Sophy slipped away into the back room.

'I'll do that, Mum. I'm not leaving yet.' Alice offered, knowing that her mother was angry with Sophy because of her lost pay and hoping to smooth things over a bit.

Tilly shoved the bowl across the table towards Alice. 'You can do it 'n' all. I've got better things to do. Sophy, you watch out for Lucy 'cos Alice's got to go to work soon.' Tilly bawled that out as she grabbed her coat then barged out of the door.

Alice smiled at her little sister who was sitting in the

middle of the bed. Lucy held out her arms to be picked up and Alice went to her to give her a cuddle. 'I'm goin' to work, Luce,' she whispered into her soft brown hair. 'And when I get me first pay I'm gonna buy you a present. A big bun?' she suggested, widening her eyes at her little sister.

'Chips,' Lucy said, having removed her thumb from her mouth.

'Right, chips it is,' Alice chuckled. At twenty months old her little sister was bright as a button, especially where something nice to eat was concerned. 'Then when I'm old enough, 'n' I've got me own place, you can come 'n' live with me, Luce. Would you like that?'

Lucy solemnly moved her head up and down, her eyes clinging to Alice's face, her thumb again between her lips.

A loud groan made Alice swing about with Lucy in her arms. Swiftly she plonked the child back on the mattress and rushed in to the back room. She found Sophy doubled up on the bed edge. 'What's up?' she demanded as Sophy retched dryly.

'Don't know . . .' Sophy gasped. 'I never had the bellyache like this when I was feeling sick before.'

'Lie down,' Alice said and went to try to get Sophy's legs up on the bed.

'Don't want to,' Sophy moaned and flicked Alice away. 'I hate that Danny Lovat for this,' she sobbed. 'It's all his fault. He don't even care. He ain't even tried to see me, or asked how I am, or nuthin'.'

'Shut up about him,' Alice hissed. A knot of fear had formed in her chest for Sophy did look very queer. 'Just lie down; you'll feel better,' she added desperately as Sophy began to wail.

This time Sophy took her sister's advice and gingerly moved her legs up to the bed edge.

'What's that?' Alice breathed.

'What?' Sophy croaked, trying to lift her head from the pillow.

'There's wet all over yer skirt. Look.' Alice pointed at the darker mark on Sophy's brown skirt. She peered closer then tottered back a bit in shock. 'Think it's blood; think you're bleeding.'

Sophy struggled up and, with an appalled expression, tried to twist about to see the stain Alice had mentioned. Her searching hand encountered the warm, wet place and she drew her palm away covered in crimson. At that moment another cramping pain made her groan.

'What is it?' Alice demanded, scared. She knew it couldn't be Sophy's time. She knew her mum had calculated from Sophy's missed monthlies that the baby would be born about July or August. It was only the end of March. 'Baby can't be coming, it's not ready yet.'

The girls looked at each other with panic in their eyes as they remembered what had happened to Aunt Fran when it was her time and there'd been blood everywhere. They knew their Aunt Fran had almost died, she'd been so sick.

'It can't be the baby. Ain't big enough.' Sophy ran her trembling hand over her small mound of a belly. 'It must be me monthlies. I'm not pregnant after all,' she gasped and winced. 'They must all be coming together 'cos it never hurt like this before or come so heavy. Oh God!' she gave a muted shriek as she felt a burst of fluid drench her inner thighs. She pushed herself to sit up and scrabbled at her skirt to look between her legs. 'It's going all over the place,' she cried in despair. 'Oh, Gawd help me! What's goin' on?' Sophy raised her terrified eyes to her sister.

After a moment of petrified stillness, mesmerised by the bloody mess spreading on the bed, Alice fumbled at the end of the mattress to find the rags they used for Lucy's night-time nappies. She started ineffectually to dab at her sister's legs but as she did so another surge of blood soaked her hands. 'There's loads of it,' she whispered, horrified.

'It's been in there for months . . . it's all been in there . . .' Sophy howled. 'I weren't pregnant; I've been all swollen with all me monthlies,' she moaned. Suddenly a pain took her knees into her chest. 'Can't stand it, Al,' she whimpered. 'Why don't it stop? That's enough . . . it must be. Where's Mum? Get Mum for me,' she pleaded. 'Look at the state of it . . . she's gonna kill me . . . the mattress's had it now.'

Alice's hands were covered with crusting blood as she yanked the bottom sheet up and tried to bundle it beneath her sister's thighs and in between her legs to try to staunch the flow. 'I'll get some washing water,' she panted and flew into the front room. She dragged Lucy away from the door where she was stretching for the handle and plonked her quickly back on the bed. That rough handling from her favourite sister made Lucy start to cry.

Alice upturned the crockery her mother had stacked in the bowl clumsily onto the table then she raced outside to the tap on the landing. A groan from Sophy made her speed back quickly with the bowl only half filled with water. Some of it slopped over the sides with her jerky movements.

'It hurts, Al,' Sophy whimpered. 'Where's Mum?'

Alice tried to find a bit of clean cloth but practically all of it was now soaked with blood. She grabbed at a piece that had a clean edge and dipped it into the water then frantically set about wiping her sister's legs. Another gush of blood made her efforts wasted.

Alice shot back and for a moment just stared at the red pool that had formed beneath Sophy's hips. She was frightened and had no idea how to help her sister. 'I'll see if Aunt Fran's in,' she gulped. 'If she stays with you 'n' Lucy, I'll find Mum.'

Sophy's frightened eyes clung hungrily to Alice's face.

'Alright,' she whispered. 'If you can't find Mum . . . d'you know where Dad's gone?'

'He's looking for work down the market,' Alice said. She quickly tried to reassure Sophy who'd started to sob. 'Mum won't be far. She ain't been gone long.' She plunged her bloody hands into the bowl to get the worst of it off before dashing into the other room. She tried to quieten Lucy's howls with a few soothing words before flying out and down the stairs to Aunt Fran's. She hammered on her aunt's door with both fists. She called to no avail. With tears of frustration starting to her eyes Alice swore and dithered on the spot, unsure whether to bolt back up the stairs and see how Sophy was or to go out immediately to try and find her mother. She continued down to the street and darted searching looks here and there hoping to spy her mum close by. She didn't but at that moment Margaret Lovat came out of next door.

At first Margaret made to ignore Alice. It was the way they all went on now since Danny had got Sophy pregnant. Didn't look . . . didn't speak. But Margaret had never had a quarrel with Alice, and from her harassed demeanour the older woman could see she had trouble.

'Somethin' up?' Margaret asked, hesitating on her walk to the shop.

'Sophy,' Alice breathed. 'She ain't pregnant after all. All her monthlies have come together and it's gone all over the place and Mum's gone out.'

Margaret blanched. 'Where is Sophy?' she demanded.

'On the bed in the back room,' Alice gasped. 'Can you just stay with her and keep an eye on Lucy while I find me mum? She's gotta come back and see to her ''cos I don't know what to do.'

'Well I was . . .' Margaret began. She stepped past Alice. 'Go and find Tilly as quick as you can,' she said. 'Quick as you can!' she repeated urgently as Alice succumbed for a moment to her shock and stood riveted to the spot. 'I've left my lot up there on their own,' Margaret explained. 'I was only going to get a drop o' milk.'

Alice nodded vigorously and jerking into action she hared off along Campbell Road. Thankfully her mother hadn't got too far at all. Alice spied her in a dim hallway of a house opposite talking to Beattie Evans; no doubt they were tearing strips off the Robertson family.

Frantically Alice beckoned her mum and Tilly, sensing her agitation, rushed out straight away.

'Sophy's not well, Mum,' Alice blurted in a cautious whisper. Despite the urgency of the situation she was still conscious of keeping her family's privacy. 'Her monthlies have come after all and she's bleedin' all over the place. Mrs Lovat's with her.'

Tilly didn't wait to hear more; with her skirts in her fists she began to run home with Alice hot on her heels.

'Think it's done.' Margaret's quiet statement greeted Tilly's appearance in the doorway. She inclined her head at the bulky mess on the bed. She had been gripping Sophy's hand strongly in comfort but now extricated her fingers and moved so Tilly could come closer to the bed and attend to her daughter.

'If you pop next door for me, Alice, and keep an eye on me kids, I'll stop here and help yer mum have a clean-up.'

Alice nodded but her eyes were mesmerised by the sight of her white-faced sister lying on a bed of blood. Alice found Lucy still on the mattress where she'd left her. It looked as though she'd cried herself out. Now her little eyelids were drooping and she was hiccoughing past the thumb in her mouth. Quickly Alice stooped to gather her up and take her with her next door.

The two women worked together in silence, rolling Sophy gently to one side so they could remove the soiled wadding stuck beneath her hips.

'I'll set water ter boil, and get the bath in from out back,' Margaret said gruffly and received just a nod from Tilly in response. When Margaret returned with the tin hipbath she collected together the soiled sheets and rags. 'Washin' or throwin'? she asked bluntly.

'Washin',' Tilly replied roughly.

'I'll set 'em to soak then get the copper alight out the back 'n' get started,' Margaret said.

'I wasn't pregnant, after all, Mum,' Sophy stirred to murmur, her drained features displaying a mingling of surprise and relief.

Tilly's eyes were drawn to the purplish mess in the tin bowl. 'That's good then,' she said gruffly after a long pause. 'I'll just get rid o' this. Won't be long.' She picked up the bowl and went down into the back yard where Margaret was getting the washing copper organised. The two women exchanged a long look as Tilly proceeded towards the privy. She opened the door of the filthy brick shit house and tipped the contents of the bowl down the toilet and yanked the chain.

Tilly's eyes closed just for a moment before she turned and went back inside to fill the bath and help Sophy into it. A moment later she came back out to see Margaret vigorously plunging the washing dolly on the sheets in the copper.

'Thanks,' she said curtly.

'Least I can do,' Margaret said, equally brusque.

'Yeah . . . there's that to it,' Tilly said and, turning about, went back inside.

TWELVE

'Would you do us a favour, Geoff?'

Geoff frowned. He'd emerged in to the street and found Alice still dawdling on the pavement. Moments ago he'd been gulping down his cup of tea while watching her from a window and wondering what was up with her. She'd been pacing restlessly back and forth, frowning and chewing on a thumbnail.

He hadn't been expecting her to stop him and ask him to help with whatever was troubling her. The Keivers didn't give the Lovats the time of day and, as far as he knew, hadn't done so since the almighty ruckus that'd occurred between their families after Danny had got Sophy up the duff. Although, to be fair, he and Alice hadn't ever fallen out, and would acknowledge each other if they were passing in the street. Whenever he saw her approaching he always hoped she might stop and say a few words rather than walk on by with a gruff mutter or a nod. A couple of times he'd been on the point of putting himself in her way and inviting her to have a bite to eat at the café. But the moment always came and went and took with it his courage. Only once when he turned to look at her did he catch her out looking right back at him. Geoff had known from the day he'd hauled her off fat Louisa's back that he liked Alice and instinctively he had protected her rather than see her get hurt.

'What sort of favour?' Geoff asked. 'I'm back off to work. Only come home for me dinner.'

'Won't take long.'

'What's up, then?' Geoff asked, mildly curious.

'Are you going Thane Villas way?' Alice wheedled and looked appealingly at him. He was as tall as his brother Danny although, at nearly fourteen and a half, he was over a year younger. She was sure he'd manage to do what she wanted. Then it was up to her to do better than stutter a stupid excuse for showing up late.

'Could do, I suppose,' Geoff casually replied. 'What's up?' he repeated.

'Nothing really,' Alice said, quite nonchalant. 'Just want you to get something for me. I can't reach it 'cos I'm not tall enough.'

Geoff frowned and shrugged. 'Alright. But better get going or I'll be late back.'

'Where are you working now?' Alice asked conversationally as they walked briskly along.

'Got a job in a gents' outfitters, round in Hornsey Road. Milligan's, d'you know it?'

Alice hoisted her dark brows. She was impressed. 'That's a good place. Good pay, is it?' she enquired.

'Nah!' Geoff grunted a laugh. 'But it has . . . perks . . . if y'know what I mean.'

Alice slid him an old-fashioned look. 'You'll regret it, y'know, if you get caught out doing something daft. Milligan's is good gear and far too rich for me dad's pocket, so he told me.'

'That's why I ain't getting caught out doing something daft,' Geoff returned dryly. 'Ol' man Milligan ain't a bad old stick. So I ain't taking the piss out of him like I could if I really put me mind to it.'

'Bet Danny's pleased you got the job,' Alice said as they marched on towards Thane Villas.

It was as though the hiatus in their fledgling friendship had never occurred. They had fallen back, straight away, into a comfortable camaraderie.

''Spect him and your dad get a few nice bits.' Alice ran an eye over Geoff's neat appearance. He obviously did alright for clothes himself out of his job. Perhaps he got a staff discount because it would be really dumb in the brainbox to pinch stuff then wear it to work. And Alice reckoned that Geoff wasn't stupid at all.

'Me dad ain't exactly suited to snappy dressing,' Geoff observed sourly. 'As for Dan, I ain't doing him no favours. Me 'n' 'im fell out.' He looked off into the distance.

'You had a bust-up over something?' Alice squinted up at his averted face.

'Sort of . . .'

Alice continued gazing up at him enquiringly.

'Weren't right what he did to your sister.' Geoff plunged his hands into his pockets after giving his verdict.

Alice blushed.

'No . . . not that,' Geoff said with a grin. 'That's up to her. She never accused him of nuthin'.' He paused. 'Weren't right the way he tried to weasel out of it. He should've stood up to me mum 'n' dad and said he'd get wed to her. I know he's right upset about it all, and feels guilty at what he's done.' He frowned as he explained, 'Dan just wants to get some money and get away from here, 'fore he gets tied down with a family, and I can understand how he feels. But it still ain't right giving your own kid away. I don't reckon so anyhow.'

'No need to worry now,' Alice mumbled reflexively, a

pink stain lingering in her cheeks. It was the first time she'd discussed the matter with anyone apart from Sophy. After the initial shock of finding out she was pregnant, Sophy hadn't wanted to talk about the baby any more. It seemed her sister had wanted to forget she had a little life inside her that would never be part of her future. After the hullabaloo her parents had kept schtumm on the delicate subject of Sophy's disgrace, and if they'd talked about it between themselves Alice had never heard them doing so.

'I don't reckon *you'd* give away your own nipper,' Geoff said and slanted a penetrating look at Alice.

Alice felt the blood fizz in her cheeks again. 'I wouldn't get meself in that sort of trouble for any lad,' she scoffed. 'Anyhow,' she continued quickly, feeling odd, 'Sophy ain't in trouble; it's all come right.'

'Eh? How's that then?' Geoff shot a puzzled look at her.

'I suppose your mum wouldn't have told you,' Alice began then hesitated, feeling foolish and embarrassed. Of course Margaret wouldn't have said anything. All women's stuff was unmentionable, especially to men; Alice had picked that knowledge up from Sophy when it was her time to know a few months ago. 'Sophy ain't in the family way,' Alice muttered quickly. 'So that's alright, thank Gawd. She's just been right poorly though.'

'She got rid of it after all?' Geoff asked in surprise. He remembered the day Sophy had screeched that no skewer was ever going anywhere near her.

Alice shook her head and averted her burning cheeks. 'Wasn't got rid of, but I ain't saying any more.' In fact she wasn't really sure what had happened to Sophy. After it was all cleaned up, and Margaret had gone home, Alice had met her mum coming down the stairs with Lucy balanced on her hip. Her mum had said very little, other than Sophy wasn't pregnant; but she was allowed to rest in bed for the day to get her strength back. Then Tilly had muttered about going to the back yard to peg out the wet sheets on the washing line.

Aware of Geoff's thoughtful gaze on her Alice rushed across the road to avoid his questions, and to hide her confusion. She halted outside the factory gate and tipped back her head. She pointed. 'I want you to get that down for me.'

Geoff joined her and squinted up at the vacancy board. 'You want me to get that for you?' He started to laugh. 'You gone nuts or somethin', Alice Keiver?'

'No, I have not!' Alice said forcefully, her cheeks blooming now with a different sort of embarrassment. 'It's my job and I want it. There ain't a vacancy. I already took it. It weren't my fault our place was in uproar and I couldn't get here to start on time. Ain't fair! Mr Wright give *me* the work. I want you to take down the notice before someone else sees it and goes in and gets me job.'

'You was supposed to start work here today?' Geoff asked in surprise. 'Didn't think you was old enough to be out to work.'

'Nor was you old enough, Geoff Lovat, when you was first out to work,' Alice came back quickly at him.

Geoff gazed down at her pretty, fierce features then up at the notice. His amusement died. 'You late turnin' in 'cos Sophy weren't well earlier?'

Alice nodded and frowned into the distance. 'Just my luck, ain't it, to lose me first job before I even started it.'

Without another word he pulled a penknife out of a pocket and, flicking it open, worked at each corner of the block of wood until the board came loose. A yank with both hands and it was off. 'There y'are,' he said and handed it over.

Alice gripped the cumbersome board to her small chest. 'Thanks,' she mumbled and gave him a sweetly shy smile.

'Right, I'm off then,' Geoff said, having given her a long, contemplative look. Without further ado he turned and sprinted off up the street.

Alice watched him disappear round the corner, feeling a surge of warmth steal over her at his kindness. She'd always liked him but never before noticed that he had a nice smile and long, strong fingers. She turned back and stared at the factory gate. With a deep breath she walked through it with the vacancy board wedged under a slender arm.

'Give that to me at once!' Simon Wright snatched the board from Alice's grasp and leaned it against the office wall. Inwardly he tried to keep an astonished smile from softening his expression. She had a lot of guts for a girl of her age. He looked sternly at her. 'I told you earlier, young lady, that timekeeping is of the utmost importance at this company. You're not hired. Now go away, Alice Keiver, or there'll be trouble.'

'But you gave me a job. It weren't my fault I couldn't get here on time. Why won't you let me explain? Please!' Alice demanded, sounding angry.

After the awful events that morning she'd set out for work, having first poked her head into the back room to see how Sophy was. Her sister had been flaked out on the bed, face white as chalk, so Alice had called a soft farewell and started off at a run for the factory. As soon as she had turned in the factory gate she'd noticed that the vacancy board was up. She'd stretched up for it but was unable to reach it, let alone remove it.

She'd found Mr Wright in his office. He'd scowled at her and gestured her away muttering she'd had her chance and it was obviously more than someone from The Bunk had deserved. Alice had taken the dismissal meekly and started off home again. But slowly a simmering sense of injustice had overcome her depression. She'd decided that she wasn't going to accept her fate so readily, or her mother's wrath when she came home later and found out she'd lost a good job. As Alice had paced back and forth on the pavement outside her home mulling it all over, she'd decided to go back and hope to find Mr Wright in a better mood after his dinner. Perhaps he might let her start on the afternoon shift for half a day's pay. She'd work late and wear her fingers down to the bone if he'd agree to that.

But now, as she took a wary glance at the manager's forbidding face, she realised he didn't look any more lenient than he had earlier. Nevertheless Alice tried one final time to put her case. 'It weren't my fault. Honest. I was all ready and about to set out early this morning when something dreadful happened to me sister. I had to find me mum and bring her back home to look after her so's I could come here to work. That's why I was so late. It won't ever happen again, promise.'

'And what was dreadfully wrong with your sister?' he asked in a voice that sounded sarcastic. Alice hesitated and looked away. If she told him she'd be revealing her family's private business to a stranger and she hated doing that. But she desperately wanted this job. 'She was in the family way . . . now she isn't,' she reluctantly muttered while her cheeks flared.

For a moment Simon Wright remained quiet. He coughed and stuck a couple of fingers between his neck and his shirt collar. 'I see,' he eventually said. 'And is she . . . er . . . feeling better now?'

Alice nodded. 'Think so. She's home in bed. Looks like death warmed up though.'

'Well . . . that is a very . . . unusual circumstance,' he said gently.

Alice recognised the change in his tone. She looked at him with a glimmer of hope shining in her blue eyes.

'One more chance then, Alice Keiver. If your timekeeping is bad again . . .'

'It won't be, swear,' Alice interrupted breathlessly.

'As you know Annie Foster, I think you can start this afternoon in Room 4, with her, when she gets back from dinner. She can show you what to do.'

Alice suppressed an urge to leap forward and hug him. She simply nodded vigorously then blurted, 'I'll wait by the gates, shall I, and catch Annie when she gets back?'

'Yes, you do that, Alice,' Simon said and watched her go out, carefully closing the door behind her.

'How di't go?'

Alice speeded up along Campbell Road when she saw Geoff leaning against the railing outside their houses, waiting for her to reach him. She grinned. 'I got me job back,' she told him, and, less inhibited than she'd been with her boss, she grabbed one of Geoff's long arms and gave it a squeeze that incorporated her gratitude and excitement. 'Ain't easy work,' she bubbled on. 'Ain't half noisy there 'n' all. But Annie's showing me what to do, and I'm pickin' it up already.' She turned to go in. 'Must tell Mum.' She swung back to Geoff. 'Thanks for helping me earlier. Think me boss knew I wasn't muckin' about when I took the notice in with me. Think he was quite impressed I did that. He knew I was serious about keeping me job, you see.'

'Glad to help,' Geoff said. Suddenly he pulled a piece of fabric from a pocket. 'Dunno if yer dad might make use of this. I already got a few scarves and me old man'll never suit it.' He held out a length of charcoal-grey silk.

Reverently Alice touched the slubbed silk, running her fingers over it. She could tell it was of beautiful quality. 'You don't want it?' she murmured in awe.

'Got no use for it,' Geoff said bluntly. 'And Dan ain't

havin' it, that's fer sure.' He looked at Alice as she hesitated in taking the gift. 'Don't have to have it. I can sell it on. Just thought as your dad's got a sort of gentleman way about him, he might wear it on occasions; you know, weddings 'n' funerals. But if it ain't his sort of thing . . .' He made to withdraw his hand, and his gift, but Alice snatched at the scarf.

'No . . . he'll like it . . . he will . . . I know he will.' She folded the soft silk neatly and held it. 'Thanks,' she said quietly, for a moment keeping her eyes lowered from his. She knew that really the gift was for her. But Geoff was right; her dad did have a gentleman way about him, and he deserved such a splendid thing. She must find a private moment to give the scarf to him. If her mother saw it she'd have it down the pawnshop first thing in the morning then she might spend the afternoon drinking whiskey in the Duke with Aunt Fran.

With a shy smile for Geoff she turned to go in. Looking back, she gruffly repeated her thanks before she ran up the stairs.

'Back room,' was her mother's greeting and instruction when Alice burst in to tell her the good news about her job.

Alice swung a glance between her parents. She understood why she was banished from their presence. Her mother had obviously not finished telling her father what had happened to Sophy earlier. Such conversations between them were, as far as possible considering the cramped condition of their home, done in private.

Alice gave her dad a tiny smile then went to see how Sophy was. She found her looking pale but sitting on the bed brushing little Lucy's hair. When she asked about Bethany's whereabouts Sophy said she thought she was on an errand, getting Beattie Evans some snuff from the shop.

Having seated herself beside Sophy, Alice pulled out the

scarf from her pocket then related how she'd come by it. 'Don't tell Mum, or she'll have it off me soon as she can.'

Sophy took the silk and, holding it up, twisted her wrist to look at it from different angles. 'It's really nice.' She gave her verdict and handed it back.

'Yeah; and it's a present for Dad.'

'Why'd Geoff give it to you?'

Alice shrugged, keeping her expression neutral. She wasn't about to tell Sophy that she thought Geoff had taken a fancy to her. For some reason that seemed private, just for her and Geoff to know. 'He said he don't want it,' she explained airily. 'And he won't give it to Danny 'cos they've fell out over him not treating you right.'

The mention of Danny's name made Sophy's eyes narrow to slits in her white face. 'Good. He don't deserve nuthin',' she said spitefully. 'All he deserves is a good thumping.'

'Perhaps when he finds out you're not having the baby after all he'll come round to see you. Geoff reckons he feels right guilty about it all but he doesn't want to be tied down.'

'Well, I don't care anyhow; he can fuck off,' Sophy choked out on a sob.

Alice looked shocked on hearing her sister's bad language.

There were three rules the Keiver kids must obey on pain of a thrashing: no swearing, no thieving and no drinking. It didn't seem to matter that their parents, especially their mother, indulged liberally in at least two of those sins. If Tilly had also been light-fingered on occasion, when working as a charwoman for wealthy clients, she'd been shrewder than those colleagues who brazenly boasted that having a few of their employer's little bits was their right considering the pittance they were paid. She'd also kept any hint of it from her family, including her husband. Keivers didn't lower themselves to steal; that was Tilly's motto.'Don't let Mum hear you talk like that,' Alice cautioned with a grimace at the door.

'Is Dan really sorry, d'you think?' Sophy asked forlornly.

Alice shrugged. She wished now she'd not let on what Geoff had told her. She felt as though she'd broken a confidence even though he'd not asked her to keep their conversation to herself. 'Hope they're not gonna be long chin-wagging; I'm starving and want me tea.' She stood up abruptly, shaking off a feeling of melancholy. Besides, it had just occurred to Alice that, what with the commotion earlier, and her fight to keep her job, she'd gone without a morsel to eat all day.

'Won't be nothing much to have,' Sophy said morosely. 'Bit of bread 'n' scrape if we're lucky.'

'Fancy chips,' Alice said, smacking her lips. 'Chips with loads of salt 'n' vinegar. I wish it were Friday and I'd got paid. On Friday I'm eating me tea in a caff down Blackstock Road. I'll treat you too this week.' Alice knew that Sophy always took her payday tea in a café, despite her mum insisting she come straight home with her wages. Sophy knew better than to do so: she could end up losing the lot if their mother was in a particularly foul mood. Several times Sophy had treated Alice to a cup of tea and a big sticky bun too out of her wages. Alice thought it was only fair that she returned the favour now she was able. But the thought of such delights now, when she was hungry, simply made her stomach grumble noisily.

'D'you reckon Beth'll get a few coppers off old Beattie for running her errand?'

Alice nodded, knowing at once what Sophy was thinking. 'How much you got?' she asked bluntly.

'Enough for a ha'penny and a ha'porth.' For those two coins she'd get a piece of fish and a portion of chips.

'I got sixpence,' Alice said triumphantly and pulled the coin out to show her sister.

'We got enough for a drink 'n' all then,' Sophy said with a giggle.

'You fit to go out?' Alice asked anxiously as her sister got up feebly from the bed edge.

'Yeah, already sorted meself out,' Sophy said succinctly.

'We'll catch Beth outside, before she comes back in, and say we're all off up the road to tell Sarah Whitton about me job. If Mum thinks we're out for fish 'n' chips she'll have our pockets turned out.' She added as a solemn afterthought, 'Then Dad'll lose his scarf fer sure.'

THIRTEEN

'Just as well neither of them's old enough to join up and be a sailor in the navy. They'd sink a ship before the war's properly started.' Alice's rueful comment made her two companions burst out laughing as they observed the boys' unsuccessful efforts to row their boat in a straight line.

It was a hot Saturday at the beginning of August and Alice, Sophy and Sarah Whitton were lounging on scratchy parched grass that sloped up and away from the Finsbury Park boating lake. They had walked from Campbell Road the short distance in the blistering heat and found a shady spot beneath trees. Gratefully they'd collapsed down on the ground to have a rest. They had begun to pool pennies to see if between them they had enough cash to take a boat out on the lake and still have some left to stop off at a café for a bite to eat on the way home.

A long, low whistle had curtailed their calculations. A moment later a group of youths had bowled up and sat down close by. Danny and Geoff Lovat – who were on friendly terms again now Sophy was back to normal – had been amongst a quartet of young hounds. Herbert Banks, also from Campbell Road, was with them; so was a boy Alice recognised as being out of Queensland Road.

A session of good-natured catcalling back and forth had taken place between the groups of boys and girls for some while. Bored with that, Geoff and Herbert Banks had stood up and wandered off towards the lake. A little while later Alice had watched the two of them – in possession of an oar each – rotating a boat in clumsy circles towards the centre of the lake. It was that amusing sight that had prompted her to make her remark about the war that'd recently been declared on Germany.

The news that they were at war had been shocking, and oddly exciting, but it all seemed very distant and unreal, especially on a glorious carefree summer day such as this.

'I saw me dad in the week,' Sarah said. 'He reckons now he's lost his job he's going to volunteer for the army. It's regular pay 'n' grub, he says. And he wants to do his bit for his country.'

Alice frowned. 'He's a bit old, ain't he?'

'Thirty-seven, I think. I hope they don't let him in. I don't want him to be hurt or nuthin'.'

'Me dad brought in the newspaper and we read all about it. It's all going to be over by Christmas anyhow,' Alice told her friend reassuringly. 'So even if your dad does go to war he'll be back home before you know it.'

'I heard Herbert Banks's been boasting he's going to go to the recruitin' office and pretend he's nineteen so's he can join up.'

Alice snorted derisively. 'He don't even look fifteen even though he is. He won't get away with that, not even if he draws on whiskers.'

Suddenly the two younger girls realised that Sophy had been unusually quiet during this lively discussion. Presently it was the main topic of conversation for most people. In the factory where Alice worked all the talk at dinnertime was about how the Hun were due a good thrashing.

Alice and Sarah turned their attention on Sophy. She blushed and pouted defensively as she was caught out exchanging a significant stare with Danny.

Danny suddenly leapt up and strolled the few yards over towards them.

'Wanna take a boat out?' He directed that exclusively at Sophy. 'I got the money to pay for it,' he added with gruff persuasion.

Alice glanced at her sister, expecting to hear Sophy tell him where he could stick his boat and the oars too. But after a moment, and looking bashful, Sophy sprung up and, with a mumble for the girls, went off with him towards the water's edge. Alice rolled onto her stomach and watched them. Danny helped Sophy get in then they were off and he was having more success than his brother had managed in getting going into deep water. Soon they had caught up with the little craft carrying Geoff and Herbert.

The boy from the Land, stranded alone on the grass, sent Alice and Sarah a hopeful look. But getting no encouragement he obviously came to the conclusion he'd be wasting his time. He got up and slouched back towards the park gate.

'Thought your Sophy weren't having no more to do with Danny Lovat.'

Alice raised herself up lazily onto an elbow and gazed again at the sight that had prompted Sarah's sly remark. Danny looked to be heading towards a secluded part of the lake sheltered from prying eyes by low branches that in places skimmed the still water.

'Bet Sophy's glad she weren't expecting after all. She'd better hope she can keep it that way.'

Alice continued plucking grass stalks and chewing on them. She ignored Sarah's deliberate comment. She wasn't getting into that conversation with anyone. Of course, Sarah had known about Sophy thinking she was pregnant. Everyone who'd been home in Campbell Road that Sunday dinnertime had known about Sophy thinking Danny Lovat had got her into trouble. The fight between the two families had been furious enough for the noise to carry out to Highgate Hill. But Alice had never confirmed or denied anything to anyone about it. And now, even her mum had mellowed a bit over it all. Since Margaret Lovat had helped Tilly clean Sophy up they'd started to talk again. Her sister Beth had done a bit of babysitting for the Lovats to earn ha'pennies and Margaret and Bert had started turning up again to the Saturday night singsongs around the piano.

Although the families were no longer at loggerheads Alice was nevertheless rather annoyed that Sophy had gone off so readily with Danny. Clearly she still had a yen for him despite the way he'd treated her, and she wasn't able to resist when he paid her a bit of attention. Alice felt regretful that she'd not got up and followed them and told Danny Lovat that he'd better treat Sophy right this time.

'Did you get taken on at the biscuit factory?' she asked to change the subject. If Sarah continued probing and hinting an argument was sure to erupt between them and Alice felt too warm and lethargic to get involved in any of that. Ever since Alice had started full-time work Sarah had been keen to get a proper job too. But although Ginny Whitton was keen to appropriate Sarah's part-time earnings from odd jobs she was reluctant to let her youngest daughter be too independent. Sarah was the only child left at home now, and Ginny wanted her to be on hand to do her fetching and carrying. Only on odd occasions when she was desperate – usually for a bottle of medicine, as she called it – could Ginny be seen outside the house, hobbling up the road towards the off licence.

'I didn't even go for an interview,' Sarah said sulkily. 'Me mum put the block on it. Said she'd get the truancy officer on me if I took on full-time. She'd do it too, the cow. Still got me doorsteps in Tollington Park. I did three this morning.' She looked at Alice. 'Your Beth got any spare she don't want to do? I could use another couple to boost me takings.'

Alice briefly shook her head. 'What will you do when you get to fourteen and she still won't let you get a proper job?'

'I'm gonna be off, that's what I'm gonna do!' Sarah said emphatically. 'Ain't staying with the mad old bag and livin' off charity 'n' scraps forever. 'S'not fair. It's time Connie or Louisa come back and took a turn with her. I don't see why I should be the one looking after her till she pegs it.'

Alice sat up. She put her arms around her knees and rested her sharp little chin on them. 'Is Connie really going to marry that copper?'

'Dunno. They're meant to be getting engaged, but that don't mean nuthin'. No plans for a wedding been made as far as I know. She don't like his people. All airs 'n' graces. Yet she said they've not got much to brag about.'

'At least she got away from The Bunk,' Alice remarked reflectively.

'Yeah. Can't blame her for that, even if she is with a rozzer.'

'You'll be a bridesmaid if it's a fancy do,' Alice said with a grin. 'You'll get to wear a frilly frock and hat 'n' all that.'

Sarah scowled unhappily at the thought.

'Don't want to imagine how your Louisa'd suit a frilly frock and hat though.' Alice began to chuckle as she imagined Sarah's fat bruiser of a sister kitted out all dainty.

'Bleedin' hell! What a fright!' Sarah gasped and joined in with Alice's increasingly uproarious laughter.

'Geoff's on his way back with Herbert.' Alice wiped her streaming eyes and grinned. 'Looks like the boat's home 'n' dry after all.' She watched as the two boys jumped lithely onto dry land.

'I reckon Geoff's sweet on you.' Sarah looked at Alice. 'I reckon you 'n' 'im are going to be walking out together soon.'

'Don't be daft.' Alice blushed. 'He's me friend . . . like you.' She turned her head away from Sarah's astute gaze and met Geoff's eyes. A pleasant little sensation rippled through her as he smiled.

'I reckon he'd like to be more'n yer friend. You'd best hope he ain't like his brother with the girls, or you'll be sorry, like your sister was.'

'He's nothing like Danny.' A firm shake of Alice's head stressed that. 'He's much nicer than Danny. Generous 'n' all, he is. Treated me 'n' Sophy to something to eat in Blackstock Road last Friday when me mum was on the warpath. She had every penny off us both to square her rents for Mr Keane. Cheek she's got! She came looking for us after work before we could spend any. Said she'd give us a bit back in the week but she's not.'

'Well, he would do, wouldn't he?'

'Eh?' Alice said.

'Geoff was showing off 'cos he's keen on you.'

'Oh, shut up!' Alice said irritably. The thought of her and Geoff as sweethearts . . . well, it was daft. As far as she was concerned, she was never marrying anyone tainted by The Bunk. Not even someone as nice as Geoff Lovat. She was going to work hard and save as much as she could and escape to clean air and flowers in the garden.

Besides, Alice impressed on herself, she didn't have time to bother with romance. What occupied her thoughts was getting better work than she had at the toy factory. Not that she was unhappy there. Although the work was demanding and boring her colleagues were nice enough and she'd struck up quite a friendship with Annie Foster. Annie had helped her no end when she'd first started and had found keeping up with the production rate difficult and the machinery cumbersome to use.

Constantly in Alice's thoughts was the interesting rumour she'd heard that a new factory was opening up in Isledon Road to make stuff to do with the war. She'd heard that there might be jobs going soldering hand-grenade cases. She'd also heard that the pay was likely to be about twelve shillings. That was more than she was getting in the toy factory. She might still be young but she knew she was an experienced factory hand now. If she needed a reference she was sure that Mr Wright would give her one. She'd worked hard and kept her nose clean. She'd seen a nice skirt and blouse down in Chapel Street market. She'd had enough of her mum buying her stuff second hand. If she was old enough to work full-time she was old enough to buy her own clothes.

'Bleedin' hot!' Geoff exclaimed then flung himself down beside Alice on the grass.

Herbert sat down too before lying back and shielding his eyes with his arm. 'We goin' off to the flicks this afternoon?' he mumbled against his sleeve to Geoff.

'Nah,' Geoff replied, squinting into the distance. 'It'll be sweltering in the fleapit on a day like this.'

'We were just saying,' Alice ribbed him, 'hope you two ain't about to apply for a job in the navy. You'd sink ships.'

'Weren't that bad,' Geoff jovially protested. 'Got back on dry land alright. Anyhow Dan can be skipper.' He concentrated his narrowed gaze on the spot in the lake where his brother was smoothly rowing. 'He looks like he's got the hang of it alright.'

'That ain't all he's got the 'ang of by the looks of it.' Herbert smirked insinuatingly. He peered from under his arm at Alice. 'Your sister don't never learn, then.'

Alice jumped up. She didn't like Herbert much at the best of times. She remembered him sticking his oar in on the day that Louisa had set about Sarah over her missing blouse. 'You want to mind your own business, Banksie,' she said. She looked at Sarah. 'I'm going to walk down to the water and wait for Sophy. Coming?'

'What for?' Sarah sighed and used a hand to fan her warm face. 'Be better off waiting here in the shade. We'll get roasted by the sun.'

Alice knew that was true but she simply wanted to avoid any more hints or questions concerning her sister and Danny Lovat and what they thought they were playing at, considering all the trouble they'd caused.

'See you later then,' she said and started to walk off towards the water.

Geoff levered himself up. He fell into step beside Alice. Obliquely she was aware that Sarah had got up too and was following them, probably to avoid being left alone with Herbert.

'Me mum'll kill her if she finds out she's knockin' about with him again,' Alice suddenly burst out in a low hiss and slanted Geoff an angry look. 'She's a bloody fool going off with him like that!'

'He ain't exactly using his head either,' Geoff said quietly. 'P'raps he's just got something he wants to say to her and that's why he's took her off alone.'

'What? Like sorry?' Alice suggested sarcastically.

'Yeah . . . like sorry,' Geoff replied. 'I know he is and I know 'n' all he wouldn't have the guts to do it with all of us around.'

'D'you think that's it, then?'

Geoff nodded. 'Yeah . . . I do. He says he's going down the recruiting office to volunteer. Dunno if he was being serious or larkin' about.'

'He must be larkin' about,' Alice scoffed. 'He's not yet seventeen. They won't take him till he's nineteen.'

'Well, he's not going to say his right age, is he?' Geoff gently pointed out. 'He could pass for quite a bit older than he is. Peter Slater out of the Land who works down the market with Dan got took on. He's sixteen and he's already been over Woolwich Common on drill.'

'You look as old as Danny.' Alice glanced at Geoff, her expression solemn, an ache tightening beneath her ribs. 'Are you going down the recruiting office too?'

'Not sure yet. What I do know is that there's not much in a shit hole like Campbell Bunk to stay put for, except me family 'n' friends . . . like you.'

'You've got a good job,' Alice said quickly, hoping to dissuade him from going to enlist. 'You'll get on and get out of The Bunk. That's what I'm going to do. I'm going to get on and get out.'

'Can't see me mum 'n' dad being pleased to see me get on 'n' get out,' Geoff remarked wryly. 'Not when they've got four little 'uns and none of them close to leaving school. They'll want me 'n' Dan to hang around fer years yet.'

Alice nodded slowly. She knew that was true. Her parents – especially her mum – had the same view on things. They wanted their older kids – the ones bringing in a bit of pay – to stick around for ever so they could put all their earnings in the family kitty.

They had reached the water's edge and both stood staring out over its glittering grey surface. The boat with Danny and Sophy glided closer and beached some yards away. With self-conscious courtesy Danny helped Sophy alight.

'We're goin' off down Blackstock to get something to eat,' Geoff yelled at his brother.

'I never said I would, Geoff Lovat,' Alice shrewishly reminded him.

'They'll come too,' he said with a private smile for her. 'Then we can find out all what's goin' on between them.' Geoff looked back at Sarah and Herbert who were dawdling about behind, looking bored. 'Best get rid of them two or we won't find out nuthin'. Dan'll clam up.'

'Sarah's me friend. I can't just tell her to get lost,' Alice protested.

'Tell her you're going home. We'll take a detour up The Bunk then when her and Banksie's shook off, we'll keep on going and find out what these two are looking so pleased about.'

Alice took a look at her sister and knew straight off that indeed she was looking secretly pleased with herself, so she must be up to something. Sophy's eyes were shining and she could barely tear her gaze from Danny's face.

'Alright. We'll get rid of Banksie and Sarah,' Alice agreed, 'and carry on down the caff.' As Geoff turned to walk back she fell into step beside him. 'If Sophy says her 'n' Danny are walking out again me mum'll have her guts fer garters. Then after that she'll murder him,' she warned Geoff, not wholly joking.

'Certainly don't look like he's said he's off fighting the Hun. Your sister looks right happy about something.'

'She did say . . . a while ago . . . that she reckoned he deserved a good thumping. Perhaps she's hoping the Germans'll give it to him.' With that parting shot Alice speeded up and, linking arms with Sarah, the little party proceeded towards the park gate.

FOURTEEN

'You said you was goin' away 'cos you was joinin' up.'

'Well, I ain't. I'm goin' away to train 'orses. Can help fight the war that way 'n' all. Transport's as important as soldiers.'

The two brothers locked eyes in combatant stares across the table in Kenny's café in Blackstock Road.

'What are you going to tell Mum 'n' Dad?' Geoff hissed at Danny. 'All hell's gonna break loose when they find out. They're relying on you putting in the pot.'

Danny shrugged. 'Don't know yet what I'll tell them. But I'm going back home to Essex. That's definite. Sophy's coming too, 'cos there's a job for her 'n' all in me boss's house.' He glanced at Sophy and she smiled encouragement at him.

'They won't let you go,' Alice warned her sister. Sophy's soppy love-struck expression was making her feel as needled as Geoff sounded. 'When Mum finds out what you're planning she'll go crackers. Anyhow you don't know anything about working as a servant in a big house.'

'Soon learn,' Sophy returned obstinately. 'Danny says that Peter's sweetheart didn't know about working in service either. She's a shop girl. But she got took on all the same.' She paused. 'Anyhow, s'long as I send them a bit of cash now 'n' again Mum 'n' Dad won't worry. If anything I'll be doing yers all a favour. Could do with a bit more room about the place what with Stevie 'n' Bobbie always under all our feet.'

Alice looked dubious but fell silent. She still felt dazed by what she'd just learned from Danny and Sophy. Their infectious enthusiasm for the new life they were planning, far from London, had failed to excite Alice. She could see only trouble ahead caused by their abrupt determination to move away to Essex together to work for a well-to-do family.

A sudden fierce resentment trembled through Alice as she brooded on the fellow who'd brought it all about. Peter Slater had worked in the market with Danny before joining up. Prior to that he and his fiancée had been on the point of starting afresh out in the Essex countryside. Peter's boss had dozens of costermonger stalls and shops around the city but he also had a big house and a farm, close to the coast in Essex, where he reared livestock. Horses were needed for the war in France and Peter Slater had been due to go to the farm to learn to train the animals before they were ferried abroad for the military.

But Slater had got a bit too merry and patriotic one dinnertime in the pub and, full of Dutch courage, he'd gone to the recruiting office and joined up. Soon he'd be on his way to France. At Danny's request – and to keep his boss sweet in case he needed him again – he'd recommended Danny as his replacement for the training job in Essex. Danny had been keen to have his ticket back to the county he classed as home. From the moment he'd arrived in Campbell Bunk it had always been his intention to escape and return to his roots.

'So you two are courting again then, are you?' Alice asked abruptly.

'Sort of . . .' Danny said bashfully and slid a glance at Sophy.

'You'd best make sure you don't do anything stupid this time,' Alice warned Sophy. 'Ain't going through all that chaos again!'

Sophy mumbled something beneath her breath and averted her red face.

'Well, thanks very much,' Geoff snapped sarcastically at Danny. 'You scarper and leave me stuck working me fingers ter the bone providing fer 'em all. You selfish bleeder!'

'Ain't nuthin' preventing you from scarpering too when your time comes,' Danny replied defensively. 'You stick it for another year then it's your turn to leg it.'

'What they all supposed to do then?' Geoff 's expression was thunderous with disbelief. 'You know Dad'll never pull enough in collecting pots in a pub to keep them all.' Geoff leaned closer to his brother and spat through his teeth, 'He's a bleeding cripple in case you've forgotten! He ain't ever going to get a good paying job. And you know Mum can only take in washing while she's got kids hangin' on her skirts.'

'I ain't letting that worry me!' Danny roared with equal ferocity. 'Sod the lot of them! It's me chance 'n' I'm takin' it!'

'So am I,' Sophy said and flicked at Alice a defiant look.

'You'd best make sure you do send something back then out of your wages,' Alice retorted. ''Cos if you don't, I wouldn't put it past Mum to come and get it off yer.'

That observation wiped some of the confidence from Sophy's face. It was no idle threat. She knew her mother was capable of anything; even travelling to Essex to take her wage packet off her if she believed herself entitled to it. She'd wrestle it from her new boss if necessary.

Geoff gave his brother another filthy look then without a word he pushed back his chair and stalked off. Alice shot her sister a scowl then got up too and followed Geoff out into Blackstock Road. She caught up with him in a few seconds. For a minute or two they walked side by side in silence.

'Can't really blame 'em,' Alice eventually said on a sigh. 'Truth is, I think I'm a bit jealous.' She glanced up at Geoff but his profile remained set in hard lines, his lips clamped together. 'We'll get our turn,' she said quietly, 'I know we will.' She touched his arm but he shook off her empathetic fingers.

Suddenly Geoff crossed the road, leaving Alice stranded on the pavement alone. 'Where you going?' she called after him. She had assumed they were heading home to The Bunk.

'Nowhere,' he snarled and kept on striding along.

With a tut of exasperation Alice ran to catch up with him. 'No use sulking over it.' She suddenly realised that the more Geoff fumed on it the more she accepted, in a resigned sort of way, what Sophy and Danny had done.

Her sister was going away . . . moving on . . .

Alice had always known that someday it would happen. Hadn't they at night, whilst huddling beneath the coats to try and keep warm and muffle the noise of drunken arguments preventing them sleeping, shared whispered hopes and dreams of just such escape routes as the one Sophy was set on taking? Sophy's time had come and she'd found the courage . . . and the person perhaps . . . to help her snatch at her new life. But her sister's good luck had come too suddenly. It had startled her into feeling resentful because now she understood how much she relied on Sophy's friendship, and how much she would miss her when she was gone.

But it wasn't Alice's way to be envious for long. It was her way to make sure that she worked towards the same opportunity. And if fate were to be less kind to her than it had been to Sophy, she'd make her own luck.

Abruptly Geoff sat down on a low brick wall that fronted a small rectangle of grass. Alice retraced a few steps and plonked herself down beside him.

'I'm going for a new job,' she told him, as much to take his mind off their families as to get his opinion on what she planned to do. She realised she did value Geoff's opinion on such things.

'Where's that?' he asked, without looking at her but sounding vicious. 'Timbuctoo?'

'Don't be daft,' Alice said with a giggle and punched his arm. 'I heard that a new factory is opening round in Isledon Road to make stuff for the war. Soldering weapons like hand grenades and so on. It's more money than I get now. Me 'n' Annie's going for jobs there next week.'

'How d'you know you'll take to soldering?'

'Don't know,' Alice admitted truthfully. 'Don't need to like it that much if it's more pay. It's worth a try.'

'Yeah . . . it's worth a try . . .' Geoff echoed, staring off into the distance.

'Don't be mad about it,' Alice said quietly. 'You can't blame them for what they've done. I'd do it . . . so would you, y'know you would.'

'Too right I would!' Geoff gave a hollow laugh. 'Just wish it'd been me heard about the job back in Essex.,' He grimaced in disappointment. 'He don't know nuthin' about horses. I do.'

'Do you?' Alice asked interestedly.

'Used to work with the stable boys at the local pub back home. They'd let me groom the horses and sweep out the stalls 'n' feed 'em. Got to take a look in some fine carriages wot pulled in there.'

'Get paid much?' Alice asked, ever practical.

'Nah!' Geoff chuckled. 'Didn't get paid nuthin' at all. Got tips off the customers sometimes. Couldn't have been more'n about seven when I started hangin' about round there just to see and touch the horses. Love 'em, I do.'

'You should join up for the cavalry then,' Alice said with a grin.

'Yeah . . . or the mounted police,' Geoff suggested dryly. 'I'm sure the constabulary'd like havin' a kid out The Bunk on the police force.'

They exchanged a look and both burst out laughing at the farce of it. Acting the clown, Geoff fell backwards off the wall and kicked his legs in the air. They noticed a middle-aged couple strolling arm in arm along the pavement stare at them. Their obvious disapproval served only to set them off guffawing again.

'Come on . . .' Alice urged him finally, wiping her eyes. ''Fore we get in trouble. They don't like Bunk kids round here. They might call the coppers to get rid of us. I've had a bucket of water thrown on me before to clear me out of it down Seven Sisters. Shouldn't go about monkeying around, the rozzers tell us.'

Geoff brushed himself down and shook his head to clear it. He then stood looking at Alice, his expression slowly becoming quite solemn. 'If it had been me got that job with the horses in Essex, would you have come with me?'

'What . . . to work in a big house?' Alice gave a thoughtful frown and a final scrub at her clumpy wet eyelashes. She stood quietly, seriously considering it. 'Might not like being a servant and fetching 'n' carrying all the time. Don't mind keeping things clean though. I like things clean and tidy. I like gardens too.'

'So . . . you would've come, then?'

'Might've.' She raised her eyes to meet his. 'Suppose anything's better'n sticking around here.'

Geoff continued to claim her gaze until Alice fidgeted and said, 'Come on, let's go. It's getting late and they like me to see to the kids before the neighbours turn up for the Saturday night singsong.'

Suddenly Geoff bent and pressed his lips hard to Alice's, making her skitter back in surprise. It was her first proper kiss.

'What's that for, you daft ha'porth?' she said, squinting up at him. She wasn't sure whether to laugh it off or give him a slap.

'You would've come with me, right? We'd have been courting. That's what you do, Alice, when you're courting.' He sounded quite casually amused by her flustered reaction.

'How do you know what courting couples do?' Alice scoffed as they started to walk on. 'How much courting have you done, Geoff Lovat?'

'A bit.' Geoff didn't sound amused any more.

Alice looked up, about to find something crushing to say, but as their eyes met she found the little jibe died on her lips. Instinctively she knew that Geoff's knowledge of what went on between men and women was far greater than hers, and she wasn't sure why knowing it unsettled her, or made her mouth pulse as though his still moved against it. For a moment they walked in silence. 'You know what's really annoyed me about those two?' Alice said, having shaken off her odd mood.

'No . . . what?'

'I left me cake. I never got to eat me cake or drink much of me tea, and I'm starving, and I paid for it.'

'We can go back past the fish shop,' Geoff suggested. He pulled out a few coins and counted them out. 'We'll have to share the fish.'

Alice grinned up at him. 'Thanks. When I get me new job soldering I'll treat you to a fish supper, promise.'

'Don't work like that when you're courting.' Geoff

grinned back at her. 'I always got to treat you 'cos I'm a real gent.'

'Shut up about courting, you daft sod, or someone'll hear and think you mean it. Then there'll be trouble. And I reckon we got enough of that comin' our way when our parents find out about . . . Oh, here they come,' Alice said as she took a glance behind and saw Danny and Sophy catching up with them.

'As they've had our grub in the caff, they can shell out for the fish 'n' chips,' Geoff said.

'Don't work like that when you're courting and you're a real gent.' Alice impishly echoed his words back at him then turned and scampered off, laughing.

'I'll be sorry to lose you, Alice. You're a good worker and if things don't come right for you round in Isledon Road I'd take you back if I had a vacancy.'

'Thank you, Mr Wright,' Alice said. 'I'll remember that.'

'We've had lots of orders come in because of the war. Kiddies like to play with toy soldiers at such times. We'll be as busy as the new factory. Overtime might be available . . .' Simon Wright dangled the carrot, in his own way trying to make her change her mind about leaving. Oddly he'd miss her, he realised, and her sweet, mischievous way. He'd never forget the sight of her marching into his office on her first day at work with the vacancy notice tucked under her thin little arm.

Alice waited for Annie and they went out into the muggy evening together. Alice felt oddly nostalgic yet excited too on knowing that her final shift was behind her. At the gate she and Annie stopped and turned to take a look back at the building.

'Ain't sad to see the back of that place,' Annie said flatly.

Alice looked up at the wall where the notice had been

pinned. She remembered how months ago Geoff had got it down for her and she'd gone in, quaking, to plead for her job. She wasn't glad to be going. She'd liked working there. But it had just been her start; it had never been where she'd finish.

FIFTEEN

'I'm gonna miss you so much, Al.'

'Going to miss you too,' Alice muttered hoarsely and kept on folding her sister's few new clothes. Neatly she put them in Sophy's travelling bag. She sniffed back the dew that threatened to drip from her nose and blinked away blurring tears. 'Can't believe you're really goin',' Alice choked out through the lump in her throat. 'It's come around so quick. Seems like only yesterday you announced you was off when we was in the caff with Geoff and Dan.'

Almost a month had passed since Sophy and Danny dropped the bombshell about leaving London for Essex. Now it was a Saturday in late September and at midday Sophy was getting on a train and leaving The Bunk to start her new life in service at a manor house in Essex.

'It don't seem real,' Sophy said, her quavering voice betraying her nervous excitement. 'If I don't like it there I'm coming home,' she added. 'Don't care what Dan says; if they're horrible, mean sorts I'm coming back here, 'n' that's that.'

Alice looked up, her blue eyes glistening, but she smiled encouragement at Sophy. She knew her sister would never be back, mean people or no mean people. Sophy had in her pocket her ticket to ride away from the worst street in North London. Her future was fresh air and regular grub and, please God, when the time was right for them, perhaps a family of her own with Danny Lovat. Despite all the argy bargy that had gone on between Sophy and Danny Alice knew her sister had always, deep down, never stopped loving him. 'You'll be alright,' Alice mumbled. 'It's not as if you're going alone and don't know nobody. You've got Dan.'

'Yeah . . . I've got Dan,' Sophy said softly and followed that with a crooked little smile.

Suddenly Alice hugged Sophy tightly to her. 'Don't go doing nothing stupid for him though,' she said gruffly. 'Don't go letting him persuade you to misbehave again before you're properly sorted out together. You'll both end up with no roof over your heads. Posh lady'll put you off soon as look at yers if you're knocked up at your age and livin' in her house.' She let go of Sophy and resumed packing her clothes.

A sheepish look and a quick nod was Sophy's agreement to her younger sister's wisdom. 'I already put him straight on it all, don't worry about that.' She gazed intently at Alice. 'You think I was in the family way, don't you, not just late with me monthlies.'

Alice shrugged and glanced away, not wanting to upset Sophy on this day of all days.

'I've been thinking about it a lot,' Sophy said. 'All that blood 'n' stuff . . . it were a tiny baby, weren't it? I lost me baby, before it was ready, didn't I?'

Alice's small teeth sank into her lower lip for a moment as she considered her answer. 'Not sure,' she finally said. 'If you did it's called a miscarriage.' She looked gravely at her sister. 'I heard Annie talking with some of the other women at work. What they were saying about this friend of Annie's sounded similar to what happened to you. They called it a miscarriage.'

'Kitty at Star Brush kept dropping hints like that. I didn't want to listen to her 'cos it made me stomach turn to think of me baby getting tipped down the bog even if he was dead. Anyhow Mum found out what she'd been saying and told her to shut her gob, and keep her nose out, so I never found out no more.'

The sisters gazed solemnly at one another, each lost in private memories. Six months ago they'd been two frightened girls bewildered by what was happening to Sophy. Now they knew what women knew and prayed they'd never need to struggle through such a time again.

'So don't go doing nothing stupid,' Alice repeated hoarsely.

Any further conversation on the subject was prevented by their mother's appearance in the doorway of the back room. 'Ready?' she asked Sophy. 'Don't want to be late and miss your connectin' train at Fenchurch Street. Danny's already out on the pavement waiting.'

Sophy quickly stuffed the last few remaining bits in her bag. 'Will you come to the station with me?' Her eyes were pleading as they met Alice's.

'Try 'n stop me,' Alice answered huskily.

'We'll all come,' Tilly announced shortly. 'Bleedin' hell! Ain't every day one of me daughters gets a job takes her miles away across the country.' She rolled down her blouse sleeves and buttoned the cuffs. ''Sides, Margaret and Bert 'n' all their kids are seeing Danny off. So we're seeing you off 'n' all. And that's that.'

Jack took Sophy's bag from her and the Keiver family trooped down the dank stairs to join the Lovats congregated on the pavement. As the little party set off in a festive mood in the direction of Finsbury Park railway station some of the neighbours came out to lean shoulders on doorjambs and watch the families pass. Old Beattie Evans called out good luck and farewell to Sophy from across the road and Sophy acknowledged her with a wave and a smile. She then skipped ahead and walked beside Danny at the front of the human convoy, her expression proud and her chin high. As Alice watched the couple she felt a warm contentment bathe her insides. It looked like Sophy had subdued her butterflies and settled down already.

Alice and Geoff fell into step together, right at the back of the group, behind their parents and a clutch of their boisterous younger siblings.

'Glad he's off at last,' Geoff muttered. 'He's been driving me up the wall goin' on about having proper riding boots. Thought I could get him some from Milligan's. It's a gent's outfitters in Islington, fer Gawd's sake, not a nobs' shop up Savile Row.'

Alice chuckled and angled her head to see Danny's smart, poker-straight back as he marched on with her sister towards their new life. 'Well, you've done him proud. He might not have his riding boots but he looks ready for anything all the same.'

'Yeah . . . don't he just.' Geoff grunted wryly. 'Give him all them togs as a going-away present. Had to pay fer it 'n' all. Old man Milligan's been watching me like an 'awk. He ain't daft. He knew I'd be eyeing a bit of new clobber.'

'You're a big softie, Geoff Lovat.'

'Not where Dan's concerned, I ain't. Just glad to see the back of him.' To avoid Alice's mocking look he added gruffly, 'Still don't know why there weren't no big ruckus over it all.' He frowned. 'I was expecting me mum 'n' dad to kick up a helluva lot more over losing him and his pay.'

'Me 'n' Sophy have been waiting for the same in ours. Even up to this morning when we were packing her things we were expecting round one to start. We was afraid me mum might decide she'd got to stop home after all.' She gazed into the distance. 'Strange really . . . but it seems since the war started things've been a bit different. It's hard to explain what sort of different,' she said slowly, reflecting. 'I can't put me finger on it 'cos the fighting's all a long way away and it'll probably be over soon in any case. But it seems like everyone's expecting something big might happen so they're not bothering making a song 'n' dance over other stuff like they would normally. Hope what's coming turns out to be good.'

'Can feel it all in yer bones, can you?' Geoff's tone was lightly teasing, but his thoughtful frown displayed he'd attended intently – more closely than he was willing to let on – to Alice's simple, jumbled philosophy.

'Yeah . . . suppose I can feel it in me bones. It's peculiar just waiting, knowing it could turn out bad, but really hoping it'll be good instead.'

Having reached the station the group trooped onto the platform where the train was standing. A lot of people were milling around and Margaret and Tilly ordered the kids to be still and not hare about and get lost.

Sophy turned and rushed back along the family queue to where Alice was standing with Geoff. She snatched her sister in a determined embrace.

'I want some letters off you,' Alice mumbled against Sophy's shoulder. 'I want to know all what's going on in Essex. Especially want to know what the people's like, and what your digs are like 'n' so on.'

Sophy nodded then, rubbing at her streaming eyes, she pushed away and moved amongst the other members of her family to give them hugs and kisses.

Having given her eldest daughter a perfunctory cuddle Tilly pushed Sophy away. 'Geddoff with you,' she fondly chided. 'Ain't much to tell you that ain't already been said.

Just make sure you behave yourself and keep yer job,' was her blunt maternal advice. 'Don't forget: if you can spare it send it 'cos we need it. And come back and see us soon as you can. That's all.'

Sophy nodded at her mum and cuffed her nose. She turned to her dad and went immediately into his open arms.

'Be a good gel,' he whispered achingly softly against her temple. 'Keep safe. God bless you.'

'And you . . .' Sophy choked.

Bert and Margaret Lovat were bestowing similar advice on Danny while he attempted to free his legs from his clinging little siblings and Geoff hung back, looking amused. Finally Geoff approached his brother and shook Danny's hand and then rather self-consciously he found his place at the back of the family group again.

At last the goodbyes were done and the couple boarded the train with moments to spare as the guard paced officiously up and down, whistling and signalling. As the train pulled away a thicket of waving hands sprung up and some of the little ones shot along the platform to follow in its juddering black wake. Even little Lucy trotted a few steps after her big sister Sophy before Beth caught her up in her arms and nuzzled her pink cheek.

'That's enough. Let's get going,' Geoff muttered gruffly to Alice.

She understood his reasons for wanting to be off now. She wanted some time away from the rest of her family too on what seemed to be a particularly significant day. An ending and a beginning . . . perhaps not just for Sophy and Danny, Alice mused as she nodded agreement to Geoff's suggestion that they make their escape.

'Off down the caff fer a cuppa,' Alice called out to her mum. She'd chosen the right time to slip away. Tilly was preoccupied and simply acknowledged Alice's shout with a wave. She was in the process of comforting Margaret over the loss of her firstborn by planting two work-raw hands on Margaret's shaking shoulders. Margaret continued to weep loudly into her hanky as Geoff and Alice made their way out of the station.

Before they disappeared round the corner Alice glanced back to see her father and Bert Lovat were already marshalling the kids into some sort of order for the tramp home. In the distance she could just see the train that was carrying her sister away. 'Bye, Sophy,' she murmured before the view was lost to her.

SIXTEEN

'Why ain't you in uniform? Too yeller to go to war?'

Alice snatched the white feather that the woman had thrust against Geoff's chest and threw it on the ground. 'You stupid old fool!' she hissed. 'He ain't even old enough to join up. He ain't even sixteen yet.'

The woman showed no sign of remorse. Her features remained contorted by bitterness. She was dressed head to toe in black and it was easy to guess what caused her spite: she'd recently lost her husband or son to the war. Women of all ages, sour of countenance, dressed in mourning clothes, were an increasingly common sight on the streets.

Alice marched on, urging Geoff to do the same by clutching tightly at his elbow. Her hostile glare clashed with the woman's belligerent stare until they'd passed her by.

'Me husband's gawn and me son were short of seventeen when he joined up,' she yelled after them. 'Brave as a lion, he were. Now he's dead fighting fer the likes of them's too yeller to go and do their bit. You're big enough to do your bit.'

'Don't take no notice,' Alice mouthed at Geoff as they kept walking. She took a keener look at Geoff's strained features. He *was* too young to officially join up but Alice could tell he'd been affected by what the widow had shouted at him. There were tales going around of boys as young as twelve who'd lied about their age and gone off to help win the fight against the Germans. The street was crowded and people were turning to stare at them. 'Gotta make allowances,' Alice announced loudly. 'The poor old soul's grieving and it's done her a damage in the brainbox.' Alice gave Geoff a playful nudge to try and coax a smile from him.

Geoff obliged with a little grunt of laughter. 'Times like this I wish I weren't so tall. That's the second time this week some old gel's said I should get meself to France in uniform.'

'Good job your mum weren't about. She'd have something to say about it!'

'Bleedin' hell . . . would she,' Geoff agreed in alarm. 'If I decided to go down the recruiting office, and she found out, she'd be down there after me to drag me home. She's still not got over losing Dan's wages.'

'I've got a letter from Sophy in me pocket,' Alice told him, glad to change the subject to something more pleasant. 'When we get to the caff I'll read it to you. Well, the bits that aren't personal, that is.' Alice qualified her offer with a cheeky grin.

A sleety rain started to fall. Pulling up the collar of her coat, Alice speeded up her pace and urged Geoff to keep up and trot with her.

It was an icy afternoon in April and they'd been out for the afternoon browsing with friends in Chapel Street Market. Sarah Whitton had been with them but Sarah and Herbert Banks had decided to go somewhere dry and warm when the weather took a turn for the worse. They'd headed off to the flicks for the matinee while Geoff and Alice dodged the showers and continued looking at what was on offer on the stalls. Finally having decided there was nothing she liked enough to pay good money for – apart from a toffee apple for each of them – they had been on their way to the café for a nice hot drink when the widow had accosted Geoff.

As Alice turned to look over her shoulder she saw in the distance the widow stoop and collect the feather from the wet pavement then wander off, darting looks here and there as though seeking another young fellow to embarrass with it.

Alice knew the attitude of the people to the war was changing. Christmas had come and gone months ago and still there was no sign of the Germans being defeated. Every evening she sat at the table with her dad and they scanned the paper to find out what was happening over there . . . and over here. She remembered reading over and over again, open-mouthed, the article about something called a Zeppelin that had flown over the Norfolk coast to carry out a raid. That had been a long while ago – back in January. Then just last month the allied fleet had lost two ships and thousands of sailors and retreated from the Hun around a place called Constantinople. The allies were struggling and people at home were not now so confident as they'd once been of a fast, easy victory. Feelings were beginning to run high over it all as the casualties increased.

A swift glance at Geoff told Alice he was still looking a bit morose after being unfairly called a coward. 'Gasping for a cuppa,' she said cheerily. 'Let's get in there and have a warm-up.'

They entered Kenny's café and found seats. While Geoff went off to fetch the drinks Alice fished in her pocket and pulled out Sophy's letter. She spread it on the table and smoothed her fingers gently over her sister's spidery writing.

After warming her cold palms on the hot cup and taking a few sips Alice picked up the note.

'Sophy's having a grand old time of it. She says she might get promoted from the kitchen and be a proper housemaid in a month or so when one of the women leaves to get married. Then she gets to stay upstairs and polish all the lovely furniture. She says here,' Alice pointed at a place on the letter, 'she'd like to eventually train up to be a lady's maid and do hair stylin' and sewing. The pay's better, of course, and like that, when her mistress or her daughters go here 'n' there on visits, the lady's maid sometimes gets to go too to keep them all neat 'n' tidy.' Alice gave Geoff a twinkling smile. 'If she manages to pull that off, I bet she'll get to see some smashing places. Might even get took on holidays abroad.' Her eyes swooped back to Sophy's letter. 'And listen to this, what they had for dinner last week when guests come up from London and stayed over at the Manor.' Alice cleared her throat to recite, '"We had a sheep butchered for that weekend and also a goose and lots of chickens. Even us servants got to have a three-course dinner in the evening with puddings and cheeses. Oh, Al, you should've been here, it was wonderful grub."' Alice's wide eyes met Geoff's. 'Coo, she's lucky . . .' Alice had already read the letter several times since it arrived in the post yesterday but the part about the delicious food her sister was enjoying, she could feast her eyes on time and time again.

Once in a blue moon in The Bunk, they might, when times were good, have a joint of beef or lamb roasted with potatoes on a Sunday dinnertime. She was usually the one to rush up to the baker's with the tin containing their dinner. Along with most Bunk families lucky enough to occasionally have a Sunday roast they paid the baker to cook it to perfection in his big oven. The hob grate at home wasn't adequate to do justice to such a fine meal. The last time Alice could recall having such a lovely feed was about the same time as the piano turned up. It had been ages ago: the weekend when her dad first got good work doing up Basher's houses to satisfy the sanitary inspector. Alice tore her mind from the memory of more bountiful days and back to the letter in her hand. 'Then Sophy just says that the housekeeper's alright and lets her and Dan sit close together at the big table in the servants' hall 'cos they're sweethearts.'

Alice folded the paper and put it away. 'You had any letters from Dan yet?'

'Nah!' Geoff said and gulped his tea. 'Think me mum got something from him on her birthday earlier in the month. Weren't expecting him to keep in touch with me in particular.'

'Perhaps when the summer gets here . . . if we save up the fare . . . we could go on a trip and see them. I'd like that,' Alice added dreamily. 'It'd be nice to go to the seaside.'

'Yeah . . . p'raps,' Geoff said quietly. He knew full well the expense of such an outing was beyond him now Dan had gone and he was the main breadwinner at home. 'Anyhow,' he said roughly, 'the amount of food the two of 'em are tuckin' away we probably won't recognise them. They've probably turned into a right couple of fatsos.'

Alice's gurgle of laughter was soon fading away. 'Oh no! Not him!' she muttered in a dejected tone.

Geoff turned to glance over his shoulder to see who had entered and upset Alice with his presence.

Jimmy Wild was brushing rain from his coat and shutting the door with a clatter of the bell that hung on the back of it. He was with another man who Geoff recognised. He'd seen the fellow hanging around on the corner on Paddington Street when gambling schools were out. He believed his name to be Benny.

Jimmy caught sight of the young couple and with a grin he immediately sauntered over to their table. 'Alright, young Alice?' he greeted her cheerily.

Alice dredged up a smile, hoping he'd then go away again. She hadn't seen her uncle Jimmy for very many months.

Nor had she wanted to. Now she was older she understood much more about him and his mean, selfish ways. She knew he'd gone off with a fancy woman and abandoned her aunt Fran when she was very ill from giving birth to their dead daughter. He'd left Bobbie and Stevie for Tilly to deal with, for he must have known that Fran couldn't cope with them considering the state she'd been in. Alice understood too that her uncle wasn't really a happy chappie who blew his top once in a while and found it necessary to chastise his kids, or return the slap his wife had given him. And Alice knew that husbands and wives did come to blows. She'd seen her mum and dad go at it like cat and dog on occasions. She'd seen her old Nan try and separate them with a broom. As she brooded on those occasions the song that her dear departed Nan would croon came in to her mind and refused to budge:

Sally, roll your sleeves up,
Take your mother's part,
Father's come home drunk again
And he's broke your mother's heart.
They're fighting one another
And he's give her two black eyes,
But he'll tell her he still loves her in the morning.

'So, how've you been, Alice?' Jimmy's loud enquiry brought an abrupt finale to the ditty rotating infuriatingly in Alice's mind. 'Ain't seen you in a good while. Gettin' big now, ain't you?'

He slowly inspected her in a way that made Alice feel uneasy and unpleasantly hot.

'You gotta be fifteen now, ain't you?'

'Fourteen,' Alice told him quickly and picked up her cup and drank from it.

'I know you too, mate.' Jimmy turned his attention to Geoff. 'You live next door, don't yer?'

Geoff simply nodded and sat back in his chair, ready to push it back and get to his feet in an instant.

'You two walkin' out, are you?' Jimmy went on, swinging a leer between the young couple, oblivious or uncaring of the fact that they clearly wanted him gone.

'No . . .' Alice said.

'Yeah . . .' Geoff said.

They'd spoken at the same time and Jimmy chuckled. 'Right . . . right . . . geddit.' He gave Geoff a jokey punch on the arm. 'Gotta try harder, mate. Change her mind. Little Alice'll be well worth the trouble, I reckon. Pretty as a pitcher, ain't she?'

Geoff stood up swiftly in a way that made Jimmy back off a step. They locked eyes for a minute then Jimmy chuckled again. 'How old are yer, son? Never could tell who was older out of you 'n' your brother. Both lanky sods. Surprised you ain't got yourself off fighting the Hun. You'd have no trouble passing yourself off as nineteen.'

'He's not yet sixteen.' Alice slid that in quickly. She could tell just by glancing at Geoff that he was getting riled.

'Right . . .' Jimmy drawled in a sarcastic tone. 'Gonna wait are you, till you get a bit taller?'

'Surprised you ain't got yourself down the recruiting office,' Geoff said through his teeth. 'Fit bloke like you, who's keen on using his fists, is just what they're after for a bit of hand ter hand in the trenches.'

Despite the sneer in Geoff's tone Jimmy couldn't resist flexing his toned biceps at the backhanded compliment. 'If I weren't a family man with me kids relyin' on me to provide for 'em I'd be enlisted. But I got responsibilities, y'see . . .' he added on a sigh.

'Yeah,' Geoff said. 'I see alright.'

Jimmy stepped closer, his chin poking out pugnaciously but at that moment his mate called him from where he was sitting at the bar. ''Ere . . . drink's going cold, Jim.'

'Comin', Ben. Done 'ere.' Following a lopsided smile for Alice, that went unreturned, Jimmy swaggered off.

'Finished your tea?' Geoff asked Alice quietly.

Alice nodded and stood up at once.

'See yer then, Al.' Jimmy called that from the bar as Geoff opened the door.

'Coming over to see the boys someday soon. Might see you later then. Mind how yer go, sweet'eart.'

Alice simply gave a nod before she went out into the drear afternoon.

'He back with your aunt then?' Geoff asked as they set out at a fast pace for home.

Alice huddled in to her coat. 'Not as far as I know. If he is you can bet it's only 'cos his fancy woman's had enough of him and chucked him out.' She cast a look up at Geoff. 'Either that or he's pretending he's a family man with a wife 'n' kids, instead of a cheating layabout, so he don't have to explain why he's not joined up.'

'You won't get the likes of him to join up till the Hun send out armies of *frauleins*,' Geoff observed sourly.

'That what you're waiting for?' Alice joked then regretted her remark. 'Didn't mean that . . . sorry,' she mumbled, thoroughly ashamed. 'You must be sick of people dropping hints about you joinin' up when you're not even old enough to go.'

''S'alright,' Geoff said. 'I know you don't mean no harm.' He smiled thinly. 'Got a feeling your uncle don't like me though,' he added.

'Well, don't worry about that!' Alice returned forcefully. 'None of us like him! He's a pig and I hope he don't come round The Bunk to see Bobbie 'n' Stevie. I hope he gets himself back down Finsbury Park with that old bag and stays put with the ponces!'

'I saw Uncle Jimmy when I was out,' Alice told her mum as she sat down at the table. 'He came in to Kenny's café when I was in there with Geoff.' She watched her parents exchange a look. Her dad then continued reading the paper.

'You just ignore him,' her mother firmly instructed. 'We're well rid of the likes of him round here.'

'He said he's coming to see Bobbie 'n' Stevie,' Alice informed her.

Again her parents exchanged a look.

'He won't be by,' Jack reassured Tilly. 'He'll be too worried Fran'll want money off him fer the kids.'

'If Nellie's kicked him out he'll be by,' Tilly responded roughly. 'He'll come crawling back as soon as he needs a bed to stick his boots under.'

Alice could sense the atmosphere getting a bit strained between her parents and wished she'd kept her news about Uncle Jimmy to herself. 'Who's coming over tonight? Same lot?' she asked cheerily about the Saturday night singsong.

''Spect so,' her mother replied grumpily.

Alice tried another diversion.

'Some Belgian refugees started at the factory. Some of them can't hardly talk any English. Feel right sorry for 'em, I do.' Again this got no more response from her mother than a grunt. Alice looked at her; she could tell that the news that Jimmy was prowling about close by had unsettled her mother.

In fact it was six weeks later that Jimmy put in appearance in Campbell Road.

Alice came face to face with him as she was setting off at a fast pace for work one morning. She'd forgotten all about his talk of coming back there to see his sons. Too much that was sensational and important had gone on for her to bother thinking about the likes of him and his pathetic promises. Everyone thereabouts had been preoccupied with the war because it had come close to home: houses in the East End of London had been bombed and people killed and injured and made homeless. Added to that had been the awful news weeks ago that a ship called the *Lusitania* had been sunk off the coast of Ireland with such a great loss of life that it was hard for Alice to comprehend something so dreadful.

So the sight of Jimmy Wild slinking along with a dog end drooping from his lips came as an unwelcome interruption to the brooding thoughts circling in Alice's head. The most important of those currently was that her beloved dad had started dropping hints that he felt it his duty to go and help the war effort as the situation was getting grave. And that had started an almighty row with her mum. She'd got very little sleep last night as they carried on shouting at one another into the small hours.

As Jimmy greeted Alice she came to a halt and mumbled a response.

'Bobbie 'n' Stevie gone off to school yet?'

'Dunno,' Alice said. 'Probably.' In fact she did know very well that they were still at home. But she hoped that by saying she thought they'd left already their wastrel father might turn around and take himself off elsewhere. Alice understood now that there would only be trouble wherever Jimmy was.

Jimmy looked Alice up and down. 'You're all grown up, Alice, and quite a looker. Off to work?'

Alice nodded.

'Where's that?'

Alice felt an odd reluctance to tell him. 'Munitions factory,' she said. 'Soldering stuff like weapons 'n' so on.'

'Yeah?' Jimmy affected to look impressed. 'Doing yer bit for the war effort; that's my gel.'

'Gotta go. Be late,' Alice said swiftly. A weak smile was slanted up at him then she was on her way and uncomfortably aware that he'd turned to watch her walking away.

'Wot the fuck d'you want?'

Jimmy carried on up the stairs towards his wife's rooms. 'That ain't a nice way to say hello,' he sneered, sending a sidelong look up at Tilly. 'Specially when you ain't seen me for a while. Bet you missed me, ain't you, Til?'

'Yeah . . . like I missed getting smallpox,' Tilly snapped. 'Why don't you just turn around and piss off.'

'Why don't you just mind yer own business?' Jimmy responded. 'You know if you don't, I'll have to make you . . . just like before. Remember?' A menacing smile followed the warning and he stopped climbing the stairs to pose against the banister. 'Y'know sometimes, gel, I think it's why you goad me so much. You're after a repeat performance, 'n't yer?'

Tilly's features hardened into a mask of utter loathing. 'You disgust me. But you'll never beat me down so you can poke yer threats right up yer arse. Fran's me sister 'n' I'll look out for her when needs be. We're family . . . something you'll never be, you evil bastard.'

As the door to her room opened and Jack came out Tilly fell silent. Jack's features set into stone when he noticed who was talking to his wife.

'Alright, Jack?' Jimmy asked chummily as though he'd never dream of threatening the fellow's wife.

'I was till I saw you.'

'That ain't nice, Jack,' Jimmy protested in a whine. 'We're brothers-in-law, you 'n' me.'

'Yeah . . .' Jack intoned. 'And I wish we weren't 'cos I've

had more'n enough trouble with you being part of me family.'

'Bleedin' hell,' Jimmy huffed, all indignation. 'I come to see me kids and hand over a bit of me wages and get nothing but aggravation off the pair of yers.'

As though she'd heard the magical word wages Fran appeared in the doorway. For a moment all four people stood still and silent.

'Come on,' Jack told Tilly firmly. 'We ain't getting involved in this. I'm off to work. You're up the shop. We ain't got no milk or tea. Beth'll look out for Lucy.'

With that Jack caught his wife by the arm and hurried her down the stairs. Surprisingly, Tilly allowed him to steer her past Jimmy without incident despite her fingers curling at her sides. It was only when they reached the bottom of the flight that she broke free of her husband's restraint and wheeled about. She simply looked up at Fran. 'Alright?' The single word was heavy with significance.

A nod was all the answer she got from her sister.

'I'll be back shortly . . . don't you worry about that.' Tilly turned and went out with Jack.

SEVENTEEN

'Is Jack thinking of going down the recruitin' office and volunteering?'

'What makes you say that?' Tilly thrust one end of the damp sheet at Fran and backed off with the other until the linen was pulled tight. Deftly they folded and came together. Tilly took the neat rectangle and dropped it into the basket at her feet.

'Jimmy heard it on the grapevine,' Fran said, and plonked her hands on her hips while waiting for Tilly to unpeg the final sheet hanging limp on the line.

'Oh . . . yeah?' Tilly scoffed as she gave an expanse of cotton to her sister and they repeated the process of stretching and halving. 'Where'd he hear that? Couldn't have been off the recruiting sergeant 'cos the weasel ain't got it in him to turn up there himself and take the king's shillin'.'

'Yeah . . . well, I'm glad of that 'n' all.' In pique Fran let go of the sheet and let Tilly fold it on her own. 'Jim's a family man. He's just being sensible, stopping home and lookin' out for his own. What's needed is bachelors in the army.' Fran's defensive stance wilted. 'Why are you always so against him? Way you carry on you'd think that you 'n' Jack never had a cross word between you.' She gave her sister a significant stare. 'I heard the two of yers last night going at it like the clappers.' Fran's hands again found her hips. 'Kept me awake half the night.' That peevish complaint drew no response from Tilly. 'Anyhow, Jimmy's been good lately, giving me regular money every week. He took the boys boatin' on the lake down Finsbury last weekend.'

A snort of derisive laughter met that. 'Well, if he's trying *that* hard the old bag's thrown him out fer sure.'

'You're wrong!' Fran cried, quite agitated. 'He's still living with her. She won't let him go, he says. Keeps causing a right scene when he says he's moving out and coming back home where he belongs.'

'I reckon she wants shot of him, first chance she gets. And he knows it. Soon as he can't ponce off her no more he'll be back and running you ragged instead to keep him in booze 'n' bacca.'

'He's changed . . .'

'Ain't listening to none o' that crap, Fran,' Tilly announced bluntly. 'Heard it all before so don't tell me no more 'cos we're gonna end up arguing.' Tilly contemptuously clicked two fingers. 'He ain't worth that as far as I'm concerned.'

For a few minutes the small back yard crackled with tension. Tilly turned back to Fran. 'If you must know Jack has said a few things about enlisting. I put him straight on it. He's needed here, with me 'n' the kids. He reckons if things over there ain't better after Christmas he's going. Always been patriotic and brave, has my Jack. Them sodding Kitchener posters stuck all over the place don't help. *Your country needs you!*' She spat. 'Perhaps it do; but when you live in The Bunk your family's needs are greater. So Jack still ain't going, and that's that.'

'Well . . . now you understand how I feel about my Jimmy stoppin' around with me and our boys.'

'No I don't,' Tilly responded flatly. She scooped up the washing basket overflowing with damp cotton. 'Gotta get going and get me rents collected.' She shoved Fran's washing at her then made for the back door. 'I'd get that lot ironed if I was you and get it back over Highgate before the kids get home from school.'

Geoff looked out of the window of Kenny's café at the steady drizzle.

Alice shook his arm to get his attention. 'Why don't you try and get a job too at the new factory that's just opened up? Me and Annie are going to be drilling and tapping. But best of all we can get night work. Good pay for night work. We heard they might pay up to sixteen shillings to start off.' She clattered her cup to rest on its saucer. 'Bet the pay's better than what you get in Milligan's. Be nice to have good money for Christmas.'

Geoff wrinkled his nose. 'Nah, I just got a rise. Me wages ain't far short of fifteen shillings and I've still got me perks to take into account on top. Anyhow, don't fancy factory work, nor working nights. Might tell me dad though. If he can sit at a bench drillin' it might do him. He used to do night work in a factory back in Essex.'

'Lots of girls'll be working there for you to chat up,' she ribbed him.

'Hah, hah,' Geoff said and leaned back in his chair. 'Like you don't know that there's only one girl I'm interested in.'

'When I'm older . . . I reckon I'll be interested in you right back,' Alice answered with a jaunty grin that nevertheless held a hint of flirtation. 'But for now I've got to get meself a good job with good pay so's I can save up for a few nice clothes and a decent place to live. Can't wait to be grown up enough to get out of here.'

'How old d'you reckon you'll be before you're grown up enough?' Geoff asked acidly.

'Keep on like that, Geoff Lovat, and I'll make sure I never grow up enough.' Alice narrowed her eyes on him to let him know he'd annoyed her. 'Not for you anyhow.' She looked away, feeling a knot tightening in her guts that she sensed was guilt. Sometimes she knew she wanted nothing more than to have Geoff put his arms about her and kiss her. But . . . she'd seen where that could lead, and she wasn't ready to give up on her dream of a decent life in a nice area. Getting yourself in the family way led to a swollen belly and a lifetime of drudgery in The Bunk.

Geoff stared back at her from beneath his lids then laughed to lighten the tension between them. 'Coming to the flicks this afternoon?' he asked.

'Alright,' Alice said immediately, glad they were again on an even keel. It was one of the things she loved about Geoff: he never stayed sulky for long or bore grudges. Whereas at home her mum had seemed to be in a vile mood since her dad had said that after Christmas, if things still looked bad, he was going to definitely join up.

Every time the German planes whined overhead in the night sky her mum and dad would wake them and get her and Beth and Lucy to huddle beneath the table. There was no room for their parents too so they'd dive under their iron bedstead. Her dad had fashioned quite a sturdy little shelter for the two of them by putting planks of wood on top of the springs. So far they'd been lucky and the planes had carried on over the rooftops. But her dad always muttered the same thing on all clear. 'It's only a matter of time . . . only a matter of time . . .'

'D'you reckon the war'll end soon?' Alice asked wistfully.

'Nah,' Geoff said dully. 'No chance.'

'Me dad's going off to fight after Christmas.'

Geoff looked at Alice's gloomy face. He'd heard the rumours too that Jack Keiver was ready and willing to do his bit for his country. 'He'll be alright; be back before you know it,' he gruffly reassured her. 'He'll know how to keep himself safe and come home. He's got it up there.' Geoff tapped his head indicatively.

Alice smiled weakly. 'I know he has . . .' she murmured.

'Dry yer eyes, Al, there's a good gel.'

Alice turned on the bed to see her dad leaning over her. She took the handkerchief he was holding out to her and scrubbed her eyes. As she pushed herself onto an elbow he sat down on the bed beside her. Gently his tobacco-tinged fingers pushed back the dark hair that was sticking to her damp cheek. 'Come in with all of us.' He tipped his head to indicate the front room where a New Year's Day party was in full swing. The piano keys were being tickled with far less skill than Jack would have brought to the rendition of 'Pack Up Your Troubles'.

'Don't want you to go, Dad,' Alice snuffled and ducked her face to his hanky to blot fresh tears.

'I know. I don't want to go neither, Al.' Gently Jack gathered his distraught daughter into his arms. 'But sometimes things you don't expect just come along and put a spoke in your life . . .' He paused, let out a sigh. 'And you have to forget what you want and what you like and just do what you know's right. All us men as can fight got to stand up and be counted now. Ain't going right for us over there. We've got to stop the Germans soon as we can or it might not be planes goin' over but Hun marching up the street.'

Alice blinked bloodshot eyes at her dear dad's face. 'You'll come back, won't you? They'll let you come back on leave 'n' so on?'

'Of course!' he promised. 'If they say I can't have no leave, then I'll have to run off.'

Alice whimpered a laugh. 'Then you'll get shot, right enough, and it won't be Germans doing it.'

'I'll be back,' he promised. 'Got this to keep me safe, ain't I?' From an inside pocket he pulled out the silk scarf she'd given him as a present. 'Me keepsake . . . lucky charm, ain't it. Where I go, it goes.' He folded the soft material and reverently put it back whence it came. 'Keep me warm too, it will.'

Alice nodded and sniffed. 'Wish Sophy had come back to see us for Christmas. Miss her, I do.' It was true. Sophy's absence at this special time of the year had heightened Alice's feeling of melancholy. The usual excitement of Christmas Day had seemed to be lost without her.

Weeks ago Sophy had written to say that her employers wouldn't give time off to staff over the holiday as they had guests to stay till the New Year. Alice could read between the lines. Her sister and Danny were happy to stay where they were. Alice didn't begrudge Sophy her comfort and Christmas feasts in Essex.

'Your big sister's got a new life now. We all gotta be glad that she's fallen on her feet. After what went on . . .' Jack coughed and fell silent. 'Well, it's good to know she's happy and settled, that's all.'

'I know; I'm glad she's got such a good job. It's just . . . I miss having her to talk to.'

'Beth's getting older. Soon you and her'll be good pals like you was with Sophy,' her dad suggested kindly. 'She'll be finished school before you know it and out workin'. Your mum'll make sure of that.'

'Yeah . . .' Alice chuckled wryly. 'Mum'll make sure of

that alright.' She looked at her dad intently as though imprinting his beloved features on her mind. A surge of adoration prompted her to hug him round the neck. Before he could return the embrace she just as quickly let him go. Slowly she raised a finger and tickled the mark on her father's jaw. 'Freckles!' she teased him.

'Monkey!' he mocked her back and dropped a kiss on the top of her dark, silky head. 'Come in the other room,' he urged her again. 'Come 'n' join in a song with your old dad.' Jack winced as a few off-key notes were strung together making a discordant noise. 'That's old Prewett havin' a turn on the pianer. He's a cack-handed sod, I'll give him that!'

He lifted Alice off the bed and onto her feet. 'Come on, Monkey. You and me'll show him how it's done.'

The front room was crowded, musky with the aroma of ale and tobacco smoke. Tilly immediately gave her husband a tipsy smile. Jack slid onto the piano stool, good-naturedly butting Bill Prewett off the end with his hip. Before Alice could sit beside him Tilly had plonked down close to her husband and leaned her head on his shoulder.

As Alice watched her parents tears needled the back of her eyes again but she blinked them away. Her mum was keen to show her dad how much he meant to her. The fond display seemed sweeter for being so rare. It reinforced Alice's fears for her dad's safety. Normally her mum was sparing with her affection. But the arguments between them over him joining up had now stopped.

Tilly had accepted Jack was going; she'd had to, for when Jack made up his mind on something, that was that. All Tilly could do now was wring every last drop of enjoyment from the time remaining to them. Even the presence of Jimmy Wild, sitting with an arm around his wife, all cosy and quiet like butter wouldn't melt in his mouth, couldn't rile Tilly today. She wouldn't let it. So, as her sister Fran gave her a tentative smile that begged her tolerance, Tilly raised her glass in a salute and smiled right back.

Geoff strolled over to Alice, a bottle of beer in his fist. 'Alright?' he asked, tactfully avoiding staring at her bloodshot eyes fringed by clumpy wet lashes. 'Want a drop?' He offered the bottle.

'Ain't allowed,' she told him with a wrinkled-nose smile. Lucy had trotted up and clutched her about the knees. Alice swung her little sister up in her arms and began to dance with her despite that at three and a half years old she was now quite a weight to carry. They swirled around laughing to their dad's gay tune. Round and round they went in uninterrupted rhythm till Alice felt quite giddy and nauseated and Lucy was shrieking in delight.

Geoff took a step forward and steadied Alice as she stumbled. 'Daft . . . you'll drop her.' The chiding was kind. Then with the child between them he lightly held Alice and they adopted Margaret and Bert's posture. Quite sedately they followed their elders' steps and executed an approximation of a waltz whilst dodging the furniture.

Jack unobtrusively watched his tipsy wife watching their daughter as she danced. 'New start for Alice at Turner's engineering come next week.'

Tilly nodded. 'Good job she's making her way 'cos I'm gonna need the extra money once you're gone.' Her voice was thick with alcohol and emotion.

Jack turned and pressed his lips to his wife's temple. 'Won't be gone long, love,' he crooned, rubbing his cheek against hers to comfort her. 'When I come back on leave I'll fetch you something fancy from France,' he promised. He looked back at Alice and Geoff. 'Won't get no better than him,' he said quietly to Tilly. 'That's a good lad.'

'Yeah . . . I know,' Tilly slurred and, after a deep sigh, she snuggled up to Jack again. 'She's found someone like her dad.'

Tilly tilted her head, gave her husband a searing look. 'Don't want no fancy French stuff brought back. Just want you back. You come back home in one piece!' she whispered, her fierce whiskey breath burning his cheek. 'Don't you dare leave me on me own, Jack Keiver!'

EIGHTEEN

'You should've stopped home today,' Alice said to Sarah Whitton. Gently she drew her sobbing friend into her arms to comfort her.

'Ain't stopping home with me mum, the wicked old cow,' Sarah choked. 'She laughed when Louisa told us about dad. Wicked old cow, she is,' she repeated forcefully. 'Ain't surprised he ran off and left her when he did. Told her so 'n' all.' She scrubbed a hand over her streaming eyes. 'Rather be with the women at work than with her. At least they said nice things like sorry to hear about your dad, and so on.'

Alice had just discovered from her friend that this morning Sarah's sister Louisa had called round to Campbell Road to break the awful news that their dad had been killed in the fighting. Despite her grief Sarah had gone to work as usual and come to meet Alice at one o'clock as they'd arranged, outside Alice's workplace.

The two girls were stationed outside the gates to Turner's engineering factory in Blackstock Road. Sarah now worked in Kemp's biscuit factory despite her mum's initial objection to her taking on full-time. The amount of broken biscuits that found their way home in Sarah's bag had helped sweeten her attitude to her youngest daughter becoming independent.

'Do you still want to go to the caff?' Alice asked quietly. 'We could just take a walk about instead if you don't feel up to eating anything.'

Sarah gulped an agreement to a walk and, shoving an arm through one of Alice's, they turned and began to proceed along the road.

Alice glanced at her friend's bent head. Dread rolled in her stomach as she thought about her own dad, and the danger he was in. He'd been gone so long and just once had he had home leave so far. It had been so good to see him! But that visit had been months ago and they must wait many more months before he came home again.

Sometimes Alice wondered if she'd forget what her dad looked like, and she'd panic and grab from the top of the piano the photo of him in his uniform. She'd stare deep into his eyes as though he could see her too and she'd reassure herself he *was* smiling. She'd written him a letter two days ago. Would he ever read it? Had *he* been injured or killed?

A few little cards had arrived from him posted from France. On those he would always write that he was thinking of them all and hoping soon it would be over so he could come home for good. When he'd come back on leave, she knew he'd deliberately avoided truthfully answering probing questions about the peril all the troops were facing. There was no complaint; nothing at all that might have worried them about his safety. But Alice read the newspaper every day and scoured the columns for news of the war. She knew how dreadful were the conditions for infantry soldiers in the trenches. As a private in the Fusiliers her dad was no doubt right in the thick of things. She closed her eyes and a soundless prayer trembled over her lips. *Please God, take care of Jack Keiver and soon bring him home safe.*

Feeling a bit guilty at allowing horrible imaginings make her forget Sarah's real distress Alice squeezed her friend's arm in sympathy. 'Does Connie know?' she asked quietly. 'Did Louisa go and see Connie too and tell her about your dad?'

'Dunno,' Sarah whimpered and cuffed her nose. 'Since she broke up with the rozzer and moved out of his house nobody sees much of her. Don't even know where she's living now or what work she's doing.'

Alice murmured a neutral response. She knew that Constable Franks had broken off the engagement to Connie because Sarah had told her at the time it'd happened. Nobody seemed to know why the engagement had come to an abrupt end. Alice had also heard quite recently – from Annie Foster who'd got it from her sweetheart, Tommy Greenfield – that Connie had been seen with a fellow who looked old enough to be her father, but who'd acted more like a sugar daddy. *Had his hands all over her, he did, and she didn't seem to mind,* had been the way Annie had recounted it.

Alice hadn't passed that on to Sarah. It was only gossip after all that Connie Whitton had been spotted acting like a pro.

'Who's that over there with Geoff?'

Alice immediately looked in the direction that Sarah had indicated. They'd just turned the corner and on the opposite side of the street was Geoff and with him was a petite blonde-haired girl.

As Alice watched them an odd, unpleasant sensation flipped her insides. Geoff was gazing intently at the girl and the two of them seemed to be standing very close together whilst talking.

'D'you know who she is?' Sarah asked with a frown. 'Not seen her about before. She's pretty, ain't she?'

'Might be a customer out of his shop,' Alice mumbled

unconvincingly and urged Sarah to walk on. If she was a customer it didn't explain why the girl looked to be upset. Now they were closer Alice could see that the blonde was dabbing at her eyes as though she might have been crying. Immediately Alice was reminded of Sophy's tears when Danny had got her in the family way and she turned cold. A moment later she was inwardly chiding herself for jumping to conclusions about them.

Geoff noticed Alice and Sarah and raised a hand in greeting but he kept on talking to the girl he was with and made no move to leave her side. In fact he moved a little closer to her, inclining his head as though listening intently.

'Best be turning around in a minute,' Alice said gruffly to Sarah. She felt piqued that Geoff hadn't immediately rushed over to her. She also felt determined to discover who the girl was and why she seemed to have so much to say to Geoff, who was her . . . Alice's thoughts petered off. Geoff was just her friend, she realised. She'd never let him be more than that. She knew he'd like to be. He hadn't tried to kiss her again, nor had he so much as given another hint that they were sweethearts walking out. So if he found another girl he liked, why shouldn't he get close to her and pay her attention? 'Got to get back to work,' Alice said huskily. 'I'm only taking a short break today.'

They turned about and started walking back the way they'd come. A few minutes later Geoff caught up with them and fell into step.

'On yer dinner breaks?' Geoff asked airily and cast a curious look at Sarah's red and blotchy face. 'I am 'n' all.'

'Just heard this morning that me dad's got killed in the fighting.' Sarah croaked an explanation for her appearance for she could sense Geoff's unspoken question. She'd always had a soft spot for Geoff and she'd rather tell him why she looked a mess than have him ask.

'Bloody hell . . . not another one!' Geoff exhaled loudly in sympathy. 'I was just talking to Peter Slater's fiancée. She just told me that they heard a few days ago he's got reported missing, presumed dead. In a right state, she is.'

'Peter Slater's fiancée?' Alice sent him a sharp sideways glance. 'Is *that* who she is?'

'Yeah. You remember him, don't you? Dan got his job training horses when Peter had a few too many bevvies one dinnertime and joined up. Poor sod. If he'd stayed out of the pub he'd probably still be alive and in Essex. He'd only just turned eighteen.'

A guilty sensation rolled in Alice's stomach, making her feel quite sick. She'd felt annoyed on seeing Geoff talking to Peter's fiancée and all the poor girl had done was to tell him she'd had bad news about her sweetheart.

They stopped at the corner and after a brief goodbye Sarah went off back to work at the biscuit factory.

Alice and Geoff continued on along the road towards Turner's. Still Alice felt oddly unsettled. She slid Geoff a look. Having sensed her eyes on him, he turned his head. After a moment his quizzical expression altered and a glimmer of understanding replaced it. A corner of his mouth tilted in what could have been amusement or satisfaction.

Alice felt her face getting hot for she knew she'd betrayed her jealousy. She speeded up towards the gate of the factory. 'See you later then?' She swished past and kept walking towards the factory entrance. After a moment of silence she swung about to see if he'd rudely gone off without even bothering to reply to her mumbled farewell. He was standing watching her from behind the railings. For a moment they stood quite still, their eyes locked together.

'Ain't interested in her,' Geoff said softly and planted a large hand on the iron bars.

'Ain't bothered if you are,' Alice returned.

'I reckon you are.'

'You can reckon all you like, Geoff Lovat,' Alice snapped. 'We still ain't walkin' out.'

'I reckon we are,' he said and with a grin he pushed away from the railings and walked on.

'Dad!'

The chorus of joyous shouts issued from Alice and Bethany. Simultaneously the two girls launched themselves forward and hugged their father in a tangle of limbs before he was properly through the door. They'd been up early that morning doing what they could to tidy the place whilst awaiting his arrival.

Jack dropped his kitbag. He struggled to free his arms from where his daughters had pinned them to his sides so he could grip them tightly to him. He swung his face planting his lips on two dark heads, then another fierce kiss was bestowed on both girls before he let them go.

'Got a surprise for you, Dad,' Alice said. 'Close your eyes.'

Jack looked from Alice to Bethany but neither was giving anything away. He swiped his hat from his head and put it on the table.

'Go on, close them,' Beth said excitedly and cupped her palms over her father's eyes until he moved up his hands to replace them.

The door to the back room opened and Sophy and Danny crept out.

'Can open 'em now,' Sophy said softly. As soon as her father's fingers had dropped away from his face Sophy launched herself at him, hugging him tightly about the waist and burrowing her face into his neck. Danny watched the scene indulgently before he approached Jack to shake his hand.

'So good to see you both,' Jack croaked through the tears in his throat. 'Lovely surprise . . . lovely . . .' he mumbled.

'I'll be back later,' Danny said tactfully as Jack withdrew a handkerchief. 'I've gotta go next door and see them all. Me mum'll be on the warpath else.'

Jack nodded in understanding but kept Sophy clasped against his side as he dropped a kiss on her hair. 'You're looking bonny, Sophy,' he choked out. 'They've been feeding you well, I see.'

Sophy blushed. She knew she was getting plump. But she didn't care too much because she was content. And besides, Danny said he liked her better with a bit of meat on her.

Finally Jack walked further into the room and gave his wife, who'd been sitting on the piano stool watching the scene with a smile, a searing look. But he went to Lucy who had jumped from the bed, giggling, and had been patiently awaiting her father's attention. 'Are you the birthday girl who's gonna be five tomorrow?' Jack teased Lucy with a grin. 'Your daddy's got you a present.' He put his youngest back down on the floor and Lucy bounced up and down excitedly, barefoot, on the boards while Jack dug in his bag and brought forth a floppy doll with yellow wool hair and a red dress. 'Come all the way from France that did, Luce,' he told her as he handed it over and ruffled her soft curls.

Lucy hugged her present to her and climbed back on the bed to examine it.

Finally he turned his attention to Tilly. 'It didn't cost much at all,' he said easily. 'Worked out at just a few coppers . . .' He knew how hard things had been for his wife trying to cope alone. Kids' toys were no bloody use to people with empty bellies.

Tilly shrugged and continued to feast her eyes on her husband. She'd sooner have had the cost of the doll – and she reckoned it was shillings, not pennies – jangling in the kitty but she was too pleased to see Jack to start a row today. Besides, Sophy had brought her some money from her wages and handed it over before she'd had to ask. Jack sat down beside her on the stool and put his arm around her. He waited till she'd cuffed the wetness from her eyes before he bent his head and gave her a kiss on the lips.

Alice watched them. Now she was older she understood why they sometimes liked to have a bit of time alone. Despite yearning to stay with her dad and question him immediately about how he was, and what he'd been doing since they'd last seen him, she announced cheerfully, 'Me 'n' Beth 'n' Sophy are going to get a cake and some pop so's we can have a birthday party for Lucy.'

Tilly gave her a startled look that begged to know where the money for *that* was coming from.

'We've all been putting a bit by from our wages, even Beth's chipped in,' Alice explained and avoided her mother's eye. If Tilly had known a few savings were around she'd have turned the place upside down looking for the little stash.

'We've ordered a sponge cake from the baker's in Hornsey Road as a surprise,' Beth said with a beam. 'We arranged to collect it this afternoon.'

Once the sound of their older daughters clattering down the stairs had died away Jack gave Tilly another kiss, then another that was hungry enough to take her head back against his arm.

'D'you reckon Fran 'ud do us a turn and look after Lucy for a bit?' The words had been whispered against Tilly's thick, fiery hair. Jack touched the crisp collar on her best embroidered blouse and tenderness flowed through him. She'd tidied herself prettily for him and he knew taking that sort of trouble wasn't easy for a woman in a place like this.

Jack knew that once Lucy's birthday tea party was over there'd be entertainment for the adults in the Keiver household. The neighbours would come by and it would be like old times; a warm feeling bathed his insides as he remembered those good days. Life was never easy in The Bunk but compared to what he'd experienced on the Somme it seemed wonderfully carefree.

'I'll see if Fran's in and will have Lucy in hers for half an hour,' Tilly breathed against his cheek

'Half an hour?' Jack growled with a wolfish smile. 'Better make it an hour, love, I've not seen you in a while.'

'Wish Dad didn't have to go back,' Beth said as they walked along in the direction of Hornsey Road.

It had been exactly the phrase that had been rotating in Alice's mind. She sighed and nodded. 'Got to keep cheerful though and make it a nice break for him,' she warned her younger sister.

'Sounds like it's dreadful over there, don't it?' Sophy said, biting her lower lip. 'He looks really tired and much older, don't he?'

Alice nodded and blinked her eyes. They'd been reading in the newspapers for months about the terrible carnage in France. Having their dad back, and looking whole and healthy, if a bit grizzled, was a huge relief. The dreadful battles on the Western Front had killed and wounded so many. Their dad's leave was less than a week this time so Alice knew they must squeeze every last drop of enjoyment from his visit.

'Let's hurry up 'n' get the cake and pop and go home,' Alice blurted, suddenly unwilling to waste a precious minute more than was necessary that could be spent with her father. Her sisters nodded and linking arms the three of them huddled together in affection before breaking apart and trotting on.

'Want to go for a walk round and about?'

Alice raised her eyes to Geoff's face. They were standing out in the street, getting a breath of fresh air. It was summer and still light and warm despite the lateness of the hour. The atmosphere upstairs in the Keivers' front room was stifling due to the crush. Sophy and Danny were having a fine old time regaling pop-eyed people with the wonderful life they enjoyed in Essex.

'I'll get me coat,' Alice said and darted back inside. A moment later she was back at Geoff's side. 'Little Lucy's had the best day,' she told him as they strolled. 'Dad got her a present from France; a doll with yellow hair and a red dress. Pretty little thing, it is. Can't imagine how she's sleeping through all that din!' She chuckled. 'Out like a light she is with her dolly in her arms . . .'

'Did she like her party?'

Alice nodded vigorously.

'You were right about Sophy and Dan,' Alice said.

Geoff gave her a quizzical look.

'They've both turned into a right couple of fatsos,' Alice said on an impish chuckle.

'He's got four chins,' Geoff said with a guffaw. 'Glad now I didn't go,' he said self-mockingly. 'Sooner stop here 'n keep me figure.'

Alice gave him a playful punch. 'Well, I'm glad you stopped here 'n all . . .'

Suddenly they both started to attention and chorused, 'Oh, no!'

They'd hardly got to Blackstock Road when the air-raid siren had started, prompting Geoff to grab Alice's hand and jerk her around. They began to run back towards Campbell Road.

Breathlessly they hared up the stairs and hollered over the racket, 'Air raid!'

Music and singing died away and a score or more faces stared at them. Jack's fingers had stilled on the piano keys; now he lifted them to hover just above, and everybody tensed and listened. The whine was audible, and so was the much fainter drone of engines.

'Lights out,' Jack bawled and quickly candles and lamps were extinguished. An unspoken consensus of opinion seemed to have been reached by all: stay put and hope for the best, for nobody moved.

By touch alone Jack started to play the piano in the dark and then he started to sing too. He broke off to bellow, 'Well them Hun buggers can't hear us, can they?'

Laughter rippled through the room, getting more raucous as Jack continued to play with great zeal. After a moment everybody had joined in singing 'Pack Up Your Troubles'.

Alice was in front of Geoff and as she felt his arms come about her in the dark, she sensed the reverberation of his singing voice through her coat. She leaned back against him, closing her hands over his, clasped together on her waist. She felt suddenly warm and unafraid and glad that her dad and Sophy were here with them. If the worst happened, and a bomb was dropped on them, at least she'd be with the people she loved and they'd all go together. When the droning was at its loudest, so was the choir, rising in a defiant crescendo of sound that seemed to shake the house. When danger was past, and the lights were eventually relit, the company seemed rather subdued. Within half an hour the party had finished and the neighbours had dispersed.

NINETEEN

''Ere, Til! Wait up!'

Tilly swung about to see Beattie Evans pounding the pavement behind her. She halted at once for her neighbour looked flustered and that indicated she had something important to tell her.

Beattie wobbled to a stop and wheezed in air. 'Never guess who I just seen. Strutting bold as yer like up the top end . . .'

Tilly raised her eyebrows in enquiry.

The exertion of catching Tilly up and delivering that little speech seemed to have taken all Beattie's breath and for a moment she simply fanned her face.

Impatient to be on her way Tilly made a guess. 'If you've caught sight of Jimmy 'n' his tart out walking you don't need to tell me nuthin' about them. I know they're still carryin' on, and I don't need nobody telling me my sister's a fool.'

Despite Jimmy's promises that he'd soon escape Nellie's clutches and be back home with his wife and kids, Fran still tolerated him spending most of his time with his fancy piece. Tilly reckoned that it was Nellie who was keen to be rid of Jimmy. She'd glimpsed her recently in Holloway Road with heavy powder clogged on a puffy eye. Tilly could put two and two together. Jimmy would cling onto Nellie while she was earning and he could take a cut of the money. He was obviously employing his fists if necessary to ensure he got as much as he wanted.

'Ain't him!' Beattie blasted out a cackle. 'Nah! This is a *real* sight fer sore eyes. Jeannie Robertson. Didn't reckernise her straight off. All dolled up to the nines, she is. Just saw her up the other end. Saw me right back, she did, and didn't look too concerned about getting spotted neither. That's a brass-faced baggage to turn up after what she did!' Beattie exclaimed.

Tilly's eyes narrowed. She hadn't forgotten the Robertson family. How could she? They'd done a bunk with the blouse she'd loaned Jeannie for pawning, and with Mr Keane's rent and furniture. But what really niggled Tilly was that she could have lost her job over it all.

'Up there, is she?' Tilly echoed and her mouth set in a grim line. 'I'll have her . . . the thieving cow.'

'Hang on,' Beattie whispered in shock. 'Bleeding hell. Look! Here she comes. She's heading straight for us.'

Tilly turned to see that indeed Jeannie Robertson was marching purposefully in her direction. Tilly eyed her from head to toe. She didn't appear to be in need of anything now. *Dolled up* hardly did justice to her elegant attire. She'd always been an attractive woman for her years – Tilly guessed Jeannie was about her own age, thirty-seven. It was the first time Tilly had seen her spruced up and she realised Jeannie Robertson wouldn't have looked out of place sauntering along Bond Street. She certainly looked to be a misfit in Campbell Road, yet a few years ago she'd been glad to take a room in one of the worst houses to be had in this slum. A blue velvet hat was perched on Jeannie's head and she was garbed in a smart dark outfit with a leather bag dangling from an elbow.

'Got somethin' fer yer,' Jeannie stated as soon as she stopped. Her voice hadn't undergone the same transformation and was as coarse as ever it had been.

Tilly elevated her chin. 'Well . . . let's know quick what it is, 'cos I got something for you too.' One of Tilly's clenched fists was raised to hover by her waist.

A small smile writhed over Jeannie's lips then disappeared. 'Can't blame you for how you feel,' she said simply. 'Let's go in there.' She nodded to an open doorway close by. 'Nobody else's business anyhow what went on,' she said, slinging a significant glance at Beattie who was listening to proceedings with slack-jawed avidity.

A shrug confirmed Tilly's willingness to speak with Jeannie in private. In the shelter of the doorway she swung about immediately to confront her.

'Got a few things to say and this to do.' Jeannie pulled out of her stylish handbag some bank notes. 'Should be more'n enough there to cover what I took. Furniture were crap anyhow but it served a purpose. Blouse you let me have to pawn kept us fed when we had nothing. So I'm saying I'm obliged to you. I'm saying too that it's up to you what you do with old man Keane's share of that there cash.'

Tilly continued staring at the fifteen pounds she held as though she couldn't quite believe it was hers. A hint of floral perfume wafted from her fingers and Tilly was tempted to move her fist to her face to acquaint herself with the scent of plenty.

'You want to pay Keane for his back rent and that pile o' shit I carted off, that's yer own business.' Jeannie turned and walked away a few paces. 'Another thing . . . you done me a good turn and I pay back favours.' It seemed Tilly was intent on ignoring the offer so Jeannie turned away.

'You done alright for yourself, then?' Tilly rasped.

'Doing better than I was,' Jeannie answered wryly over

a shoulder. She swung about. 'Got hooked up again with a bloke I used to know out of Lorenco Road. He's done alright. He's got a few clubs now up west and he's right generous. That's enough for me for the time being.'

A dry chuckle rolled in Tilly's throat. 'That's enough for any of us, I reckon.'

'I heard your husband's gone to fight.'

'Yeah . . . he's in France. But he was back a few months ago.' A smile tipped Tilly's lips as she remembered the wonderful time they'd had on Lucy's fifth birthday.

'Well, as I said, you done me a good turn 'n' I won't forget it. Both me sons joined up,' Jeannie added as an afterthought. 'One navy . . . one army, neither of 'em old enough ter go.'

''Spect you miss 'em,' Tilly said, her fists finally relaxing at her sides.

'Yeah . . . but not as much as they miss each other, I reckon.' With that Jeannie turned and set off up Campbell Road.

She'd got a few yards when Tilly hissed after her. 'You mean it? You'll not let on if I keep all o' this?' She discreetly wagged the cash, half-hidden in her skirt. 'What if Mr Keane goes after you for it? He don't forget nuthin'. If he sees you about he'll have yer.'

'He won't . . . not when he finds out who my bloke is.' Jeannie retraced her steps. 'Keane might think he's something round this poxy hole but he ain't in the same league as Johnny Blake.' Her top lip curled lightly. 'I won't have no trouble off him so you won't have no trouble. I'll make sure of it.' Jeannie paused. Her shrewd eyes flitted over Tilly's rough, faded clothing. 'Might have a bit of business for you. I know you 'n' your husband used to do a bit of street selling from time to time. As I said, Johnny's generous; buys me stuff I don't pertickerly like. So, I got a few nice bits I got no use for . . . coats and boots 'n' so on. I'm looking to shift 'em so . . .'

'Don't want no charity off yer,' Tilly butted in brusquely.

'Ain't giving yer no charity,' Jeannie retorted. 'I was going to offer to sell 'em to you. If you flog it on at a profit . . .' She shrugged. 'I ain't bothered. I just want shot of it so's I got room in me wardrobe for stuff that suits me.'

Another discreet squint at Jeannie's attire told Tilly that if the *stuff* were as good as what she had on it would be a payday. 'I'll take a look at it, if you like,' she said with gruff nonchalance. 'I don't mind doing a bit of hawkin' so I'll have the lot off you if the price is right.'

'Right,' Jeannie said briskly. 'I'll be back one evening next week with it. Just so's you know in advance, I'll be wanting a guinea for the lot.'

Tilly's eyes slew to the velvet hat perched on top of Jeannie's head. It looked to have cost all of that and more. Jeannie Robertson was doing her a good turn in the only way she could . . . by making out it wasn't much good at all.

This time when Jeannie set off Tilly watched her go then emerged from the doorway and walked in the opposite direction. Beattie hove immediately into view to trot after her. When Tilly continued to smile, but remained uncommunicative, curiosity got the better of Beattie's usual caution with this woman.

'What's she want?' she demanded.

'To pay her dues.' Tilly's good mood remained unspoiled by her neighbour's crude inquisitiveness. So she didn't advise Beattie to keep her snout out.

'Bleedin' hell, Fran! Knock next time, will you?' Tilly snatched up from the table the money that Jeannie had given her earlier in the week and thrust it into a pocket.

But her sister had seen it and her eyes darted to the place into which the notes had just disappeared.

'You done alright for yourself, then. Where d'you get that sort of cash?' Fran came further into the room and closed the door that lead onto the landing.

'Jeannie Robertson's been by to pay back what she owed.'

Fran's eyes opened in wonderment. 'She's come back after all this time to pay you what she owed?' she echoed.

'Yeah; surprised me 'n' all. She's doing alright now. Got a rich fancy man, she has.'

'Lend us ten bob, will you?'

Tilly stood up and said curtly, 'Already lent yer, Fran, and you said Jimmy was going to pay you something last Friday so's you could give it me back this week.' Tilly looked at her sister. 'Take it you ain't seen him, and you've got nothing for me, then.'

'Don't look like you need it,' Fran remarked sullenly.

'This here's gotta last. Jack ain't here helpin' out now, Fran. It's just me 'n' the girls. Ain't got a man's wages coming in.'

'Neither have I.'

Tilly sensed that Fran had a complaint to make and was waiting for the right moment to slip it into the conversation. 'Jimmy's done the dirty on you again.' She wearily stabbed a guess.

'I'm done with him.' Fran curled her lip. 'He ain't never going to leave that cow and come home for good. Ain't seen him or his wages in weeks. Done with him for good, I am.'

Tilly grunted a laugh. 'Well now, I ain't even going to ask if you mean it. But if I really believed that he *was* gone for good I'd say keep the money wot I lent you and take this 'n' all as a thank-you present.' She drew the fifteen pounds out of her pocket and slapped it down on the table. 'It'd be worth all of that to see the back of the bastard once 'n' fer all. Trouble is, I know you don't mean it this time any more than you did the last. So you can leave that cash where it is.'

Jimmy Wild yanked up his coat collar as he emerged from the King's Head pub and sloped off towards Seven Sisters Road. He kept his head down. By hiding what he could of his face he hoped nobody closer to home would spot the beating he'd taken. He'd been a figure of fun in the pub because of it. But he'd needed a few drinks so he'd taken the stares and whispers while he knocked back a couple of pints and whisky chasers and mentally licked his wounds. Rage and resentment made him grind his back teeth. In turn that made him flinch and curse as his skin tightened on bruises that were constantly throbbing.

Earlier that evening he'd been to see Nellie to collect what he liked to call his commission from her. He'd known for a while that the bitch was keen to ditch him. She wasn't as docile as Fran who'd take a painful lesson in obedience then open her legs for him an hour later without too much complaint in case the boys got a taste of his temper. Nellie, he'd learned to his irritation, was a brooder. She'd carry on sulking and moaning for days at a time. But her resistance to accepting a bit of discipline, or to handing over the thick end of her earnings, wasn't the reason she wanted rid of him. Nellie liked a man around to warn the other working girls and their pimps she'd got someone looking after her interests. The reason she no longer wanted Jimmy was that she'd found someone to take his place.

Saul Bateman had taken care of Jimmy too when he'd showed up unannounced and caught the two of them in bed. Jimmy had unwisely thought he'd got the fellow at a disadvantage seeing as how he was stark bollock naked, pumping away on top of Nellie and breathing heavily. So he'd confidently left the knife in his pocket and landed the first punch. But in a leap his younger rival was on his feet and impressing on Jimmy he was the better man in every way. Nellie, the silly tart, had started shrieking and grabbing the sheet to cover herself as though she'd revealed something he'd never seen before.

It hadn't taken long – a few to the face and a couple of body blows – for Jimmy to realise he was outmatched. He'd fled with Saul's bellowed threat to kill him following him down the stairs and out into the dusk. Now, as he ambled on, instinctively towards The Bunk, Jimmy brooded on when and where he might be able to again catch the bastard by surprise, and on that occasion use his blade rather than his fists on him.

His plans for revenge brought little consolation. Unendurable humiliation still savaged his mind and Jimmy's instinct was to find a whipping dog to buck him up a bit. As he turned in to Campbell Road he saw just what he needed.

Fran saw him right back. She'd been out in the street looking for Stevie and Bobbie to order them indoors as it was late. She'd had a bad day too and was in no mood for any nonsense from her sons or from the useless git she'd married. Jimmy had given her no wages for over three weeks. Adding to her money troubles was the tight-fisted client who had promised to pay her today for last week's washing, but hadn't. Nevertheless if she'd known what sort of mood Jimmy was in, or that he'd been in a fight, she might have proceeded with caution. As it was Fran just gave him a scowl, two raised fingers and a contemptuous, 'Fuck off.'

Her attitude was like a red rag to a bull. But Jimmy used his soppy smile as he approached. He was still looking pleased when he landed a short jab to the side of her face. Taken by surprise Fran reeled back with little more than a grunt.

Deftly he caught her and dragged her out of sight into the hallway before any neighbour started taking an interest in what was happening. With grim determination pursing his mouth Jimmy started up the stairs dragging Fran, dazed and groaning, with him. He quickly shoved her inside the room and used a boot on her buttocks to propel her towards the bed. She hit the edge and collapsed, neatly avoiding the fist he'd swung at her. Annoyed at that, he yanked her up by the hair and deliberately aimed to split her nose and lip.

Fran stayed sprawled where she was, eyes closed, bleeding mouth agape. Even when Jimmy drew the belt from around his waist, slowly, as though savouring the slither of leather on his hips, Fran remained unresponsive.

Jimmy tested her with a vicious lash across the legs but she was out cold and didn't murmur or flinch. Fired up and frustrated he kicked her for good measure then prowled back and forth. His lips drew back against his teeth as he began cursing the stupid bitch for being so pathetically weak that a couple of smacks had finished her off too soon. If he hung around waiting for her to come round so he could give her a bit more Bobbie and Stevie were sure to turn up and create a commotion. The boys were older now, not so inclined to cower quietly in a corner when he was on the rampage. He didn't want old Prewett poking his nose in, or Tilly bloody Keiver for that matter.

Suddenly he stopped pacing to listen. Another bump from above could be heard and a slow, crafty grin split his face. He went to the door and crept onto the landing, looking right and left, alert to being spotted, as he made for the stairs. He knew the sound of Tilly Keiver finishing off a bottle of whiskey. He knew what the thuds and clunks meant after so many years living in close proximity to her. He knew too that, drunk or sober, she wouldn't even open the door to him unless he gave her good reason.

He knocked and called softly. ''Ere, Til, it's Jim. You seen Fran? She ain't in. I come by 'cos I got some money for her fer the lads.'

Tilly stuck a hand through a tiny opening. 'Give it 'ere then,' she slurred. 'I'll make sure she gets it tomorrer.'

'Ain't she with you?' Jimmy enquired, all friendly, whilst keeping his bruises turned away from the aperture.

'No, she ain't,' Tilly muttered, getting annoyed.

'I was gonna knock at old Prewett's, before I go. Say hello.' He paused. 'Know if the ol' git's about, do yer?' It was a sly probe to discover if anyone was home and might bear witness against what he had planned.

'He's gone to Bethnal Green. Funeral,' Tilly muttered succinctly. 'Now give us Fran's money 'n' piss off, will yer. I'm done in.'

Jimmy put his shoulder hard against the door and Tilly staggered back to crash into the table. 'Wot the fuck yer doing?' she spluttered, frowning incomprehension. Her inebriated state made it difficult for her to regain her balance and she clutched at a chair back.

An encompassing glance about the room told Jimmy what he needed to know. She was on her own. It was late and the kids were probably all akip in the back room. Nevertheless he kept his voice silky and soft. 'I'm doin' what I should've done a long time ago, you mouthy bitch. No Jack now to hide behind, have you?' he taunted through his teeth as he back-kicked to flick the door to. 'Got two things for you, Til,' he purred with sadistic relish. 'Got this . . .' He raised a fist. 'And got this . . .' He started to unbutton his fly. 'Now how you take this . . .' he handled his groin lewdly, 'is gonna determine how much of this you get.' He suddenly let fly with a punch that whipped Tilly's slack head sideways. He licked his lips as he heard her stunned gasp.

'Now that didn't hurt,' he mocked. 'That were just a little tickle.'

The throb of agony in her jaw had dispersed some of the inebriated fog in her mind. Tilly blinked and with a guttural cry launched herself at him. Her drunken state made her clumsy and Jimmy floored her with ease and stood grinning down at her semi-conscious figure.

He used his boot to turn her onto her back and came down astride her. 'Want it here, do yer?' He pounced on her heaving breasts, double-handed, then ripped the buttons from her blouse. Her skirts were already awry and he tugged them higher while she bucked beneath him, cursing and crying in frustration and rage. But try as she might she was too drunk and stunned to stir her senses into action or shift the weight on top of her.

Jimmy levered himself up a bit to yank down his trousers and as he surged forward again Tilly recovered just enough to spit in his face. Jimmy cuffed her spittle from his cheek and drew back that same arm, intending to give Tilly back what was hers.

'What's going on?' The voice, faint with shock, came from the threshold.

TWENTY

'What's going on?' Alice cried and rushed into the room. She'd just returned home from a walk to the café with Geoff. Only moments ago they'd parted at the foot of the stairs. She bent to her mum and gasped as she saw the state of her battered face. She then raised her eyes to her uncle; their faces were almost level. 'What have you done to her?' she whispered, aghast. Her fearful gaze fell to a puce part of him that poked jauntily out of dirty white cotton. With a shudder of revulsion she sprang up and tottered back a step.

Jimmy whipped to his feet and caught her as she turned to run for the door. 'Where you off to, Al?' he asked, his voice guttural with lust. The arm about her waist tightened and he slid a hand up to squeeze a small breast. 'Stay fer a bit and be nice to yer uncle . . . eh? Got a little kiss for me, have you?'

Alice shrieked and one of his brutal hands quickly muffled her cries. She could feel hot pressure behind her and felt the bile rise in her throat as he ground himself against her buttocks.

'Come on, li'l Alice,' he crooned. 'That streak o' piss boyfriend of yours ain't old enough to know how it's done. What you need is a real man. I'll show you a better time'n he can manage.' He dragged her back with him to the iron bed and forced her down on the dirty mattress.

Alice felt as though she were suffocating. She twisted her head away from his boozy breath, tried to squirm from the rough hands tearing at her clothes to reach her skin. She wanted to see her mum. She could hear her groaning but not locate her on the floor.

Tilly dragged herself to her knees and lunged for the bed. 'Get off her! Get off her, yer filthy bastard. She's yourn. What you doin' to yer own daughter?'

Jimmy turned his head as Tilly pounded ineffectual punches at his thigh. 'What you on about?' he snarled.

'She's yourn . . . your kid . . . get off her, you . . . evil . . . fuckin' . . . bastard.'

As the hand that had been gagging her slackened Alice jerked free and screamed. When Jimmy turned back to stare at her drop-jawed she drew a breath to yell again. The disbelief in his eyes at what her mum had said was already being dimmed by lust. His rough fingers pinched her lips again to quieten her. 'She's a lyin' bitch,' he mouthed close to Alice's ear. 'Don't you take no notice. I ain't yer daddy . . .'

Geoff was taking a final drag from his roll-up, leaning against the railings, when he heard Alice scream. He thought for a moment he must be mistaken, for only a minute or two previously he'd kissed her goodnight in the shelter of the doorway and she'd gone off humming happily. But this was The Bunk and God only knew anything could happen in it. A second later he was bounding up the stairs.

The sight that met his eyes as he burst in to the Keivers' room momentarily petrified him to the spot with shock.

Tilly was on her knees at the bed edge, dragging at Jimmy's legs and crying, her features mired in blood and snot. Alice had seen him over Jimmy's shoulder and her eyes were dull with humiliation and misery. Jimmy turned his head and spat a curse at him. Aiming a backward kick at Tilly to get her off his legs he vaulted to his feet, closing his trousers.

Geoff quietly pushed to the door. 'What d'you think yer doing?' He sounded oddly polite yet tight-lipped wrath had drained his complexion of colour and narrowed his eyes to slits.

'What you can't, sonny. I'm gonna give her a good time. And when I've done with you I'll finish her off 'fore she goes cold on me.'

Geoff continued into the room and circled as Jimmy started to navigate the furniture.

'He's got a knife, Geoff,' Alice choked out. She'd seen Jimmy's sly movement and the flash of silver as one of his hands withdrew from a pocket. She swiftly yanked down her rucked-up skirt and scrambled to the edge of the bed.

'Stay where you are, Alice.'

It was uttered with such quiet authority that Alice obeyed Geoff and froze into immobility.

Slowly Tilly's numbed senses were surfacing though a mist of pain and alcohol. She tried to pull herself onto her feet. But her legs buckled beneath her and she cried out in anguish and frustration. Her head was reeling, her throat clogged with blood and mucus, making her retch and gag. She sank again to her knees.

Jimmy lunged and Geoff dodged sideways. Jimmy chuckled and licked his lips on seeing he'd got a lucky hit and drawn blood. Red beads had sprung up on Geoff's forearm and stained his shirt.

'Come on . . . you can do better'n that, can't you, sonny?'

he taunted then feinted with the knife a couple of times, showing off.

Alice had also seen the stain on Geoff's shirt and she jumped off the bed, her darting eyes searching for something with which to attack Jimmy.

'Stay where you are!' Geoff roared at her. 'Stay!'

Alice sank back on the bed edge.

Again Jimmy used the distraction to his advantage and got the blade glancing off Geoff's left shoulder. The wound was deeper than the first but Geoff barely felt it for he'd got what he wanted. He'd drawn him in enough to strike. He jabbed a brutal fist at Jimmy's nose with his right hand then followed it quickly with a left cross before dancing out of range of the waving knife. As Jimmy started to collapse he stepped in again and brought his knee viciously in to his groin then followed it through to slam under his chin. As Jimmy sagged to his knees he swiped out wildly at Geoff, spitting curses.

Nobody had seen Fran appear. From behind a half-open door, and a half-open eye, she'd watched the scene for minutes in silence. She'd seen her niece pulling down her skirts and her sister's bloodied face and torn clothing. She'd seen Geoff Lovat's heroic defence of her female kin. Now her husband was on his knees she walked in and raised, two-handed, the heavy pot she held. She brushed past Geoff and swung the vessel sideways, with all her might, into Jimmy's cheek. He rolled away groaning, trying to avoid another blow from her. She followed, wordlessly, doggedly, and smashed the pot down again on his head as he writhed at her feet.

Geoff tried to push Fran clear as he saw the knife rising in Jimmy's fist but he was too late and it scored Fran's belly, finally drawing a rasping sound from her. Geoff came down on top of Jimmy, pinning him to floor to try and wrestle the blade from his grip. A moment later there was a loud grunt followed by a cough.

Geoff struggled to his feet and looked down at Jimmy's rapidly blinking eyes. Suddenly the lids fell and his head sagged to one side. Geoff turned to the women in the room. All three were looking expressionlessly at the man sprawled on the floor.

'Is he dead?' Tilly croaked.

'Dunno . . . Think so . . .' Geoff answered hoarsely.

'Good,' Tilly said tonelessly. She finally managed to drag herself to her feet using the bed edge. One of her hands rested on her daughter's down-bent head, just briefly, before she staggered over to her bleeding sister.

'Let's see,' she said and, dragging Fran's trembling hands from where they covered a crimson stain, began to pull apart her clothes.

Geoff went to the bed and sat down next to Alice. 'You hurt?'

'No . . . I'm not . . . no, I'm not . . . he didn't . . . I'm not . . .' she whispered through chattering teeth.

Geoff put his arm about her and drew her head down onto his shoulder.

'Thought Dan was the boxer out of yers.' A hysterical giggle followed Alice's words.

'Used to spar with him. Was always better than him. Never let on though. Didn't want to get roped in.'

Alice clung to him, feeling him shaking as violently as she was herself. Suddenly she started to keen quietly, her hands clutching at her face.

'Wot in fuck's name's gone on here . . .?' Jeannie Robertson took a hesitant step into the room. Her eyes flitted over the carnage, settled on the young girl weeping on the bed being supported by a young man with a face as white as a sheet. Finally she gazed at the man on the floor, a dark pool spreading under him on the floorboards.

Quietly she closed the door behind her. Hoisting up her smart skirt to keep it clean she stepped over Jimmy's body and stood by the table. For some long moments she stared at the two women who seemed to be propping each other up. Their features were almost unrecognisable because of the battering they'd taken.

Tilly blinked back at Jeannie through an eye that was puffed to a slit. For almost a minute nobody spoke and Alice's weeping was the only sound.

'He the one done this to you all?' A jerk of Jeannie's head took in Jimmy's inert form.

Tilly nodded. Moisture slid from the small crack hiding her eye. She winced as she knuckled it away. 'Tried to rape me 'n' me daughter too,' she croaked.

'He weren't no good,' Fran mumbled with such absurd understatement that Jeannie raised her eyes heavenwards.

'Well, he ain't gonna bash or rape nobody no more, is he?' Jeannie said gently. She looked at the young couple still huddled together on the bed edge. She could stab a guess at what had gone on, and how Jimmy Wild had finally got what he deserved. 'You intending getting the police involved?'

As though the consequences of Jimmy's death had not occurred to any of them, four people lifted their heads to stare at Jeannie before they exchanged glances with one another.

'It were self-defence,' Fran mumbled through her swollen lips. 'He had a knife and Geoff tried to take it off him after he cut me. Look what he's done to me,' Fran moaned and opened her blouse to show the long gash on her belly.

'Ain't done yer face no favours either, love,' Jeannie observed as she frowned at the lump of flattened flesh that was Fran's nose. 'So you gonna get the police involved then, and hope for the best?'

'No . . . we ain't!' Tilly whispered forcefully, spitting blood. 'Not if we can help it. Could go bad for Geoff and he don't deserve to . . .' She stopped but everybody knew what she'd left unsaid.

A court case, a trial, a jury . . . Geoff could be found guilty of murder if things went against him.

'Ain't swingin' fer him,' Geoff said quietly. 'Ain't even risking getting locked away for that piece o' shit.'

Beside him Alice retched, and crossed her arms over her belly as though to contain its contents. Fresh tears dripped from her eyes.

'We got to somehow sort it out,' Tilly muttered, agitated, and knuckled again at her blurry vision.

'Looks like you need a favour doin' after all.' Jeannie dropped the bag that contained her unwanted clothes onto the table. 'Wish now I'd never bleedin' offered,' she wryly added. 'Can you get him down the stairs and out the back to the shit house?'

Geoff looked up, realising Jeannie was addressing him.

'Yeah,' He agreed automatically. 'I can do that.'

'Good. With luck I'll get him gone by morning.'

Geoff made a move to get up then sat down again and turned to Alice. 'I'll be going in the morning too, Al. Looks like I'm off to fight after all,' he said with a bleak, twisted smile.

Tilly slipped out into the back yard at dawn.

She'd not slept and neither had Fran. They'd done what they could to clean themselves up while Alice went down to tell Bobbie and Stevie that their mum had had a little accident and was going to sleep up in theirs. The boys had accepted the news, as they always did – wide-eyed and close-lipped. If they thought it odd that Alice looked weird and white and shaky they said nothing. No questions. They undressed quickly then huddled together in bed, whispering about their game of football.

Alice had wearily climbed the stairs again to join her mum and aunt. The three of them had lain down on the bed in the front room and waited for the dawn light so they could grapple with a new day. Dazed with shock and exhaustion there'd been no further conversation between them, just intermittent moans from Fran as her injuries throbbed and she tried to ease her position on the mattress.

Tilly raised a hesitant hand to the door of the shit house. Her eyes closed as she pulled it, groaning, open. It was vacant and stinking dirty as usual. Staggering relief swamped her. She shoved the door closed and leaned back against it for a moment. Then quickly she went back inside.

'Going to work Al?'

Alice nodded and looked at her mum. A dreadful question hovered in the air between them and it seemed neither could find the courage or energy to mention it. There were so many dreadful thoughts, urgent thoughts, battling for attention. A deceit, possibly of more than sixteen years standing, could wait a little longer.

'He's gone,' Tilly gruffly told Alice, eliminating one of the torturing uncertainties from her daughter's head. 'Jeannie's done what she promised. Gawd knows how . . .'

Alice nodded in thankfulness. Neither of them wanted to voice their dead tormentor's name but a train of thought had been set in motion, prompting Alice to plaintively burst out, 'Mum . . . what you said . . .?'

'Gotta go down 'n' see how Fran's coping with the boys,' Tilly brusquely interrupted. 'Reckon her wound needs stitches but doctors ask questions. See to Lucy for me if she wakes before you leave. I'll see you later.'

* * *

'I hoped you wouldn't go without saying goodbye.'

'Nah . . . wouldn't do that,' Geoff said and smiled at her through the iron railings. 'Got time for a little walk?'

Alice nodded vigorously. It was her dinnertime at the factory and she'd hoped and prayed that he'd be there as she emerged into autumn sunlight. Throughout the morning she'd worked like an automaton, shutting dreadful memories from her mind. She'd concentrated solely on whether she'd get a chance to see Geoff before he went away. She desperately wanted to see him and try to make him change his mind about going off to fight. As they started to walk along, Alice slipped her hand through the crook of his arm. Geoff glanced down then placed his fingers over hers.

Last night Geoff hadn't taken much notice of his injuries. He'd let Alice bathe away the blood and cover the wounds in clean rag. He'd taken up the offer of one of her dad's shirts too. He couldn't go home wearing his own and risk inevitable questions so he'd left it, torn and bloodstained, on the floor.

'Are your cuts hurting?' she asked in quiet concern. She had felt him wince just now as she touched him. 'Are they worse than we thought?'

'Nah . . . just scratches. Sting more'n anything.'

'I don't want you to go . . . you don't have to go,' Alice burst out with quiet passion.

'I do . . . you know I do, Al.' Geoff blinked to clear the moisture that had sprung to his eyes. 'I can't get locked up . . . or worse. I could swing for it if a jury saw it different to how it was.' He sniffed. 'I'd sooner take me chances in France, and if it's me turn to die . . .' He smiled down at her. 'At least it'd be for something worthwhile. At least me mum could feel proud instead of ashamed. Jimmy Wild ain't worth dying for.'

'Has your mum gone mad over you leaving?' Alice croaked through a throat that felt blocked with tears.

'Just a bit,' he said ruefully. It was his way of letting Alice know there'd been ructions in the Lovat household. His expression grew sober. 'They know I mean it. That's all I want them to know.' He slanted a glance down at Alice.

She nodded her understanding of what he'd left unspoken whilst the heel of a hand smeared over her wet cheeks. 'We all agreed, only us lot that was there will ever know what went on.' She paused before gulping out, 'Jeannie's done it somehow.'

'Yeah, I know. I was up watching for 'em. Looked like professionals. Knew what they was doing alright. In 'n' out real quick 'n' quiet. Used a handcart.'

Alice felt sick at knowing it, and immensely relieved. 'I'll do what I can for your family, promise,' she choked out through the painful lump in her throat. 'There's vacancies in Turner's. I'll ask the supervisor if you like; put in a word about your dad getting a job. You can earn well on nights.'

'Thanks.'

'Me mum'll do what she can for Margaret too, I know it.'

They passed an alley and Alice's step faltered. She tugged Geoff towards it and down the narrow path then looked up at him earnestly. 'Got so much I want to say to you,' she gasped out. 'Don't know how. Don't know how to say thanks or sorry or anything. I know I've not always been fair to you.' A rosy bloom warmed her cheeks. 'We could've been proper sweethearts sooner. I know that's what you wanted and it's not too late.'

'Thanks for the offer.' Geoff raised a hand to her face and cupped it tenderly. 'But I got a train to catch. Ain't got time for no canoodling with you, Alice Keiver.'

She flung herself at him, hugging him fiercely about the neck.

'Ain't risking getting you in the family way, much as I'd like to take you up on it,' he whispered against her soft hair. 'I ain't me brother, remember it. I love you and when I come back for you it'll be with a wedding ring.'

Alice plunged her mouth against his, trying to show him how much he meant to her and with sweet restraint he kissed her back.

'Make it up to you when you come back on leave, I will,' she said with a watery smile.

'I'm gonna keep you to that . . . so do you want to change yer mind?' Geoff asked hoarsely whilst a finger trembled, outlining her lips.

Their eyes locked and Alice felt a thrill ripple through her. She shook her head and went on tiptoe so their faces were close.

'Love you, I do,' she whispered, then plunged her mouth firmly on his. 'You're the best friend I ever had,' she murmured against his cheek when their mouths had parted.

Geoff gazed deep into her eyes and a tinge of sadness was in his voice as he croaked, 'Yeah . . . I know . . .'

'Just come by to see how you're doing.'

Tilly had cautiously opened the door a fraction, peeped around it, then let Jeannie in.

'You look better than expected, all things considered,' was Jeannie's verdict once she'd given Tilly the once-over.

Tilly grunted a humourless laugh and instinctively probed at her tender cheek with her finger. 'Just brewed. Want one?'

Jeannie nodded and took the tea. 'People are gonna be asking why you're in the state you are. Best give 'em an answer rather than let them find their own.'

It was sensible advice. Tilly knew that she and Fran couldn't hide indoors for many weeks till their faces healed.

'It's well-known round here that I done a runner a while back. Well-known too that you was well 'n' truly narked about it. Good enough reason for a fight between us, I reckon.'

Tilly chuckled faintly. 'So how come you got off so light? I'm known as a bruiser and you ain't got a mark on you.'

'Caught you at a bad time, didn't I?' Jeannie replied. 'On an evening when you was legless.'

Tilly's smile faded and she looked away. She knew if she hadn't been drunk when Jimmy turned up things might have turned out differently. She'd not been able to think straight or defend herself when he'd crept up to her door. Yet Jimmy was dead now and she couldn't but be thankful for that. 'I was pissed alright, so we're halfway there.'

'When I go I'll call you a few choice names and make it seem we're still at loggerheads. A bit of pushing 'n' shoving outside might be useful. Old Beattie's on watch, so let's give her something to look at. Your sister will need her own story. How's she look?' Jeannie tacked on the end.

'Bad; nose is broke and her belly needs to be stitched. She won't go to hospital. Best not to anyhow. Doctors'll be suspicious.'

'I know a quack who'll take a look at her. No questions.'

'Why you doin' all this for us?' Tilly's fierce demand flew through her fat lips. 'I let you have a poxy blouse, that's all. Weren't nuthin' special.'

'Were at the time,' Jeannie said succinctly and sipped from her tea. 'Where I come from we return favours best we can.'

'I take it your bloke got the body took away.' Having received a nod Tilly muttered with a frown, 'How d'you persuade him to get involved in something as bad as that?'

'Usual way,' Jeannie returned dryly.

Tilly chuckled until her cuts smarted.

'We was sweethearts way back, when we was little more'n

school kids,' Jeannie explained. 'Then I chose the wrong bloke and married Gordon Robertson instead of Johnny. Regretted it ever since. Johnny seemed a rough handful and Gordon seemed a charmer, but he turned nasty early on. By then Johnny had gone away. I hadn't seen him in fifteen years when we run into each other and hooked up again. Lucky it was that he never married.'

'Sounds like he never got over you. You must have him right round yer finger for him to do what he done that night.'

'Nah; weren't nuthin' for someone like him. Getting corpses shifted . . . just another day at the office for Johnny Blake.'

'You know what it's like to take a beating, don't you,' Tilly stated quietly.

Without a word Jeannie took off her smart jacket and opened her silk blouse. She moved her camisole aside exposing a breast . . . or what remained of it.

Tilly stared at the shrivelled scarlet skin and then raised sorrowful eyes to Jeannie.

'Me husband. Used an iron on me. Reckoned I'd been flirting . . . showin' off me tits.' She buttoned herself up again. 'I'd took it all up till then. Left with the boys the same day though I was fainting in pain. Kept going though till I got here.' She finished her tea and put the cup down on the table. 'Fuckin' good job actually that Johnny's an arse man.'

TWENTY-ONE

'So you can't suggest where your husband is or what might have happened to him in his absence?'

'Already said, ain't I, he'd left me. We're separated. Don't know nuthin' about what he gets up to no more. Don't care neither. You can ask anyone round here if you don't believe me. They all knew he'd cleared off to that tart Nellie Tucker.'

'Why wouldn't I believe you, Mrs Wild?' Constable Bickerstaff tapped his pencil on his notebook. Swiftly he started writing. He flicked a look up at Fran just as she cast an appealing look towards her sister.

Tilly was sitting at the table, nursing a cup of tea.

'You heard what she said. If you want to know about Jimmy, best get yourself down Finsbury Park and question Nellie,' Tilly suggested harshly.

'We intend to,' Constable Franks said. 'We've come first to inform next of kin.'

'You just said you ain't sure it's him you've found. Me sister might not be next of kin in that case.'

Ralph Franks coloured slightly beneath his colleagues' withering look. He'd jumped the gun on that one and he knew it. He coughed. 'That's right. We're not sure. It's a headless corpse . . .' He hesitated as he saw Mrs Wild gag. He received another glare from Bickerstaff.

'The man had obviously been in a fight and had been stabbed. He looks to have been your husband's size and height. He had a distinctive tattoo on his left arm that's still visible,' Constable Bickerstaff interjected. 'A snake . . . your husband had a tattoo like that as I recall, Mrs Wild.'

'Lots of men got snake tattoos,' Tilly butted in and put an arm about her sister's heaving shoulders. 'Get going, will you. You've upset her now and it might not even be for a good reason.'

Twitch stared thoughtfully at his notes while he pondered on making the request. The body wasn't a pretty sight. It had obviously been in the water for weeks. He knew too that what the women had said about Jimmy Wild and the tart was true. He could recall the street fight that had gone on between these two women and Nellie Tucker when Jimmy had first started knocking about with the prostitute. He decided to ask the question. 'Would you be able to identify your husband's body from that snake tattoo, Mrs Wild?'

Fran shook her head vigorously and suddenly swung around to spurt vomit on the floor.

'Look what you've done to her!' Tilly blasted. 'Why should she look at it? Might be someone else's old man.'

Constable Franks studied the mellowing bruising on Fran's face. He then looked at similar yellowing on her sister's cheek. They'd taken a beating at about the same time, it seemed. As the bruises were quite faded he'd guess that they'd got them at about the same time Jimmy Wild – if it was him – got dumped in the Thames. 'You two been scrapping?' he asked dryly.

'Yeah . . .'

'No . . .'

'Well, which is it?' Bickerstaff asked with a spasm. He

knew what Franks was thinking. He'd already mulled that one over. He knew that Jimmy liked to use his fists. He knew he'd frequently set about his wife and kids, although he'd never known him to assault his sister-in-law. But Jack Keiver had gone to war and was no longer able to protect his wife from a man who got off on punching women.

'I had a fight a few weeks back,' Tilly blurted, keen to disperse the awkward quiet that had settled on the room. 'Woman called Jeannie Robertson did a flit owing back rent and got me in the shit over it all with me guvnor. She's been back here, ain't she, and I went for her over it.'

'You came off worst by the looks of things,' Bickerstaff remarked. He knew that Tilly Keiver could hold her own in a fight so he remained sceptical. But she'd given him a line of enquiry if he cared to check.

'And you?' He turned his attention to Fran. 'Were you helping to even the score with this . . . er . . .' He referred to his notes. 'Jeannie Robertson?' The sorry sight of Fran's wonky nose drew his eyes.

'Not me,' Fran said. 'Ain't my business.'

'She fell down the stairs here, pissed,' Tilly stated. 'Been drinking too heavy since that bastard up 'n' left her with the kids and no money.'

Bickerstaff glanced thoughtfully at the floor then put away his book. 'Well, I think that's all. If the necessary evidence that it is your husband . . .' This time Bickerstaff looked a trifle embarrassed. The proof they needed was a severed head, and referring to it had made Fran look as though she might again throw up. Briskly the two police constables took their leave, stepping daintily to avoid the mess on the boards.

Outside in the street the police officers started walking immediately in the direction of Lennox Road. Stares and catcalls followed them. They'd been seen going into the tenement house. Now quite a crowd had gathered to watch for them to leave. Rozzers weren't liked walking the streets round here. They certainly weren't wanted poking around inside the houses.

'I reckon they're lying and know more than they're letting on. I reckon they might be guilty as hell.'

'Yeah?' Bickerstaff answered sardonically. 'What makes you say that?'

'Wild's given the two of them a painful seeing-to once too often and they've had enough. They've got someone to make sure it doesn't happen again. If they managed to catch him unawares they could even have done it themselves.'

Ralph's eyes slid sideways as they passed the Whittons' house. Of course he knew that Connie wasn't in there. She hadn't moved back with her family when he kicked the lying, cheating whore out of his parents' home. She'd moved into a swish apartment in the West End provided by her rich lover. He should have known that, having been bred in this dump, she'd be a no-good greedy tart out to take him for a ride. After she'd got her claws into him he'd even risked his career and his liberty trying to increase his earnings to buy her what she wanted. He'd become a bent copper for the bitch! Ralph's eyes swerved ahead again, a bitter sneer visibly distorting his mouth.

Bickerstaff had noticed the change in his colleague's demeanour and he understood the reason for it. Ralph Franks had been the butt of ribald humour at the station when word got around that his fiancée had been humping an old man. 'You don't want to let any personal grievances get in the way of how you judge people around here,' he said. 'The Whittons and the Keivers might be neighbours but they're not necessarily out of the same mould . . .'

'Shut up, will you,' Ralph snarled, his face darkening in rage. 'It's got nothing to do with you.'

'Take it easy . . .' Bickerstaff shrugged. 'All I was going

to say is, be careful how you approach this investigation or you'll give some of them back at the station a reason to start chin-wagging all over again. I'll let you know my theory on it all, shall I?'

'If you want to, go ahead,' Ralph muttered and averted his florid face. The old bastard always had something to say that got too near the mark.

'This is Campbell Bunk we're talking about here, so if every woman who'd had a fight with a neighbour – or an ex-neighbour – or every person who got drunk and went arse over tit down the stairs got arrested because they look a bit bashed-up and suspicious, we'd run out of cells to house them all in under an hour.' He clasped his hands behind his back. 'Mrs Wild's distress was genuine enough; I've got the proof of that stuck to my shoes.' He glanced with a grimace of distaste at vomit-spattered leather. 'It's a coincidence that those two look like they've come a cropper about the same time as Jimmy.' Bickerstaff frowned thoughtfully. 'I reckon we'll find the answer to all of this from Nellie. If it is Wild . . . and it probably is . . . I think he got into trouble trying to punch above his weight. I've made a few enquiries here and there with nonces that know what goes on. Saul Bateman's got involved in a prostitution ring. He's been pimping for Nellie. I think Nellie got involved with him while she was still with Jimmy. Jimmy wouldn't have liked sharing Nellie's money three ways. In fact a little dickie bird told me that a fight between the two men took place in Nellie's flat, and Bateman was heard threatening to kill him next time. Jimmy was spotted running off with blood on his face and his tail between his legs.'

'Saul Bateman?' Ralph had gone pale.

'Yeah; he might be a second-rate rogue but he's a nasty piece of work nevertheless. Jimmy wasn't in the same league. If Jimmy refused to bow out gracefully when he was told to, he was a bloody fool. Saul wouldn't have any qualms about making mincemeat out of Wild and feeding him to the fishes.'

'I told you not to come here.'

'Yeah, I know what you told me. I remember what I told you 'n' all. I ain't caring for Mum on me own no more.' Sarah Whitton glowered at her sister Connie. 'Gonna let me in, then? Or we going to have a chat about it right here? Don't matter to me. I'll do it here . . . there . . . anywhere . . .'

Connie chewed her lower lip in frustration, regretting the day she had ever let either of her sisters know where she was living. She'd only passed on her address in case Ralph might come by Campbell Road, asking after her. She'd cherished a hope that he might perhaps send her a message via her family, or write to her because he wanted to know how she was.

Their parting had been extremely bitter; her pleas for another chance, her apologies for being greedy and stupid, had all been chucked back in her face. Connie had known what he'd really wanted to give her was a right-hander for making him a laughing stock in front of his family and his colleagues in the force. So she'd stayed with Mr Lucas, let him spoil her, as he liked to put it. But she knew it was only a matter of time before the old goat was spoiling someone else.

'Shove off,' Connie spat through her teeth at Sarah. 'Me bloke will be here soon and he won't want to see the likes of you hangin' around making the place look untidy.'

'It's *you* don't want the likes of me hangin' around,' Sarah snapped back. 'Scared he might take a fancy to me, are yer?' she sneered.

A spontaneous laugh erupted from Connie. 'Sod me, if he did I'd know his sight's failing along with the rest of him.

You seen yourself lately?' She gave her younger sister a derisive top-to-toe inspection. Sarah had a pleasant face but her figure was skinny and flat-chested. Today she had scraped her lank, mousy hair back from her features into a drooping bun. As for her clothes . . . it looked as though the rag shop in Fonthill was still getting her custom.

'Fresh meat though, ain't I?' Sarah jibed, fired with indignation. Connie's contempt hurt because it was genuine. But she'd wiped the smile from her sister's face with that last comment. From Connie's reaction Sarah guessed her sugar daddy had a roving eye. Knowing it unsettled Sarah too. She wanted Connie in clover almost as much as Connie did herself.

Connie's apartment was on the first floor of an elegant whitewashed building on the outskirts of Mayfair. Having just climbed a wide, curving stairway Sarah now took a glance about the luxuriously carpeted hallway where was to be found apartment number twenty-three. When she'd turned up a short while ago the porter had given her the once-over followed by a threatening finger indicating the exit. It was a different doorman to the one who'd been on duty last time she'd called. This one was a burly hatchet-faced type. Sarah had thought he might kick her out but he'd reluctantly let her pass when she'd said her sister lived at number twenty-three and then carried on to describe Connie.

Hatchet-face had known her alright. Connie had always been a looker; with fine clothes and expensive grooming at her disposal she was beautiful. Even the scowl distorting her features couldn't disguise that fact.

'Get in here then fer Gawd's sake, before someone sees you,' Connie whispered in exasperation. Her eyes darted to left and right to spot if a nosy neighbour might be observing them.

Sarah whipped past her sister, a satisfied expression on her face. As she entered the scented apartment Sarah wondered how Connie's gentleman friend liked taking her out and about in company when she spoke the way she did. Perhaps he didn't give a hoot . . . or perhaps he'd warned her to keep her gob shut. Sarah was old enough to know a sugar daddy didn't keep a girl in style so he could listen to her gabbing.

It was the second time Sarah had visited Connie here but the first time she'd been allowed over the threshold. The last time she'd turned up at a bad moment and Connie, on opening the door in just a flimsy silk wrap, had looked like she might faint in shock. Sarah had glimpsed at a distance some little old man with silvery hair peering down the hall at her. Sarah never had found out what yarn Connie had given him. Probably she'd said she was the char or some such thing.

Now Sarah stood in the sitting room gawping at the wonderful things her sister enjoyed. A glittering chandelier was above her head; plush, deep carpet beneath her feet. A pair of huge velvet-covered sofas were scattered with cream silk cushions that had tassels and beads that caught the light. Slowly Sarah caressed the cool jewels, ran her fingers through the silky fringes. She moved on to where a small side table held a long-stemmed glass half-full of what looked like a gin and tonic with a piece of lemon floating in it. Connie snatched it up and downed it in two gulps as though scared her sister might get to it first.

'Done alright, 'n't yer?' Sarah finally sourly observed.

'Yeah. And that's the way it's staying so say your piece and get going.' Connie put the back of a hand to her moist mouth. 'Mr Lucas'll be here any minute.'

'Mr Lucas?' Sarah chortled. 'Is that what you call him?'

'He likes me to be formal with him . . . respectful, he calls it. Gentlemen that age got manners 'n' things,' Connie continued defensively.

'Got money 'n' things 'n' all, some of them old gentlemen like your Mr Lucas,' Sarah jibed.

'He's a nice old stick; treats me well anyhow,' Connie snapped.

'Yeah . . . I can see,' Sarah replied with increasing sarcasm as she deliberately studied evidence of Connie's lucrative profession.

'Oh . . . just piss off, will you.' Connie flounced about.

'I will, don't worry, soon as I've told you what I want,' Sarah said. 'And just in case you think I'm pickin' on you 'cos you've turned flash and tarty I'll tell you now I'm going after Louisa 'n' all over this.'

'You're going after Louisa, are you?' Connie twisted about and hooted in amusement. 'Weren't so long ago you was scared witless of her.'

Sarah reddened but jutted her chin. 'I was a kid then. Now I ain't. I'm working me fingers to the bone full-time and I ain't giving up all me wages to that old cow indoors so's she can lay on the couch and swig from a bottle all day. It's time you 'n' Louisa took a turn shellin' out for her.'

'Or what you going to do? Get your own place?' Connie crowed. 'Got enough put by from packing biscuits to set up on your own, have you?'

'Yeah,' Sarah lied. 'I have. Me and Alice Keiver have been talking about it for a while. She's had enough in hers and I've had a bellyful in ours. If you don't give me a decent bit of cash to help out Mum's getting left on her own.'

'You wouldn't dare,' Connie taunted. She knew that Sarah and Alice were close friends. They'd bunked together before when Sarah went to live at the Keivers' for a while. Connie had got out of The Bunk and intended never to return. She was selfish enough to leave Sarah to deal with their mother, but she wasn't heartless. Their mother might not survive long if abandoned in that fleapit. 'You wouldn't dare go off 'n' leave her on her own,' she repeated, less chirpily.

'Watch me,' Sarah challenged. 'You and Louisa have got away with blue murder long enough. You've both pissed off and not even lobbed half a crown my way to help out every so often. It's you and Louisa's in the wrong and you know it.'

'How much d'you want?' Connie grabbed up her bag from the sofa and scrabbled inside. She wanted her sister to go and leave her in peace so she could numb herself with a few more gins before Mr Lucas turned up and put her to work. A handful of silver was thrust towards Sarah.

'That's not enough.' Sarah cast a withering look at Connie's fistful of coins. 'That's taking the piss . . .' She suddenly broke off as there came a loud knock.

'That him?' Sarah whispered, her eyes widening in alarm.

Connie's panic was evident in the way her head had jerked towards the door. 'It's too early. Anyhow he's got a key,' she mouthed. She took a few hesitant steps down the hall then turned to hiss, 'Stay there, out of sight, just in case . . .'

Sarah did as she was told but felt lightly amused. What was Connie expecting her to do if it was the old geezer? Hide behind the couch?

'Gawd's sake! What is this? Piccadilly Circus or something?'

That raucous complaint from Connie drew Sarah to the doorway of the sitting room. Her spirits plummeted as she saw her sister Louisa stomping over the threshold.

'What you doing here?' Louisa snarled at her over Connie's silken shoulder.

'Could ask you the same thing,' Sarah flung back as her shapeless lump of a sister bore down on her. She went back into the sitting room, Louisa and Connie following close behind her.

Connie planted her manicured fingers on her slender hips and cast a frustrated look heavenward. 'Two minutes . . . then if yers ain't gone willing I'm calling downstairs and having yers thrown out.'

Now her slob of a sister's odour was fouling the atmosphere the room seemed to have lost most of its gloss. Sarah was as keen to be gone as Connie was to be rid of her. But she wanted what she'd come for: a decent sum of money and a promise of more in the future. Considering the lifestyle Connie now had Sarah knew she'd be a mug to settle for less than a fiver today.

Connie must have got downwind of her fat sister too for she wrinkled her nose and wafted a hand in front of her face. ''Struth! How long since you had a bath, Lou?'

'What's she doing here?' Louisa ignored the implication that she stank. Her greasy head jabbed forward to indicate Sarah.

'She's come for money and she wants some off you 'n' all. Ain't that right, Sar?' Connie elevated her plucked eyebrows, her expression mischievous. 'She's going to move in with Alice Keiver and leave Mum to fend for herself if we don't chip in.'

If Connie had been expecting Louisa to immediately cut up rough she was to be disappointed. Louisa looked Sarah up and down. 'You 'n' Alice in love?'

'What?' Sarah frowned in startled incomprehension.

'She thinks you might be queer . . . like she is,' Connie explained whilst picking at a frayed fingernail. She glanced up and snorted back a laugh. Sarah's dawning comprehension was slowly transforming her youthful features in to a mask of utter revulsion. 'Well, let's face it, no bloke was ever going to fancy her, was he?'

'Give us a fiver and I'll get going. For now.' Sarah extended a palm. She quickly moved towards the door.

'Ain't got a fiver.'

On hearing that both Sarah and Louisa cast on Connie an extremely old-fashioned look. All things considered it seemed like a blatant lie.

'It's true,' Connie exclaimed. 'I don't have much money.' She whirled a hand about at the lavish surroundings. 'None of this is mine, is it? I have to get everything I want on his accounts; clothes, make-up, grub. Even the bleedin' hairdresser sends him in a bill. Don't think he trusts me with me own money. He's a tight fist with his cash.'

'Thought he were a nice old stick.' Sarah sarcastically reminded Connie of her recent praise for Mr Lucas.

'He's not bad as punters go,' Louisa butted in. 'Plenty worse'n him.'

'How d'you know?' Sarah demanded. Her eyes veered between her sisters. 'How does she know?' she asked Connie, bewildered. 'You introduced her to Mr Lucas?'

A snort of mock horror erupted from Connie. 'He ain't never seen her, thank Gawd, but she knows punters alright. Her lady friend's on the game up west.'

A sullen stare from Louisa met that sly dig at her love life and her employment as a pimp.

'So what you after this time?' Connie asked Louisa. 'And if it's money you can sod off along with her.' She flicked her head at Sarah.

'Want a decent dress ter borrer if you've got one going spare.'

Sarah stuffed a fist to her mouth to stifle her spontaneous hilarity. 'You'll never squeeze in Con's dresses, you silly fat mare.'

'Ain't fer me, is it?' Louisa snarled, her face contorting in rage and her fists clenching. 'It's for me friend, Sonia. She's got a special on tonight and needs to look the part.' Louisa knew that a ruckus in Connie's lovely sitting room was out of the question. She visibly made an effort to control herself and turned her back on Sarah.

'Sonia?' Sarah echoed. Inwardly she digested that Sonia must be Louisa's lady friend who tonight had a special punter to entertain.

Sarah hadn't seen or heard from Louisa in many months. And that was the way she liked it. They might be sisters but Sarah was quite sure she hated the ugly slob. She'd been on the receiving end of most of Louisa's bullying over the years. Connie was closer to Louisa in age and had been able to give back almost as good as she got. And that was encouraged in Bunk kids. It was their duty, as far as their parents were concerned, to stick up for themselves. It was especially true when family pride was at stake and they were expected to win scraps with neighbours' kids. Children were often to be seen being dragged up or down the street by their elders to confront an opponent and settle an argument with their fists in full view of an appreciative audience. Louisa and Lenny, God rest his soul, had been their father's pride and joy in that respect.

'Give us the cash so's I can get on me way,' Sarah pleaded.

'Christ's sake! How times I got to say I don't have a fiver!' Connie automatically reached for her glass, forgetting it was empty. She banged it down on the table again in frustration. 'Here! Have something to take down the pawnshop. But you'd better make sure it comes back sharp.' She twisted about, eyes darting here and there, then snatched up a figurine from the mantelshelf and thrust it at Sarah.

Sarah contemptuously waggled the shepherdess in her hand. 'That's no good! How much is it worth?' She studied the porcelain more carefully.

'I dunno, do I?' Connie fumed. 'Well take this 'n' all! Just get lost before Mr Lucas turns up and kicks the lot of us out!'

Sarah stuffed the two ornaments into her bag. She could tell Connie was getting frantic and close to tears. Louisa was looking anxious too. They all wanted the same thing: Mr Lucas kept sweet for as long as possible, so he'd keep Connie for as long as possible, and they might all benefit from the randy old goat.

'I'll get you something out me wardrobe,' Connie flung at Louisa. She whirled towards the bedroom door, knuckling her eyes. Before she disappeared she hissed over a shoulder, 'Then get going and don't come back here no more.'

'Are we goin' . . . going to go out for dinner this evening, Mr Lucas?' Connie tried very hard to remember to talk properly, as she'd been instructed. She remembered what else she had to do too to please him. Her small pink tongue circled her lips wetly and she snuggled up to him on the sofa. Her eyes focused steadily on the buttons on his smart dark jacket. Despite the sight of his spindly white legs being quite repulsive, her eyes were often involuntarily drawn to them. 'I am so very hungry for something nice to eat,' she recited in a breathy tone then exaggeratedly sucked a thumb.

'Are you, my dear?' the silver-haired gentleman asked in his quiet, cultured voice. 'Well, let's see if Mr Lucas can do something about that for his little girl. What do you fancy to eat?'

'I'd like a nice juicy steak, please sir, if I may.'

Mr Lucas rubbed the backs of his freckled fingers over Connie's smooth, flushed cheek. 'Would you indeed?' he purred. His arm crept along the back of the velvet sofa and he tugged her closer to him. 'I think my little girl is greedy. I'm not sure you shall have steak.'

Connie lifted wide eyes to his face and blinked rapidly.

'Have you been naughty, my dear, while I've been away?'

Connie put a hand to a hot cheek, glad the old fool would

think her blush meant she was excited rather than guilty. She nodded, while his bony fingers tightened on her neck, slunk over a shoulder to squeeze a breast beneath silk. Connie steeled herself not to wince as he tugged at her nipple. Her eyes darted to the mantelpiece. She was sure he hadn't looked once in that direction or noticed anything missing. It would be best to work hard to distract him and make sure it stayed that way. The atmosphere was cloying, heavy with scent, making it hard for her to breathe. She'd sprayed so much perfume around the sitting room to cover Louisa's stink that she'd have to ask him to buy her a new bottle.

'Naughty girls don't get steak, do they?' Mr Lucas cooed against her cheek, his fingers writhing on her breast. 'What do naughty little girls get?'

'Something better,' Connie whispered before her head lowered towards his naked groin.

TWENTY-TWO

'It's a right pretty little thing.' Alice touched a finger to the smooth porcelain. She took the shepherdess from Sarah's hand and turned it over, examining it, before putting the statue on the table next to its mate. 'Reckon they're worth a bob or two.'

'Yeah; but not round here. Who in Campbell Road's going to have enough spare to buy a shepherd and shepherdess to stick on the mantelpiece?'

'You'd be best off taking them up west to a pawnbrokers that posh people use.'

''Spose . . .' Sarah sighed. 'All I asked for was a fiver and the crafty cow's give me these buggers to shift instead.'

Alice levelled on her friend a dubious look. All the while she'd been admiring the dainty china a worry had been in her mind. Had Sarah been narked enough by Connie's refusal to hand over some cash to have stolen them? Even to Alice's inexperienced eye they looked to be rare and valuable things.

'You're not going to get in bad trouble over this, Sar, are you?' Alice frowned at the beautiful ornaments. She knew Sarah was always broke. Sometimes she didn't have a few coppers left from her wages to buy herself something to eat in her factory dinner break. Alice was constantly paying Sarah's way for her in the café or lending her a little bit so she could nip to the shop for tea or bread. 'You've not pinched 'em off Connie, have you?'

''Course not,' Sarah declared, indignant. 'Connie said her Mr Lucas is a tight-fisted old git and won't give her no money of her own. She's got no cash to help out with Mum so she's given me these to pawn. If she gets in trouble over it with him that's her look-out.' Sarah flicked at the base of one of the ornaments before adding charitably, 'Mr Lucas can't be that bad; you want to see where he lets her live, Al.' Sarah shook her head slowly, her expression veering between wonder and envy. 'Quite close to Hyde Park, she is, in a place wot's got a doorman and carpets right along the passages. Got one of those big shiny lights in her sitting room, she has, all made of glass drops; and two long sofas covered in blue velvet with masses of cushions on top, some even got beads 'n' tassels on them. Never seen anything so lovely as them cushions.' Sarah plonked her elbows on the table and rested her chin in her hands. 'He's a horrible little pipsqueak though, he is. I know 'cos I've seen him before. Must be fifty or even might be sixty, with grey hair and a thin weasel sort of face. But Con reckons he's good to her.'

Alice grimaced in a way that made words unnecessary.

'Yeah, I know. I couldn't do it neither,' Sarah said. 'Ain't enough fancy cushions in the world to make me do that!' She frowned in revulsion as another memory struck her. 'You'll never guess what's even worse . . . Louisa's turned queer. Her and some woman have set up together down Finsbury Park. This Sonia's on the game and Louisa's acting as her pimp. Turns your stomach, don't it, just thinkin' about it?'

'Quick! Put them away!' Alice hissed, abruptly interrupting Sarah. She shoved the two ornaments towards her friend.

It was a Saturday morning and they were sitting at the table in the Keivers' front room. Alice had heard her mother's key just go into the lock. If Tilly caught sight of Sarah's booty she'd know straight off it was worth a bit and wheedle to buy it for a pittance. Alice knew that Sarah was daft enough, and desperate enough for a bit of cash, to let her have it, too.

The figurines were swiftly slipped inside Sarah's bag.

'Thought you two would be off out down the market this morning.' Tilly dumped a bottle of milk on the table and turned to give Lucy, who was grizzling, a light cuff round the ear. 'Lovely morning, it is,' she carried on. 'Sun's out . . . quite warm for this time o' the year . . .'

'What's up with you?' Alice softly asked her sister. She'd immediately sprung up from the table and pulled little Lucy down to sit beside her on the bed. She gently eased Lucy's head onto her shoulder and soothingly stroked her hair.

'We was just going off down the market, Mrs K,' Sarah said, sending Alice a speaking look.

'Well, you can take Lucy with you,' Tilly ordered Alice, ignoring Sarah's disappointed look on learning they were to be burdened with a kid. 'She's been under me feet and whining all morning. Get her out of me sight fer a while or I'll give her something to snivel over.'

'Can't stay out long, Sar, I don't think Lucy's feeling well.'

Alice and Sarah had been walking through the market browsing the stalls, keeping an eye out for a trader who looked likely to be interested in boosting his stock by buying Sarah's china figures with no questions asked. But Alice had been aware for a good while that Lucy was dragging her feet and pulling back on her hand. Her little sister was now grizzling again, and loud enough to make people frown and mutter at them. Alice bent down to examine Lucy's face and was quite concerned to notice a feverish flush on her cheeks. She put a hand to Lucy's brow. It was very hot. She gave her sister a cuddle and whispered, 'Let's get you home, shall we?'

'Hello . . . who's making all that noise?'

Alice turned her head to see Jeannie Robertson a yard or so away, smiling down at her and Lucy. Alice hadn't seen Jeannie since the dreadful night Jimmy had attacked them, but she knew that Jeannie had been back just after that awful episode to see her mother and tie up tight any loose ends. The further the horror receded into the past, the more Alice allowed herself to believe her mother's reassurances that Jimmy was gone and forgotten and the coppers wouldn't be back to bother them any more.

Alice slowly rose from her crouching position and returned Jeannie's smile, feeling awkward and nervous. What did you say to a person you barely knew but who had nevertheless, to return a simple favour, helped cover up a killing and dispose of a dead body? Alice realised Jeannie was just being friendly. She'd been passing, heard Lucy howling – as had everybody in the vicinity – and had stopped because she felt a bit sorry for her. It would be daft to suppose the woman might be about to comment on the carnage they'd both witnessed that night, especially considering Sarah's presence.

'Don't think she's feeling too well.' Alice placed a hand on Lucy's hair. 'Taking her back home to get her into bed. Reckon she's caught a chill.'

'Best place for her if she's brewing something up,' Jeannie agreed. 'How's your mum doing?'

'Alright, thanks.'

'Your aunt Fran?'

'Yeah . . . she's doing alright too.'

A wail erupted from Lucy and she clung to Alice's legs, burrowing her snotty little nose against her big sister's coat.

'I'm gonna have to go and take her home, Sar. She's poorly alright.'

Sarah gave a long, irritated sigh. ''Spose I'll have to carry on on me own then. I want to get shot of these as soon as I can.' She impatiently twitched the bag she held. 'I'm fed up of lugging them about.' She peered inside at the troublesome china. 'Might try down Solly's secondhand shop if the pawnbroker won't give me what I want for them.'

Alice shrugged and started off home, leading Lucy by the hand. A moment later she felt compelled to look back. She saw that Sarah had opened the bag containing the ornaments and was showing them to Jeannie. An odd feeling stirred in the pit of Alice's stomach. She wished Sarah had just left the bloody things at home. Of course she knew why she hadn't done so. If Alice had been given such nice things to pawn she wouldn't have left them indoors either for her mother to find. Another glance over her shoulder and she saw Sarah and Jeannie move to a secluded spot by a wall. It was obvious they'd repositioned so Jeannie could take a better look at Sarah's treasure without any passers-by getting a gander at it too. Alice lifted her shoulders in an imperceptible shrug. Jeannie was smartly turned out. She looked to be still riding high. If she had the seven pounds Sarah wanted for the ornaments why shouldn't she buy them? In fact Alice knew that Sarah had been prepared to haggle and accept four pounds for a quick no-questions-asked deal. As Lucy's distress increased Alice stooped and picked her up in her arms despite the fact that she was quite a weight to carry. She hurried on home with her sister bawling against her shoulder and the thought in her head that it wasn't her business what Sarah did with her ornaments.

* * *

'You're drinking rather too much too often, my dear.'

'So what if I am?' Connie had impetuously snarled that, her judgement clouded by the amount of alcohol she'd swallowed during the afternoon. Even in her semi-inebriated state she realised she'd acted rashly. She gave Mr Lucas an appealing little smile that mingled her apology and welcome.

With every week that passed it was becoming harder to act the girlish flirt to keep him sweet. She'd been lounging, dishevelled, on the sofa wearing silk pyjamas and reading a journal when she'd glimpsed his dapper little figure stationed in the doorway. Now, with the support of the chair back, she got rather unsteadily to her feet. Inwardly she cursed that she hadn't heard the old duffer arrive. If only he'd stick to turning up when he was supposed to she'd be prepared for him and done up to the nines.

She was coming to suspect he might be checking up on her. Once or twice when he'd startled her by creeping in she'd felt so irritated by his weedy, unwanted presence she'd nearly swung around and given him a slap. But even when she was gin-dulled she knew when to button her lip and cosy up to him. She tried to do so now but he shrugged her off, his top lip curling, as though she disgusted him. He strutted off to pour a small whisky from the decanter. Connie weaved after him and again tried to entwine their limbs and mould her pelvis against his.

'I'm a little weary, my dear.' His clipped tone sounded bored. His fingers drummed on the mantelshelf.

'If you're tired shall we go straight to bed, sir?' Connie suggested in a slurring lisp. Her frantic tongue darted over her lips before she butted them against one of his dry cheeks. Her small tongue teased over his ear, recoiling from the bristles it encountered.

'I don't think so. You see, it's *you* who is making me tired. *Sick* and tired,' he stressed before tipping the shot of whisky down his throat. 'I think it's high time you moved out.' Again Mr Lucas avoided her gin fumes and her persistent clasp. 'Let me tell you why you weary me, Connie,' he added, calmly swatting her off again. 'I didn't mind that occasionally your sisters came here to visit you . . . oh yes, I know about that. The porter, Jenkins, told me two coarse young women describing themselves thus have been here quite recently. I don't even mind putting up with your deplorable lack of breeding.' That was the truth. In Gilbert Lucas's experience ambitious young gutter sluts made excellent paramours. They would strive to postpone their tumble back in to squalor by being amenable to providing any sexual service he suggested. The good life once tasted was as heady as any drug to such girls. Unfortunately, his experience had also taught him that common tarts often drank, lied and stole more than their classier counterparts.

He'd recognised Connie Whitton's ambition and her allure from the first moment he'd clapped eyes on her. She'd been with her fiancé at the time but had nevertheless responded slyly to his admiration when they'd been introduced at a family party. Ralph's mother had made little effort to conceal the fact that she despised her future daughter-in-law because she was beneath them. Gilbert had been attending the party with his wife but that hadn't deterred the little minx from encouraging his interest in her. After a seemingly innocent invitation from him to dance, in full view of their partners, they had enjoyed a waltz. Connie had immediately agreed to meet him for lunch later in the week. And so their affair had started.

Now Gilbert regretted getting involved with her and wasn't sure why he had. A sixteen-year-old virgin was his preference when taking on a new mistress. Connie Whitton didn't qualify on either count. She'd said she was eighteen but he guessed her to be at least twenty. But Connie had an angelic face, a heavenly body and an impish nature that had appealed to Gilbert. Although she was saucy and knowing she was not a particularly skilled lover. But she'd made up for that with her enthusiasm, at first. Now she was getting too familiar and too comfortable. She thought she could relax because she had it made. He was about to shatter the silly girl's illusions.

He knew it was his own fault that he'd lost his Dresden china. He should have removed the figures before Connie took up residence. He'd been neglectful because the two previous girls he'd allowed to live in the apartment had left them untouched. Neither of them had given any indication that they appreciated the figurines' quality or value. They had been more eager to filch the silver teaspoons or condiments, no doubt thinking that small items that disappeared went unnoticed. Gilbert Lucas noticed everything and, when it was the right time, he used that knowledge to his advantage. When he'd finished with a mistress she always went quietly rather than face a police investigation.

The figures were his wife's property and had come to her as heirlooms. She'd disliked them and had asked Gilbert to sell them. He'd given her fifty pounds and told her that was what they'd made at auction. He had been therefore reluctant to take them home again and explain that he'd lied. He'd also have needed a yarn as to where they'd been housed since they'd been removed from the china cabinet. Gilbert had an eye for a good investment and knew that such fine, early pieces would increase in value over time.

Obviously he had underestimated Connie. She'd stolen the most valuable items in the place then not had the sense to pre-empt and soothe his suspicions with a tale about them getting knocked over and broken. He'd been waiting for her to come out with that pathetic excuse. Forlornly he'd hoped she might have pawned them and would soon replace them.

They'd been missing for a week. He wasn't prepared to wait any longer to find out what the little bitch had done with them. Impatiently he swiped Connie off as she again clung to his arm. She bounced back onto the sofa and looked stunned by the power he'd used to propel her onto her back.

'What's up?' Connie gasped, frightened. 'Won't yer tell me what I done?'

'No! *You* tell *me* what yer done.' He viciously mimicked her whining accent. 'I'd like to know where my Dresden pieces are, Connie.'

'Eh?' Connie frowned and raked her fingers against her forehead as though it might help unscramble her befuddled thoughts. 'What you on about?'

'I'm on about my figurines, my dear.'

Realisation dawned on Connie, making her jaw unattractively slacken as she ferreted for some excuse. 'Got broke . . . they got broke,' she spluttered. 'I know what you mean now. The little shepherds . . . they got broke. Sorry.'

'Got broke, did they?' he parodied. 'So why are they listed as entries in an auction catalogue?' Gilbert didn't know that for sure but he guessed that was where they would end up. Any pawnbroker or dealer worth his salt would know to put them up for the highest bidder. The idea of buying back his own property infuriated him. 'You've sold my Dresden, haven't you?' he hissed through his teeth. 'One thing I won't tolerate is a thieving whore.'

'I ain't lied or fieved!' Connie lied, her cheeks reddening and her bottom lip trembling. She struggled to sit up straight and concentrate.

'You can tell the police that.'

'No!' Connie screamed and shot to her feet. 'Alright . . . I gave them to me sister to pawn,' she rattled off. 'She wanted money for me mum 'cos she's poorly, 'n' as you never let me have none,' she slung at him a blaming look before continuing, 'I give her them ornaments.' She hung her head. 'I didn't know you was so attached to them.' Her lids fluttered up and she peeped at him appealingly. 'I'll make it up to you . . .'

Gilbert barked a laugh. 'If you understood their value, my dear, you'd know just how stupid you sound.'

'I'll get her to bring 'em back.' Connie nervously twisted together her fingers. 'I'll go and see her and fetch 'em back for you.'

'That's my good girl.' Gilbert smiled and approached her. He patted his thin fingers on her cheek and momentarily allowed Connie to playfully catch one between her lips. A moment later five fingers had pinched on her chin and jerked it up. 'Get dressed and go and tell her now,' he ordered silkily.

'Can't I go tomorrow?' Desperately Connie slid a hand to the puny bump between his legs. She sensed that, whether she got the china back or not, unless she was very careful her good times might be over. She sagged to her knees and unbuttoned his fly.

As her head bounced and bobbed and her teeth and tongue worked determinedly a ferocious hatred for her sister Sarah welled in her mind. It would be Sarah's fault if she lost all she'd gained. If she hadn't come here whining for cash the blasted figures would still be on the mantelpiece. It would never have occurred to Connie to risk all she had by stealing from Mr Lucas. Her rising anger made her unusually energetic and the hot spurt hit the back of her throat early, making her gag. Quickly she swallowed, choked and swallowed again, her face lowered and screwed up against the sour muck in her mouth. As she retched he strolled off, buttoning himself up.

'Fetch them back, Connie, or I'll fetch the police.' He was already in the hallway when he called out to her, 'Go and get them now, my dear. I'll be back for them tomorrow. Oh . . . and if you fail, make sure you're packed and ready to leave. I'll have Jenkins downstairs assist you, if necessary.'

TWENTY-THREE

'Is Saul Bateman here?'

'No, he ain't; what d'you want?' Nellie balefully eyed the copper. He was out of uniform but she recognised him from walking the beat in Campbell Road. She'd never seen him nosing around here before. Certainly Saul hadn't mentioned him. 'What are you after him for?' she repeated, trying to close the door to her flat and keep him out.

Ralph Franks wedged his large leather boot on the threshold. 'It's urgent business, so if he's in there you'd best fetch him.'

'He's not here, I tell you,' Nellie protested, banging the bottom of the door against his foot.

'When you see him tell him Franks needs to speak to him.' Ralph removed his boot, allowing Nellie to slam the door in his face. He stomped back down the flight of stairs and into the dusk. His heart was hammering with anxiety and frustration. He'd taken a chance coming here and it looked to have been in vain.

It was damnable bad luck that the fellow reported to have been involved in a fight with Jimmy Wild just before he went missing was the petty villain who'd given him backhanders. In the past Ralph had tipped Bateman off if the police were starting to show too much interest in his activities. He'd got twenty pounds per nod. But Ralph hadn't known about Bateman's association with Nellie or a prostitution ring. It had been suspected down at the station for some time that Bateman was fencing stolen goods and running a small-time drinking and gambling club. No firm proof had turned up. The war had depleted personnel and there were no resources to pursue petty criminals. But a murder investigation was a different kettle of fish.

Ralph knew that if Saul were arrested, possibly charged with Jimmy Wild's murder, the weasel would have no hesitation in dropping him in it if he thought it might help his cause. He could lose his career and get a prison sentence. The thought of spending time behind bars with some of the vicious scum he'd helped to convict made his mouth dry and his temples throb. He ground his teeth in rage. He'd landed himself in a minefield for a poxy hundred quid. And practically all of it had been squandered on Connie.

He turned the corner and spied just the man he wanted to see, jauntily bowling along in the direction of Nellie's flat. Saul might be a second-rate rogue but he was a first-rate swank. He was tall, flashily dressed in an expensive overcoat, his blonde hair sleeked down under a natty hat. Ralph relished knowing he was about to deflate the jumped-up prick.

As soon as Saul saw Ralph cross the road and deliberately disappear up an alley between two shops he knew the copper had something to say to him. He wasn't happy to be waylaid out in the open. Even out of uniform it was obvious Franks was a flatfoot. Saul believed himself to have a fearsome reputation and he didn't want it ruined by being spotted hobnobbing with the likes of Constable Franks.

'What are you doing round here? What's up?' Saul snarled before he'd properly caught Ralph up.

'Big trouble,' Ralph bit out on swinging around. 'That's what's up. And it's coming your way.' Ralph glanced right and left but nobody seemed to be about. 'Jimmy Wild's gone missing. A body believed to be his has been recovered from the river.'

A sly, closed expression began tautening Saul's features and Ralph knew that Bickerstaff had done his homework. The two men had had a violent run-in over Nellie's earnings. Possibly he was talking to Jimmy's murderer. He felt his insides turning stone cold. *If you lie down with dogs* . . . ran through his mind. It was a favourite expression of his mother's. The last time she'd spouted that at him had been when they'd found out he'd got engaged to a common scrubber.

'Nothing to do with me. I've not seen Jimmy Wild in a while.'

'Nobody's seen him in a while . . . probably because he's been floating down the Thames minus his head,' Ralph drawled sarcastically.

Saul nervously licked his lips and thrust his hands deep into his overcoat pockets. 'Now look . . . I'm telling you . . .'

'No, you look, and let me tell you. You're in the shit. Wild separated from his wife ages ago to move in with Nellie Tucker. It's also on record that you and him had a fight and you were overheard threatening to kill him next time you saw him. He was seen running out of Nellie's place covered in blood. You were seen coming out of there a short time later. Don't need to be a genius to put two and two together and come up with a prime suspect for this case.'

Saul Bateman's lips disappeared into a thin white line as the significance of what Franks had said penetrated his mind.

'I just thought you might appreciate knowing that you

and Nellie are about to get a visit. You would have got a knock on the door sooner but the body's not yet formally identified.' Ralph felt more at ease now Bateman was chalk-faced and visibly agitated. 'Whatever Nellie says in your defence won't count for much. You've been on borrowed time for a while. There are people who'll gladly pin this on you and see you swing.' Franks could tell he had him on the run now. 'If I were you I'd disappear where I won't get followed. I hear France is the place to be.'

Saul drove a hand into a pocket and brought out some bank notes. He thrust them at Franks in quivering fingers.

'As it's serious, have this one on me,' Ralph said and brushed past him feeling quite perky. He casually emerged from the alley and started off at a brisk pace along the road.

When he got older, wiser, he'd notice those subtle clues that needed looking into. As it was he'd missed them and Twitch was glad Franks was still an inexperienced tosspot with his brains lodged in his trousers.

The nervous, speaking look that had passed between Jimmy's wife and her sister; the scrubbed spot on otherwise filthy floorboards . . . Bickerstaff had noticed them, but not so obviously that his colleague might too.

He watched Ralph stride away into the distance and glanced at Saul Bateman as he hurried off, puffing on a cigarette, in the opposite direction. Bickerstaff could have shopped Franks to their superiors a while ago, for he'd been stupidly lax. If you were going to be a bent copper you should at least do it with a semblance of style, so he thought. But Bickerstaff felt a bit sorry for Ralph. He knew he wasn't inherently rotten. He'd glimpsed the misery that haunted the back of the boy's eyes. It was just that the poor sap couldn't think straight, he was so eaten up with bitterness over Connie.

A few years back Sidney Bickerstaff wouldn't have hesitated in blowing the whistle. But he'd mellowed recently. Another fifteen months and he was for the pipe and slippers. So he'd decided he didn't want to see Ralph get into deep shit because he'd fallen for a girl who'd grown up hungry for the good things in life. Connie Whitton had seen a way to improve her lot and Sidney didn't blame her for grabbing as much as she could while she could. He'd watched all those Bunk kids growing up in squalor and deprivation. He'd seen some of them barefoot and begging for farthings for the shop when their parents were too pissed to stay on their feet, let alone put a meal on the table. Connie might be riding high at the moment but he knew it wouldn't last. At some time she'd be joining the likes of Nellie Tucker, open to all comers and plying her trade from a tatty room with a pimp on her back.

All in all Sidney was content, untroubled by conscience at having wound Ralph up and pointed him in the right direction. Jimmy had been a sadistic brute and if he was dead . . . good riddance. Mrs Wild and Mrs Keiver would be left in peace to battle on with life in The Bunk. Bateman would remove himself from the manor. In that respect he'd done them all a favour back at the station. Nellie would be questioned. Once she knew there were witnesses who'd seen Jimmy scarper with blood on his face she'd lose her nerve to deny the fight had taken place, or that Bateman had threatened to kill Wild next time he saw him. So . . . he'd tidy the loose ends and put in his report that, if the body was ever identified as that of Jimmy Wild, he'd reason to suspect Saul Bateman guilty of killing him.

Sidney ground out his half-finished cigarette beneath the tip of a shoe while his ear swept his shoulder. He started to stroll, smiling at twilight. They'd get him a mantel clock when he went. Everyone got a bloody mantel clock. After thirty-three years in the force he reckoned he'd rather bow out smug in the knowledge he had a sweet reminiscence to while away the time.

'That's us.'

Geoff looked up. He strained to catch what one of his comrades, closer to the exit, had heard. A faint rumble of sound separated into two words. 'Stretcher-bearers!' The call had been passed along the trench from tommy to tommy until the urgent message finally reached the post where the stretcher-bearers waited for just such a summons.

The two men opposite who had been playing an idle game of rummy threw in their cards and scrambled upright. Geoff and his pal, Vinnie Cartwright, had been sharing a smoke, now they too shot to their feet and darted for the exit. Outside their post rested the stretchers: lengths of canvas slung between two poles. Having grabbed an end each of one of these they started to splash along the trench in the direction indicated by pointing fingers, jerking thumbs, nodding tin helmets. All soldiers were keen to help in getting aid to the casualty. Every man knew there but for the grace of God . . .

The stretcher-bearers' stampede along the trench was hampered as the rough duckboard underfoot petered out into sucking sludge. Geoff, in common with every fellow around him, had at some time lost his boots to the greedy grip of the yellow mud. He'd seen men struggling to recover stockings and puttees too from the bog that had become a detested dwelling place.

During the slither and splosh onwards over clay hummocks and through fetid water, a foot deep in places, Geoff's thoughts turned to home. An acute longing always swamped him whenever he was on the way to help a wounded comrade. Was the fellow's injury severe enough to get him his ticket home? Would he be a lucky bastard?

As the infernal fighting continued, and bodies stiffened and stank on miles of no-man's land, the same thought cluttered so many minds. Which of them would return to see their families? Few begrudged those that did escape. It gave hope and encouragement to those who remained that soon it might be their turn.

It certainly gnawed ceaselessly at Geoff.

He'd thought Campbell Road was hell. Now he knew what hell was he'd call The Bunk heaven.

'To the right.'

The bellowed instruction came from a corporal in the Royal Army Medical Corps who'd been waiting for them. He started to jog alongside them. They changed direction and hurtled on over some welcome even ground before abruptly again plunging onto perilously slippery clay that forced them to a stumbling walk. Abruptly they came upon the invalid.

Geoff had undergone some training when he was plucked from the rank and file of his regiment to become a stretcher-bearer. He'd been in France now for several months. He was the youngest and the least experienced of the group of men whose duty it was to get the wounded to the regimental aid post, with as much care as was humanly possible given the environment. On learning he'd been selected for the duty by his sergeant he'd tried to refuse the position. He'd sooner stay on the front line and fight with his comrades, he'd nobly said. That patriotic stance got short shrift from Sergeant Jones who'd swiftly disabused him of the notion that an easy ride was in the offing. Strong, courageous young fellows were needed to get fallen men to aid posts, sometimes under the very noses of the enemy, he'd been told.

Geoff had learned very quickly that what the sergeant had said was only mildly true. Attempting to negotiate quaggy, uneven terrain while carrying a thirteen-stone groaning man – sometimes on your back if it was the only way to negotiate the ground – was harrowing and exhausting beyond belief. At such times all a stretcher-bearer might pray for was dusk and luck to be with him.

Sinking to his haunches Geoff lit a smoke while the corporal from the RAMC took a look at Private Matthew Ratcliffe. He'd taken a sniper's bullet in his calf and blood had oozed from the wound to turn his filthy puttees into a crusty bandage.

'Saw 'im just as 'e clocked me,' he earnestly explained to them. 'Bugger were on 'is belly ready whereas I 'adn't got properly into position. I come down headfirst, bleedin' sharpish, I can tell yers. Still copped one in the leg. Saved me bonce though.' He grimaced and fell silent, closing his eyes against a wave of pain.

Geoff removed his cigarette from his lips and gave it to the injured man. Private Ratcliffe sucked on it energetically, spluttering, 'Ta, mate,' in between drags.

The corporal was searching in the rifleman's tunic for his field dressing. He found it in the wrong pocket and shaking his head, in mock exasperation, whipped it out. 'Just hold still and we'll have you quickly out of it,' he soothed in his calm, paternal tone while running his hands over the injured lad for any other damage he might have sustained while diving down the trench to escape a bullet in the brain.

Matthew Ratcliffe looked to have passed out so the corporal set to speedily patching him up and Geoff regained the cigarette that now hung limply between Ratcliffe's slack lips.

'Right. Let's get him lifted and get going, before he comes to,' the corporal instructed the stretcher-bearers after a few minutes of deft handiwork. If they could get the worst of the journey behind them before the patient regained consciousness it was best for everyone. Nobody – not stretcher-bearer, not tommy in the trench – relished hearing a wounded man's anguish. Certainly the poor fellow himself should be spared the ordeal of knowing about his bone-shaking ride if at all possible.

They reached the aid post in good time even though at one point they'd had to leave the trench because the mud-holes were unpassable. Two by two they had scrambled to the ridge. They'd tried to protect Private Ratcliffe from as much bumping and jerking as possible despite at times he seemed to have been perpendicular, held against the stretcher by able, grimy hands. Thankfully he just mumbled in delirium and for the most part slumbered blissfully on.

The light had been fading and the snipers seemed to have retired for the day. Still they'd spent an hour loitering, checking and watching then checking again before they'd emerged gingerly onto the ridge. As souls pursued by demons they'd sprinted over yards of no-man's land, keeping their eyes grimly on the horizon and away from the wretched men beyond help. On one such run Geoff had been convinced he'd sensed the claw of fingers on his leg as they'd hared by. Tortured by the thought that the fellow might have been imploring for help he'd later that evening squirmed back on his belly to find him. By ghostly moonlight he'd identified that hand stiffly outstretched in supplication. Little comfort was to be had from knowing he was many nights too late. He could think of nothing to do other than to cover his fallen comrade's taut white visage with a helmet to try to protect it from the rats.

Geoff crouched down against the wall and dug in a pocket for tobacco. He was still breathing heavily after the dash with Private Ratcliffe; nevertheless he took a long, deep drag on the cigarette, filling his tortured lungs with smoke. The aid post was set a distance behind the lines in a village.

He leaned his head back against the whitewashed wall of the farm building that served as a field medical centre and looked up at the sky as the first star shells sent up by the Germans cast an eerie luminescence on inky ground. Somewhere close by he heard the thud of a shell that was quickly followed by another. The working parties that came out under cover of darkness to do their bit always drew enemy fire.

Vinnie strolled up and settled down beside Geoff. To one side of them was a doorway and stairs that led down to the cellar. Several patients were waiting down there to be seen by the doctor. Their man, Ratcliffe, was one of them. Having watched a lazy smoke ring drift into the twilight Vinnie said, 'D'you reckon he's a Blighty one?' It was every casualty's hope to be a Blighty one. It meant he would be going home for rest and recuperation, perhaps never to return.

Geoff sucked on his cigarette. ''Spect the poor bleeder hopes it is. Don't look very old, does he?'

'Not old enough, I'd say.' Vinnie gave Geoff a sly look. 'How old are you?'

'Old enough,' Geoff said on a wry smile. 'That's what the recruitin' sergeant told me anyhow.'

After a pause he asked Vinnie, 'We hangin' around or gettin' back?'

'Got to wait and see what the doc says about him. Might be taking him tonight further up the line to the ambulance station.' A sudden loud explosion made them both duck despite the lee of the building and cellar into which they might dive for protection.

'Fritz is enjoying himself tonight,' Geoff remarked dryly.

They listened for returning fire and exchanged a joyous grin when they heard it. 'That'll learn 'em,' Vinnie said with a chuckle as the allied bombardment continued chuntering away.

'Let's go 'n' see if the doc's seen our bloke yet.' Geoff stubbed out his cigarette end and turned to go down the steps to the cellar. He hesitated on seeing that an injured fellow, leaning on a comrade, was being helped towards the aid post. Geoff got himself out of the way so they could pass unhindered. He crouched down against the wall again. He'd noticed the fellow had a head wound; almost half of his face was swathed.

The casualty squinted at them with his one uncovered eye. 'Geoff? Geoff Lovat?'

Geoff turned in astonishment and stared up at the grinning fellow. He shot to his feet and took a hesitant step towards him.

'It's you . . . Geoff Lovat . . . ain't it?'

Geoff pushed his helmet back on his head and gazed at Jack Keiver. 'Bleedin' hell!' he breathed in shock.

'Joined up then?' Jack said casually as though they'd been having a chat, leaning on a railing, in Campbell Road. 'Be alright now,' he muttered to the pal who'd been supporting him. He took an unsteady step towards Geoff. 'Nice to see a familiar face, I can tell you. Ain't seen nobody from back home fer so long.'

Geoff strode across the space that separated them and grasped Jack firmly by the hand. He pumped it up and down then curbed his enthusiasm as Jack winced. 'Come on, let's get you down them stairs. Doctor'll soon have a look at you.' Slowly they took the stairs one step at a time. On reaching the bottom Geoff grabbed a chair and gently eased Jack down onto it. He eyed the bloodstained bandage that angled over Jack's forehead, scalp and right eye. He hunkered down by the side of his chair so their faces were level. 'Do you want anything to drink?'

'Nice cup o' tea if a whiskey's out the question,' Jack answered wryly.

Immediately Geoff sprung up and returned in a moment with a tin mug of steaming tea. 'Stuck yer six sugars in that. Just what the doc ordered,' he said on handing it over. He went down again beside Jack's chair. 'What you done to yourself?'

'Ain't much. Bit of shrapnel flew at me. Knocked me out cold.' Jack sipped at his brew and closed his eyes, blissfully smacking his lips as though he'd just tasted nectar. After a moment he pressed a hand to his bandage. 'Looks worse'n it is, I reckon. Be right as rain soon.'

Geoff snapped his head towards Jack. 'You don't want to go saying that,' he hissed low and urgent. 'Play yer cards right and you could be going home. Keep shaky on yer pins. Tell 'em you got blinding headaches and can't see straight. It's a Blighty one. You make sure of it!'

'Could do with some leave. Promised Alice I'd be back again on leave. How are they all? How's all my gels?'

Geoff swallowed, wiped a hand across his face. He nodded. 'Fine,' he finally croaked. 'All fine when I left. I've been gone a few months. But they was all fine and missin' you, of course.'

Jack blinked his one eye at Geoff to clear misting water from it. 'Miss 'em all right back.' He coughed, collected himself. 'And how's your lot? Your mum 'n' dad alright? What about Dan and Sophy? Was nice to see 'em, wasn't it? Right surprised I was that day.' His eye clouded dreamily as he added, 'It was a good party, wasn't it? One of the best.'

'Yeah, it was,' Geoff agreed softly. He cleared his throat. 'They're doing alright, still in Essex, of course.' He fished in his pocket and drew out a crumpled envelope. 'Got letters off Alice here somewhere.' He'd read the letters, touched his palm to the paper, so many times the edges had become frayed.

'Tilly's never been a scholar so Al writes to me too,' Jack said with a smile. 'She's a good gel.'

'The best,' Geoff answered hoarsely. 'If you get yer ticket back home . . . tell her . . . tell her . . . you know . . .'

'Yeah . . . I know,' Jack said kindly, with a smile for Geoff's inarticulate sentiment. 'Reckon she do too,' he added. 'And same applies. If you get back before me . . . tell 'em . . . you know . . .'

Geoff nodded.

'I want to say that I'm pleased about you and Alice. You're a good 'un, Geoff Lovat. I know you'll always take care of her for me.'

'Die for her if need be,' Geoff said quietly, staring at his hands.

Jack nodded and drew forth from an inside pocket his silk scarf. Tenderly he touched it with bloodied fingertips. 'Give me this, Alice did, bless her. Got it from you fer me, I know, she did, when you worked at Milligan's.' He folded it back inside his breast pocket. 'Me lucky charm, it is. Keep it close to me heart.'

'Private Keiver.' A medical orderly beckoned. 'Come along with me now. Let's get you seen to and properly patched up.'

'I'll come back 'n' see how you're doin',' Geoff blurted as Jack followed the fellow. 'Soon as I can I'll come back 'n' see how you're doin', he promised fiercely.

Jack sent a one-eyed glance over his shoulder. 'You take care of yourself, son.'

'Ratcliffe's going onto the main dressing station,' Vinnie called to Geoff.

Geoff knew immediately what that meant. He'd be asked to act as runner and get a message to the motor station to bring an ambulance closer.

Vinnie grinned at him. He'd read from Geoff's grimace

that he knew his work wasn't yet finished for the evening. 'Hope you're feeling energetic. Shouldn't be so nippy on yer pins, should you, then they wouldn't ask you.'

Geoff carefully folded Alice's letter and slipped it inside his tunic, to rest with the others warming his heart.

TWENTY-FOUR

'Mum . . . you must tell me . . .'

'Gotta get going and get me rents.'

'No!' Alice flew to the door and pluckily flung her back against it, blocking her mother's exit. She saw one of Tilly's hands being raised and, anticipating a blow, swiftly ducked and turned her head.

Tilly dropped her arm and stomped away, muttering.

'Please tell me,' Alice implored. 'You've got to! I want to know.'

'I can't tell you 'cos *I* don't know,' Tilly bellowed in raw pain. She dropped her face into her hands. A moment later she tossed it back up and met her daughter's eyes with bleak defiance. 'I don't know if he's your father, Al. He'd forced himself on me before. Finished what he'd started that time,' she whispered, her voice haunted by vile memories. 'It were about the time that I fell pregnant with you, so I never knew if you was his or your dad's.' Tilly gulped down the lump in her throat. The dreadful news had sent her daughter crumpling to her knees. 'I don't know, Al,' Tilly repeated miserably. 'I can't be sure.'

'I thought you just said it to get him off me,' Alice whispered in anguish. 'Never thought it might be true. Not really. Thought you was protecting me . . .'

'I was!' Tilly thundered. 'He were evil and he'd have finished what he started with you given the chance. I hated him. I'm glad he's gone . . . glad he's dead, even if he is your . . .' She bit the final word off and took a step towards her sickly looking daughter.

Alice scrambled up and flew sideways away from her.

'For what it's worth I believe Jack's your dad,' Tilly said gruffly, hoping to comfort Alice with words if a touch wasn't allowed. 'When you was born he took to you straight off, natural as can be. You're his favourite, you know you are.'

'Did he know what happened . . . what Jimmy did to you?' Alice gasped through her tears. 'Does he think I'm not his daughter?'

'Never could've told him what went on.' Tilly vehemently shook her head to stress her denial. 'He'd have gone after Jimmy and killed him. Never would've let someone as good 'n' decent as Jack get strung up for putting down the likes of Jimmy Wild.' She clicked two fingers, her features contorted in contempt. 'He never were worth that. You mustn't say nuthin' neither, Al,' Tilly instructed fiercely. 'When your dad gets back home you leave him in peace over it, you hear? Leave Fran in peace too.' Tilly pressed a hand over her forehead and squeezed shut her eyes. 'Your aunt's livin' on her nerves as it is. She never knew what Jimmy'd done to me neither. She'd have blabbed to Jack for sure, saying it was my fault. That's what Jimmy would've said: that I'd wanted it.' Tilly grasped double-handed at the table edge, seeming to sway into it. 'Took a long while, and a beating that could've killed her, for Fran to come to her senses over Jimmy,' she continued in an odd, whimsical tone. She suddenly shoved away from the table, strode to the door and went out.

Alice sank to the edge of the bed and gazed at the wall. She felt too numb to regret what she'd done. She'd held her tongue for a long, long while. But she'd never forgotten what her mother had screamed at Jimmy as he'd dragged up her skirts. She'd simply concentrated on other things. But always it had been there at the back of her mind, niggling away at her consciousness.

Today, out of the blue, she'd decided to come home on her dinner break rather than go with Annie to the café. She'd known Lucy would be at school and just her mum at home. She'd convinced herself that there was nothing to it. She simply wanted her mum to confirm that she'd bawled a load of nonsense at Jimmy so the beast would leave her alone. Then she could rest easy in her mind. Instead her mind now was darting crazily here and there as consequences of this shattering news crowded in on her. Bobbie and Stevie might not be her cousins but her brothers. Her sisters might only be half-sisters. Fresh tears streamed from her eyes as she allowed the worst possibility of the lot to overcome all others. Her beloved dad might not be related to her at all. She slowly sank sideways and wearily lifted her legs up so she could lie, sobbing, on the mattress.

She was still there at four o'clock in the afternoon when her mother returned, leading Lucy by the hand.

'You not been back to work this afternoon?' Tilly demanded incredulously as soon as she spotted Alice. In the past Alice had never missed her shifts no matter what calamities occurred to put a spoke in the works.

'No,' Alice said dully. Wearily she pushed herself to a sitting position then got up. Just before she went in to the back room she said plaintively, 'Why didn't you just tell me a lie?'

'If you hadn't asked I wouldn't have said,' Tilly returned roughly. Her antagonism crumbled beneath her daughter's mournful gaze. 'It's been burning me guts for too long,' she added quietly. She tipped out of her bag and onto the table a loaf of bread and a paper twist containing tea. 'You're old enough now to take a share of the burden.'

'What on earth's happened to you?'

Alice opened the door wider and gawped at Sarah. Her friend looked as though she had been bawling long and hard; her features were puffy and her pale complexion was dark with blotches. The last time Alice had seen her in this state was just after Sarah found out her dad had been killed in France.

'Need to speak to you urgent,' Sarah mumbled through her hanky. 'I got meself in big trouble, Al.' Sarah made no move to come in. She retreated a few steps, still pressing at her face with her sodden handkerchief.

Swiftly Alice pulled the door to behind her and stepped onto the landing with Sarah. She put a finger to her lips. 'Keep it quiet. We just got Lucy off to sleep. She's right poorly again. Seems she gets one chill after the other lately. Mum's so worried about her she's sent Aunt Fran to fetch the doctor.' Alice glanced over her shoulder as though to satisfy herself she wasn't causing a disturbance to those inside. 'Mum's in a state 'cos she thinks it might be diphtheria. A kid in Lucy's class at school's gone to hospital with it.'

'Diphtheria?' Sarah's bloodshot eyes were widening in shock. Diphtheria could be a killer. It was also catching. 'D'you feel alright?' The question was garbled out as Sarah took a wary step backwards to put space between them.

'Yeah, I'm alright. So's Beth and Mum.' Alice could tell from Sarah's reaction that she knew the situation was serious for Lucy. 'Mum got her some jollop but the poor little mite can't hardly swallow it, her throat's so sore.' Alice pressed together her lips to stop them trembling. She was dreadfully worried about her little sister.

'I'm sorry now that I've come 'n' bothered you but . . .' Sarah miserably snuffled into her hanky.

'What's up?' Alice asked kindly, squeezing Sarah's shoulder in comfort. 'Your mum gone bonkers at you?' Now she'd got a closer look at Sarah she could detect a bruise on her face. Alice knew that it wasn't unusual for Ginny Whitton to hurl bottles, or whatever was to hand, in her efforts to get Sarah to hand over her wages.

'I'm in real big trouble, Al,' Sarah burbled through fresh tears. 'Ruined things for Con, ain't I, and *she's* gone bonkers. Do you remember the statues I showed to you?'

Alice had felt queasy with anxiety over Lucy. Now a new worry was churning her insides. She had thought at the time that something bad might come of that episode with the statues but soon she had forgotten all about it. Far graver matters than that had since been jostling for attention in her mind.

The atmosphere between Alice and Tilly had been strained since her mother's explosive disclosure about her parentage. They were avoiding each other's eyes and spoke only when necessary. They weren't at loggerheads exactly but Alice was still unable to fully take in the devastating news that Jack Keiver might not be her father. In an odd way she was glad that she had her little sister's health to fret over for it drove one nightmare away. Certainly another replaced it but she had some respite from dwelling constantly on the hideous possibility that Jimmy Wild might have sired her.

Now Alice sent her mind back to that walk she'd taken through the market with Sarah on the day her friend had been trying to sell the china figures. She recalled Jeannie Robertson showing an interest in the contents of Sarah's bag. Alice recalled too that she'd suspected from the start that Sarah might have filched them when Connie's back was turned. 'Did you steal them, Sar?' she asked quietly.

'No! Connie give them to me. All I wanted was a bit of cash. Stupid cow, she is. She's found out they're sort of treasures and her Mr Lucas's gone up the wall over losing them.' Sarah's agitation had made her voice shrill.

Alice put a finger to her lips, miming that Sarah must be quiet. She gripped one of her friend's elbows and urged her closer to the head of the stairs.

'How was I to know they was worth such a lot?' Sarah squeaked plaintively. 'If she'd have said I wouldn't have let Jeannie Robertson have 'em for a measly six quid, would I?'

Outside the door-less entrance at the foot of the stairs was a street lamp. As Sarah fidgeted about a silvery light from it striped one side of her face, accentuating her injuries. Alice gasped and peered closer. It looked like her friend had been beaten up rather than dodging missiles launched by her mother. 'Did Connie set about you over it?' Alice frowned in disbelief. Connie had never been known to be violent.

'Wasn't her. She's brought Louisa with her this time, ain't she. Bitch's given me a right thumping. If they don't take them shepherds back soon Connie's out on the streets. Mr Lucas told me that himself.'

'You've spoken to him?' Alice gasped in astonishment.

Sarah confirmed she had by nodding. 'Connie come over here one evening, all hysterical. Didn't have nothing to give her; not even the cash Jeannie give me. I bought meself a few nice bits: new winter coat 'n' so on,' she explained sheepishly.

'Connie never brought him here?' Alice's astonishment had increased. The idea that a rich, posh bloke had entered Ginny Whitton's hovel, even if it were to recover some valuable ornaments, seemed absurd.

'Nah . . . don't be daft!' A watery little chuckle clogged

Sarah's throat. 'Con made me go back with her to explain to Mr Lucas that she weren't lyin' over what happened to them.'

'Did she say straight off she wanted them back off you?'

Sarah nodded, looking ashamed. 'I should've pawned them and given her the ticket. Too late now though.'

'Did he . . . this Mr Lucas . . . did he go mad at you?'

'Not really; weird sort he is, all quiet and creepy. Don't trust him one bit. I reckon Connie's out on her ear anyhow whether he gets back his shepherds or not.'

After a short, reflective pause Alice gave a long sigh. 'Don't see how I can help. Wish I could.' She gazed into the distance, said wistfully, 'Wish Geoff was here; he'd know what to do about it.' Alice turned quickly to shield her expression. It had been thoughtless to bring up a mention of Geoff.

Although in the past Sarah had questioned Alice over it she was too distracted today by her own troubles to make any comment on Geoff's hasty decision to go to war. 'D'you know where Jeannie Robertson lives now?'

'Mum might know,' Alice said, guessing at once what Sarah was thinking and reckoning it to be a lost cause.

'D'you reckon she might let me have 'em back if I promise to give her back her money?' Sarah's forlorn expression told Alice she already knew the answer to that one.

'No,' Alice said simply. 'I don't.'

Sarah burst out crying, stuffing a fist to her mouth to muffle the noise.

'Shush . . .' Alice flapped a hand. 'I'll try and find out off Mum where Jeannie lives. I'll come and see you tomorrow.'

'You coming down here or am I coming up to get you?'

Both Alice and Sarah whipped around and peered over the banisters. Louisa had stationed herself at the bottom of the stairs. Her podgy fists were planted on her hips and she was staring up belligerently at them. Behind her, in the doorway, was outlined Connie, dressed in a stylish coat and hat. She appeared beautifully incongruous in such seedy surroundings . . . until she opened her mouth. She surged forward and snarled up at Sarah, 'You'd better get down here. Mr Lucas'll want some answers so you can come back with me now and give them to him, you thievin' mare.'

'Shut up, the lot of you.' Alice had leaned over the banister to hiss at the two sisters. 'We've got the doctor turning up any minute. Lucy's got diphtheria. She might be going off to hospital. You know it's catching, don't you?' Her warning had the required effect and sent Louisa and Connie scurrying back outside.

'I'll come and see you tomorrow if things aren't too bad with Lucy,' Alice promised. With a sympathetic grimace for Sarah she turned away and went back inside.

'Ah . . . you've brought Sarah to see me again; how charming,' Mr Lucas drawled. He rose slowly from the sofa but from impatience rather than any sense of weary courtesy as the two young women shuffled into the living room. He had been waiting for Connie to return to hand over his Dresden pieces. As soon as he had them she would be ejected for good, to return where she belonged . . . the gutter. His lips tightened as he noticed neither of them was carrying anything.

'Me sister's come to give you some good news,' Connie blurted nervously and tried to pin a winning smile to her lips. 'Sarah reckons she can get off her friend the address of the woman who bought the ornaments. Soon as we know where she is we can go and buy them back for you.'

'Is that so?' Gilbert drawled, his scepticism at them achieving any such thing crushingly apparent. He was quite sure that, unless the woman who'd bought them was as dense as these two, she'd try to hang on tight to them. But they'd been pilfered so the woman could possibly be classed as a receiver of stolen goods.

However, he was reluctant to cause a stir over it all in case his wife got wind of what was going on. She lived at their country estate in Hampshire but news travelled through relatives eventually. The idea that a police investigation might bring him into close contact with Constable Franks, Connie's humiliated fiancé, made him run a finger between his collar and his hot neck. He wanted the figurines returned but without anybody knowing how a common tart had tried to fleece him. His eyes rested on Sarah, making her shift uneasily beneath his scrutiny. Finally she met his eyes and grinned in an attempt to curb her apprehension.

'How much did you get for them, my dear?' It seemed an idle question as though he was unconcerned as to her answer.

'Six pounds,' Sarah whispered, then jumped at his bark of outrage.

'They are worth considerably more,' he advised, an aggressive glitter in his eyes. Gilbert continued looking at her, savouring her fright. She wasn't as pretty and curvaceous as Connie but she had the sort of adolescent appearance that oddly appealed to him. In fact that eager, ingratiating smile she had given him had stirred a movement in his trousers. She looked a lot younger than Connie and was still a virgin, he guessed. It was a long time since two females had simultaneously pandered to his needs. The fact that they were sisters added an extra little frisson to the fancy. The buoyancy at his groin increased and his tongue snaked over his lips.

At that well-known alert Connie immediately shot a look at his crotch. Her relief on glimpsing his erection was short-lived. Her satisfied expression began to transform to one of disbelief as she realised she was not the one arousing him.

Her sister was oblivious to the fact she was giving him the horn and was avoiding his eye by staring at the cushions on the sofa, a finger twiddling at a silky fringe. Connie's eyes darted back to Mr Lucas, her mouth twisted in disgust.

He coolly returned her look, his tongue again poking between his lips. 'You'll need to work hard and be extremely obliging to me, my dear, if I'm to wait longer for my property. I've been more tolerant than you deserve as it is. I'd sooner not get the authorities involved but . . .' He sighed. 'It's for you . . . and Sarah . . . to persuade me that there is another way for this all to end.'

'Yeah, I'll decide what happens alright,' Connie snarled. 'We'll get your fuckin' stuff back and then you can take a runnin' jump, you pervert.' She grabbed one of Sarah's hands and started to yank her backwards towards the door.

Sarah stumbled over her own feet, staring up at her sister as though she'd taken leave of her senses. One minute they were to be nice as pie to the old bloke; next Connie was giving him lip. Having conquered her surprise, Sarah decided that giving him lip was much better. 'Yeah . . . take a runnin' jump, pervert,' she echoed and sent him a dirty look over a shoulder.

Having belted down the stairs, giggling hysterically, they were outside the building standing on the pavement in a matter of minutes.

'What were all that about?'

'Nothing,' Connie snapped grumpily. Her amusement had withered with the first blast of cool air on her flushed face. It was obvious that the doorman was not coming after them, and slowly the enormity of what she'd sacrificed filled her mind. She'd reacted impetuously on seeing Mr Lucas leering at Sarah. Now she was calmer, more logical, she knew she should have played the old lecher at his own game. She should have strung him along a bit with sly hints that she'd eventually supply what he wanted while she had from him all she wanted.

It hadn't been purely to protect Sarah that she'd turned on him. Jealousy and indignation had played their part. The idea that skinny Sarah, who was nowhere near as pretty as she was, or as experienced as she was, might steal a man from under her nose made Connie seethe. Sarah was too clueless about men and sex to have cottoned on to Mr Lucas's intentions, but if she had known the old goat fancied her, what would she have decided to do? Sarah wasn't clueless about the offer of nice things.

'So . . . are we going to bother getting the figures back off Jeannie Robertson now you've told him to sling his hook?'

Sarah's idle question irritated Connie even though she'd been pondering on the same thing. 'Dunno . . .'Course we are you dunce,' she spat nastily. 'If we don't get his china he'll get the coppers.'

'Don't get snappy with me 'cos you've given him lip and regret it . . .'

Connie swiped a hand across Sarah's face. 'You've had that comin' off me for ages,' she bawled over Sarah's surprised howl. 'You've ruined everything, you stupid sod.' She stalked off, shouting over a shoulder, 'I'm going down Finsbury Park to stay with Lou. If you know what's good for you get that address off Alice tomorrow or I'll send Lou round looking for you.'

'How's Lucy, Mrs K?'

Tilly turned to see Sarah approaching the top of the stairs. 'Better than we hoped,' she answered. 'Doctor came and said he thinks it's tonsillitis. Got some proper jollop for her now. She's poorly but at least it ain't as bad as we thought.'

'That's good.'

Tilly was on the landing by the sink, filling the bowl to wash up. Now she gave Sarah a longer sideways look for she'd noticed her face was marked.

'Your Louisa been at you?' Tilly was curious; she hadn't seen Louisa in the neighbourhood for some while.

Sarah gave a little nod. 'Alice back from work, is she?'

'Yeah . . . she's done an early so she can help me out keeping an eye on Lucy this afternoon.'

'I'll carry on up then,' Sarah mumbled. 'I just want a few words with her.'

'Would you come with me, Al?' Sarah's eyes were on the address that Alice had scribbled down on a scrap of paper.

Alice frowned. 'What for?'

'You know her better than me. When we saw Jeannie in the market that day she seemed quite friendly with you.'

'Well . . . I don't . . .'

'Please,' Sarah wheedled.

Tilly came into the room carrying the bowl and immediately the conversation ceased between Alice and Sarah. 'Something goin' on, is it, that you don't want me to know about?' Tilly put the bowl down on the table.

'What makes you say that?' Alice asked and slid a look at Sarah.

'Your two sisters are hanging about downstairs, Sarah. I just caught a glimpse of Louisa in the doorway. Size of her, she's hard to miss. Connie's all done up to the nines, so I take it she's still doing alright for herself with that rich bloke.'

Sarah shot an apprehensive look at Alice.

'Is it alright if I pop out for a while, Mum?'

'Yeah . . . go on. I'll stop in with Lucy till Beth gets home from her shift to look after her.' She plonked the kettle on the hob then gave Alice a steady look. 'You can tell Louisa from me if she's got a beef with any of the Keivers she can come 'n' see me and I'll help her sort it out.'

'Ain't me she's after, Mum,' Alice reassured her mother. She didn't want Tilly coming downstairs too and sticking her oar in. A full-blown ruckus would only make things worse. 'It's Sarah she's got a beef with.'

'I see,' Tilly said. 'But I take it you wanted Jeannie's address 'cos she's somehow involved in this 'n' all.'

'No she's not,' Alice said quickly. 'Not really . . . it's just that . . .' Alice glanced at Sarah. She didn't want her mother falling out with Jeannie over this. A conspiracy of silence bound them together as allies if not real friends. It was too precious a relationship to risk destroying it for any of the Whittons.

'Jeannie bought some stuff off Sarah. Turns out it weren't Sarah's to sell so she's got to ask Jeannie for it back.'

Tilly nodded slowly, her eyes shrewd and narrowed. 'Well . . . better get off and get it sorted out quick as you can then.'

'Why d'you tell her so much?' Sarah grumbled as they hurtled down the stairs.

''Cos she's not daft, that's why,' Alice returned. 'You're the daft one,' she shot irritably at Sarah, making her friend wince. 'I'll come with you today to see Jeannie but if it don't work out I ain't getting involved again.'

TWENTY-FIVE

'You'd better start again at the beginning and tell me all about it.'

Jeannie Robertson had already been bombarded with Sarah's garbled version of the reason she and Alice had turned up, uninvited, on the doorstep of Johnny Blake's Belgravia townhouse. Jeannie had heard visitors arrive and gone into the hall to investigate. She had been inquisitive as she rarely had callers yet had detected familiar North London accents, intermingling with Noreen's Irish burr. Jeannie thought it daft to stand on ceremony and wait while a servant did what she was perfectly capable of doing for herself. But when Johnny was about she curbed her impatience and let the housekeeper make announcements. They had standards, he'd said, and should stick to 'em now they'd come up in the world.

Once Jeannie had sent Noreen away, and while still in the tiled hallway, she'd got the gist of the fact that the porcelain figures hadn't been Sarah's to sell but to pawn as they belonged to her sister's sugar daddy. She'd also got the full force of Sarah's grovelling apology for troubling her about it all. Jeannie had been feeling at a loose end and was therefore quite disposed to being diverted by an intriguing tale about a randy old goat called Mr Lucas and how all the Whitton sisters and Alice had become involved in stealing statues and settling sibling rivalry. She invited the two young women to go into her front sitting room so they could talk some more.

'We're really sorry to be here bothering you, Mrs Robertson . . . especially as . . . that is, we didn't know about . . .' Alice glanced at Jeannie's son, Peter. He was sitting in an armchair in a corner of the room, a blanket about his hunched shoulders, staring at the wall. As Alice watched him he began to rock back and forth on the seat, his hands gripped tightly in his lap.

'We shouldn't have come,' Alice whispered, turning to give Sarah a fierce frown full of blame.

'Don't worry, he can't hear,' Jeannie said quietly. 'Even if he could he wouldn't understand a word we're on about. He mostly stays in a world of his own. It's shell-shock; severe case, the doctor said.'

'Sorry,' Alice murmured. 'We're so sorry to trouble you like this.'

'Nice to have company for a change,' Jeannie reassured briskly. 'Don't get out as much as I used to. Before Peter came back home I used to go to Oxford Street quite regular and help out in one of Johnny's clubs. But I've not been in weeks.' Jeannie cast on her sick son a long, melancholy look.

Peter Robertson didn't look now anything like the young hound he had been a few years ago when he'd gone on a rampage with his brother smashing windows in the vicinity of The Bunk. The two Robertson boys had been known as a couple of thugs it was best to avoid. Now Peter looked frail and vulnerable; a prime target for the sort of bully he'd once been. Alice doubted if he was even nineteen years old.

Immediately Alice's mind was crammed with fears for her dad and Geoff. The horrors they were facing every day – which Peter would surely describe to her, if only he was able – made the reason for their visit seem ridiculously petty. Alice realised she felt ashamed to be there, taking up Jeannie's time, to talk about something as stupid as china shepherds that had been filched from an old roué.

Already she wanted to go home. She wanted to lie down on the bed next to Lucy and give her a cuddle. She wanted to write letters to Geoff and to her dad. She wanted to tell them both she loved and missed them dreadfully. She wanted to warn them . . . beg them . . . to keep safe from deafening shells, for she'd seen now with her own eyes what dreadful damage they could do.

'Sit down, the two of you, and I'll get us some tea,' Jeannie said. On the way to the door she crouched by Peter to murmur a few words and tuck the rug closer about his gaunt frame. He seemed unaware of her and when he shrank back it was not due to her touch but to escape whatever torments were behind his closed eyelids.

Jeannie rang for service and quickly gave Noreen an order for tea.

'Is your other son well?' Alice politely asked.

'I pray he is,' Jeannie replied as she came and sat down. 'He's serving in the navy. He's been reported missing. Now start again at the beginning,' she added swiftly as though she couldn't bear to be drawn into discussing the uncertain fate of her other son.

After a stuttered few words from Sarah, which made little sense, Alice came to her rescue. She could tell that her friend was now tongue-tied. Sarah's eyes were being drawn, involuntarily, every few seconds to Peter as he mumbled and swayed, plucking at the blanket covering him.

Quickly Alice blurted out all she knew, sending glances

Sarah's way every so often as though to check with her that she was giving a reasonable account of the facts. Sarah simply nodded at her at intervals while chewing agitatedly at her lower lip.

'I bought them fair and square.' Jeannie's abrupt response came as soon as Alice concluded the tale and fell silent.

'Yes . . . we know . . .' Alice blurted. 'We know none of it's your fault.'

'I'll give you your money back, promise I will,' Sarah whispered. 'So sorry to trouble you with it, Mrs Robertson. But this Mr Lucas . . .' She frowned at her fingers fidgeting in her lap. 'He's threatened to get the police involved if Connie don't return the ornaments. I reckon he's finished with her whether he gets them back or not. But if we all get roped in I'm gonna lose me factory job and won't get took on anywhere when it gets round I've been to court for thieving. Might even get sent to prison.' Sarah snorted back a sob.

'I don't reckon he'll want it to go that far,' Jeannie soothed. 'If he's married he probably won't want it all made public, will he? He won't want no fuss.'

'He *is* married,' Sarah burst out, looking a bit brighter. 'Connie saw his wife at a party. That's where she first met Mr Lucas. She says she was surprised that he made a play for her 'cos him and his wife seemed happy enough.' Sarah paused. 'It was the fact that they seemed alright together that made her wonder whether she could try a sort of blackmail. You know, tell him that she'd spill the beans to his missus about being his bit on the side.'

An approving chuckle erupted from Jeannie on hearing of Connie's likely tactics.

'Trouble is, Mrs Lucas don't live round here and Con ain't got her address to write a note,' Sarah said. 'The woman's living a long way off out in the countryside.' She wrinkled her nose. 'If Connie was still talking to Ralph she might be able to get Mrs Lucas's address off him as they're some sort of distant cousins. But Ralph and his family won't have nothing more to do with Con. If they knew she'd got herself in bad trouble with old Mr Lucas, they'd probably laugh themselves silly.'

'It'd be best telling nix to a flatfoot with an axe to grind.'

Alice and Sarah exchanged a look that indicated they thought Jeannie's statement very wise.

'Nothing worse than a vindictive copper,' Jeannie added before beckoning Noreen, bearing a tea tray, into the room.

The housekeeper poured tea and distributed the delicate china cups. Alice and Sarah accepted them politely then glanced around. The interruption had given them a chance to appreciate their surroundings. Jeannie Robertson had done very well for herself since she'd left The Bunk was the thought that ran through both their minds. Alice wondered whether those big houses down Highgate way, which she'd always longed to see inside, were as fine as was Jeannie's home.

'Nice, isn't it?' Jeannie said wryly after watching the two young women dart admiring looks here and there. 'Just wish I owned it.'

'Knocks livin' in The Bunk into a cocked hat,' Sarah observed, making Alice chuckle at her friend's droll tone.

Jeannie smiled too but, as Noreen closed the door, she put down her cup. 'Back to business,' she said as she got up and went to open the top of a bureau. She took some photographs out of a drawer inside. 'I got these done recently.' She showed the two young women the images of the ornaments side by side on a table. 'I was going to take them to an auction house and get an idea what they're worth.' She tapped the snaps against a thumbnail. 'P'raps if Lucas wants them back bad he'd like to make me an offer for his statues.'

'But . . . what if he ain't bluffin' about the coppers?' Sarah burst out, alarmed. 'We'll all still be in bad trouble whether he agrees to buy them back off you or not. It's bound to make him even nastier if he has to shell out for 'em.'

'I don't want the law involved either,' Jeannie stressed. 'I might be accused of receiving stolen goods. Lucas might even believe that I put your sister up to it.'

'We didn't think of any of that.' Alice shot an anxious look at Sarah. 'We don't want you getting dragged into it.'

'Bit late for that, Alice,' Jeannie muttered ruefully. After a thoughtful pause she said, 'I'll let you have one back. I realised when I bought them off you that just one's worth a lot more than what I paid you for two. But that's business. So I'm not feeling guilty and I'm not giving up the pair of them. If you want to give one back to Mr Lucas, that's up to you.'

'Where did you get them photographed?' Alice asked, a seed of an idea germinating in her mind.

'There's a place on the corner of the street,' Jeannie said. 'A fellow 'n' his wife have set up a studio there.' She went to the dresser in the corner and, opening the lower cupboard, took the shepherd out. 'You can take this one.' She handed Alice the figure. 'I like the other one better.' She looked at the two young women, her eyes distant as she shrewdly mulled things over. 'I'm bankin' on Lucas wanting this all sorted out quietly . . . no fuss. Sounds like him 'n' his wife rub along alright together even if she do know he's got a roving eye. I'm guessing he won't want her upset.' Jeannie sat back down. 'If he's a fellow with money he's probably got a bit of standing; he won't want to be made a laughing stock. He will be if it's known a brass's turned him over.' She hesitated and shrugged, unconcerned. 'Sorry love, but it's true.' Jeannie had noticed Sarah wince and redden as she heard her sister so described.

'Anyhow, if he's interested in buying back the other one you can tell him that he can contact me through Johnny Blake's Club in Oxford Street.' Jeannie was reasonably confident that no aggravation would come her way. She guessed that Mr Lucas lived in London and left his wife in the country so he could enjoy the fleshpots on offer in the capital. Johnny Blake was involved in running most of the gentlemen's clubs; even the ones that he didn't own outright. Mr Lucas would probably know of Johnny's reputation. If he decided to cross him, even to get back his valuable statue, he'd be a fool.

'How much does he charge up the corner for his photos?' Alice asked abruptly.

'Why? Thinking of getting one done?' Jeannie asked, interested.

Alice nodded, looking thoughtful.

Suddenly Peter let out an anguished moan, making Jeannie jump to her feet and go to him.

Alice swiftly got up too, gesturing to Sarah that it was high time they left. 'We'll get off now,' Alice whispered quickly, edging towards the door. 'Sorry again to have bothered you, and thanks for everything.'

'Noreen'll show you out,' Jeannie said distractedly over her shoulder from her crouching position by Peter's chair.

'Thanks very much, Mrs Robertson,' Sarah mumbled.

'Remember me to your mum, Alice,' Jeannie called just before the two young women slipped out of the door and into the corridor.

As soon as Alice and Sarah had descended the stone steps that led to Jeannie's front door Connie and Louisa bounded up to meet them.

'Got 'em?' Connie gasped in jubilation. She had noticed that Alice was carrying something in a bag.

'Only got one,' Sarah answered.

'Shall I go and bang on the door, Con?' It was a pugnacious-sounding offer from Louisa.

'Don't be stupid, fatso,' Sarah spat.

'Who you calling stupid?' Louisa snarled.

'Shut up, both of you,' Alice hissed, on noting they were drawing attention from passers-by. 'You're lucky that Jeannie's given even one back. She didn't have to give you anything at all. She bought them fair 'n' square.'

'Yeah . . . but she must've known they was nicked,' Connie remarked darkly. 'Why else would this one . . .' she gave Sarah an ungentle shove on the shoulder '. . . be walking about with them down the market trying to sell them all hush-hush?'

Alice looked at the shop on the corner of the street. The sign over the front advertised speedy snaps. 'I've got an idea that might be a sort of insurance policy in case Mr Lucas ain't satisfied with getting just this one back and paying Jeannie for the other one. I reckon Jeannie's given us good advice. She reckons he definitely won't want to upset his wife or be made to look a fool. So we'll have to get something that could do that. Then, if you're lucky, he won't get the law on you.'

A few days later the four young women were standing on the pavement outside Connie's apartment. Connie was holding a bag that contained the figurine and two photographs. She still had a key but she knew it would soon be taken away. She knew Mr Lucas would be pacing about up there now, waiting for her and his ornaments. Once he had them she'd be shown the door, probably without even a chance of clearing out the wardrobe and taking all her lovely new clothes with her.

'You coming up to see him with us, Al?'

The drizzle had turned to sleety rain and Alice decided

she would sooner be somewhere warm and dry than pacing the pavement while the Whittons confronted Mr Lucas. Besides, now she was fully involved in this little drama she was curious to know how it would all end. She and Sarah were to catch the bus back to Islington together when it was all done and dusted. Alice was curious too about the swanky apartment that Sarah once had described to her and had a yen to see it. 'Alright. Not hanging about long in there, though,' she warned Sarah. 'Want to get back home soon as I can and see how Lucy's doing.'

The doorman, Jenkins, gave them a filthy look as they all trooped by. Connie stuck her nose in the air. Louisa stuck two fingers in the air. They knew after today they'd never see him again.

'Ah . . . quite a contingent with you this time.' Mr Lucas sarcastically observed as Connie, Sarah and Alice trooped in to the sitting room.

Louisa had been told to stay outside the apartment in the corridor. All the rushing about had set her to swearing and sweating and Connie didn't want her fouling things up in any way.

Already Gilbert Lucas's eyes had dropped to the bag in Connie's hand. They then darted to Alice's exquisitely pretty face before sliding over her body. The fact that he found her attractive was obvious even before he drawled, 'I see you've brought another sweet young lady to see me, Connie. I'm coming to think perhaps you're not such a bad girl.'

'I'm coming to think you're a randy ol' git who needs to keep his fly buttoned,' Connie spouted. Again she'd been thoroughly riled on witnessing Mr Lucas's interest in a girl she considered less attractive than her.

'Have you something for me, my dear?' Apart from a look of contempt creasing his face he seemed unperturbed by

Connie's coarse talk and he continued looking at Alice as though he expected her to reply to his question.

'It's one of the statues. Got it from the lady I know who bought them both fair 'n' square,' Alice answered clearly.

Mr Lucas's mouth set in a thin line when he heard he was not to get back both figurines. Connie seemed pleased to witness his annoyance and insolently started swinging the bag in her hand.

'Mrs Robertson said that she'll sell you back the other if you like,' Alice quickly told him. She darted a glance about. The embellished cushions Sarah had liked drew her eyes. The apartment was as beautifully impressive as her friend had said. Nevertheless she wished she'd stayed outside in the cold. Alice understood now what Sarah had meant when she said he gave her the creeps. She felt uneasy in his presence too and wished he'd stop staring at her with his piggy little eyes.

'You can tell Mrs Robertson that I don't buy property I already own,' he purred. 'So you leave me no choice. I shall need to get the police involved after all.'

'Don't think Mrs Robertson would be pleased about that,' Alice said politely. 'She not done anything wrong, y'see.'

'Don't reckon your wife'll be too pleased about this neither,' Connie piped up. She drew from her bag a photo. 'We got you this. Nice, ain't it?' she jeered as she held up the picture for him to see.

The photo of Connie, sitting on a chair holding the statue on her lap, drew Gilbert's eyes. For a moment he gawped unblinkingly at it while the full significance of its existence began penetrating his mind.

'I'll let you have this 'cos I've got another copy of it for meself,' Connie said saucily. She'd noticed straight away the effect the photo had had on him. His complexion had whitened before wrath darkened it. 'It was nice of you to give them statues to me as a present but now I'm moving out you can have one of 'em back,' she taunted. 'Nice things, they are; your wife not missing them?'

Gilbert shot her a poisonous look. 'Are you trying to blackmail me, my dear?' he asked exceedingly quietly.

'Not me . . .' Connie said with wide-eyed innocence. 'But I think Ralph might like to get back at you. He never did get over losing his fiancée, y'know.'

'He called you a fucking whore, as I recall,' Gilbert said in his quiet, cultured way. 'He said he never wanted to see you again. I know how he feels.'

'Yeah, and he called you a few choice names 'n' all,' Connie returned. 'If he was feeling right nasty I reckon he'd make a point of going 'n' seeing your wife and telling her a few things about yer habits.'

'My wife knows a few things about my habits, as you so charmingly put it,' Gilbert sneered.

'Perhaps she does know you're a randy ol' sod,' Connie conceded. 'But she's not seen this, has she?' She waved the photo at him then looked smug when his angry flush returned.

Sarah and Alice exchanged a look. They'd been listening with bated breath to the slanging match. It seemed Connie had edged ahead. It had been an outside chance that the photo might have an impact, but the ploy seemed to have paid off better than they'd hoped. Mr Lucas appeared more annoyed about the photo than only getting back one of his statues.

'This Mrs Robertson . . . where does she live?' He fired the question at Alice.

'She said you can contact her at Blake's Club in Oxford Street. Johnny Blake is her very good friend, you see.'

Gilbert Lucas seemed momentarily too stunned to speak. His chin was jutted out and he ran a finger inside his collar as though he were perspiring. He turned away to conceal his expression from the three girls.

'Give me your key,' he blasted icily over his shoulder at Connie.

She lobbed a piece of metal onto the table.

'Leave the statue and get out, all of you,' he commanded.

'Any chance of getting a few clothes first?' Connie began cheekily.

'Get out!'

''Ere . . . catch . . .' Connie called. She drew the shepherd out of the bag and threw it up in the air, laughing as he scrambled forward, arms outstretched.

'You shouldn't have done that,' Sarah gasped out in between chokes of laughter. 'It might've got broke.'

They were all out on the pavement again, trying to subdue their hilarity. It had been quite a sight to see the old fellow tumble over the sofa in his haste to field the china shepherd and save it from smashing. Even Louisa had been guffawing as they'd raced down the stairs, recounting to her what had gone on. For those few minutes they might have been children again, back in Campbell Road, haring about and having fun.

Now the comedy was over. They shivered in their coats, pulling the collars up against the cold.

'I'm gettin' off,' Louisa said. 'Sonia's waiting for me in Piccadilly Circus.'

''S'pose I might as well come with you,' Connie said. 'Can I put up at yours, Lou, for a while till I get me own place? Ain't going back to Mum's, that's fer sure.'

''S'alright for me to keep going back there though, ain't it?' Sarah shouted angrily, waving her arms. 'This is what started it all in the first place. All you two ever do is please yourselves and leave me to look after Mum. Ain't havin' it no more.'

'Well, come with me 'n' all then,' Louisa said. 'I'll find you something.'

'Right . . . I will.'

Alice shot a startled glance at her friend. She knew very well why Connie and Louisa were going to meet Sonia in Piccadilly Circus. Sonia and Connie were undoubtedly going to let Louisa find clients for them.

'You don't mean that,' Alice said quickly to Sarah. 'Come on, we've got to catch the bus home.'

'Had enough . . .' Sarah choked. 'Ain't fair . . .'

'Yeah; I know,' Alice said soothingly and put an arm around her shoulders. She drew her determinedly along the pavement. 'Come on, we'll talk about it on the way home.' The idea that Sarah was prepared to go on the game to escape her home life had shocked Alice to the core.

Louisa glared at Alice for interfering. The more girls she had the more she earned. 'You don't have to listen to what she says. You coming with us or not?' she barked at Sarah.

'No! She ain't!' Alice yelled back. 'She's coming with me.' She held on tight to one of Sarah's arms as though she would forcibly restrain her if she made a move to go with her sisters.

'Come on, leave them. Let's go,' Connie muttered irritably. 'I need some money. I'm bleeding skint after payin' out for them photos.'

TWENTY-SIX

'Gonna go potty if I stay around here much longer. Might as well be dead.'

'Don't be daft, Sar!' Alice put a comforting arm about her friend. Sarah had been depressed and tearful most of the way home. They'd just got off the bus close to the top of Campbell Road when Sarah had spouted that out.

'It were all for nothing,' Sarah added bitterly. 'I only went to see Connie to get some help with Mum. Now I'm back where I started and all I done is messed things up for Con. 'Cos of me she's lost her rich bloke and she's got nowhere to live.'

'Louisa'll let Connie stop with her till she finds somewhere of her own,' Alice said buoyantly.

'Yeah; the fat cow'll get rent off Con by pimping for her like she does for Sonia,' Sarah said bleakly. 'Louisa never does nobody no favours. Connie'll want to kill me over this.'

'You've got nothing to feel bad about,' Alice stressed and squeezed her friend's arm in comfort. 'You're entitled to a bit of help with your mum off your sisters.'

Sarah nodded but snorted back fresh tears.

As they turned the corner into Campbell Road Alice sensed

that, with her detested home in sight, Sarah needed bucking up more than ever. 'We'll get away from here, you'll see,' she enthused. 'Just need to wait a bit, 'n' work a bit, 'n' save a bit.' A glance at her friend told Alice her encouragement had had no effect. Sarah's head was bowed in defeat. Sarah was sick and tired of waiting; she earned peanuts packing biscuits; she would never be able to save because she barely made enough to keep her and her mother housed and fed. With every step that took them further into the bowels of Campbell Road Sarah's dejection seemed to increase. Alice could hear her again softly weeping.

'You and Herbert will sort things out between you in time,' Alice said in desperation.

'He's worse'n useless,' Sarah choked. 'He likes living round here. He's happy up the corner gambling with his old man. He's never got no money. He's got the cheek to ask me to lend him and gets nasty when I won't.'

Alice was aware that Herbert Banks gambled a lot. He was also a bookie's runner. She didn't recall him ever having had a proper job. Unfortunately whatever little amount he earned or won was soon back on the pavement as stake money.

Sarah and Herbert Banks had been walking out for a while but Alice knew that it was no great romance. Sarah was regularly heard to say that she was ready to ditch Banksie because he was a loser. Herbert reckoned all the Whittons, including Sarah, were nuts. But they continued to stick around together while half-heartedly hoping someone better might turn up.

They had reached Sarah's home and for a moment the two young women stood quietly, facing one another, on the pavement.

'You wouldn't really have gone off up west with Louisa today, would you, Sar?' The question burst from Alice unbidden. It had been niggling in her mind throughout the journey home yet voicing her suspicions seemed like delivering an insult to her friend.

'Nah . . .' Sarah mumbled.

'Sar?' Alice whispered, aghast.

'Dunno . . .' Sarah said dully. 'Dunno nuthin' no more.'

'But you said you never would do that.'

'I know what I said,' Sarah hissed, agitated. 'I know what I done 'n' all. I messed everything up for Connie. I'm bleedin' useless, I am.'

'You're not . . .'

'Goin' in . . .' Sarah mumbled and, without another word, disappeared through the open doorway.

'See you then . . .' Alice called, trying to sound bright. She shoved her hands into her coat pockets and with a sigh carried on down the street towards home.

She found Beth at home looking after Lucy. She took off her coat and lay down next to her little sister, cuddling up close to keep her warm.

'Where's Mum?' she asked Beth.

'Gone downstairs to see Aunt Fran. She got a few nice bits off Billy the Totter. She reckons the coat might do Bobbie or Stevie a turn. Been a while she has; they're probably knocking back a few.'

'Luce been alright today?'

'She seems a bit brighter. Had a bit o' bread 'n' jam earlier, didn't you, Luce?'

Lucy nodded her small head against the pillow.

'Soon be right as ninepence, won't you?' Alice leaned towards her sister and planted a kiss on her dark curls.

Again Lucy nodded her head and snuggled against her big sister. Her thin little arms came out from under the blanket to clutch at Alice.

Alice closed her eyes as a strange feeling of contentment

settled on her. For what was left of today she'd happily count the few blessings she had. As far as she knew, and please God let it be true, her dad and Geoff were alive and well; her little Lucy was slowly getting over her illness; she had a job and decent wages. What she cherished too was the knowledge that her spirit still thrived. Unlike Sarah she still had hope and determination. She *would* improve her lot.

'Did Sarah get things all sorted out with Jeannie?'

Alice had been about to head off to work. It had been a few days since she'd gone with the Whittons to see Jeannie about the statues. Her mother's question therefore came out of the blue and as a bit of a surprise. 'Yeah; glad to say Jeannie was alright about it all.'

'She turned out to be a good 'un, did Jeannie,' Tilly said, pulling on her coat. It was her rent collection day and she too was heading off out. Lucy was still weak and Tilly was taking her downstairs to be cared for by Fran while she was working. 'Jeannie ain't a mug though,' she added significantly whilst gesturing for Lucy to button up her coat. 'It wouldn't do for us to get on the wrong side of her, you know that, don't you, Al? 'Specially not on somebody's else's account.'

'Yeah, I know that,' Alice confirmed quietly. Never would she forget that the secrets they shared with Jeannie must remain secret. 'Oh . . . not had a chance to tell you that Jeannie asked to be remembered to you when we said goodbye.' It was Alice's way of reassuring her mother that she'd parted from Jeannie on good terms that day. 'Not had a chance to tell you either that she's got one of her sons back home from the war.' The memory of Peter's frailty caused Alice's eyes to cloud in pity. Of course, she'd seen on the streets poor souls invalided home, their gaunt faces and crippled limbs testament to the horrors they'd endured. But never before had she been unavoidably close to the human wreckage of the war. For the half an hour or so that they'd spent talking to Jeannie she'd been made conscious that minds were being shattered as badly as bodies. 'Peter's got shell-shock. He does look a poor, tormented soul.' Alice's voice sounded gruff with sorrow. 'He just sat there in the chair, fidgeting and mumbling to himself, as though nobody else was in the room. Jeannie said he couldn't hear us. It were as though he couldn't see us either.'

Tilly let out a sigh and closed her eyes.

'And her other son's been reported missing.'

'You going to write to your dad for me?' Tilly hunched into her coat and, having scrubbed at her burning eyes, shoved her hands into the pockets. She'd obviously been affected by the news about Jeannie's boys. But she continued to grimace at her shoes, unable to express the emotion welling within her.

'Started a letter to him last night,' Alice replied gruffly. 'And one for Geoff too.' A soft smile shaped her features as she thought of him. After a short pause when they both seemed lost in their own thoughts Alice said briskly, 'Well I'd better be off or I'm going to be late.'

As she hurried up the road she automatically looked towards Sarah's house. She hadn't seen Sarah since they'd travelled home together on the bus. Alice had been doing extra shifts at work and babysitting Lucy while she convalesced. She'd not had an opportunity to pay her friend a call. As she got closer Alice could see a stooped figure in the doorway. Her step faltered as, amazed, she realised Ginny Whitton was up and about. She hadn't seen the woman in an age. When Alice did call on Sarah she was reluctant to enter the Whittons' malodorous hovel and usually loitered on the landing talking to her friend.

'Hello, Mrs Whitton,' Alice called and speeded up, hoping to whip past.

'Alice . . . Alice . . . spare a minute?'

Alice hesitated but didn't move closer. She regretted now not having crossed the road when she saw Ginny huddled there. She had no wish to run errands and she guessed that was what the woman was after. Alice had been caught out before by Ginny when she was out of booze and couldn't wait till Sarah got home from work for her next tipple. Alice didn't want to be unneighbourly, but if she didn't hurry she'd be late for work. She also had no money to lend to get Ginny's drink for her.

'Can't stop, Mrs W,' Alice called, edging away. 'I'm late for me shift as it is.'

'Won't take you no more'n a minute,' Ginny whined. 'Only want you to nip to the corner and back. Got money,' she wheedled. 'Look . . . got money . . .' She let go of the doorframe and tottered forward a few steps, thrusting out an open palm. 'I'd go meself, you know I would, but me leg's paining me summat awful.'

'Sarah'll be back dinnertime,' Alice said desperately, determined not to weaken and move closer.

'Sarah's fucked off,' Ginny spat with surprising vigour. 'Ungrateful little cow's gawn and left me all on me own. All wot I done for her 'n' all.'

That information first shocked Alice into immobility then drew her quickly forward. She retreated again as the stench of mingling body odour and alcohol hit her nostrils. 'Where's Sarah gone?' she demanded.

'Got a job waitressin', ain't she. Her and Connie both got jobs in a fancy place in the West End. Thought she'd of told you, being as you're best pals. Get us a half bottle o' gin, will you, Al?' One of Ginny's grimy hands opened again to reveal some coins. 'Whatever's left over, you can keep it, yer know,' she said as though the bribe of a penny or two was a great inducement.

'Don't want your money, Mrs W,' Alice replied. She held out a hand and let Ginny tip the coins into it rather than touch her dirty skin. She stared sightlessly as her cupped palm caught the silver and copper. Her mind was in turmoil. She knew why her friend hadn't told her of her plans to go away: Sarah knew that she would have done her utmost to stop her leaving.

'I'll just hang on here and wait for you,' Ginny said, unsubtly prompting Alice to go and fetch her gin.

As Alice hurried away she saw Beattie Evans approaching her from the opposite pavement. The woman started to walk briskly with her towards the shop. 'See you got nabbed, Alice,' Beattie said sympathetically. 'I crossed over the road to avoid her. Ginny owes me two bob from earlier in the week,' she huffed. 'Don't want to be unkind or nuthin' but I ain't got two bob to spare. Fact is I could do with it back. Gawd knows what'll become of Ginny now they've all up 'n' left her. Dunno how she'll take it if she finds out the truth neither. Waitressing my eye!'

Alice slid a look at Beattie; she realised she was hinting heavily that she knew about Sarah's defection, and the nature of the work that had lured her away. Any lingering uncertainty Alice had about the full extent of Beattie's knowledge was soon put to flight.

'I know Ginny ain't the full ticket,' Beattie started. 'I know it must've been hard for Sarah putting up with her, but bleedin' hell, who'd have thought *all* them Whitton gels would end up on the game?' Beattie suddenly shot Alice a look. 'When Ginny finds out she'll be glad they took themselves off. Shame of it! 'Course you was friendly with Sarah, weren't you, so you'd probably know better'n me about . . .'

'Yeah, she *is* me friend and always will be,' Alice harshly interrupted. 'And I can tell you that Sarah ain't on the game,' she added forcefully. 'If she's gone to live with Connie 'n'

Louisa it's 'cos she got herself a better job and needs a place to stop. She's said she's waitressing and that's what she's doing.'

'Yeah . . . 'course . . . 'course,' Beattie said in a mollifying tone. 'Just repeating what I heard, that's all. I ain't starting no rumours, you understand. Just repeating what I heard.'

'Who d'you hear it off?' Alice demanded.

'Herbert Banks was spouting his mouth off down the Duke. Said some bad things about Louisa, I can tell you. Said she's a queer ponce.' Beattie gasped a shocked laugh and her eyebrows disappeared beneath her curly fringe. 'Well, we all know she's ugly 'n' fat but I reckon Louisa'd put out his lights if she knew he'd said she ain't a proper brass. Ain't right to go saying such terrible things about folk.'

'Changed your tune, ain't you?' Alice said. 'It was good riddance to bad rubbish a moment ago.' She was angry and frightened that perhaps what Beattie had naturally assumed to be true *was* true, and it had made her agitated and snappy. Was Sarah a waitress, or had she finally become desperate enough at being burdened with her mother to join her sisters in living off vice?

'No need to get narky wi' me, Alice Keiver!' Beattie remonstrated. 'Like I said, I'm just passing on what I heard.' With that the woman stomped off, leaving Alice to enter the shop alone.

'Not a lot more we can do for you here, Private Keiver.' The doctor suddenly glanced up from writing his notes and gave Jack a penetrating look as though pondering on making too hasty a decision. 'The wound's healing quite well, but better to be safe than sorry with a head injury,' he finally declared. 'Don't want you keeling over on your colleagues and making yourself more of a hindrance than a help. I think it's time you were convalescing down the line.' He resumed scribbling on Jack's ticket then strode on to his next patient.

Geoff slanted Jack a subtle, satisfied smile. They were sitting together, Jack in a comfy chair, Geoff perched on a stool, in the smallest of the basement rooms situated in the farmhouse that had been commandeered for service as an aid post. In the background could be heard the dull whines and thuds of mortar fire. But neither man winced as a moment later the building shook from an explosion close by. The welcome news they'd just heard from the doctor reverberated in their minds, drowning out all else. Jack was going down the line. The further he travelled towards the coast of France and a base hospital the more likely it was to be sent to a Blighty one and get sent home to convalesce.

The Germans had been relentlessly bombarding the allied positions over the past few days. Geoff and Vinnie Cartwright had just brought in to the aid post a sapper who'd had his left foot blown clean off. Once they'd got the injured man settled Geoff had quickly slipped off to find Jack and have a chat. He knew there'd be scant time for conversation. Soon he would be summoned to act as runner to get transport to take the injured sapper to a main field hospital. No serious casualty stayed for long at the aid station. As time had passed and Jack had remained where he was Geoff had come to fear he might arrive and find Jack gone – passed as fit to return to duty.

'You're on yer way.' Geoff cackled quietly. 'Soon be home.' He gently tapped the small, neat dressing on Jack's head. 'And you ain't getting no favours neither. That's a kosher bad'un if the doc's said so. Had yer tetanus?'

'Done straight away, it was. Day I got here.'

'Make sure it all gets noted down on yer ticket,' Geoff advised earnestly as he flicked the docket attached to Jack's coat. 'The more stuff you've got written on yer ticket, the further along it'll take you.'

'What's happening up there?' Jack asked, eager to have news from the front line. 'Sounds like the end o' the world.'

'Nothing new really, just more of it,' Geoff told him with a grimace. 'They got in reinforcements 'cos they know we got 'em beat. But the bleeders just won't roll over. They've been shelling us like mad, so we shell 'em back. They snipe at us, we snipe right back.' Geoff leaned forward on his chair, rested his elbows on his knees. 'Downpours we got earlier in the week ain't helped, of course. Knee deep in places, it is, and perishing cold especially at night.' He twisted his fingers. 'Few of the poor blighters got the gammy foot; you know, toes turned black. Horrible, it is. Crippled, they are. Then there's the stinkers they've been sending over. Got to keep your gas mask on you at all times or you're for it . . .' He broke off on seeing his colleague beckoning to him. His partner Vinnie had appeared with a rueful expression. Geoff had seen it too often not to know it meant it was time for a sprint.

'Gotta go.' Geoff stood up abruptly. 'If you're gone next time I'm back here, take right good care of yourself. Remember me to 'em all back home.'

'You take care of yourself too, son,' Jack said and just for a moment gripped tightly at Geoff's closest hand. Abruptly he shook it then rested his head back against his armchair and quickly closed his glittering eyes.

TWENTY-SEVEN

Alice was about to give up and go home when she suddenly spotted a face she knew. She'd been wandering around and about the environs of Finsbury Park for more than an hour, hoping to spot Sarah or one of her sisters. She knew if Sarah had turned to streetwalking she would probably emerge after dark to do business. It was late afternoon and dusk had already settled. A few working girls were already about and sending Alice very aggressive stares as they loitered beneath the street lamps. They were obviously wondering if she was intending to poach their patch. Alice huddled into her coat, trying to seem inconspicuous and innocent to avoid trouble. She was constantly feeling tempted to give up and get going home, not simply because she felt vulnerable, but because if her mother ever found out that she'd been hanging around street corners in Finsbury Park she'd give her the hiding of her life.

It had been a week since Ginny Whitton had told her Sarah had moved out. Alice had wanted to come looking for her sooner but had waited until Lucy was well enough to resume school before tackling a new problem. She'd lost a few hours' wages by finishing her shift early so she could come and look for her friend with the intention of persuading her to go back home. Added to that was the guilt she felt at having hoodwinked her supervisor, Mr Chaplin. She liked and respected him yet she'd lied and told him she must get off early because she was needed at home to nurse Lucy. She'd risked a great deal in coming here and was thus reluctant to give up and allow it all to have been a squandered effort.

Now, as Alice glanced again at Nellie Tucker, stationed on the opposite pavement, she realised the woman had recognised her too. Alice was tempted to rush across the street to question her before she disappeared. She knew that Nellie had worked this area for some time now so might know where the Whitton sisters were living. On the other hand Alice realised it would be sensible to avoid the woman at all costs. Nellie had been Jimmy Wild's fancy piece and Alice didn't want to be involved in any discussion about her uncle's disappearance. Nellie might probe for answers to awkward questions.

Indecision kept Alice where she was and it also made Nellie dither on the spot. Nellie knew the Keivers hated her, and with good reason. They were a close-knit clan and she'd caused trouble for Alice's aunt by going off with Jimmy Wild, no matter she now regretted having ever become involved with the nasty bastard. That aside, Nellie was keen to cross the road and speak to the girl for two reasons: firstly, she wanted to discover if the body in the river had been identified as Jimmy's. If it had, she knew she ought to make tracks out of London in case she got dragged into an investigation. Saul Bateman had scarpered, she knew not where. But if the police had reason to pursue the investigation they'd hound her for information as to his whereabouts. Secondly, she was feeling inquisitive. She wanted to know what a nice girl like Alice Keiver was doing loitering about in a red-light district. She was definitely not a girl Nellie had down as a novice brass. But then she *was* out of The Bunk so anything *was* possible . . .

'You're Alice Keiver, aren't you?' Nellie had spontaneously made a spurt across the street and blurted that out.

'That's right,' Alice answered, torn between edging away from Nellie and firing off a question of her own. 'Looking for me friend . . .'

'Got any news of your uncle . . .?'

They had simultaneously rattled off what was on their minds then fallen silent.

'I'm looking for me friend,' Alice quickly recommenced before Nellie could get in first with her question. She wanted to find out what she could then depart before Jimmy's name was mentioned again. 'Don't know if you might remember the Whitton sisters?'

A laugh from Nellie interrupted her. 'Yeah; I know the Whittons alright,' she confirmed. 'Me and Louisa got a business arrangement.'

'Oh . . . I see . . .' Alice said whilst quickly digesting that Nellie must mean she was one of the girls Louisa pimped for. 'I'm not looking for Louisa,' she informed her swiftly. 'Her sister Sarah's me friend and it's her I want to find.'

'Yeah; I know who you mean. Young 'n' skinny and not been with them long. Gawd knows how they stand it, all cooped up in that poky place together.' Nellie's expression displayed her distaste. 'Got a room to meself, I have,' she added proudly.

'Where are they?' Alice bluntly demanded. In her desperation to have the information she'd sounded quite rude. 'Is it far?'

'Just up there.' Nellie pointed across the road to a draper's shop. 'They've got a room above that shop.'

Alice's mouth dropped open. She'd been standing within

sight of their door. If they'd looked out of the window they would have seen her. 'Thanks,' she mumbled and swung away.

Nellie caught at her arm. 'Any news about your uncle?'

Alice swiftly slipped free of her clutch. She shook her head. 'Don't want none neither,' she muttered.

'Know how you feel,' Nellie said and, with a satisfied smile, she crossed the road again.

It was getting cold and dark and Alice wanted to be on her way home. She never stayed out willingly at this time of the evening in case of an air raid. Nervously she hopped from foot to foot whilst waiting for someone to answer the door. She knew someone was up there because a faint light was flickering behind the thin curtain covering the window. Quickly she pressed closer to the door as a fellow ambled by, eying her from beneath the brim of a hat pulled low on his forehead. He'd been loitering about for a while. She'd noticed him watching her while she'd been talking to Nellie. Now Alice was keeping a furtive eye on him too. He turned at the top of the street then started to saunter back towards her. Alice hammered long and loud with the doorknocker then muttered in relief as finally she heard a clatter of footsteps on wooden stairs.

'What you doin' here?'

'I'm looking for Sarah.' Alice answered that snarled question whilst peering through the dusk at Louisa's heavy jowls propped on the door-edge.

'She ain't going back with you to The Bunk; so if that's what you're here for you can piss off.'

'If she's in there I want to speak to her,' Alice insisted. 'Sarah's old enough to do her own talking.' Louisa might intimidate her sisters but she didn't frighten her. Alice knew she had her mother's intrepid spirit in that respect. In fact she felt tempted to shove at the door and breeze right past Louisa.

Louisa jerked open the door and pugnaciously sized Alice up. 'Don't poke yer nose in, Alice Keiver, I'm warning you. Both me sisters are old enough to stop here with me if they want.'

'Who is it?' a voice called from above.

Alice angled her head to try and see who was standing in the shadows at the top of the stairs. She hadn't recognised the voice as Sarah's. A young woman started to descend the treads then she came up behind Louisa and linked arms with her in an affectionate way.

This, Alice guessed, must be Sonia. She tried not to show her astonishment at the sight of a slender blonde-haired girl of about eighteen.

'She's here to see Sarah,' Louisa growled out in explanation. Without another word she turned about and stomped back up the stairs, bawling, 'Sar, you've got a visitor.'

'Come in then,' Sonia invited and opened the door wider.

Alice took a step over the threshold, aware that Sonia was giving her the once over. Suddenly Alice's palms felt quite clammy yet she wasn't sure why a petite woman should unnerve her when a foul-mouthed bruiser couldn't. She guessed it must be because Sonia was nothing like she'd imagined she would be.

After her initial revulsion on learning Louisa was a lesbian, who acted as a pimp for her girlfriend, Alice had given the matter scant thought. She'd simply assumed Louisa must have paired up with a person who was her equal in hideous looks and character. But Sonia couldn't have been more different to Louisa. She seemed polite enough. She was also pretty enough to attract a man should she want a proper boyfriend rather than a punter. Alice's contemplation was disturbed as, from the corner of an eye, she glimpsed the fellow who'd been stalking her. He was loitering outside the half-closed door as though he'd been listening to their conversation. Quickly she pushed the door shut behind her in case he tried to come in.

'Go on up,' Sonia prompted her in the gloom of the corridor. 'Sarah'll be getting her clothes on. She was only half-dressed when I come down here just now.'

Alice shot a startled look at Sonia.

'Oh . . . I ain't interested in her skinny arse,' Sonia declared on a chuckle. 'Sarah was gettin' ready to go to work, that's all.' She planted her hands on her hips. 'Go on . . . don't be shy . . . go on up if you want to speak to her.'

'Ain't shy,' Alice returned sharply. 'Just ain't got much time to be hanging around or going up 'n' down stairs.' She felt annoyed that Sonia had sensed her uneasiness.

'Oh . . . right you are,' Sonia said, still sounding amused. 'Well, if it helps at all I'll let you know, I ain't interested in your skinny arse either.' At that she flounced past with a grin and ran lightly up to the first floor.

Alice followed behind. She wrinkled her nose at the sulphurous smell of boiled cabbage that became stronger the higher she climbed. It was a similar stale odour to the one that clung to The Bunk and no more pleasant for being laced with cheap scent.

Several doors lead off at the top of the first flight, but Alice headed directly towards the room leaking light onto the landing. She took a tentative step over the threshold. By the glow of an oil lamp she could see that it was a larger room than she'd expected, and that an attempt had been made to spruce up battered furniture with bits of colourful cloth. There were two beds covered in gaudy satin eider-downs pushed against opposite walls. On the largest bed Connie was lying on her stomach, her chin propped in her hands as she read a book, a glass of gin by her side on the floor. In the centre of the room was a table at which Louisa and Sonia had now taken seats opposite one another.

'Alright, Al?' Connie called and gave her a little tipsy wave before she looked back at her book.

Alice mumbled a response, her eyes searching for Sarah. Her friend suddenly appeared from behind her. She was in plain dark clothes; the sort of uniform a waitress might wear.

'Privy out back,' Sarah said by way of explanation for her absence.

'Oh . . . right,' Alice mumbled, spinning about to face her.

'Ain't going back to The Bunk with you,' Sarah announced sullenly and perched on the edge of the small bed. She began to pick listlessly at her nails.

'Don't be daft!' Alice hissed. 'If you don't turn in at Kemp's soon you'll lose your job fer sure.'

'Don't want me job back. I've got a job waitressin' and I'm off there to work in a minute.'

Sarah certainly looked to be dressed for the job, but Alice suspected there was more to it than that. She jerked her head and gave Sarah a speaking look to indicate they should go out of the room to talk privately.

'She told you, she's got a job.' Louisa scowled threateningly at Alice.

'Show Al what you've earned, Sar,' Connie piped up without looking away from her reading matter. Deftly she leaned over the edge of the bed and refilled her glass from the gin bottle on the floorboards.

'Take it easy on that stuff,' Louisa flung at Connie, who was already gulping back a mouthful of her fresh drink. 'Yer gent's gonna be here in less than an hour. He won't pay up if you're too pissed to perform.'

Alice felt her stomach turn on hearing that. She grasped one of Sarah's arms and tugged her up off the bed and towards the door. When they were on the landing Sarah tried to free herself but Alice held on tight as though to prevent her running back to her sisters.

'You can't stop here, Sar!' Alice blurted. 'It's enough to make anybody feel sick. Don't tell me that you don't think so too 'cos I won't believe you mean it.'

Sarah looked away, her eyes glistening suspiciously. 'You don't know the half of it,' she muttered. 'You want to hear the sound comes out of Louisa's bed at night. Don't get no sleep, not even with the covers over me head. Con reckons she needs to drink so much so she can't see or hear 'em at it. Goes through gin like it's water, she do.' Sarah wiped a hand over her dribbling eyes. 'Still reckon it's better than living with Mum in The Bunk though.' Sarah fished in a pocket and withdrew a fistful of silver coins and two ten-shilling notes. 'Got all that in under a week and only got to give Lou one ten-bob note out of it. Never had that much money to meself in all me life.'

Alice abruptly let go of her arm but Sarah stayed where she was. 'Your mum thinks you're doing waitressing with Connie,' Alice whispered hoarsely. 'Don't reckon you got all that as wages for waitressing. Did you?'

'Some of it's tips,' Sarah said defensively. 'Nice place it is, off Piccadilly. Wages are rubbish but staff can get a good dinner on the cheap.' Sarah raised her chin to a defiant angle. 'But most of it ain't restaurant tips; it's what I've earned off clients Louisa's got for me.' Her eyes slid away from Alice's. 'I'm working half 'n' half if you must know. Don't see why not. Banksie's been gettin' a hand job free for ages and I ain't that keen on him. Now I got some old bloke who can't get it up gives me six bob just to watch me take me clothes off.'

'You got to come home,' Alice whispered. 'You'll get your factory job back and nobody'll know for sure what you've been up to. Please, Sar . . .'

'Connie got me the job waitressing,' Sarah bluntly interrupted Alice. 'She was doing a bit of waitressing there too but she don't need it now she's got a couple of real good clients. Lou reckons she can get one of them to set Con up in a flash place just like Mr Lucas did.' Sarah let the cash fall back into her pocket. 'Have you seen Banksie? Has he been saying bad things about me?' Sarah wiped her face again. 'Called me a whore when I told him I was going to live with Con. That was before I'd even decided to go on the game.'

'Not seen him at all,' Alice said truthfully. She didn't want to let Sarah know that it was already doing the rounds in The Bunk, courtesy of Banksie's big mouth, that Sarah and her sisters were all living off vice. If Sarah knew she'd be returning home to stares and whispers she'd never show her face in Campbell Road. 'I've seen your mum though,' Alice added quickly. 'She got me to fetch a bottle of gin from the shop. She's missing you, of course.'

'How much was her booze?' Sarah drew her money out again.

'You don't owe me,' Alice speedily said. 'Ginny paid for it straight off.'

''Spose she called me a few choice names. She went bonkers when I told her I was leaving.'

'She's missing you,' Alice repeated. 'She's worried too, I expect, that she'll end up in the workhouse. She seemed a bit doddery on her feet . . .'

'Ain't only my problem!' Sarah howled in anguish. 'Ain't fair! Those two don't give a toss about her, why should I?'

'I knew you was gonna cause trouble soon as I opened the door and saw you standing there,' Louisa bawled from the doorway of the room. Connie was hovering in the aperture too, trying to peer over her sister's meaty shoulder and discover what the commotion was about. Louisa started towards Alice with her fists raised. 'Now get yourself off out of here, Keiver, or I'm gonna kick yer down them stairs.'

Sarah jumped in front of Alice as though to protect her from her sister's temper. 'She's going . . . she's going right now.'

Alice received a sharp dig in the ribs from Sarah to hurry her on her way. Still she hesitated. She didn't want to cause a ruckus but neither did she want to go and leave Sarah behind.

'Get going, Al,' Sarah hissed urgently. 'Con's gent'll be turning up soon anyhow. You won't want to be around when he comes in. Dirty ol' sod might like the look of you 'n' think you're new here.'

Shaking her head in defeat Alice turned and went down stairs and let herself out into the night. She was walking briskly and almost home when she heard a faint voice calling her. She whipped around and frowned into the darkness. Out of the gloom Sarah suddenly appeared, huffing and puffing, struggling to carry the carpetbag in her hand. Alice stopped and let Sarah catch her up then catch her breath.

'Ain't saying I'm gonna be back with me mum fer long,' Sarah gasped. She dumped the bag on the floor and sucked in air. 'Might only stay for a couple of weeks, I dunno yet. Soon as I can't stand it no more, I'm off.' She shoved her straggly, matted hair behind her ears. 'Lost me job in the restaurant now. Should've turned in half an hour ago. So if I can't get back me job in the factory, I'm gonna be in Queer Street in any case.'

Alice hugged Sarah to her, tears prickling at the back of her eyes. 'We'll sort it out,' she promised gruffly. 'Kemp's isn't the only factory around. I'll have a go getting you in Turner's and if that doesn't work . . . well . . . there's other munitions factories taking on.'

Breathing more easily now Sarah picked up the bag that contained her few possessions. 'D'you reckon Banksie might've calmed down a bit and might take me back? Or d'you reckon he might've guessed what I've been up to while I've been away?' Pessimism was apparent in Sarah's tone.

Alice linked arms with her friend and they began to walk on towards The Bunk. 'So what if he has?' she said breezily. 'He was never good enough for you anyhow.'

Getting Out

1917–1918

TWENTY-EIGHT

'You takin' the night shift next week, Alice? Only one's wanted from our section.'

'Do you want it?'

Bert Lovat nodded vigorously. 'Could do with it . . . if you don't mind, that is.' He stepped closer and used the workbench as a prop to ease his bad foot. Bert was still deeply grateful to Alice for helping him get a job at Turner's. As soon as a vacancy had turned up that would suit him she'd made sure he was first in line for an interview. To show his appreciation he continued, after many months in the job, to ask her permission before he put himself forward for the plum shifts.

'I don't want it,' Alice lied. 'You help yourself.' She nodded towards the supervisor's office. 'You'd best get in quick and see Mr Chaplin 'cos I know Annie Foster spoke about applying for it.'

Night work was sought after despite the fact that factories, lit up at night, were targets for German bombs. That was considered a paltry deterrent to people trying to earn enough to keep a large brood fed. Most people were conscious too that millions of fathers, sons and brothers were facing untold peril on foreign soil. They therefore considered keeping the munitions and engineering works going round the clock to be the least they could do to demonstrate support for those brave souls.

Alice watched Bert hobbling away towards the supervisor's station, grim determination etched on his features. She had wanted next week's night shift. Christmas was almost on them and she could have done with the extra money. But she'd promised Geoff she'd do what she could for his family. She and her mother and aunt owed him so much. Letting his father take the pick of the shifts was next to nothing in return. In protecting them all, and braving Jimmy's vicious attack, he'd risked his life and his future. Alice always grew cold when pondering what would happen if Margaret and Bert Lovat discovered the hideous truth about why their son had so suddenly decided to enlist. But they mustn't ever know. Nobody must ever know.

'Mr Chaplin's son's come to see him. He looks nice, don't he?'

Alice whipped about, startled. She'd been so lost in guilty thoughts she'd not heard Annie Foster come up behind her. She continued unbuttoning her overall with unsteady fingers while blood thundered in her ears.

'Look . . . over there . . .' Annie nodded sideways, nudging Alice to gain her attention. So interested was Annie in the young soldiers that she'd not noticed how unsettled Alice seemed.

Alice glanced obligingly at the young men talking to their supervisor. Their blue flannel suits and red ties made it obvious they were home on convalescence.

'Mr Chaplin's son's the taller one,' Annie whispered.

He *did* look nice. If he were like his father he probably was very nice. Mr Chaplin was a good boss, well-liked and respected. You could have a laugh and a joke with him but not take liberties, if you knew what was good for you.

'Let's go over and say hello,' Annie hissed. 'The son's quite a looker, ain't he? Better-looking than his pal.'

Alice gave Mr Chaplin Junior a closer inspection. He was probably only a few years older than she was. He wasn't as dark, or as tall and stocky as Geoff. But he was tall and broad enough. His hair and complexion were fair, like his father's, and his profile promised pleasing features.

He turned and looked their way. Immediately he smiled and Alice was struck by the gentle friendliness in his expression.

'Come on,' Annie hissed. 'Don't need no more invitation than that. I reckon he'd like to get to know us too.'

Alice, for a reason she didn't understand, shrugged away from Annie's grip. 'No. I told Mum I'd get straight home. Besides, I want to write a letter to Geoff.'

Annie shrugged and walked over to the group of men as Alice negotiated a maze of workbenches until finally she got to the factory exit. Before she left she glanced over her shoulder. Annie was chatting to the soldier she hadn't thought that good-looking. Mr Chaplin's son was watching her leaving. Alice received another mild smile, perhaps tinged this time with a little disappointment.

Quickly she slipped out of the door and set off home.

'Keep away, yer bastard . . . keep away, yer bastard . . . keep away, yer bastard . . .'

The peculiar chanting was undoubtedly in her mother's voice and it prompted Alice to speed down the remaining stairs. She burst out of the hallway and onto the pavement where she spied Tilly straight away. Her mother hadn't got very far in her trip to the shop. In fact she was retreating backwards towards her own doorway as though to seek its shelter. Alice peered beyond Tilly in search of an explanation for her odd behaviour. When she found it she felt her knees weaken and she gripped at the iron railing to one side of her for support.

Cycling towards them was a telegraph boy, or a messenger of death, as they were known, for they delivered news of those fallen in the war. They were the most alarming sight to people with men in the armed forces.

Tilly dropped her head and stared at her shoes as though praying that if she didn't look, he wouldn't be there. Alice watched him, transfixed, as he drew nearer and nearer then pedalled past. Obliquely she realised she felt sorry for him. He looked as nervous as she felt. People came only reluctantly to Campbell Road at the best of times. This lad was hated simply for doing his job. As Alice exhaled her pent-up breath he creaked to a stop at a house on the opposite side of the road.

'It's the Forbes' . . . he's knocked at the Forbes'.' Tilly audibly gasped in a relieved sob. She crossed herself muttering an oath of thanksgiving. 'Poor Dolly. Could be Walter or Gregory.' She named the woman's sons, both of whom had joined up. 'I'll go across and see her later. Don't suppose she'll feel like company now.'

Other women in the street had been dawdling; watching and waiting in trepidation. A fellow removed his cap and bowed his head in anticipation of a bereavement being made public. A wail of anguish sounded and the telegraph boy was seen to skitter back and quickly mount his bike. He sped off down the road while the women dotted about shook their heads, cuffed at their eyes then went solemnly about their business.

Tilly started off to the shop again then cast a glance back over a shoulder at her daughter. Alice hadn't moved; her sad blue gaze was resting on the woman who had sunk to her knees on her doorstep.

'Going to work now, Mum,' Alice finally murmured and trudged off in the opposite direction.

'I didn't get a chance to introduce myself the other day.'

Alice swung about. She'd been on the point of hurrying, head down, through the factory gate when that greeting made her snap up her chin and draw to a halt.

Mr Chaplin's son strolled up and leaned a shoulder on the black iron. His easy smile, very like the one she remembered from his previous visit to the factory, warmed her upturned face. Close to he was more handsome than she'd thought. His grey-blue eyes twinkled at her.

'Can't stop now,' she said quickly. 'Don't want your dad telling me off for being late for me shift.'

'Won't keep you more than a minute. I'd just like to properly introduce myself. I'm Joshua Chaplin.'

His fingers, as they closed around hers, felt long and firm. Her hand remained cradled in his for a moment before he gave it a businesslike shake.

'Well . . . nice to meet you. I'm Alice Keiver, but I reckon you might already know that.'

'I confess I do.' He grimaced apology. 'I asked my dad your name. Hope you don't mind.'

'No . . . I don't mind,' Alice said with unusual shyness. He was again in his hospital uniform so she added politely, 'Hope you soon get better. Is it bad?'

Joshua shook his head on glancing down. 'Leg wound.' He started to walk with her as she approached the entrance to the factory. 'It got infected. If it heals properly this time I expect I'll be sent back.'

Alice noticed then that he had a slightly awkward gait. She stopped, not because of his limp but because he had an air of restfulness about him that she found appealing. She realised she'd like nothing better than to linger in his company and talk. The idea that he might soon rejoin the fighting, and she might never see or speak to him again, saddened her. 'Well, in that case, I hope it takes a good while before it's right,' she blurted.

'Thanks,' he said. 'I'd sooner stop here too now I know what's waiting over there.'

'It's dreadful, isn't it?' Alice said and angled an earnest look up at his profile.

Joshua nodded but his affable smile remained unaffected by whatever harrowing memories he had.

'Me dad and me friend, me best friend that is, are in France,' Alice gruffly told him.

'I hope they'll both be safe and back soon.'

'I pray for it every day,' she replied vehemently.

The door to the factory beckoned but still Alice didn't yet want to use it. She wanted to stay with Joshua a while longer. And that's what he wanted. She could read from his steady grey gaze that he liked her. She knew it would be easy to flirt with this fellow yet felt ashamed of even thinking it when Geoff was in France fighting, risking his life, because of her. The last time she'd seen Geoff had been right here. He'd come to see her at work, in her dinner break, to take a walk with her and say goodbye. They'd kissed. She'd offered him more than that. A less worthy man than Geoff would've taken what she'd offered. She'd known for a long while that Geoff loved her. And she loved him dearly; but she wasn't sure it was in the way he wanted. Now she was standing here with another man and she knew that, if he asked, she'd like to take a walk with him. But she mustn't.

A short while ago her mind had been filled with the memory of the telegraph boy. He might have brought news today that her dear dad or Geoff had been killed in the fighting. She'd set off to work with her heart still thumping and a sense of momentous relief trembling her limbs that some other poor soul had got the news she'd dreaded. Now that feeling was lost to a sense of guilt and shame. 'Got to go in. I'm late,' she mumbled and hurried into the building, leaving Joshua standing quite still, watching her.

When Alice emerged into midday sunshine she immediately glanced about. Joshua Chaplin was nowhere to be seen. A sense of disappointment washed over her despite that she tried to convince herself she was glad.

'Going round the caff?' Annie Foster had strolled up beside her.

Alice nodded. They started to walk along Blackstock Road in the direction of Kenny's café.

'I saw Joshua Chaplin hangin' around by the gate this morning,' Annie said with a sly glance at her friend. 'He seemed keen to find out off his dad what your name was. Reckon he took a shine to you straight off. Did he ask you to the dance?'

'Dance?' Alice looked sharply at Annie.

'He didn't ask you, then.'

'What dance?'

'Dance being arranged next month over the Wood Green Empire for the servicemen home on sick leave. I wished he'd asked me. His pal asked me instead. D'you remember the one was here with Joshua last week? Paul O'Connor is his pal's name.'

'Are you going with him?' Alice asked. She knew that Annie and Tommy Greenfield were sweethearts. She knew too that Tommy had enlisted over a year ago.

'Might do,' Annie said. 'Can't sit about moping forever. Tommy wouldn't want me to, I reckon.' She slid Alice an astute look. 'Geoff wouldn't want you to neither.' She stuck her hands in her coat pockets and shivered. Although it was sunny it was January and very cold. 'Just a dance anyhow,'

Annie added with a shrug. 'That's all it is. And I reckon we owe the poor blighters a bit of lighthearted fun before they get shipped off again.'

'Well, I've not been asked,' Alice said flatly. 'So that's that.' They'd reached the café and she pushed at the door. 'Let's get something to eat.'

'Off to a dance, are yer! That's nice! Geoff's fightin' in France and you're out gallivanting with a feller.'

'He's not a feller. Not the way you mean anyhow.' Alice continued brushing her hair then pinned it neatly to frame her face. She turned her head to inspect her reflection in the mirror and tidy a few wisps. 'It's a works outing, that's what it is. Annie's going and so are some others from Turner's. Mr Chaplin and his wife and son are going too.' Joshua had asked her to the dance the next time she'd seen him. After a little gentle persuading Alice had accepted. She was looking forward to it because she'd realised that what Annie had said was true. It was just a dance, and heaven only knew the poor souls who were invalided home deserved a little bit of enjoyment before they were sent back to the trenches. *They can't hardly dance with themselves, poor sods,* one married woman on Alice's section had declared. A moment later she had volunteered to make up the numbers, saying her sailor husband wouldn't mind a bit.

'But it's Mr Chaplin's son you're interested in, ain't it?'

'Don't be daft,' Alice told her mother crossly. 'Don't you think these fellows have earned a little bit of enjoyment before they get sent back to the fighting?'

'He asked you to go, didn't he?' Tilly ignored Alice's reasonable enquiry.

'How do you know that?' Alice asked sharply. She knew her mother wasn't above checking up on her.

Tilly tapped her nose. 'Got me spies, don't you worry about that.' She slanted a shrewd look at her daughter. 'I know a fellow in hospital blues has been hangin' around the factory gate waiting for you at dinnertimes. I know you've been several times down the caff with him.'

'Well, as you know all that, you should also know that Annie's been coming too. And you should know that what we talk about most is Geoff and Dad and Tommy Greenfield and all the men we know who are serving out there, and how much we miss them and want them back in one piece,' Alice rattled off angrily. 'And it's usually a big party of us meet up. Some of Joshua's friends join us at the caff . . .'

'Oh . . . *Joshua*, is it?' Tilly interrupted triumphantly.

Alice shrugged and rolled her eyes.

It was inevitable that sooner or later her mother would get wind that a man was showing an interest in her. A lot of people from The Bunk worked at Turner's. And her mother collected rent from many of those families.

'You look nice, Al.' Fran had come up from downstairs. She stood on the threshold, admiring her niece in her pretty best clothes.

'Going to a dance with a feller, ain't she? Fine carry on after all wot Geoff done for her.'

'He did it for us all,' Alice stated quietly. 'And well you know it.'

'No harm in it, Til, is there, for her to go out and enjoy herself fer once?' Fran looked awkward. 'Wish I was going out to a dance.' She slunk dejectedly down into a chair at the table but gave Alice an encouraging smile.

Since Jimmy's death Fran seemed to be a different woman. Initially the terrible shock of what happened that night had laid her very low. Then, just as she seemed to rally enough to appreciate the vital benefits of a life without a sadistic, bullying husband, the visit from Twitch and Franks had sent her again into a decline, confidence plummeting. But that had been a long while ago now. Tilly and Fran, in one of their rare intense talks about that night, had come to the conclusion the headless body in the river had not been identified as Jimmy's. The police would have returned to Campbell Road by now if it had. Fran was officially his next of kin even though they'd separated. If the constabulary hadn't managed to find out from Nellie what had become of Jimmy it seemed right to assume they would consider him a missing person. It was wartime and unexplained things happened. A lot of men had joined up and been killed or reported missing. People had perished in air raids . . . not all of them recognisable or accounted for.

Bobbie and Stevie had happily accepted an explanation that their father might have gone to fight the Hun as he hadn't been seen for a while. They rarely asked about him and had, as had their mother, blossomed in his absence. Fran had gained steadily in confidence and got herself a job soldering in the factory in Isledon Road where Alice had worked.

'Any chance of a job at yours yet?' Fran asked Alice. She had enquired a few times whether Turner's were taking on. The money there was better and she was getting ambitious.

'Keeping me ears 'n' eyes open for you,' Alice replied. 'Soon as I hear anything I'll let you know.'

'Beth needs a job too,' Tilly ordered bluntly with a quelling look for Fran. 'And I don't mean as a tea gel neither.'

'She's too young for nights, Mum.'

'I know that. Just get her a foot in the door on a daytime shift. The rest'll follow in due course.'

'Won't be late home,' Alice promised by way of farewell. Quickly she caught up her coat and went out.

'You don't want to be late neither!' Tilly's bawled threat followed Alice down the stairs.

Alice knew that her mother didn't like her going out spending even a little bit of money. She was now earning very well at Turner's and making the largest contribution to the kitty. With regular night shifts she could earn as much as two pound ten shillings a week. Her mother demanded two pounds for housekeeping despite the fact that Alice rarely ate at home and didn't want the old clothes her mother tried to fob her off with from the rag shop or from Billy the Totter. The amount her mother demanded she hand over was a constant cause of friction between them because a lot of the housekeeping pot went on booze. As much as she hated seeing so much of her hard-earned wages tipped down her mother's and Aunt Fran's throats – Tilly liked to have a drinking chum both at the Duke and at home – Alice felt less able to summon the energy to tackle her mother over it. She knew that the terrible circumstances of her uncle's death, and the revelation of the secret surrounding her birth, had increased her mother's need to seek comfort in the bottle.

Alice now had her own inner demons to subdue. Lurking constantly at the back of her mind was the hideous worry that Jimmy might have fathered her. Time and again she had taken Jack's photograph from the piano and stared into the mirror with it pressed to the side of her face. Sometimes she could find similarities that made foolish her fears; at other times she was sure not one of his features resembled hers. She didn't want to blame her mother. She'd first-hand knowledge of what a violent brute Jimmy Wild had been. But niggling at her was the thought that perhaps Tilly might have been drunk when she'd needed to be sober on that awful occasion too . . .

Alice hadn't wanted Joshua coming to Campbell Road and

being disgusted by the squalid place in which she lived. She had impressed on Annie that she'd meet her and their escorts at her place in Playford Road. But standing on the corner of Paddington Street were three people she recognised.

Joshua smiled warmly on seeing her. He had been lounging against the wall, head down, dragging on a cigarette while he waited for her. Now he stepped on the dog end on his way towards her. Annie and Paul O'Connor started off up the road towards the bus station and Alice and Joshua fell into step behind.

'Thought we agreed to meet outside yours,' Alice called sharply to Annie.

'Yeah, we did,' Annie answered, unconcerned. 'But as you was a bit late we walked round to save time.' She swung about and walked backwards, a grin on her face. 'We've been asked to take tea with Mr and Mrs Chaplin before we go off to the dance. Nice, eh?'

Alice shot a startled look up at Joshua's profile. 'Is that right? Are we going first to yours for tea?'

'Only if you want to. It was my mum's idea.' An apologetic look shaped Joshua's features. 'I wanted to invite you myself,' he said quietly. 'I didn't get a chance to mention it, though.'

It was the first time Alice had seen him look a bit annoyed about something. She took pity on him. 'A word of warning,' she said conspiratorially. 'Annie can't keep anything to herself.'

'Would you like to come for tea at ours?' Joshua asked.

'Yes . . . thank you,' she answered politely.

As they strolled on Alice was sure Joshua was glancing about at the grimy tenement houses and the ragged children hopping on and off the kerbs. It was probably his first experience of such a slum. A group of youths were playing dice on the opposite pavement in between regarding them with sullen hostility.

'It's a dump, ain't it?' Alice sounded defiant, as though she'd sooner mention it herself than have him do so. 'And that little lot are staring at you 'cos they don't like strangers round here.'

Joshua shrugged. 'Once I've been back a few times perhaps they won't think me a stranger round here.'

'Think you'll get invited back, do you?' Alice said, still sounding defensive. She couldn't curb her frustration that he now knew she lived in a hovel. 'You think it's a dump, don't you?'

'I'm not interested in the houses,' Joshua said mildly. 'I'm interested in someone who lives in one of them.'

Alice sent a fierce blue gaze up at him. 'Well, I ain't going to be here too much longer. I'm saving up . . . moving out . . . just as soon as I can.'

'Funny that,' Josh replied. 'Just before I came out tonight, I said more or less the same thing to my mum and dad.' He stuck his hands deep into his pockets. 'I told them that just as soon as this war's done, I'm getting my own place. Reckon it's time.'

'How'd they take that?'

Joshua slanted her a quizzical look. 'Oh . . . they don't mind. Probably be glad to see the back of me. Got a brother and sister still at home too, you see. It's a bit cramped.'

'Me mum won't be glad if I go,' Alice sighed. 'She likes me wages too much to want to see the back of them. Don't know how I'll tell her when the time comes.'

'I'll tell her for you if you like,' Joshua suggested quite seriously.

That provoked such a hearty, spontaneous laugh from Alice that the couple in front swung about in the hope of sharing the joke. 'You'll need to put your tin hat on when you do!' she finally said, wiping her eyes.

'As bad as that, eh?' Joshua grinned, unfazed by the hint that Mrs Keiver was a right dragon.

'Worse than you could ever know,' Alice murmured, turning her head. Her amusement had withered and she'd sounded quite depressed.

TWENTY-NINE

'Hello, stranger.' Tilly opened her door wider and looked Jeannie up and down. 'Still doin' alright then, I see,' she slurred with an admiring look at Jeannie's expensive outfit. 'Come in. Want one?' Tilly held out a bottle of whiskey. She'd been drinking since Alice left for the dance and Fran went back downstairs to get the boys their suppers. She was pleased to have an unexpected drinking pal.

Jeannie accepted with a smile and a nod.

Tilly was already tipsy but she was still canny enough to be seeking reasons for this odd visit. 'Nice to see you, Jeannie, but I reckon you're here 'cos something's on yer mind. That business with Sarah Whitton, is it?'

'Nah!' Jeannie chuckled. 'Just come by to say goodbye. I'm goin' away.' She sat down at the table.

Tilly shoved a half-filled glass towards her guest. 'Gone sour for you with Johnny Blake, has it?'

'Sort of.'

'You don't sound that put out,' Tilly said in surprise. A fellow like Johnny Blake would sound like a godsend to most of the women who lived in The Bunk.

'It's me wants to move on.' Jeannie sipped from her drink.

'He said I can go back any time. He'd take me in tomorrow. He's a good bloke in that respect. But I want to get Peter away from him,' she said quietly. 'He might be good for me but he ain't good for him.'

'Alice told me about your son being shell-shocked,' Tilly said and grimaced her sympathy. 'Very sorry to hear it, I was. And your other lad . . . the one reported missing?'

Jeannie shook her head, eyes glistening with tears.

'Has Johnny been mean to Peter 'cos he's not right?' Tilly asked with gruff gentleness. She could tell Jeannie would rather not speak about her other, lost son.

'He's been kind to him . . . too kind,' Jeannie said. 'Treats him like he would his own son.'

'That ain't bad, surely?'

'Yeah, it is when you're in the kind of business Johnny's in. Peter's getting better slowly; Johnny's been promising to bring him into the business and Peter's lappin' it up. Ain't what I want. All feuds and rivalry and gang wars, ain't it? Nature o' the work.' Jeannie took a large swallow of whiskey. 'Peter's all I've got now. I ain't losing him to some South London thug who wants to make a name for himself with his boss. I don't want Peter facing no more danger. He's just about survived one war; that's enough for him, I reckon.' Jeannie stood up, preparing to leave. 'Me husband's family's from Scotland. We used to take holidays there when the boys were little. Peter's forgot a lot, but not that. He speaks fondly of his grandma still. Weren't her fault her son turned out to be a nasty bastard. Gordon's enlisted anyhow so no danger of running into him. So that's where we're going.'

'Not stoppin' fer another?' Tilly waved the bottle.

Jeannie shook her head. 'Thanks all the same but I'm getting off. You take care of yourself, Tilly.' Jeannie looked at the bottle, tightly clutched, then at Tilly's glassy gaze. 'Ain't gonna find the answer in that, Tilly,' she said softly.

'I know. I've had a fuckin' good look in more whiskey bottles than I can count. Ain't there.'

Tilly looked at the whiskey in her fist. 'Hard to give up on hopin', though, ain't it, when you live round here?' She shoved unsteadily to her feet. 'Take care o' yourself, and hope it goes right fer you both.'

'You take care too, Tilly.' The hand that rested on Tilly's shoulder suddenly pulled her into an embrace that Tilly returned in full measure. They broke apart suddenly and Tilly immediately went to sit back down.

Just before Jeannie left she said, 'Oh, tell Alice for me that I got what I wanted for the statue. She'll know what I mean.'

Alice stood on the threshold to the small, neat dining room, her eyes immediately lured to the table. Upon its surface lay a crisp snow-white cloth and a veritable feast. As wonderful as the food looked it was the atmosphere of cosy tranquillity that had entranced her. For so many years she had dreamed of escaping from the clamour and decay of The Bunk to live in a place such as this. It was by no means a posh house; it was small and set in a terrace. The furnishings were not new or elaborate. But to Alice it was as fine as any palace.

'Glad you come now, ain't yer?' Annie grinned at her friend.

Alice felt her face heating at her friend's crude comment. At that moment she could have slapped Annie simply for cutting short her quiet appreciation of her surroundings.

'Let me introduce you to my mum.' Josh took her lightly by the elbow and drew her into the room.

A fair-haired woman had risen from her chair by the fireside. She immediately gave the newcomers a friendly, welcoming smile. Mr Chaplin came in through a door that Alice assumed led to the kitchen as he was bearing a large teapot.

'Well,' he said, 'You lot timed that to perfection. All ready and waiting for you.' He set the teapot down on the table.

'Mum,' Josh said, 'This is Alice . . . Alice Keiver.'

Mrs Chaplin took Alice firmly by the hand. 'So pleased to meet you, Alice. I've heard a lot about you. My husband tells me you're a good hard worker at Turner's.'

Alice smiled, tried to think of something to say but she still felt awkward and overwhelmed. 'How d'you do,' she blurted and briskly shook her hostess by the hand.

'Now, do tuck in, all of you,' Mrs Chaplin instructed the assembled company. She took a stack of china plates that had been resting on a corner of the table and handed them out.

Alice took one automatically with murmured thanks. She watched as Annie went immediately to the table and began to fill her plate with sandwiches, small cakes and pastries. The red jelly, soaring out of the centre of the spread, quivered as Annie's darting hand knocked its dish.

Josh poured two cups of tea then pulled out a chair for Alice to sit next to him at the table. He pushed one of the filled cups towards her.

'Tuck in,' he quietly encouraged her. He moved a plate of sandwiches and cakes within her reach. 'Don't want to be late for the dance.'

Daintily Alice took one sandwich and one cake and placed them on her plate. 'Thanks,' she gruffly muttered. 'This is very nice,' she added and raised her blue eyes to Josh's steady grey gaze.

'Good, I hope you enjoy it,' he answered softly. 'Because I'd like you to come for tea again before I get sent back.'

Geoff sank down in the trench with his back against the sucking mud and his boots disappearing into a bog. He could feel the cold sludge seeping into his socks and was glad.

When sensation was gone so might be his toes. He hung his head, tried to block out the sound of moaning calls from the wounded on no-man's land.

Earlier that week the Germans had broken through the Allied lines in several places and the result was a grotesque landscape of twisted bodies scattered as far as the eye could see. Things had since calmed down and both sides had again dug in. But a daring raid to try and take out a deadly accurate German sniper had brought new Allied casualties.

'Keep yer nut down,' Vinnie gutturally ordered.

Geoff had been peeping over the top of the trench into the mustard-coloured dusk, his squinting vision darting to locate twitching uniformed figures. He crouched down again beside his comrade. 'Can't stand it, I tell yer,' he hissed. 'Can see arms and legs moving; hear 'em wailing. Can't stay here and do nothing!'

'We can all hear 'em,' Vinnie muttered roughly. 'There ain't no point in us going to help and coppin' a bullet too off that bastard. Be no bleedin' use to them then, will we?'

Geoff knew what Vinnie was saying was true. But wounded comrades were close by; a few of them just yards away. Some might have minor wounds yet they would bleed to death if left too long. The stretcher-bearers must wait for the cover of full darkness before making their move. German snipers had already cruelly despatched several brave souls who'd made a heroic dash to recover their wounded pals. Even after dark it would be far from safe. The Germans would try to foil a rescue mission by sending up star shells and flares to illuminate the grisly scene.

'Fuckin' Fritz!' Vinnie gritted through his teeth. His eyes were screwed shut and he clapped his hands over his ears as a particularly awful scream rent the air. It was followed by an eerie, echoing silence. A boyish voice started to call for his mother then the sound of his anguish was drowned out as a shell whined overhead. Instinctively Geoff and Vinnie ducked but the fellows further along the trench took the brunt of that one. Energetic yelling filled the air and acrid smoke billowed their way. A group of men were shuffling through the sludge towards them, away from the damaged part of the trench.

Geoff and Vinnie struggled up and, grabbing their gas masks and a stretcher between them, they waded through the mud towards the newly injured, the wretched souls momentarily abandoned on no-man's land.

Now things were less frantic – and please God stayed that way, so many weary soldiers were heard to mutter – Geoff and Vinnie and several colleagues were being relieved. They were going into the village to be billeted and rested up for a few days. As they struggled on through the slime towards the injured Geoff concentrated on the comforts that were only twenty-four hours away. A hot bath and a good long sleep were almost his. Suddenly he felt his eyes sting with tears and felt silly and childish for being overwhelmed by the prospect of something good coming his way. Fiercely he sniffed and blinked and urged Vinnie to a faster pace along the trench.

'Keiver?' The medical orderly was unknown to Geoff. He hadn't seen him at the aid post before. The fellow searched up and down his list. 'Ah . . . Jack Keiver, Royal Fusiliers . . . yes, he's gone.'

Geoff grinned at the fellow. 'Lucky bleeder'll be home soon.'

The orderly frowned. 'Don't think so. Discharged as fit to return to duty,' he read from his clipboard. 'A lot of those borderline cases were passed fit when Fritz started acting up again. Everybody needed, see.'

Geoff's smile froze on his lips. 'Yeah, know that, don't I.

But not him. Doc said he was going down the line. Said he didn't want him keelin' over. That's what he said.' Geoff sounded quite belligerently insistent.

The orderly shrugged but looked sympathetic. 'New doctor's seen him, I expect. Old lot have all been relieved.' He looked at Geoff's easy attire. 'Same as you. You're off on rest leave, aren't you?'

Geoff nodded. His face was grim with disbelief. When he'd been relieved of duty he hadn't set off towards the village with his colleagues. He'd come straight here to the aid post to see if Jack had yet started his journey towards home. He'd been expecting to hear the welcome news that Jack had been taken by motor ambulance towards the railway line that ferried casualties towards the coast.

'Sorry there's no good news for you, mate,' the orderly said kindly. 'Friend of yours, is he?'

Geoff swallowed the bitter disappointment that seemed to trap speech in his throat. 'Yeah . . .' he finally answered. 'A good friend.'

THIRTY

'I'm being sent back.'

Alice had been staring dreamily into her tea. Now she jerked her head up and stared at Josh. 'Back? Back to the fighting in France?'

Josh nodded. 'Heard yesterday. I've been passed as fit.' He smiled wryly. 'Can't deny my leg is much better. Bit stiff, though.' He tested that limb's flexibility by wobbling it under the café table. He smiled reassuringly at Alice. 'I won't be in the thick of it straight off like I was before. Not exactly fast on my feet, am I?' he added ruefully. 'I'll be on light duties to start.'

'Wish you weren't going,' Alice finally gulped out. 'Wish this bloody war was over with!'

'Me too,' Josh agreed with quiet vehemence. He comfortingly squeezed Alice's fidgeting fingers as they flicked at a teaspoon. 'It can't go on much longer; since the Yanks came in last year everyone's been saying it's just a matter of time. Just needs a final few scraps on the Western Front and we'll have the Hun on the run. No point in stopping now, not when so many people have died. Can't let it all have been for nothing, can we?' he said on a sigh.

Alice knew what Josh had said was true. Every available man was needed for that final push to get the enemy retreating back to Germany. How else would her dear dad or Geoff ever get to come home? Still she didn't want Josh to go. She had come to like him very much.

'I hate this war! I bloody hate it!' she spat. 'Wish it had never started. Wish we'd never got involved in it.'

'You're not alone in that,' Josh said. 'Come on, I'll walk with you back to work.'

They stopped by the factory gate and finally Alice blurted out the question that had been buzzing in her head. 'Will I see you before you go?'

Josh shook his head. 'Will you write to me?'

Alice nodded vigorously.

'My dad'll let you know where to send letters.'

Again Alice nodded. 'I know it's not likely but if you were to come across me dad, or me friend Geoff Lovat . . .' Her words trailed away and she cuffed impatiently at her watering eyes.

'I'll keep a look-out for them both, promise,' Josh said. 'Royal Fusiliers and Middlesex Foot.' He reminded himself of what she'd told him about those two beloved fellows.

'Thanks,' Alice mumbled.

'You take right good care of yourself, Alice.' Slowly Josh took her hands and dipped his head towards her. He lightly touched his mouth to her soft cheek.

She had known him now for over three months. In that time they had gone out to the pictures and to dances and concerts for the servicemen. But never had they done so unaccompanied. Usually Paul O'Connor and Annie Foster or other young people from the factory joined them. And never before had Josh tried to kiss her. Josh knew about Geoff, of course, and that he held a special place in Alice's heart. But he'd never probed for information and asked Alice if her very good friend Geoff was also her sweetheart. And Alice had not said. Alice realised that she'd warmed to Josh even more because of it. It was as if he understood that there was far more to the bittersweet relationship between her and Geoff than she was able to explain. He was waiting, as was she, for fate to determine all their futures. Alice went on tiptoe, briefly brushed her mouth on Josh's cheek, mimicking the affection he'd shown her. She turned and wordlessly sped in through the factory gate.

'Post's arrived.'

Geoff sprung to his feet, a rare smile splitting his face. He'd been billeted in the village for several days and appreciated not one of them. The usual comforts of warm water, bedding and hot food held little cheer. Since he'd discovered Jack's misfortune nothing had bucked him up. Until now. One of the best, longed-for moments on rest leave was getting letters from home.

The corporal who'd been to the small post office to collect the treasure-filled sack started to delve inside and bark out names.

Vinnie Cartwright heard his name called and bounded forward.

Geoff gave his friend a smile while his heart thumped and he prayed he might soon be summoned. The corporal leaned in to scoop from the bottom of the sack for it was quite clearly now almost empty. 'Geoffrey Lovat!'

For a moment Geoff remained numb with thankfulness then he strode forward to take his two letters. A lingering look at the small, neat writing on one of them made a lump form in his throat. It was from Alice. The other bore his mother's spidery scrawl. He tore open that envelope and greedily read the news from home and his whole family's sincere wish that he was keeping safe and well. He smiled, slipped it in his tunic pocket. Then he looked at the letter from Alice.

'Not opening it?' Vinnie asked. He was folding up his own note and carefully replacing it in its envelope.

'Nah . . . saving that one fer later,' Geoff replied quietly. He put it away inside his breast pocket whilst withdrawing from the same place his crumpled packet of cigarettes. At his leisure later, in private, he would savour reading Alice's letter. Presently there were too many people milling about and too much distracting noise to dilute the precious moment.

Geoff got a foothold in the wall just as a star shell went up, silvering the slaughter on no-man's land. The Germans had begun a fresh onslaught and again broken through the Allied line just a day after he returned to the trench. It was night time; dark enough to try and recover what poor souls they could. 'I see him,' he whispered urgently to Vinnie. 'See him moving. Thirty yards I reckon, off to the right.' He hoisted himself up and slithered on his belly to the first bomb crater and dropped into it. His heart was pounding fit to burst his ribs. He poked his head up, alert to any sight or sound. Charred trees, mangled to death by shellfire, impeded his view here and there. Then he heard the faint call again and heaved himself from his shelter. He kept his head down, helmet leading the way. Using knees and elbows he moved forward as fast as he could, ignoring the flesh-ripping debris beneath him and praying that the boy's voice would continue to guide him with its faint cries.

Something gossamer-smooth, evocative, touched his hand and he'd scrambled on a foot or two before suddenly stopping. He wormed backwards, blindly patting at the corpse he'd moments ago gingerly avoided as it loomed in front of him in the mist. His scrabbling fingers again encountered silk fluttering lightly in the breeze. His hand slipped to where the material was clawed. He ran a hand from those cold fingers to an arm and up, up to a shoulder, to a head facing away from him. The man's skull refused to turn towards him. Geoff ran trembling fingers to an icy forehead, splaying them to locate a ridge of a scar high up beneath a lock of hair.

Despite the water flowing from his eyes, clouding his vision, Geoff could feel that Jack's face was otherwise unmarked. He pulled himself round in the lee of Jack's body to stare down into his face. A German flare bathed the body in pearly light, confirming its identity. Instinctively Geoff tried to close Jack's sightless eyes to protect them from rats but couldn't and he sobbed in frustration and anguish. With his forehead resting on Jack's frozen chest he felt for the silk scarf and carefully removed it from his fingers, trying not to tear it. Geoff folded the silk and placed it in his breast pocket, aware then that Vinnie was swearing and hissing at him to hurry up from somewhere in front. Geoff gasped in a lungful of fetid air and crawled on. He was sure he was close to the shell hole in which Vinnie was sheltering and pushed back on his elbows to properly clear his eyes of stinging brine and locate him. A bullet hit him in the chest, bouncing him over onto his back.

'Sehr schön,' the German soldier said and pulled the length of silk across a grubby palm. He'd just ransacked Geoff's pockets and found the scarf. He scrunched it in his fist, about to pocket it, when he felt stiff fingers on his leg. He shrieked, skittered back, making his comrade bellow a laugh. *'Jeder ist sehr tot! Windig, nur windig,'* he scoffed and carried on to salvage, as he'd been ordered, what he could from the carnage.

The soldier with the scarf glanced fearfully down into staring eyes. He wasn't sure the Tommy was dead or that the wind was responsible for moving him. When he'd leaned over the body, the young soldier had been on his side. Now he was on his back, wild eyes glaring fiercely at him.

He chanted a prayer and swiftly bent, replaced the scarf where he'd found it, in a pocket with a hole by the dead soldier's heart. With a swift, backward glance he moved on.

THIRTY-ONE

'Got a minute, Al?'

Alice turned to see Margaret Lovat hovering by her doorway, one of her chapped hands clenched on the iron railings. Alice had been about to dash back to work. She was a bit late but she smiled at her neighbour and went to see what she wanted. 'Just on me dinner break.' It was a gentle hint that she had little time to spare.

'Won't keep you more'n a minute,' Margaret said.

Alice sensed that the woman was uneasy and after a moment it occurred to her why that might be. Bert Lovat worked at Turner's and he knew, as did most of the staff, Alice had several times gone out with their supervisor's son. Recently Alice had noticed the stares and whispers increasing. Alice had suspected Bert or Margaret might have something to say about her friendship with Josh. They'd known that Geoff had started walking out with her before he went to fight.

'Just want to say that I ain't taking no notice of the rumours goin' about,' Margaret blurted.

'Rumours?' Alice echoed.

'Yeah . . . those bleeding good fer nuthin's trying to cause trouble. I ain't taking no notice of what they're saying and neither is Bert. We just wanted you ter know that. You've been real good to us since Geoff's been gone. Your mum has too and we don't forget favours. Just want you to know it.'

'What rumours?' Alice had grown pale. Suddenly those stares and whispers she'd noticed had taken on a sinister significance. Had it somehow become known . . . gossiped about . . . that her dad might not be her dad at all? Was the talk something to do with Jimmy's odd disappearance? Alice's imagination darted here and there. 'Who's been saying what?' she demanded rather rudely in her agitation.

'Thought you knew, Al.' Margaret sighed regretfully. 'I wouldn't have said nothing but Bert told me that there's been gossip at Turner's that you're in the family way. They're saying that you 'n' yer sister Sophy are out of the same mould where fellers are concerned.' Margaret pursed her lips. 'Your Sophy's alright. Her and Danny just had a bad start, that's all.' She put a motherly hand on Alice's shoulder. 'Talk is Josh Chaplin's got you pregnant 'n' done a runner rather'n stand by you.'

Alice let out a laugh of relief. 'What a load of rubbish!' She emphasised her disgust with a dismissive gesture. 'Josh's been sent back to France. If he didn't go he'd be a deserter.'

'Are you in the family way?' Margaret asked tentatively.

''Course not! I wouldn't! What about Geoff?' It was a spontaneous denial that drew from Margaret a twist of a smile.

'Geoff thinks the world of you, 'n' all Al. But . . . it's war, ain't it? Things happen; people change, so if it changes for you we just want you to know we don't bear no grudges over it.'

'I wouldn't ever hurt Geoff,' Alice declared passionately. 'He's me best friend in the world.' She blinked back the moisture filling her eyes.

* * *

'D'you know if Mr or Mrs Lovat's at home?'

'Yeah. That's me.' Margaret turned around to see who'd spoken so nervously.

The telegraph boy handed her something yellow.

'Are the Keivers home next door?' It was another quavering enquiry.

'I'm Alice Keiver.' Alice simply frowned at the boy. Her mind was still grappling with what Margaret had told her.

The lad quickly delivered another piece of yellow paper. He backed off. He'd been spat at, thumped and chased in his time. He was taking no chances, especially in this neighbourhood. Within a moment he'd set off at a run, pushing his bike. With an agile jump he was on and pedalling furiously.

Alice and Margaret stared at the telegrams and then at each other, shocked into speechlessness. Margaret suddenly collapsed and in trying to catch her Alice dropped her sheet of paper.

A few moments later Tilly came out of her doorway to find out what the noise was about and saw Alice and Margaret huddled together against the railings, wailing.

It should have been a horrible wintry day with wind and rain, thunder and fog. Alice trudged on aimlessly with the signs of spring mocking her anguish. The sky was blue and balmy air was stroking her wet face. The trees she passed had fat, unfurling buds of bright green. The sunny scene splintered into a kaleidoscope of colour as fresh tears streamed from her eyes.

She turned into Thane Villas and instinctively trudged towards the toy factory. She looked up at the board that showed a list of job vacancies. She could see the splinters in the wood where Geoff had quickly prised it free for her and helped her get her first job. Slowly she sank to the ground, sat with her back resting against the gritty brick pillar and howled for her dad and for Geoff; she cursed and shrieked, careless of being seen or heard.

'Been looking for you.'

Alice glanced up and through red puffy eyes saw Sarah Whitton.

'Saw Beth . . . she's in a state,' Sarah quietly explained. 'She told me about yer dad and Geoff . . . so sorry, Al . . .' Sarah crouched down then turned and sat beside Alice. Gently she put a hand on one of Alice's then withdrew it. She remembered well enough that at such a time you didn't want more than a little touch. She remembered how she'd felt when she'd first heard her dad had been killed. You didn't want to be smothered or talked at. You didn't know what you wanted. Sometimes it was best just to be left alone. After a while she asked quietly, 'You ready to go home?'

Alice moved her head to indicate she wasn't.

'Sit here a while, then . . .' Sarah said, and they sat together, barely moving or speaking. When Alice's grief erupted in hysterical screams and rants Sarah dropped her forehead to her drawn-up knees and let her be. They'd be alright, she told concerned people. And they would be.

When Alice struggled, stumbling, to her feet a couple of hours later Sarah got up stiffly too and walked by her side. When Alice wordlessly slipped her arm through her friend's for support Sarah's head briefly tilted sideways to comfort her as they carried on back to Campbell Road.

'My dad told me about your father being killed.'

Alice looked up at Josh. It was dusk but she could clearly read the sincere sympathy in his gentle grey gaze. She simply nodded and pressed together her lips. 'I'm glad you've come back safe,' she said. 'I prayed every day for it.'

'Thanks for writing to me. Have you finished for today?'

Alice nodded. 'Yeah . . . I'm going home.'

'It's dark. Is it alright if I walk home with you?'

Alice hesitated in answering. He'd been waiting for her when she came out of the factory gate. She knew he'd returned from France. Mr Chaplin had told her. She'd been expecting that at some time she'd come through the gates and see him waiting for her.

It was late November and the troops were still returning. A great many had been back in time for the victory celebrations on Armistice Day earlier in the month.

Campbell Road had celebrated the wonderful news of the end of the war in its own inimitable way. At intervals Alice had watched the uproar from the window that overlooked the street: bonfires raging in the road; boozy singing and jigging around the barrel organ; children with pots and pans and spoons marching up and down from one end of the road to the other, drumming their joy that fathers and brothers had, or soon would, come home. It had carried on for more than two days before petering out.

Of course Alice was glad it was over. But she'd cried bitter tears too. Save for another eight months' grace her dad and Geoff would've been back and she and her sisters and mother would have been out in the street with the others, the loudest singers, the liveliest jiggers.

But Josh had come back. He'd figured equally in her thoughts and prayers since he'd gone away.

'Is it alright if I walk you home?' Josh asked again. When Alice remained quiet he asked, 'Are you waiting for your sister Beth to finish her shift? Or is it Annie you're walking back with?'

'No. It's not that. Beth finished earlier than me. And Annie isn't here now; she's married.' At Josh's look of surprise she gave a small smile. 'When Tommy got back they got married straight away.'

'I'm pleased for them,' Josh said.

'Me too,' Alice said softly. She paused. 'It's not that I don't want to walk with you . . . it's just that me mum's probably going to be about and if she spots you . . .' Alice glanced apologetically at him. 'Since we lost me dad she's worse than ever. Drinking all day sometimes, she is. She lost her job with Mr Keane because of it.' Alice turned her head, feeling ashamed at what she'd admitted.

'Well, that's alright. Understandable that she's distraught. I'll stop with you on the corner of Paddington Street if you like.'

Alice gave him a small smile and nodded that she'd like to have his company in that case.

As they walked Josh said, 'It must have been a terrible blow when you got news of your dad.'

'Dreadful.' The word emerged as a hoarse whisper.

'Where did he fall?'

'Hill sixty . . . that's what we were told. Geoff . . . me best friend . . . was killed there too. I don't know if they ever saw one another. I hope they did. I hope they were good company for one another.'

'I hope so too,' Josh said with a throb of sincerity. 'I always liked to see a familiar face from back home, especially if it was a real surprise. You could reminisce about people and places you knew.'

'They got on well.' Alice slanted a look up at him. 'Me dad liked him, and he liked me dad. Geoff worked in an outfitter's shop. He gave me a gentleman's silk scarf once that he'd got hold of. He said me dad could have it. He were kind and generous like that.'

'Did your dad like it?'

'Oh, yes, he did!' Alice exclaimed with a smile. 'He thought it was the best thing. He took it to France; said it were his lucky charm . . .' Her voice tailed into silence and she turned her head.

'I bet he felt lucky just having it with him. Bet every time he looked at it or touched it, it reminded him of all of you.'

'He said something like that before he went and when he came back on leave.'

They had turned into Campbell Road and Alice slowed her pace as they approached her home. She groaned beneath her breath as she spied her mother silhouetted by a weak light burning behind their doorway. Tilly was leaning on the railings and beside her was Aunt Fran. Alice cursed louder when she realised her mother had spotted them. A moment later Tilly was swaying unsteadily in their direction. Even before she'd slurred a word Alice realised she'd been drinking.

'So who the bleedin' hell's this then?'

Alice inwardly cringed and slipped an apologetic glance at Josh. 'It's Joshua Chaplin. He's just walked home from the factory with me.'

'Oh . . . has he? Well, now you're home he can sling his hook.'

'Mum!' Alice began, her cheeks hot with embarrassment.

'I'm pleased to meet you, Mrs Keiver,' Joshua said pleasantly but his eyes were drawn back to what, for him, was an odd sight. There was a piano standing in the gutter. Inhabitants of The Bunk were quite used to coming across items for sale stuck on the railings or in the road.

'Pleased to meet me, are you?' Tilly rasped. 'Well, I ain't pleased to meet you. So fuck off.' Tilly grabbed at one of Alice's arms and gave it a yank. 'Indoors, you.'

Alice jerked back. She was furious at her mother's disgraceful behaviour. She couldn't have taken against Josh for any real reason. It was the first time they'd met, and he'd been more polite to her than she deserved.

She knew that her mother was being mean and nasty because she was afraid. Alice knew once she'd realised her dream of moving on it would leave her mother and sisters in financial trouble. Beth was bringing in regular money but the only work her mother now had was charring when she was sober enough to do it. The sight of Josh, returned from the war, had reminded her mother that once they'd been good friends and gone dancing together.

'That looks like a good piano. Is it for sale?'

Tilly had been about to add to her uncouth remarks but instead her jaw clacked shut. Drunk or sober she was canny about cash. 'Why? What's it to you if it is?' she demanded.

'My brother's been after getting a piano. He's pretty good even though he taught himself to play. He often bashes a few songs out on the piano down the local pub.' Josh looked at Tilly. 'Is it yours?'

'Belonged to me husband, Jack. He was real good on it. Got no use fer it now he's gone, God rest his soul. Glad to see the back of it.' Tilly roughly cuffed at her eyes as spontaneous tears blurred her vision.

Alice knew the piano's presence at home upset her mum. Jack's clothes had been sold off to Billy the Totter quite quickly and unemotionally. But the piano was different. It'd seemed to be a symbol of good times to Tilly. Sometimes, when in bed at night, Alice and her sisters could hear their mother weeping whilst plink-plonking on the keys and murmuring to her beloved Jack. That then set the three of them to quietly crying, huddling together in the dark.

'Billy not turned up to take it?' Alice asked her mum, glad to have a topic of conversation. A couple of the lads from across the street had got it down the stairs for them that morning for a few coppers. Billy had been due to collect and pay for it this afternoon. Alice had imagined it would be gone by the time she returned from work.

'Course he turned up! He's took it and brought it back, ain't he,' her mother snapped sarcastically.

'I'll have it off you,' Josh said calmly. 'Be nice at Christmas time to have a piano for a singsong.'

'Want ten pound fer it,' Tilly said immediately.

'Mum!' Alice protested. 'Billy was going to give you four.'

'Give you five,' Josh said. 'That's fair. And as it's Saturday tomorrow, I'll bring round a cart and collect it.'

'Done,' Tilly said and stuck out a spittle-moistened hand.

Josh shook it without hesitation. He gave Alice a smile. 'See you tomorrow, then. I'll be early; about nine o'clock.'

'Suits us,' Tilly said.

'Yes,' Alice said. 'Nine o'clock'll be fine.'

With a small salute of farewell Josh turned and strode off briskly up the road.

The following morning Alice was up bright and early. She was peering out of the window at a quarter to nine and suddenly a smile curved her mouth. Josh was coming down the road, pushing a barrow.

'Here, is he?' her mother asked dryly on seeing her daughter's sunny expression.

Alice turned about. 'Yes. He's early.'

'Going with him, are you?' Tilly asked, eying Alice's neat appearance and her coat on the chair all ready for her to don to go out.

'Yes . . . I'm going with him.' Alice knew that there was more significance in their conversation than her accompanying Josh on his tramp back to Wood Green with a piano on a cart. 'You don't have to stay around here now, Mum,' Alice said. 'When I move on I'll keep helping out with money, I swear. Beth'll do her best too, I know she will till it's her time to get her own place. Why stay here now . . .?'

'Ain't going nowhere.' Her mother cut her short. She sat down at the table. 'The Bunk's for me, cradle to grave.' Tilly picked listlessly at a dirty fingernail. 'Your dad wanted to get up the other end,' she said softly. 'It were always his ambition to get one o' them better houses up the other end.' She slanted a glance at Alice. 'If I go anywhere . . . that's where it'll be.' There was a rap at the door. 'Off you go, then,' Tilly said. She shoved her chair back from the table and went through into the other room without a backward glance.

'Won't be late back, promise,' Alice said quietly to a closing door.

THIRTY-TWO

'I didn't know whether to offer to get the beast back inside your place last night before I set off home. I thought I might turn up this morning and find it'd been pinched from outside your door.'

Alice huffed a chuckle. She'd just sprinted up the stairs to hand over to her mother the five pounds that Josh had paid for the piano. Now she was back in the street, a little out of breath, standing by his side. 'Me mum said she'd kip on top of it if needs be to make sure she got her fiver. She doesn't often have a joke any more,' she added wistfully. 'Sorry she was so rude to you yesterday. It's not just you,' Alice stressed. 'She can be nasty to anyone when she's been at the whiskey.'

'I've got a thick skin,' Josh reassured her. 'It passed over my head.' He finished lashing the piano to the cart then handed the two brothers from across the road a handful of coppers for helping him lift and load it. He tested the ropes and, when satisfied they were strong and serviceable enough, he lifted the barrow by the handles and they set off.

'I thought your brother might come with you to get it this morning,' Alice remarked as they turned the corner.

Josh was not struggling with the load but she could tell from the bulge of muscle in his forearms that it was no easy task he was undertaking.

'Didn't want him to. Thought if Matthew came you might not walk with me.'

'Sure I would come with you, were you?' Alice slanted him a challenging glance.

'I hoped you would. But I know it's quite a trek.'

'I'm used to walking,' Alice told him. 'Me and Sophy used to go out and about with our mum and dad when we were little 'uns. Used to do a bit of busking for pennies.' A faraway look was in her eyes. 'I can still remember how weary me poor little legs would get.'

'If you feel tired you can hop on the cart,' Josh suggested. 'There's room and I don't reckon you weigh much.' He gave her petite figure an appreciative glance.

Alice blossomed beneath his admiration. 'Thanks for the offer. I might take you up on it later. But I feel fine at the moment. Anyhow, we should have a little rest about halfway,' she decided. 'We could have a sit down and buy a cake to eat.'

'Like a picnic,' Josh said with a grin.

'Yeah; a sort of picnic,' Alice agreed. She glanced up at the grey winter sky. 'Hope it doesn't rain.'

'I've brought along a tarpaulin for the piano, just in case,' Josh said.

'Never mind the ruddy piano, what about us?' Alice protested with a giggle.

'Well, we could dive under the tarpaulin too,' Josh said. 'I think I might like that.'

'Daft!' Alice scolded on a blush but she moved closer to him, feeling warm and content.

'I know where we can get something to eat at Crouch End,' Josh said. 'There's a place to sit and park the cart too.'

'I've brought some money for a bite to eat.'

'I'll pay, Alicc,' Josh protested gently. 'I wouldn't be much of a gent otherwise, would I?'

'Geoff used to say something like that,' Alice blurted. '"I'll pay 'cos I'm a real gent", he'd say, all mocking. He did use to make me laugh.'

'I'm glad I'm like him. Even in just that small way,' Josh said with simple sincerity.

'You *are* like him,' Alice said softly. 'But you're different too. And I'm glad about that 'cos Geoff was special and I think you are too but . . .'

'I know what you mean, Alice,' he said in a gentle voice.

She could feel Josh's eyes on her profile and knew suddenly it was the right time to tell him a little bit more.

'Geoff was the most loyal person ever and would do anything to help. We hadn't been walking out together for long when he went off to fight. Geoff was more like my best friend than my sweetheart but I loved him dearly.'

'Sweethearts can come and go.' A long moment had passed before Josh started to reply, as though he'd carefully considered his words. 'You can move on from a sweetheart and forget them. But a true friend like that you can't replace, can't forget either.'

'That's how I feel about him,' Alice whispered. 'I won't ever forget him; won't ever again be anyone like him in me life. I was so lucky to have known him.'

'I wish . . . I hope I can mean as much to you,' Josh said quietly. 'Geoff was lucky too, Alice. He had you in his life . . .'

'He wasn't lucky in that!' Alice choked. 'Ruined his life, it did, knowing me and my family. He shouldn't even have gone to fight. He wasn't old enough. He was only eighteen when he was killed. He didn't want to go but he had to get away, 'cos of us . . .'

Alice turned her head away from Josh's puzzled look.

'Don't ask me. I can't tell you. It's bad . . . can't tell you,' she dully repeated and clamped together her lips.

'That's alright,' Josh soothed. 'We've all got secrets.'

'Not like the ones I've got,' Alice choked out with a grim laugh. Swiftly she changed the subject. 'I always wanted to get away from The Bunk and get me own place. It was my dream and Geoff's too. We both wanted to earn as much as we could and get on and get out.' She stared solemnly into the distance. 'Some of the girls working at Turner's bought themselves fur coats with their wages. You could earn so well working nights in the munitions factories. Seemed like heaven to start. Now I'd give up every penny to turn back the clock to before the war and have me dad and Geoff home . . .' Her words faltered and she swiped the heel of a hand over her wet face.

'It meant a lot to the men to know their women and families were comfortable,' Josh said. 'It eased their minds; made them proud too.'

'It's all finished for us women now anyhow.' Alice sniffed, twisted a little smile. 'All the men who're back and fit to work will take the good jobs. No more munitions needed, and it would only be the devil himself who'd be sorry about that.' She suddenly winced as she felt a stone cut into the sole of her shoe.

'Hop on the cart,' Josh suggested. 'We're going on the straight so you might as well have a ride.' He slowed right down to let Alice scramble aboard.

For a while they carried on their journey in silence. Alice unlaced her boot and tipped it up to see if a stone chip might fall out. 'Have you got secrets?' she finally murmured whilst still fiddling with her boot.

'I've got things I'd rather not talk about.'

'Horrible things?'

'Yes.'

Alice raised her blue eyes to his face. He met her gaze squarely but she could see the distress moistening his eyes as he dwelled on private horrors. 'Things that happened in the war?' she guessed.

Josh nodded. 'What I saw on the Somme,' he explained gruffly. 'Still gives me nightmares . . . sometimes I cry like a baby when I'm on my own.'

'Have you spoken about it to your mum or dad?'

Josh shook his head. 'Don't want to tell anyone. Don't want to speak about it.'

'But you'd tell me.'

'Yes,' Josh said. 'If you wanted to listen, I'd tell you.' He gave Alice a searing look. 'And when you're ready, I'm willing to listen to whatever you've got to say. I won't ever betray you, Alice. You can trust me, I swear.'

'Thanks,' Alice croaked, her eyes again glistening. After a quiet moment she took a deep breath and said, 'Don't think of you as my best friend yet but I reckon I will.'

'Glad about that,' Josh said with a smile. ''Cos I've a feeling I'd like it a lot if you did.' He glanced down diffidently at one of his fists gripping a handle. 'Got a bit of money left after giving your mum that fiver. I brought it with me specially 'cos I saw something a few days ago in a jeweller's shop in Wood Green High Street. It's a pretty little ring with three small diamonds. It's not fancy, but I thought if you wanted something fancy then next year . . .'

'Don't want fancy,' Alice gruffly interrupted. 'And don't show me just yet. Perhaps when we come this way again, you can show it to me then.' She reached out a hand and placed it over one of his. She felt unable to speak. Her heart was thumping so hard she felt she might burst with happiness yet a feeling of serenity had settled on her too.

'I'm glad you've come with me today, Alice. I thought if

you did it would be a good omen and I must find the courage to tell you that I've fallen in love with you.'

'In a little while I reckon I'll have that courage too,' Alice replied, achingly softly. 'But for now I just need a bit more time for the pain inside to go away . . .'

'No rush . . .' Josh said, smiling tenderly.

With a little hop she was off the cart. She slipped a hand through one of his arms, rubbed a cheek against the straining sinew she could feel beneath the material of his sleeve. Wordlessly she gripped one of the cart handles and added her strength to his as they walked on.

EPILOGUE

Summer 1922

Like a nesting bird she'd come back to claim from her kin what was her due. As the baby stirred in her womb Alice groaned and wished they'd be quiet. Their chattering was irritating, like the low buzzing of the flies outside the closed window.

Digging her elbows into the mattress she levered herself up to look at the trio of women congregated at the foot of the bed. The heat felt stifling and her dark hair draped aggravatingly on her perspiring brow. On hearing her whimper her mother came over to her. She perched on the side of the mattress, murmuring soothingly whilst holding a cold compress to Alice's brow.

'I'm too hot . . . it hurts . . .' Alice complained and collapsed back with a groan as another contraction gripped her abdomen. She clutched at her mother's forearm as a new, urgent sensation writhed in her pelvis. 'Feels different now,' she whimpered. 'Something's different.'

''Ere . . . Lou!' Tilly summoned the woman standing with Beattie. 'Think things are movin' again. Take a look.'

Lou Perkins obligingly came to examine Alice. 'Good gel!' she praised. 'You're doing fine. Can see a head. Nearly there now. Soon have your baby. Now when I tell you to push, you push with all your might.'

Alice panted out her agreement as her mother and Beattie Evans took up position either side of her. She clutched gratefully at their sturdy hands.

'Where is he?' Alice gasped fretfully.

'Well out of it, love, and leave him there,' her mother bluntly said. 'Only get in the way, he will. Besides, only one thing gets said to husbands at a time like this . . . "don't you come near me no more".'

Alice squeezed shut her eyes and bore down.

'Will she get too hot?' Alice looked at the tightly swaddled bundle laid against her shoulder. All that was visible of her daughter was a tiny, crumpled face. Alice touched a finger to a warm pink cheek then dipped her head to touch her lips to her daughter's soft, musky skin.

'She's just right. Needs to be kept warm.' Lou Perkins beamed at her. 'Well, that weren't too bad, were it? One of the easiest babes I've helped into the world.' She came closer to peer at the tiny bundle. 'Beauty, ain't she?' She looked over her shoulder at Tilly.

Tilly nodded and came closer to look at her first grandchild. 'Ain't she just,' she choked, cuffing at her watering eyes. 'I'll call Josh up now for you. I'll be back later to take a proper look at her,' she said briskly. 'Come on, you lot, let's get shot of all this mess.'

The three women gathered together the soiled linen and pots and bowls.

A moment after they'd gone Josh appeared in the doorway, his expression a mix of joy and wonder. He came swiftly, quietly to the bed and bent to tenderly press his lips to Alice's upturned face. He laid on her belly the crimson carnations he'd bought for her. Carefully he took his daughter from his wife and cradled her in his arms. With persistence he searched amid the sheet and found her tiny fingers and toes to stroke. 'Have you decided on a name?'

'Lilian,' Alice said simply. She touched a red petal before lifting the posy to breathe in its scent. 'I like it. Do you?'

Josh nodded, his gaze roving his daughter's perfect features. Suddenly she opened her eyes and looked at him with solemn intensity. 'Is she fair or dark?' He touched the linen hiding the top of her head.

'Don't know,' Alice said. 'They've covered her right up tight.'

Josh eased back the cloth to take a look. He grinned when he saw the down on Lilian's head. 'She's fair . . .' He broke off and raised the baby's chin very gently. For a moment he remained quite still, his voice suspended by a surge of emotion. Then he came back to the bed and gave Alice her daughter. 'Look, Al.' His gentle finger smoothed a fold of flesh so Alice could see a small freckled area of skin on her daughter's throat.

Alice took in a shuddering breath, her forehead lowering to touch her daughter. 'She's got my dad's birthmark,' she sobbed. Tell Mum to come back,' she gasped. 'Tell her to come back now 'cos I've got something wonderful to show her.'

Easter 1987

'Thanks for bringing me home, Beryl.'

'That's alright, Nan. Did you have a nice time?'

'I did. Your mum always does a lovely tea. Now before you get off, I've got you some lettuce and spring onions you can take with you. They're in the pantry; come through and I'll just fetch them.'

Beryl followed her nan into the small kitchen and waited while Alice rummaged in the cupboard. She brought out jars as well as vegetables and put them on the scrubbed table.

'We're going to have a barbecue over ours for Dad's birthday in a couple of months. You'll come, won't you?'

'Ooh, yes, I'd like to,' Alice said, sorting through her homemade jams to find the blackberry one.

'It'd be nice if Aunt Sophy and Uncle Danny could come. Are they up to the journey from Essex?'

'Well, your uncle Danny has a bit of trouble getting about now,' Alice cautioned. 'He's almost ninety, you know. Perhaps they will. I'll phone and find out. You know how they love seeing all of you children and your children.'

'It's a shame they didn't have a family of their own,' Beryl said.

'It wasn't to be,' Alice answered simply. 'But they've got all their nephews and nieces instead.'

'If they don't make our barbecue, perhaps another time we'll take the barbecue to them. It'd be nice to visit them down at the coast again. The kids love it there. '

'They'd like that,' Alice said enthusiastically.

'What's this, Nan?' Beryl had wandered into the small front sitting room and held up a book she'd found in an open drawer.

'Oh . . . that's the book about the place I used to live in Islington when I was growing up; before I was married. Campbell Road, it was called. Or The Bunk as we all called it. Do you remember I told you a nice young man had come to interview me so he could put lots of past residents' memories in a book he was writing?'

'That's where Uncle Danny grew up too, isn't it?'

'Yes, that's right.'

'And his brother Geoff was killed in the Great War, wasn't he?'

'Yes. He was a smashing man; well, he wasn't much more than a boy when he was killed. But he was lovely.'

'I know you liked him . . . I've heard you say,' Beryl said, eyes twinkling.

'I did. I liked him a lot.'

'Did Granddad know?'

'He did,' Alice said with a faraway look. 'We didn't have secrets.'

'I miss Grandad,' Beryl sighed wistfully.

'Me too,' Alice said. 'But mustn't complain because we had a good life together.'

Beryl flipped the book to read the back cover. 'Can I borrow it, Nan?'

'Yes . . . if you like.'

A child's laughter could be heard followed by a wail.

'Uh . . . oh,' Alice said with a little grimace. 'Sounds like someone's come a cropper.' She moved the voile curtain to peer out of the window. 'Looks like your Martin has taken a tumble.' She gazed fondly at the sight of two handsome blonde-haired boys being urged to get into a car by their father. The youngest of her great-grandsons was clutching at one of his knees as his father dabbed at it with a hanky.

Beryl sighed. 'I told them to wait in the car.'

'Ooh . . . Boys will be boys,' Alice chuckled. 'Graham's getting tall.'

'Off to football practice tomorrow,' Beryl said. She took the vegetables and jam that her nan was handing over. A louder wail from outside drew her attention. 'Time to get those two home, I think.' Swiftly she bent and kissed her nan on the cheek and tried to hug her too without squashing the produce she'd been given.

Alice watched as her granddaughter hurried to the car to help her husband get the boys settled for the journey home. She waved out of the window as the car started to reverse along the cul-de-sac. A sudden breath of warm air lifted the voile curtain to silkily scarf her neck.

A smile touched Alice's lips at the subtle caress. Then she picked up the book and made a move as though to go after Beryl. She knew they wouldn't yet have turned out of the road. After a moment's hesitation she slipped the book in the half-open drawer in the sideboard and pushed it shut.

AUTHOR'S NOTE

As children growing up in Tottenham, North London, I and my three sisters and two brothers always knew that my maternal grandmother (see pictures at end of book) had had a 'hard life'. It was some while before we fully realised how dreadful had been her upbringing in a slum in Islington nicknamed The Bunk.

In the late 1970s and early 1980s an historian began researching the social history of Campbell Road, reputed to have been the worst street in North London. He contacted ex-residents of the street (see pictures at end of book) and my grandmother was interviewed and her recollections incorporated into a book he was compiling. On its publication in the mid-1980s my nan was presented with a copy. By that time Campbell Road was no more. In 1937 it had changed name to Whadcoat Street and finally slum clearance in the 1950s brought about the demise of the notorious Campbell Bunk.

My nan was born in 1901, just around the corner to Campbell Road, but she remembered having moved to the street when she was still an infant. Her family resided there, in cramped rooms (see pictures at end of book) in various dilapidated tenement houses, until she was a grown woman. She finally escaped in 1922 when she married my grandfather, but members of her family remained there for many more years. Her mother, my great-grandmother, lived there until the Second World War when she died in a tragic and rather mysterious accident.

The majority of Bunk dwellers suffered extreme hardship like my ancestors yet some anecdotes hint at their ambivalence about the place. Community spirit and camaraderie seemed to unite them (see pictures at back of book) in a way that justified a wry pride in their infamy. From my grandmother's narrative it's clear her regular claim to be *'a tough old bird'* was no idle boast and undoubtedly accounted for her longevity. She was still digging her vegetable patch until shortly before her death at the age of ninety-two.

When my beloved mum died several years ago the Campbell Bunk book again came to light among her belongings. We also discovered the first couple of chapters of a novel she'd started that had been inspired by her mother's wretched early life. As a family we became very interested in our genealogy and my youngest brother did some research into the family tree. My dad wondered if my mum's work could be continued and finished as a tribute to her and to my grandmother. I considered it a privilege to take on the task.

The Street is fiction but I have woven some of my grandmother's reminiscences and my mother's writing in to the novel and trust that the end result would make them both smile.

Campbell Road from Seven Sisters Road, taken at the start of the Peace Day celebrations of July 1919.

The inspiration for Jack Keiver, as a young man.

The inspiration for Tilly Keiver, as a young woman.

Three factory girls from Campbell Road and neighbouring Fonthill Road.

Brand Street. Built 30–40 years before Campbell Road, Brand Street was typical of slums cleared between the wars.

Campbell Road men on a beano to Southend.

The inspiration for Tilly, with the last of her 11 children.

Campbell Road, May 1935. The *Daily Mirror* used this photograph to exemplify patriotic enthusiasm in even the poorest areas.

The first floor back room at 27 Campbell Road, which occupied 2 adults and 4 children.

Campbell Road, the bottom end during the slum clearance.